The Führer's Time Machine

Orion's Legacy

Mike Brameld

Foreword

Although this book is predominantly a fictional piece of work there are many elements of truth included which should help stir your imagination.

It is a mixture of fact and fiction and science fiction
Let us call it science-faction.

Regarding the characters; any resemblance to any persons living or dead is purely coincidental; although many of the activities, ranks and positions held may well have been inspired by similar persons.

The story began as a short story comprising 2,000 words. Thanks to the ongoing support and gentle badgering by my wife Linda it has developed into this novel.

I hope you enjoy reading it.
If nothing else it may stir your imagination and help you to consider the possibility that there may be a ring of truth in its message.

Thank you for choosing my book.
I hope you find it as enjoyable to read as I did to write.
If you did enjoy it please recommend it to your friends.

The Sequel?
A sequel is due for publication in Summer/Autumn 2023

"The Führer's Paradox"

Acknowledgments

To Mr Gordon, an inspirational teacher who inspired me never to give up on my dreams, and whose teaching skills I endeavoured to emulate in my own career.

To Erich Von Däniken , who gave me my first insights into the possibility of early alien intervention on earth , and to his current 'apostles who continue his good work. These include .. Bill Birnes, Robert Bauval, David Childress, Graham Hancock, Jason Martell, Nick Pope, and Giorgio Tsoukalos.

Cover Design courtesy of
100covers.com

Dedicated to my wife Linda,
my constant support and 'rock' throughout this journey.

Chapter 1

The distant humming became ever more intense, so deep and strong that it rolled backwards and forwards in his stomach creating a feeling of deep nausea. It felt as if his stomach was rising up to meet his throat - he needed to retch and clear this ball which had stuck in his throat; he couldn't breathe and felt a panic growing inside. His head felt as if there was a machine inside, vibrating through his skull and making his teeth ache as they constantly vibrated against each other.

His face was pressed against the metal sides of what felt like a steel drum. The metallic taste in his mouth was his own blood, a feeling only made worse by the cold, unforgiving steel plate pressing into his cheeks. He could smell ozone. He lifted his head away from the cold, hard floor desperately looking around to find a way out but the darkness was only broken in places by small blinking lights, not enough to see by, but easy to see. As he moved forwards he bumped into a metal slab, it felt like some form of desk. The lights were blinking even faster and the humming became more intense. He looked around for a clue as to where he was. Feeling around in the semi darkness only increased his feeling of fear, he could feel nothing, no clue as to where he was; the sweat on his forehead now ran into his eyes, stinging and dulling his limited vision, then down into his mouth. The salty taste on his lips made him believe he was at sea – or was it just his sweat?

Then the humming became louder and he felt his body slide sideways and feel as if it had become attached to the walls as if by magnets. The pressure on his chest increased until he found it hard to breathe. His face was forced onto its side, his cheeks forced against a steel plate, smooth steel panels forcing into his gums. He could taste the blood on his tongue; he was suffocating, lungs fighting to pull in gasps of precious air. He was hopelessly trapped, but where?

Thoughts in his mind were racing, echoing around a brain struggling to make sense of what was happening.

"How the Hell do I get out of here, when I don't know where 'here' is?"

This was it – he couldn't go on, he was terrified and tried to shout for help, but the words wouldn't leave his mouth. "Christ, I'm gone."

Just then he felt a hand on his shoulder, gently tugging him backwards and forwards. Slowly he began to hear a voice in the distance, like the sound of conversation when trying to sleep on an aeroplane. The tugging became more intense, and the voice louder.

"Come on Johnno, wake up, it's only a dream!"

'Johnno' slowly began to wake up. His eyes blinked at the painful light invading his vision; his mouth was dry and he could still feel his heart thumping in his chest. His head was throbbing. His hair was matted and full of sweat, as was his t-shirt. He began to get back his consciousness – he felt like he used to when at the dentist as the gas began to wear off and sound began to flood back into his head. He suddenly realised where he was –back in his quarters at his air force base.

Another nightmare!

"Christ, Johnno, I realise it's an important day for us but screaming in your sleep won't help." This was his good buddy Rick – a fellow pilot aiming to get into NASA alongside his friend.

"Sorry Rick, I don't know why but stress always gives me the 'heebie jeebies'."

What Johnno didn't say was that he'd had this nightmare since he was a little boy growing up in his home town of Prescot in the UK. He can't remember when they started, they'd always been there. As a child he'd always wanted the dreams to finally end, and for him to find his way out, but he never did.

Johnno slowly sat up and apologised "I guess I'm having nightmares about beating you in today's tests – and what you'll do to me when I beat you."

Rick smiled, and then threw his pillow at his friend's head. "No chance buddy, only the best gets through, and that's ME." 'He grabbed his towel and ambled towards the shower. "Time to become the cleanest astronaut in NASA buddy", and disappeared towards his own room and his shower cubicle. He glanced back at his still woozy friend "Give your Mom's photo a good luck kiss from me – I guess we'll both need it".

Rick – full name Richard Abrahams – was Johnno's closest friend and co-pilot. He was a little taller than Johnno at 6'3" to Johnno's 'mere' 6ft, with a shock of blond hair, but they formed a perfect team, acting and thinking as one. He had distinctive Nordic features and had been born and raised in the USA by loving parents who had been born in Norway and emigrated for a better life in 1937 as the Second World War became an imminent possibility. They settled in San Diego, California, opening a bakery where they quickly gained a reputation for quality breads and pastries, eaten with relish by sailors from the nearby naval base. They worked long hours in order to generate a new future for themselves and their new family – Rick came along just two years after they arrived. The constant naval presence had an effect on young Rick as he grew up, but he wanted to be a flyer as sailing made him sea sick.

Through hours of dedication and support from his parents he managed to graduate and then attend Stanford. He successfully applied to 'be a flyer' and quickly rose through the ranks, his potential marking him out as test pilot material.

Johnno and Rick first met at flight school when both had been selected for the Blackbird programme. Rick had gained a degree in pure and applied mathematics when he studied at Stanford. This gift, coupled with lightning reactions and a similar sense of humour had made him the ideal co-pilot to have as your partner, especially in an experimental aircraft. The fact they both had ties to Scandinavia was the final 'coincidence' that helped them bond as partners. Rick could calculate and recalculate flight data with un-nerving accuracy, whilst Johnno had the reactions required to act instinctively on his co-pilots orders.

They also shared a passion for Jim Beam and Budweiser beer, and disappearing into the desert on Rick's pride and joy, his Harley-Davidson Electra Glide – old 'shovel' as it was affectionately known. Rick made a point of keeping several bottles in his panniers reminding his friend "Always carry a spare my friend, you never know when you'll need it."

In these instances roles were reversed as Rick took the lead and Johnno squeezed onto the back. It took an awful lot of trust to travel at 100mph with your friend leading the way on a pitch black desert night. That's how relationships are forged.

Once, when on leave and visiting Rick's parents in San Diego, they decided to display their unique Scandinavian bond with (almost) matching tattoos. Whilst Rick had a small Norwegian flag to the top of his arm, Johnno had the Swedish flag as a tribute to his beloved Aunt Freya.

His flight crew even gave their test aircraft the call sign OD1N, reflecting the close bond their two airmen shared.

Johnno relaxed back into his pillow. His heart had stopped thumping, the sweat removed from his brow and he gently wiped his chest and under his arms. "These nightmares will be the death of me." He glanced at his alarm clock, it was 7.17 am, he had to be suited and booted for the final flights at 10.00 am. He put his arm under his head and relaxed back into his pillow reflecting on his continued good fortune in becoming a USAF air ace. "Who'd have realised how this little orphan from England could have come so far, and may even go into space"

He leaned over and picked up the small picture frame, complete with a black and white photograph of his mother and father. He'd never known his real mum or dad, and this was his only link to his childhood.

He smiled at the fading image. "Hi Mum, I'm nearly there, thanks for looking over me for all these years," and then gently kissed the frame. "And here's one from Rick, but don't give him too much luck ," he kissed the frame again. On an impulse he took the photo out of the frame and decided to take it with him for luck. He would tuck it into the pocket of his body belt for security.

At every turn in his life he'd looked to his mother and father and the faded black and white photograph for guidance, and always believed he'd gotten it. "Tell Dad wherever he is that I hope he's proud of me, just as you are".

He closed his eyes and thought back over his charmed life.

Johnno's real name was John O'Ryan. When asked at school what his name was he announced proudly "John **O**'Ryan" - so 'Johnno' became his nickname.

His only contact through his young years was his Aunt Freya. A tall blonde haired attractive woman, she had taken John in when his mother died, though John could only ever remember her as his loving carer from the day he was born. He'd never really questioned how a Nordic lady became his surrogate mother, all she would tell him was that she had "been in Sweden with his mother during World War Two, and had promised to look after him if something happened to her". His mother and father had been killed during the second world war, and so Freya was keeping her word in raising him. And a good job she did too.

All through his years of growing up he remembered adventure and laughter. Freya would take John everywhere to learn about life. Camping, canoeing, hiking, climbing trees – a childhood dream really.

If ever he mentioned his real mother Freya would tell him to collect the photograph; she would remind him how beautiful and brave she was and a good friend too. When they were children Johnno's mother wanted to be a dancer, and her nickname was 'Tutu'. Whenever Freya heard this she would smile and reply 'Me too'. Johnno's mother thought this was hilarious and would laugh every time she said it.

Occasionally Freya's eyes would fill with tears, but she would smile and wipe them away, and suggest another fun thing to do.

If ever John mentioned his father then Freya would again treat his question with due reverence and tell him everything she could.

He had been an airman whose aircraft had crash landed in Germany. He'd been found by resistance members and spirited away to Sweden where he'd met a beautiful young girl with blond hair and freckles "all over her nose and face". Her name was Sara. "Good looks AND a gun," were he first words he said to her.

Soon her father and Sara were experiencing the harrowing side of war, fighting together and eventually they fell in love.

Sara and John senior were dropped into Northern Germany, following requests by the English RAF to check what was happening in a small town in the Northern Baltic. Strange lights had been seen in the night skies, with trails of flames and fire crashing into the Baltic Sea.

When the Germans had been seen trying to collect wreckage in the same area the RAF knew this was important.

Sara and John and their colleagues had managed to infiltrate the site,

their target being an unidentified apparatus in its Southern edge. It was believed to be some form of warning device, possibly a type of radar.

They were tasked with destroying the site in order to prevent an early warning of a planned air raid on this site. They also had to collect two of their contacts, Polish prisoners who worked as janitors, and had already supplied a plan of the site and its secrets.

The sudden development of 'so called' wonder weapons was of deep concern to the allied forces. The contacts were then to be smuggled back the Britain, via neutral Sweden, in order to pass on everything they knew.

His parents were last seen entering the structure in target area D, the unknown apparatus.

Shots were heard by their comrades waiting outside, but they were never seen again. Freya's eyes would again moisten. She would hold John closely to her chest and he would feel her sobbing. She always held him close to her heart with her left arm, and stroked his hair carefully, avoiding hurting her little charge with a large ring on her right hand. Around his neck he wore a chain and amulet, a birthday present to Freya from his mother – Freya had placed it around John's neck as he left home to realise his dream of being an astronaut – though he knew he'd have to learn to fly first!

"Wear it always, whenever you are alone, and especially when you become the pilot you've always dreamed of becoming, your Mother's spirit will keep you safe, just as mine keeps me safe." It was a promise he always kept. He felt especially proud as the design also matched that on Freya's special ring, also a gift from his mother – he realised how close Freya and his mother must have been, and that filled his heart with joy.

"And always remember, it may be just a small amulet, but in life small things matter."

Then the nightmares started.

Freya would gently wake John whenever she heard him, and would then sit in a chair in the corner of the room whilst he tried to get back to sleep so that she could "open the door of the dark room and let him out to safety".

"I wonder what Mr Gordon would say if he could see me now?" he thought.

Mr Gordon was his favourite teacher at school. He didn't laugh like all his friends did when Johnno told him he wanted to be a spaceman and fly to the moon. He was an inspiration; he constantly reassured his young pupils. 'Make time to make things happen, they will, and you WILL succeed in living your dreams'. This shy young child, who was in awe of a wonderful teacher, was now all grown up and heading for his dream of being a spaceman.

One day, in class, one of his young pupils innocently asked "What did you do in the war sir?" A tear came to his eye as he recounted the tale of a young Jewish man growing up in Poland who had witnessed many dreadful sights, including family members disappearing as the new German 'master race' began to spread over the continent. He told how he had lost all of his family, sent to a camp for resettlement, only later finding this camp had been called Birkenau. How he alone had been smuggled out of a different German work camp, where he was essentially a slave, and somehow smuggled to safety through resistance contacts, ending up in the neutral country of Sweden.

All the children sat open mouthed, listening to his tale of survival.

"I was flown to England and sent to live with a wonderful family in Lancashire, Ray and Lily Gordon. They didn't care what my religion was; I was a lost, lonely soul and they just cared for me as if I was their own. I had the luxury of playing and roaming in freedom. If I apologised for daydreaming they would just smile and tell me to 'make time to make things happen, and that includes dreaming'. The children smiled when they heard those words.

When their son was reported lost, missing in action on an RAF raid, I tried to reassure Mrs Gordon that I would join the fight and find her son". She had turned to him and smiled, holding his head gently in her hands, then gently cried. "Too many lives have been lost in this war, do what you must, I need to stay here and wait for my other son to come home again".

He told them how proud he felt when she called him her 'other son'. He had parents again who could help his heart to heal after losing his real parents at home.

"And so I, Josef Gorski became Joe Gordon. I enlisted in the RAF so I could fly over and find my 'brother'. Although I flew on several ops I never did find the Owens' missing son, but I stayed with them until I met and married a local girl. I never forgot how a young man was helped by strangers, and by becoming a teacher, it would allow me to pay back my debt. I would educate young minds and help steer them away from ignorance and warfare, and teach them how to love themselves and people they saw as enemies."

Johnno joined the RAF and became a pilot. He was seconded to the USAF in the early 1960's, when NATO was growing ever more concerned during the cold war. Naturally his Aunt Freya moved with him, ever mindful of the promise she made to her dear sister all those years ago.

His natural flair and ability saw him quickly rise through the ranks, eventually joining the secretive Blackbird project at Groom Lake. Here he was partnered with Rick and a lifelong friendship began.

As he stood there he felt a tear in his eye as he 'saw' Mr.Gordon smiling at him.

"I think he'd be really proud of me" Johnno murmured to himself, smiled and then kissed his charm for luck.

In the distance he heard the shower being turned off.

"Time to go, NASA waits for no-one." Placing the photograph on his bedside table he grabbed his towel and ran for the shower. As the water warmed up he leaned on the sink and looked at himself in the mirror. He could see a small grey streak appearing in his mousey brown hair.

He gently brushed it back whilst examining his teeth and tongue, then lifting his chin to feel if he needed a shave.

"You are one lucky son of a gun John O'Ryan. Today is the day you show the world just how good a pilot you really are." As the mirror began to steam up he turned and entered the shower.

Chapter 2

It was a hot June day and the heat shimmered on the desert runway, giving the impression of a water covered lake. It had been a lake at one time, Groom Lake, but had long since been dry and used by the US Air Force for many diverse reasons.

It seemed to take forever to strap them into their flight suits – especially modelled for their frames to counteract the effects of 'G' force. "Now I know how it feels to be in a strait jacket" – Rick was being fastened in by his ground team – the new suits had to be fastened for them, a novelty they weren't too sure about. "Some people say we're nuts for doing this job." – the ground team member smiled. "Nuts ... but brave nuts." he replied.

"This new bird we're testing must really be something – why all this fitting and padding, I bet the astronauts at Kennedy don't have this much fuss." Johnno smiled as he finished the sentence – he hoped he was another step closer to living his dream of being an astronaut.

"You not allowed to wear jewellery sir," Chuck, his ground crew lead reminded him, pointing to the pendant around his neck.

Johnno tucked it securely into his t-shirt next to his dog tags. "What jewellery?"

Chuck smiled, "Yeah, what jewellery?", passing him his helmet.

"Can you give me a clue where you're headed for sir?"

Johnno winked. "If I did I'd have to kill you."

Chuck smiled "We couldn't have that sir. Good luck."

Johnno patted his chest, and zipped up his suit.

"Here we go Rick", they both grinned and bumped fists,

"Look out ionosphere, the boys are on their way."

.....

They strode purposely towards the runway where the Blackbird craft awaited them. The heat from the desert and tarmac floor hit them squarely in the face causing them to screw their eyes behind their Raybans, but at least there was no discernible breeze to upset their flight calculations.

"Who'd have believed it?" Rick mused "two air force jockeys testing a brand new aircraft, modified specially for us to suit our mission, it's a dream come true buddy." Johnno smiled, and playfully hit his flying helmet against his colleagues'. Johnno grinned "We may not be astronauts yet but this must up our chances of showing we have the 'right stuff'."

"I'm sure we'll be on the Moon this year, JFK said so ... then the Universe had better look out – here we come!"

In the distance the matt black of the new aircraft shimmered in the early morning sun. The mirage made her look twice as tall.

"Jeez Johnno, she looks beautiful.".

The sleek lines and distinctive shape of the new Blackbird made them both grin. "She's like a rocket with wheels Rick ... and WE'RE going to fly her." This is where all the hours of practice and preparation would come together. The mock-ups of the cockpit, the hours and hours of simulation, the long nights studying the controls systems – test procedures to be carried out – even the emergency escape procedures, had all led to this day.

Tucked away in the Nevada desert – two proud, but extremely

excited, pilots, and the future of high altitude flight rested on their very experienced shoulders.

They both smiled as they met their flight crew. The tradition was to shake hands with them all and thank them for their hard work in preparing the bird for this test flight – this they duly did.

The crew then gave them a cigar each to light on their return.

"And may God hold you safe in the palm of his hands" came a quiet voice from one of the crew.

Johnno filled up with pride, a small tear in the corner of his eye. He blinked, pretending the sun was in his eyes.

"Don't worry; we'll take good care of her." Johnno tapped his flight suit where his lucky charm sat. "Here I go Mum, wish me luck."

They slowly climbed the ladders into the cockpit, Rick settling down behind his friend and colleague. Johnno patted the aircraft's fuselage. "Let's look after each other today," then clambered into his seat. They set about their pre-checks as the flight crew settled them in, fastening the harnesses that strapped them safely into their seats.

"This is for luck sir." and one of the flight crew smiled at Johnno and handed him a small Bell shaped charm. "Your Aunt Freya asked me to pass it on to you and to keep it safe with yours".

As Johnno looked up the crew man smiled and gave a knowing wink, and it seemed as if a light actually twinkled in his eye. Johnno smiled, and wondered how the hell has his Aunt Freya done this – but he reached inside his suit and clipped it on the chain alongside his other charm. He looked out again to thank the crew man but he was nowhere to be seen. "Jeez, that guy would have a future in Vegas as a magician".

Johnno tapped his chest again and looked skywards.

"Here I go Aunt Freya, wish me luck."

High in the control tower Commander in Chief Joe Pazzaro watched intently through his binoculars. In the background staff busied themselves for the coming flight tests, double checking everything. Technicians' heads disappeared into their screens, scrutinising every detail. Joe Pazzaro was a hard taskmaster and expected perfection – his pilots lives were on the line.

"Is everything ready, all pre-checks done?" he asked

"Yes sir, Oxcart is a go ... Blackbird 3 is primed and ready, new afterburners added and new fuels as well!" The sergeant stood smartly to attention, looking pleased with his efforts.

"What new fuels? I wasn't told anything about new fuels! This is purely a high altitude test – who the hell asked for new fuels sergeant?"

Quickly checking his data sheets he noted that the fuels had been authorised by Lockheed Aeronautics, and countersigned by both NASA and the CIA.

The commander spun around, and looked intently at the officials viewing the test at the back of the command tower – the CIA were present – ostensibly to ensure complete secrecy in this top level trial.

"Is this any of your doing Tesman?"

At the rear of the room a tall gent in a black suit lowered his binoculars, but leaving his gaze towards the aircraft outside. "That's on a need to know basis, and it's MR Tesman," he drawled "but I suggest that you contact Mr. Grey if you need to know more."

At that he raised his binoculars back to his eyes, obviously denying the commander the chance for any further questioning.

The commander had heard of this 'Grey' through discussions with his colleagues at NASA and operation Paperclip. Though he'd never met him he was advised not to – not a man to be questioned as he had friends in 'very high places'. He replaced the cigar in his mouth, turned around and raised his binoculars once

"Let's hope this goddam fuel doesn't cause any problems. Months of planning and millions of dollars and they change the goddam fuel at the last minute!"

Tesman looked to a colleague at his side. Unlike Tesman, who wore a black suit and highly polished shoes, his colleague wore a lieutenant's uniform, which he seemed uneasy in. He wore dark glasses, the kind worn by sufferers of photophobia and not the usual Raybans; he seemed too small to be in the Air Force.

"Are we ready Mr. Maia?" he said quietly through the side of his mouth, not for once averting his gaze from the aircraft on the runway.

The lieutenant looked up and lowered his glasses. His eyes had the look of haematite, no pupils, no whites – just a bluey-black shiny mass. He nodded. He raised his glasses back to cover his eyes and slowly moved back, at the same time pressing a small black fob in his pocket...

"It is activated, Herr Kapitan." Tesman grinned, then grimaced.

"At last – and it is Captain here, you moron". His colleague looked embarrassed, and muttered an apology.

Tesman said nothing and purposely raised his binoculars skywards.

.....

On the tarmac the two pilots completed their pre-flight checks. A thumbs-up to the control tower and the cockpit was lowered and fastened securely.

The Blackbird began its graceful drive across the tarmac, everything behind the twin engines being blown away in the dust, creating a shimmering sunlight across the runway.

The ground crew held onto their caps and glasses as their 'baby' set out to show the assembled VIPS just how good it could perform.

Johnno smiled "Its times like this I remember the poem I learned in school"

"Oh really", replied Rick with a knowing grin on his face, "is this a limerick by any chance?" he asked.

"No far from it my friend- Mr Gordon inspired me with this." He quietly began to speak softly, but with great reverence, closing with the line "put out my hand and touched the face of God."

"Sorry if I'm getting soft old buddy, but that's my favourite poem, learned by heart as soon as I found it in a school library book. You wouldn't believe it but I was a bit of a geek at school." Rick smiled. "Never!"

"A beautiful thought airman," crackled through Johnno's helmet, "now go out and not just touch his face, but let's put a smile on it." Joe Pazzaro may have been a taskmaster, but he was a leader who was proud of his men. "Wilco sir." Two voices replied in unison as they reached the end of the runway and slowly turned their aircraft, in readiness for take-off "Final checks- fuel temperature OK- recording systems on."

Johnno was looking around as he moved the flight controls "Ailerons A-OK, Backup systems active-do we have a green light to go tower?" Johnno smiled. "On days like this I remember my old teacher Mr. Gordon who told me to follow my dreams and the sky's the limit. Little did he know then how prophetic those words would prove to be to a small schoolboy all those years ago."

"Perhaps even the sky may not be the limit buddy. Who knows?" Rick's voice was calm and reassuring. "Who knows?"

"I wish he was alive today, I'd love to see the look on his face." Johnno added wistfully.

"He'd be so proud of you buddy."

"Now go ahead and make ME proud boys." Pazzaro's voice crackled through their helmets "go ahead and show me and the rest of our esteemed guests and ground crew here just what you and that technological wonder is capable of doing."

In the distance the technicians in the tower checked their radar screens intently. All air traffic in a radius of 50 miles and a thirty thousand foot ceiling had been blocked or diverted in readiness for this highly secret test. "All clear sir, you're ready to go, and God Speed."

Pazzaro smiled "If only Andropov and Kosygin could see what's coming their way"

Johnno took the throttle and put on the power. Blackbird began a steady track, gently accelerating down the runway as more power was put on.

Rick studied his control panel "Power incremental and steady – temperatures OK – let's roll Johnno." They could feel the runway below them sending slight tremors through their craft. The rhythmic 'bump-bumping' of the concrete sections began to become more obvious and more often as they gained speed. Then full power was steadily fed in and the mighty Blackbird roared along the runway and soared into a clear blue sky, leaving only wispy trails and haze on the tarmac runway.

All eyes turned skywards as she rose steadily, and was soon out of sight. The green blip on the radar showed all was well and the trials had begun. In the cockpit Johnno smiled, and whispered under his breath ... "On my way Mr.Gordon, I'm on my way."

Chapter 3

Although this was to be a high altitude flight, official orders included a low level pass over the air base to impress their high ranking guests lined up in front of the control tower. Oxcart needed billions of dollars, and much support from congress, the armed forces as well as the CIA if it was to be successful. All eyes strained skywards as the Blackbird reappeared in the distance and then gracefully soared past the tower.

Outside all the ground crew waved and cheered them on.

Inside Joe Pazzaro smiled and lowered his binoculars briefly. "Well done boys, now show them what we really can do."

The plan was to complete the 'sales pitch' around the airbase when they would then head South West towards Edwards Air Force Base and then turn and continue to the North West, hugging the coast line towards their arch enemy the USSR. Joe Pazzaro looked through his binoculars and glanced at the radar screens to monitor progress. He had been in charge of spy planes, having orchestrated Operation Rainbow and the original U2 programme.

Even after the complete re-design following the Gary Powers' fiasco he was still there, liaising with the CIA to get his new birds built. He was still amazed at how the CIA had set up dummy companies to buy the titanium required to build his babies. The USSR had been the only supplier of high grade titanium in sufficient quantities. He wondered how they would feel if they knew that good old greed had been so successful in a communist regime. "Money always talks." he mused to himself.

As Blackbird roared over the base he allowed himself a slightly smug smile as he chewed on his cigar stub. "Thank you my commie friends for allowing us to build the craft that gives up all your secrets ...."

Suddenly there came an urgent cry, echoing around the ops room.

"Bogies at 1 o'clock," shouted the radar operator at Joe's left, "and they're coming in hot sir, and I mean hot!"

"Shit – not today, of all days." Joe scanned the skies looking for tell-tale signs of foreign jets. "They could be MIGs – but how the hell did they get so close without us picking them up?"

"Captain O'Ryan - Johnno–guide your craft to ceiling altitude ASAP..." Joe shouted over his microphone "We have two bogeys approaching, let's lose these suckers."

Johnno heard the command and immediately moved the throttle forward, pulling back hard on his stick. "Hold on to your pants Rick, we're off to touch the face of God."

"Arm the Minutemen" roared Joe "If these commies want a war let's give them one ... let's blast them back to their own Gods or whatever they believe in."

The Air Defence team sprang into action at the back of the tower. No longer a drill they moved quickly to arm the missiles, lock on target and fire. Every man knew the drill, where he had to go and what he had to do. They had the look of a well ordered team of ants. However when they reached their station and flicked open the fail-safe switches nothing happened.

"No go sir, all missiles are dead – they're deactivated." screamed the controllers.

"Try again" Joe shouted back at them, sweat now pouring from his brow and an air of desperation trying to creep in past his years of ordered precision. A flurry of activity followed. There followed a frenzied resetting of switches, power and monitors. Technicians literally fell over themselves as they moved between desks and control units. Nothing was live.

"Still no go sir," screamed one of the technicians, with an air of dumbfounded resignation. "Everything was checked A-OK just thirty minutes ago – now we're dead in the water!"

Pazzaro's face contorted into one of fear. Feeling the sweat pour down his forehead he wiped it away from his eyes, trying not to show fear of what he now believed was happening. His cigar was now firmly jammed in the corner of his mouth. He then uttered, disbelievingly

"Shit – it's Malmstrom all over again, and that was a UFO – goddamit"

After the event a news blackout had been initiated, and all staff on site bound to state secrecy. Even Commander Pazzaro was included in the push for secrecy. He then thought back to his co-operation in operation Bluebook.

"Lies, and more damn lies." he said under his breath.

"Contact Edwards and warn them – they'll need to activate Dreamland, I'll give the necessary codes, just get our Aardvarks airborne - now! Order them to shoot on sight! No Goddam commie is going to ruin my day," he ordered, not wishing his team to even consider his thoughts of a UFO incursion.

"Wilco sir – they'll be in the zone within ten minutes – on the run way and prepped as we speak."

"Make that five minutes ..." Pazzaro glanced in their direction and Bellowed. Taking the ever present cigar from his mouth he sighed and squeezed his temple with his other hand. He knew that activating Dreamland would finally let the public know about America's fear of a UFO attack.

How would they react to a nuclear war over their own skies?

Would history remember him as the man who started Armageddon? Or as the man who saved the planet?

"Sir – the bogeys are moving away." Joe allowed himself a slight respite in his fear. This was followed several seconds later by a voice showing more than a mild concern.

"They are actively tracking Blackbird now sir, and closing in fast." Blackbird carried no armaments. It was, after all, a spy plane with a camera.

"Captain O'Ryan … Johnno, report." Johnno heard his commander's voice over his headphones.

"Here sir .... We're travelling at around Mach 2 but we now see the bogeys on our trail and closing fast. Just what the hell are they? Surely not MIGs at that speed, do they have a Blackbird of their own?"

"Sorry to say they are unidentified – suggest you pass directly over Edwards and let their defence systems take them out." Joe screwed his eyes in anguish, knowing full well that any nuclear blast that took out the UFO's would probably take out Blackbird as well.

"Wilco sir, we're changing our heading now." Johnno moved his stick sideways, but could see the bogeys steadfastly closing in on his radar. "Pedal to the metal Johnno," Rick shouted across the intercom, "they're almost on us my friend." his voice becoming more anxious. Johnno stared into the distance and increased the throttle. Both pilots felt a gentle surge as Blackbird changed direction and accelerated away at speed.

Back in the control tower Joe Pazzaro looked anxiously at the radar screens and could see the dots of the bogeys closing in on Blackbird.

"Edwards – come in please – status report!" The speakers just crackled

"Edwards – come in please – status report!" There was only silence.

"Shit, this just gets better and better," Joe said in desperation banging his fist on the desk in front of him.

"I trust you have a master plan." The voice of Tesman came from the back of the tower. "Or are we about to lose our billion dollar camera to little green men from Mars?"

"Sir, we are about to be caught." Johnno's voice crackled in Joe's headphones.

"Do we operate 'Shutter' and eject sir?"

Shutter was the self-destruct code. The pilots would eject, starting a self-destruct code with the aircraft. The belief was that the craft was already compromised if the pilots needed to eject, and the safest option was to destroy it in the air rather than let it fall to earth and injure the public. This, plus the top secret equipment which may just survive the crash, necessitated 'Shutter'.

"Tell Blackbird to use full throttle – let's test the new fuels to the limit." Tesman's voice came from beneath his binoculars, "and increase altitude to ceiling limit." Pazzaro gripped his chin – how could he fail so badly and possibly lose two of his best men? Ejection at that speed and that height would be suicidal.

"I repeat, do we operate 'Shutter' and eject sir?"

Pazzaro deliberated for a second or two, then reluctantly followed

Tesman's instructions "Increase throttle to max, and a forty five degree climb rate, let's see what they can do." "Wilko."

Johnno increased the throttle to max, and pulled back on the stick. The 'G' force pushed both pilots back into their seats, the pressure on their chests, cheeks and eyeballs causing them to wince and hold their breath. Blackbird's speed rose steadily ... "Jeez, we're at mach 2 and still rising, we must lose them at this rate." Almost as on cue the bogeys overshot Blackbird, rocking her from side to side.

"What the .... ?" Rick's voice was incredulous as he saw two silver 'cigars' fly past, and then conjoin into one unit dead ahead.

Johnno was struggling to talk with the pressure on his chest. "Bogeys have passed and appear to have merged into one single unit; I'll try to get images of them before we lose them completely." Rick activated the forward facing cameras, putting his cross hairs on the silver grey craft which now lay dead ahead.

"I cannot recognise the craft sir – it's a dull aluminium colour with no markings whatsoever. Its body looks to be seamless. Shit, it doesn't even have any wings! Our bogey is visibly slowing down sir. I fear we're going to collide if we're not careful. Do we take evasive action or Shutter sir? I repeat, take evasive action or shutter?" Johnno fought with the controls as he waited for a reply. The newly merged craft seemed to be coming slowly back towards them on a collision course. He veered right, then left. Both pilots kept their eyes fixed on their enemy, but still the bogey seemed intent on a holding them on a collision course, exactly mirroring their manoeuvres. Johnno could feel the sweat on his face running down into his face mask. This wasn't how it was meant to go. He didn't fear death as much as he did failure. Inside Blackbird Johnno and Rick now had new problems of their own.

"Do we take evasive action, or operate Shutter sir? I repeat; evasive action or shutter?"

Johnno took a deep breath, deeply aware of the craft in front of them and its apparent intentions, and repeated with a growing sense of urgency "Do we take evasive action, or operate Shutter sir ... I repeat, evasive action or shutter?"

Their headphones remained silent.

"I think we're on our own buddy, and this certainly isn't written in the book!"

"What I wouldn't give for a sidewinder right now." Johnno spat through his gritted teeth whilst still putting his Blackbird through the most evasive manoeuvres ever. He dragged the stick up and round, performing an unbelievable barrel roll – but still the strange craft stalked them.

"Jeez Johnno, much more of this and we'll tear apart."

"I know we're not designed for this but we're not going to die without a fight." Controlled desperation was taking over. No matter what they did in Blackbird the craft mimicked their movements exactly, all the time edging closer towards them.

"I think we're about to say goodbye to mother earth Rick – I'll throttle right back and drop as low as I can – when I give the word we'll eject – I'd rather take our chances with gravity than with a fireball." As the words left Johnno's mouth he noticed a blue light emanating from the rear of the craft ahead. Pretty soon they were both bathed in a blue light causing everything within the cockpits to shimmer and move, almost jelly like. Both men looked around themselves, their flight suits took on a strange incandescent hue. Rick lifted his hands in front of his face, his flight gloves began to radiate with strange sparkles within the light.

Joe Pazzaro scanned the skies, chomping on his cigar. "Just what the hell is that thing and how can it go so goddam fast?"

"Perhaps it is a space ship commander." Tesman replied sarcastically. Then, looking down, he spoke to his underling "What do you think Mr Maia, were we prepared for this?"

Mr Maia grinned a sardonic grin, his face taking on the appearance of a mischievous leprechaun.

The tannoy crackled and hissed back into life.

"No joy with evasive action commander, the unknown craft is slowing down visibly, but tracking our course exactly. It has us bathed in a weird blue light. I fear we're about to collide unless we can do something not in the book."

From behind him Johnno heard Rick's voice echoing Johnno's thoughts. "If they're intent on holding us and bringing us down, let's go out with a bang my friend, let's see just what our new fuel actually does and take down that bastard with us. Let's aim down its throat"

"I read you loud and clear, it's been a privilege flying with you my friend. One last try at contacting base first to tell them what we aim to do..."

Back in the control tower the intercom crackled with a barely perceptible hum. "Do we activate shutter sir?"

"Repeat – do we activ .... " the sound died away, then silence. The speakers now just crackling with static.

Now at 30,000 feet the two pilots realised they were now on their own. "No reply Rick – let's do this." Rick smiled as he heard the words. Johnno flicked open the safety catch on the experimental fuel lever. He steadily increased the throttle and felt his body thrown back into his seat.

"Jeeeeeeesus, we're up to Mach 3 - Mach 4 and still accelerating fast."

Ahead of them the unidentified craft still held them in its beam.

"Brace for impact Rick – see you in the next life buddy."

As they approached the unknown craft the beam seemed to expand all round them, gradually turning into an inky black screen. As they hit this screen they felt themselves being sucked and stretched forwards at phenomenal speeds.

There was no impact. The Blackbird entered into a black circle of nothingness with the unidentified craft leading the way. As soon as they entered the circle closed shut like a drawstring on a sports bag leaving only a clear blue sky in its wake.

And all was quiet.

Chapter 4

Back in the control tower Joe Pazzaro was about the reply to his pilots, confirming 'shutter', with a genuine feeling of dread in his heart. However, before he could reply, the radar operators called out

"Sir, bogey is merging with Blackbird ... Shutter should be operated immediately."

"I repeat Sir; bogey is merging with Blackbird ... Shutter should be operated immediately."

At that the screen went blanks – the green blips disappeared – and all went silent.

Everyone just looked at each other in amazement – shell shocked.

"What the hell has just happened? Where have they gone?"

Pazzaro and all the ground crew scoured the skies looking and listening for the tell-tale signs of an explosion – anything as evidence of what had happened - but nothing was visible. They listened but there were no sounds or shock waves that always follow a high speed collision. The skies were clear blue – and no tell-tale resonating sounds of anything.

The speakers fell silent, not even any droning static emanated from their circular mouths.

"Edwards base here – we believe you may have a problem," the speakers burst back into life. "Sorry we couldn't reply, all our comms went down, we couldn't reply or target any bogeys. Can you report back please? How is Oxcart, I repeat, how is Oxcart?"

At the rear of the room Tesman glanced at Maia. "Phase 1 complete- let us hope phase 2 is just as successful." he said quietly. He then raised his voice perceptibly as he looked across the room towards Pazzaro. "At least you haven't started Armageddon commander Pazzaro – you have merely lost a very expensive aeroplane and two extraordinary pilots."

Pazzaro winced. He had lost two good men – the plane he cared little about, that could be replaced. Two good men could not.

"I'll report back to Mr Grey – I suggest you start a search." said Tesman with a sardonic grin all the way across his face. "Oh, and I'd check the fuses on your missiles."

Tesman discarded his earphones and silently left the tower, with Mr Maia close at his heels.

"Get everything and everyone out there looking for our pilots... Did they eject safely? .... Do we have anything? .... For God's sake get everyone on their case. I want to know what happened – NOW," emphasising his command by thumping his hand on the console desk, an action he rarely took. The commander looked shocked. He quietly left the tower, moving down the steps with the air of a man with the world's troubles resting on his shoulders. He passed the assembled dignitaries, barely acknowledging their presence. He had other things on his mind, continuing the sales pitch was not one of them.

Entering the main building he then went back to his office, shoulders bent, his usual demeanour gone. He ignored his staff as he crossed the room, giving them a cursory glance as he opened his office door.

"Get me the secure line out please Sally." he said as he passed his secretary and went into his office, slowly closing the door behind him. Although quite dark it was ordered and business like. There were rows of books behind a small and tidy desk. A haze seemed to hang in the air – a result of permanent cigar smoking.

A photograph of his wife and family sat in pride of place to the right of his desk blotter. A silver case of cigars sat to the left. It was engraved with the words "To a much loved captain from a very grateful crew".

Pazzaro had been a pilot in WW2, flying B29 Superfortresses over Germany. He'd seen, and reported 'Foo Fighters' to his superiors at the end of the war, but he'd never seen one since. Today was definitely not the day he wished to see them again.

Perhaps today was the day they came back to haunt him.

He sat back in his chair, retrieving a small glass and a bottle of bourbon from one of the drawers. He poured a shot, and slowly took it back. He wiped his mouth, and took a deep breath. In the centre of the desk was the secure line - he lifted the handset and pressed the central button. After a wait of mere seconds that seemed to him like hours he drew in a deep breath and began

"Are we clean?" he spoke into the mouthpiece

"Yes Commander, we are."

"Mr President, Joe Pazzaro here at Groom Lake ... I'm afraid that I have some bad news for you sir."

Chapter 5

It was surely a dream, albeit a really bad one. He felt himself floating, flying, and falling silently. Below him he could see rows and rows of trees – they looked just like Christmas trees no less, all covered in snow. Was old Saint Nick going to appear?

As he looked down on the trees he suddenly realised they were getting bigger and bigger.

But, all too soon, he realised they weren't getting bigger at all – he was falling down towards them! And the scene was running faster and faster like the old silent movies that he loved so much as a child. He felt the topmost branches catch him as he flew, scattering the snow into myriads of crystals that looked like stars in the dark night sky. But soon the tug of these branches became more violent – pushing him from side to side, shaking his head until he felt his teeth would fall out. The noise outside grew louder and louder as the impacts became more forceful. But then, suddenly, everything stopped. He was motionless, but aware of a blue light shining all around him, bathing everything in its eerie translucent glow.

He felt he was being lowered gently downwards as if in a large, slow moving, elevator.

All movement stopped. All was quiet again.

"This must be Heaven," he thought. "perhaps I'll meet Mum and Dad at last."

He drifted gently into unconsciousness.

The translucent blue light drifted away and the inky black night enveloped him.

.....

"Hallo, woher kommst du?"

"Cześć, skąd jesteś?"

"Angielski?"

"Amerikanin?"

"English?"

"Polskie?"

Johnno could hear voices in the distance, alongside the church Bells ringing inside his head. As his consciousness slowly returned he wondered why God would welcome him in a foreign language. Slowly he opened his eyes, wincing painfully as light came flooding back in. He was aware of pains in his back and his buttocks. How could you go to heaven and still feel pain?

He felt a cold cloth pressed onto his forehead. Instinctively his hand shot up and grabbed the hand holding it.

"Where am I – in Heaven, or the other place?" He spoke in an anguished, slurring tone, determined to fight back if he was in 'the other place'.

"Don't panic, you're safe now." a woman's voice replied.

"Must be heaven." thought Johnno, and relaxed his grip.

"He's awake – he's safe." she shouted through into the next room.

"Thank God," came the reply, "but not so loud next time, remember where we are."

A tall, muscular man came in from the adjoining room where he'd been eating his lunch. He was probably in his thirties, with a shock of blonde hair, brushed back onto his head and tucked into a flat cap. Although he wore a thick woollen jumper his strong physique was easily visible beneath the bland clothing. He carried a machine gun which he seemed loathe to put down, as if it was an extension to his arm. Around his waist was a thick leather belt, the grip of a pistol tucked into this belt was just visible as he walked. He picked up a reefer style jacket, putting it on as he approached Johnno. "Welcome to the land of the living my friend – it's good to see you're safely with us."

Johnno was slowly coming to his senses, lifting himself up onto his elbows. He felt as if he should know this stranger, or at least expected to know who he was – but wasn't sure at all why"

"Don't try to get up too soon," the girl spoke softly, gently pushing him back onto the bed, "there will be plenty of time for questions, we're just pleased that you've been delivered safely to us." It was there again; how had he been delivered safely? And who to?

The tall man walked toward the door, just visible through the dim light provided by oil lamps scattered around the room. He turned down the lamps near his exit, approaching in semi-darkness. "I'll go and tell the others that Starman has arrived, and to go ahead with the next stage in our plans. Keep a close eye on him Astrild, and answer as many of his questions as safely you can, I fear he's in for a shock." He smiled, pulled his machine gun strap over his shoulder, fastening the last button on his jacket he slipped quietly out of the door into the cold night air, gently closing it behind him.

"I'll get you a hot drink, and something to eat. You need to get your strength back, and then I'll try and answer any questions you have." Astrild got up and moved towards the back room where her colleague had appeared from.

Johnno pulled himself up onto his elbows to try and see exactly where he was. The room was dark, but had a warm glow coming from the end where the log fire was burning and crackling. It reminded him of his holidays with his Aunt Freya having adventures in the Norwegian forests. He could smell the logs burning in the hearth, pine probably, perhaps even juniper – reassuring, earthy aromas first encountered as a child.

The room was somewhat similar to his holiday cabin. The bare walls showed the rough cut timber from which they were made. The curtains resembled army blankets, with red stripes just visible with the flickering light from the fire. His bed was equally rustic, with well-worn blankets and sheets almost hiding the rough wooden legs. On the wall he could just make out what appeared to be a hunting rifle hanging from a wooden peg, and was that a revolver on the table? Then he realised what the man was carrying as he left – he'd seen photos in the books he'd read about the second world war when he was reminiscing about his long lost father – it was a British Sten gun. An inexpensive machine gun made for close quarters killing. What was he doing with a world war 2 Sten gun?

The room was lit by oil lamps, positioned on tables around the room giving off just enough light to see where you were, but not enough to hurt your eyes.

His elbows gave way. He was obviously weaker than he thought. "I think I need to rest my eyes a while." Johnno lay back, resting his head on the rolled up blanket that was standing in for a pillow.

He slowly let out a gentle sigh, "I must remember to be able to remember something." As his head rested onto the blanket the mist in his mind slowly began to clear. "Fir trees and snow, and foreign accents." Johnno spoke quietly to himself, trying to put the pieces in place.

"Am I in Oregon?" he asked. A smiling voice came back "Oregon? Where's that?"

"Is this Washington State? Did I land in Canada? No, probably British Columbia. Alberta perhaps?" Jeez, don't tell me I crashed in Alaska!"

"None of those, sorry, but there's plenty of time for that. You need some warming food and a good rest. You were out in the cold for a couple of hours; your body needs to build itself up again."

The jigsaw of memories slowly began to be pieced together. He could vaguely recall an early morning shower and donning his flight suit. A hot and dusty walk across the runway to his plane

The pre-flight checks he took with Rick - Rick, where the hell was Rick?

He sat bolt upright on the bed. He scanned the room again for another bed where Rick might be lying unconscious or, hopefully, just sleeping.

He could see no-one and his heart sank.

"My co-pilot Rick, Rick Abrahams, where is he? ... Is he safe?"

"I'm afraid you were on your own when we found you – sorry"

Johnno's heart was hollow. He felt sadness, then anger. He'd not lost only a superb co-pilot; he'd lost his best friend.

"Shit!" He felt a tear in the corner of his eye for the second time today. "Shit, shit, shit!"

Falling back onto the bed he drifted back into a much needed state of restful and recovering slumber.

Chapter 6

Meanwhile, back in Washington, a seemingly concerned president was having a hurriedly arranged conversation with his chief of staff of the United States Air Force, Commander Tom Gerarty in the Oval office.

The President placed his hand over the phone as he spoke. "Tom, I've got Joe Pazzaro on the red line here, we've lost our Blackbird on a test flight – what do you think we should be doing."

Commander Tom Gerarty had risen through the ranks from an Air Force Cadet just in time to see action in World War 2. He'd seen action across the skies in Europe, introduced the jet squadrons in Korea, and graduated through the ranks by means of common sense and hard work. The President rated him highly as a leader of men, and a battle hardened veteran.

"Well Mr President I've seen some unusual sights across the Philippines, Germany and Poland, especially with the 'Foo Fighters', but we never had a physical encounter with them."

Drawing heavily on his cigarette, he watched as the blue curls of smoke rose into the air. He leaned forward in his chair, closer to the president. "We weren't sure if these Foo Fighters were German weapons, their Wunderwaffe as they called them. But we could never understand why they never directly attacked us, just flew alongside as if monitoring our actions. After the war was over we discovered that the German pilots, some Russkis too, had seen them and thought they were *our* wonder weapons." He leaned back. "Look, I'm not saying I believe in UFO's, or little green men from Mars, but I feel sure there's something out there – but I'm damned if I know what."

"Are we sure that our Russian friends don't have it?"

The president shook his head. "There's nothing to show that in the comms we've picked up on, we must assume they're lost". After a pause of several seconds he added "somewhere." He removed his hand from the telephone mouthpiece and spoke. "Sorry to keep you waiting Joe, I've got Tom Gerarty here, tell us the full story, we're on a secure line."

Commander Pazzaro related the full details, down to the disappearing radar contact. "I've been in constant touch with Edwards, Mc Chord, Fairchild, Mountain Home - all of our North West bases, even as far as Elison, Alaska and there's no report of an explosion, or wreckage found anywhere sir. We've lost her I'm afraid. One top secret plane and two damn fine pilots, and God only knows where they are."

The President looked pensive, deep in thought. He climbed out of his chair and walked around his desk, sitting on the end near his seated colleague. "We'll need to keep a lid on this; we don't want the public thinking that Russians have the ability to use our air space undetected. Nor do we want them thinking we are at war with aliens. Joe – tighten up security and implement a full blackout. Remind our staff of the official secrets act and their duty to their country."

"Tom, we'll keep eyes and ears on our Russian friends and their allies. Tell our listening sites in the UK and Germany that we need round the clock surveillance. If anyone asks why just tell them that they'll be stationed in Elmendorf before they've finished the sentence." Both Commanders gave an affirmative reply. Commander Gerarty put on his peaked cap, saluted the president, and moved to leave the room.

"I'm depending on you, Tom, as soon as we have an answer I'll get right back to you." The commander smiled uneasily and left the oval office, closing the door behind him.

"Joe, do the pilots have family that we can contact and support. We'll need to remind them of the need for total secrecy?"

"No Mr. President. Both pilots were single men with no living parents. We must be grateful for small mercies".

"God be with you Joe" said the President replacing the phone into its cradle.

All alone now in his Oval Office he knew what he needed to do. He moved back to his chair. Once he'd sat down he tapped his fingers on the desk and then on a lever on the inside of his desk leg – a small compartment swung open. Inside was a small metal object, much like a cigarette case. It appeared to be made of silver, and was smooth on both faces. He pressed on one side and the top swung open. Inside were a range of buttons with strange symbols on them. There was a small round mesh at one end, and the inside of the lid seemed to be coated in a blue plastic film.

He pressed 5 of the buttons in a seemingly random sequence. The object clicked, and a small image appeared on the inside of the opened lid. A face appeared ... the president looked mildly amused. "Well, I'll be damned, this contraption actually works"

Moving the receiver towards his mouth, and lowering his voice "Richard, it's the President here."

"Good news I hope?" Mr President.

"Phase 2 is complete. Secrecy is assured. Operation "Orion's Legacy" is officially under way."

"Thank you Mr President – 1969 looks as though it may be a very good year."

"Keep the Majic12 in the loop Richard, with just enough details to keep them at arm's length."

"Will do Mr President" There was a notable pause "When do we plan to let our colleagues in on the operation?"

"I'll check with Tom and if everything is on track for a July landing we'll call them together and let them know everything. Currently it's on a need to know basis, and we are the only ones who need to know at present. Understood?"

"Fully, Mr President."

The president closed the receiver, clicking it shut. He replaced it into the desk compartment and shut it firmly, ensuring the lever was back in place. He reached into the rosewood cigar box which had become a permanent feature on his desk, took one out and smelled its aroma, gently drawing it under his nose. He carefully lit it, drawing in several times to ensure it stayed lit. A curl of blue smoke rose above his head. He leaned back in his chair, looking worried and feeling very apprehensive.

"God help those boys, God help me and God help humanity if this operation fails"

He picked up his blue phone to contact NASA directly. The distinctive dial tone would inform NASA staff just who was calling. After several rings the call was answered.

"Thomas Payne speaking."

"Tom, its Richard here ... feedback please ... how are things looking for our Apollo deadline this year?"

Chapter 7

Back in the cabin Johnno was awakened by someone shaking his arm roughly.

"Wake up, we need to move quickly". It was Astrild tugging at his sleeve. "Quickly, we need to go into the cellar."

Only half-awake Johnno wasn't sure what the problem was, but the urgency in her voice was enough for him to act. He swung his feet out of the bed, still feeling as if he had the hangover from Hell. Astrild pressed a knot on the timber wall near the fire and the rug on the floor rolled up to one side. A hatch opened beneath them with steps leading down into the darkness. "Quickly, get down there and don't make a sound".

Johnno was unsure why there was so much urgency in her voice, but he stepped down into the darkness, moving as quickly as he could, until his feet found solid ground. The trapdoor silently closed, he heard a gentle scraping sound, which he assumed to be the rug returning, and then nothing. A blue light began to shimmer around him as he looked around. This wasn't a normal cellar; there was no brick wall or even a log wall. The sides were smooth, and had a look of aluminium. He gently felt it and was amazed that it seemed pliable, padded almost. His fingers made small impressions on the surface but then gently disappeared. It was cold to the touch, and definitely a metal and not a plastic. His face screwed in consternation and wonder, "How can you have a soft metal? It doesn't make sense."

As he paced around the room he guessed it was around twelve feet square and just over seven feet high – he could stand safely but reach the ceiling. On one side he could see symbols painted in a circle around the centre, as though around a hatch, but there was no hatch there. The blue hazy light followed him around as he inspected his new environment. Then his exploration was curtailed as he heard muffled voices above him, obviously in the cabin above. He stood dead still, trying to make out any of the conversation. His heart raced. Was it the Russians who had downed his plane and had now come for him? He didn't fancy years in a Gulag, or being paraded like his mentor Gary Powers. The voices didn't seem to be Russian.

Cubans? No, it didn't sound like Latin American or Spanish. He even considered Vietnamese or Chinese, given the state of play in the Far East.

Then he realised; "It's German, definitely German. But why the problem and why am I hiding? Germany is our ally, and has been for twenty years or more".

"Why the hell am I being hidden away? Have I been kidnapped and this Astrild is drugging me to keep me here."

He reached up to try and find the door hatch with a view to showing himself and asking for repatriation from wherever he was back home. But no matter how hard he tried he could find no way out – the door opening had disappeared. There wasn't even a handle to pull on. Panic set in – why was he down here? Why save me? Then imprison me?He banged hard on the roof where he felt the door should be, but the metal was soft to his touch and no sound appeared. No matter how hard or how often he struck the roof no sound appeared.

Then he realised that there were no steps. Where the hell had the steps gone? He felt there was no way out. His heart sank. He fell back and rested against the side wall. Putting his head in his hands he felt helpless. Was it a dream? Was it a new nightmare?

"What the fuck is happening to me? … and why?"

.....

Back in the cabin above him Astrild was dealing with the visitors.

"Are you sure that you've seen nothing? It must be very hard to miss a plane coming down in these woods."

The words were delivered in a clipped English accent, delivered by a German Oberleutnant in a black uniform. The light from the logs in the fire enhanced those given by the oil lamps in the room, one on the table and one in an alcove by the door highlighting the SS symbols on his collar. His face was quite gaunt, highlighted by the severe short 'back and sides' haircut trapped under his peaked hat. Complimented by a pair of metal framed glasses he looked as though he was trying to emulate Heinrich Himmler. As he paced around the light from the fire cast his shadow behind him, a menacing shadow with a hint of Nosferatu. The shadows cast on his face made him look even more menacing and evil. He acted as though he knew this and relished the hint of fear he was sure that he could smell in his quarry.

Behind him he was supported by two armed soldiers, both carrying the distinctive maschinenpistoles issued to the Waffen SS during WW2. He gestured to the soldiers with his pistol, a Luger Parabellum, to search the cabin and outside storage.

Astrild replied; "I'm sorry Herr Kapitan, but we've not seen or heard any more than usual. What, with the constant air raids and the anti-aircraft fire, it's hard to find silence anymore but I'm sure we would have noticed an aircraft coming down in the woods." She looked over to her colleague Manni who was standing with one arm on the fireplace, trying to look relaxed, whilst ensuring that he could reach the shotgun mounted over the fireplace should he need to.

"**Herr Oberleutnant** if you please" the German officer snapped in a tone implying his importance.

Oberleutnant Engel walked around the cabin, his eyes looking for any giveaway signs of anything that would tell him they were lying, his boots resonating on the flag floor. He stopped by the log bed at the end of the cabin, noticing the crumpled blankets. He picked up the pillow, "Who sleeps here?" Astrild smiled nervously and turned to Manni.

"It's for me. My sister uses the bedroom here." he said, gesturing to the room where one of the soldiers was still searching, lifting covers and checking the simple wooden shelves "It's much easier if I can get up and about when I need to go to the factory when I take in the supplies, wood for the prisoners' fires mostly. Oh, and some local Schnapps for your soldiers, it helps to keep out the cold."

Engel stopped by the fire, in front of the rug. He looked down at it, glancing at his hosts, looking for any signs of nervousness. He looked over to the soldier who had just finished searching the bedroom. "Nothing in there Herr Oberleutnant." he snapped, clicking his heels as he did so.

Engel looked at the rug, and gestured for the soldier to pull it back. He smiled as he looked to Astrild, and then Manni, looking for any signs of fear. They smiled as innocently as they could. The soldier leaned over and pulled the rug away from the fire, to show ... more flagstones. Engel looked bemused. He walked onto the flagstones, stamping his feet as he did so, but there was no hollow sound as he had hoped.

The second soldier entered "Nothing Herr Oberleutnant." he barked, also snapping his heels together in deference to his officer.

"If you do see, or hear, of any downed aircraft you must let us know. The plane we seek has bombs on board and could kill many locals if they detonate, and that would be .... A pity." Engel spoke in menacing tones, obviously looking to instil some fear after the fruitless search.

He marched briskly out of the cabin door, his two minions in close pursuit.

Astrild went to the door and watched the shadowy figures move down the path to the track which served as the road. Here a third soldier was waiting, opening the door to the Kubelwagen for his officer. The two others climbed into the back seats, and the car slowly made its way down the track into the dark of the woods until silence returned.

"That was close." said Manni, replacing the rug after carefully turning it back through 180 degrees. They both realised just how close they had come to being discovered, and months, if not years of planning would come to nothing.

"And here comes the first difficult part of our plan." said Astrild as she approached the wall, preparing to again press the knot on the log panelled wall which acted as a switch. Pausing briefly she looked to her colleague, and then down at the floor.

"How do we explain that our guest has travelled back in time by some twenty five years, into Poland in the middle of a World War, and just why we need him so much?"

She pressed the switch on the wall and the opening in the floor reappeared.

Johnno heard the trap door begin to slide open, and he readied himself for a possible fight.

Light slowly began to flood back into his enforced hideaway. He blinked but, surprisingly, his eyes had stayed accustomed to the light due to the blue haze which had surrounded and followed him around his 'cell'. He looked up and saw his hosts smiling benignly, proffering a hand to help him leave his hideaway. He relaxed, just slightly. The steps had reappeared from the side of the wall as if by magic, and he slowly climbed up, scanning the room as he did so. They beckoned to him to sit in a rough log armchair.

"You'd better sit down whilst we explain." his hosts voiced in unison.

"We're sorry about that, but you must be kept safe until your task is complete."

"Task, what task? Just what the hell are you talking about? Why have you imprisoned me here, and just where the hell **is** here?"

"You have not been imprisoned at all, but we do desperately need you and your special skills"

"'Here' is actually Poland." Astrild told him.

"And that is not the unusual thing you think it is, " Manni added. "you are in Poland ... the year is 1944 ... and the world is at war!"

Johnno looked startled, and a grin slowly appeared on his face.

"Whose joke is this? Has Rick organised some kind of treat for my birthday?"

He gripped the chair arms, lifted himself up, and looked around the room waiting for someone to enter and shout 'surprise'. They have taken a lot of care with the decor – it **did** look like a genuine log cabin, and Manni **was** carrying a vintage Sten gun.

Johnno then remembered it wasn't his birthday; then recalled that Rick could not be found after his test flight went haywire. He looked stunned, and put his head into his hands. "Christ, whatever this is, it just gets better and better." roughly pushing his hair back and looking upwards again at his hosts.

"Please let us explain" said Manni, "but first a question for you, if you don't mind."

Johnno's eyes opened wide, a puzzled look on his face; he nodded.

"Do you believe in life on other planets? What about Alien life forms different than your own?"

He thought a while. "I have read War of the Worlds, and thought some life elsewhere in the Universe may be possible. But they came here to kill and conquer – are they REAL?"

Manni smiled. "No, not the Martians, nowadays there is no viable life left on Mars, but elsewhere there most certainly is. There are planets, universes, Federations of beings out there who are far older than life on Earth. These Federations have come together in order to help life develop and flourish in other galaxies, on other planets. They cannot directly interfere with natural progression, but can lead by example and assist in the natural way of things."

Astrild joined in. "Many millennia ago unscrupulous cultures would visit developing worlds and rob them of their riches for personal gain. They would actively encourage wars where the inhabitants would be armed with new weapons and kill off their enemies with impunity. The visitors could then plunder materials needed for their own diminishing stocks. They took gold, platinum, lithium and copper to name but a few, and leave their well-armed squads in charge as they left, promising to return and reward them. Of course they never did."

"That's when the Federations formed." added Manni " To stop the acts of preventing civilisations from developing as naturally as they could."

Astrild continued "If they destroyed themselves, and several did, so be it. That is the natural order of things. But visitors could not, and should not, be allowed to interfere and affect natural development of any race of beings."

"That's a lovely story, and sounds very impressive, but what does that have to do with me and Rick, and my Blackbird flight?"

Manni sat down next to his reluctant guest. "Earth has been visited in the past by several alien life forms. Whilst some are here to plunder, others wish to help."

Astrild sat back against the table. "A culture you on earth called the Annunaki came here millennia ago, and helped early civilisations develop by a process of support and supposed non-intervention. Their home planet originated in what you on Earth call the Pleiades constellation, and was beginning to die due to over population and loss of natural resources. Their spacecraft's path brought it close to planet Earth, where your early Sumerian culture was developing. However when their greed began to overtake their desire to develop human resources our Federations had to act. They began to manipulate human blood lines with science – modifying what humans have just discovered as DNA. They wanted workers to mine for elements, gold especially, as this is widely used in components for their flying craft. They were forced by the Federation to return to their home planet, Nibiru, and are being constantly monitored."

"Have you heard of the ancient wars of your Indian continent?" Manni queried. "Some six thousand or so years ago your Indian continent was visited by more beings from the Pleiades cluster who decided to claim your planet as their new home. They bought aircraft with them which were able to traverse the universe at great speeds – faster than light can travel. They were also capable of moving into the 4th dimensions – that of time – at will. That made them almost impossible to deal with. Whilst they were travelling home with elements extracted from Earth several other alien cultures moved into their newly found 'home' in order to save them. These are the basis of ancient Indian Gods still worshipped and revered today."

` Astrild continued. "The eventual outcome was a war between these two rival factions, with dire results. Powerful devices were used which created explosions hotter than the Sun. Whilst this drove out the Pleiadians the Federation decreed that these weapons could never be used again by visiting beings. If Earth was to use them, it must develop and find them itself. Many beings died of terrible sickness in the aftermath of these explosions, created by manipulating nuclear energy."

"Do you know about Hiroshima?" asked Manni. "In our present time in 1944 it hasn't happened yet, but you must have heard about its death toll, even years later caused by radiation sickness."

Johnno nodded. "Yeah, we dropped two devices in Japan to end the War. We were told that we killed the few to save the many – that was its justification. They've never been used in anger since – thank God."

Astrild took over. "And there are the beings who originated from the planet you call Alnilam, one of the three main planets in your belt of Orion. In this constellation you also find Riga, and that's where the Federation of planets is based. The Federation has visited your planet in the past, the latest visits being during the rise of Egypt and its Pharaohs, followed by supporting civilisations in the Americas, dating back from the Aztecs through to modern Native American peoples. By a process of help, not intervention, methods of farming and raising crops to support the growing numbers of inhabitants were passed on. Think of them as benevolent teachers, assisting their students to develop and grow by a process of nurture and support."

"Which is where you come in" Manni spoke quietly.

"Me? How? I'm just a pilot in the US air force – I'm not a spaceman." Johnno moved towards the fire, preparing to snatch the rifle of the wall if needs be. Having his side facing the fire created a silhouette, but his contorted, querying face, could plainly be seen. It was a mixture of anger and bewilderment. "And how do I know you're not a pair of nutcases who've trapped me in a cabin telling me wacky stories? Where's your proof, give me some proof or I swear! " he gestured towards the rifle.

"It's time." said Astrild. Manni nodded.

"Excuse me, I need to provide that proof." said Manni, gesturing for Johnno to step to one side. As he did so, he moved slowly sideways, but mindful of the need to get at the rifle above the fire if needs be. He was unsure of Manni's actions, but needed to keep an eye on Astrild as well. Manni walked over and moved the rug by the fire, and pressed the knot on the wall which acted as the switch to the hidden compartment.

Once again the floor opened up slowly, an eerie blue light flooding the cabin once again.

Manni climbed down and pressed a series of lit characters on the sidewall in an apparent random sequence. There was a hiss – and Manni climbed back out of the compartment.

Johnno moved over and peered inside. He could see an opening to the side, but nothing else.

"Yeah, and what does that prove? And I'm not climbing back in there either." – he smartly moved sideways, keeping his back defensively towards the fire.

"Please prepare yourself – this may come as more than a bit of a surprise."

Astrild smiled. "Here is the proof you requested." Manni walked over to the front of the cabin, opened the door and quickly checked outside. He looked down the path and into the trees, searching for any signs of lights and people approaching. "All clear." he said, coming back inside and locking the door, the cold air causing a fine mist to come from his mouth.

Johnno felt apprehensive. He glanced back at the rifle over the fireplace, mentally checking how long it would take to grab down, fire and take them both out.

Manni and Astrild stood side by side; they took a deep breath , closed their eyes and the same blue haze that was in the compartment seem to envelop them, a translucence that surrounded them and crackled slightly. There was an aroma of ozone, an electric presence in the air.

Johnno gazed at them intently and saw the haze begin to shimmer. Their bodies seemed to move as if made of clay. Their faces seemed to slowly morph and change.

Johnno reached up and grabbed the rifle, pulled back the bolt, and swung it around towards his hosts.

"Shit," he cried, eyes opening wide, "Holy shit."

There, in front of him stood his Aunt Freya and Rick or, at least, two people who distinctly looked like them. He was distracted as voices came from the compartment below.

"Can we come up now?"

Johnno swung around, aiming the gun at the compartment opening. He feared, and was now ready to fight for, his life.

"Yes please." said Freya quietly.

From deep within the compartment, slowly climbing up the steps came two silhouettes backlit by the steady glare of the log fire. Slowly their features became more visible as Johnno's eyes managed to focus on their faces. It was Manni and Astrild!

Johnno looked both ways – over to Rick and Freya, and back to Manni and Astrild.

He felt the blood rise from his feet upwards through his body, travelling slowly as if in an elevator. He felt his legs slowly begin to buckle beneath him. As the 'elevator' reached his head he felt his scalp tighten, making his hair stand on end; his eyes closed and he passed out.

Astrild jumped forward and caught the rifle whilst Manni help break his fall.

"Well, that went well." said Rick, sarcastically. "Let's hope we can convince him that he really is our Starman."

Freya rushed over to check Johnno was OK. She felt his pulse; "Racing, but steady. He'll be OK when he comes round." She pulled a piece of cloth from her pocket and wiped his brow, hoping that the aroma from what was left of his childhood comfort blanket would somehow help.

"Let's get him somewhere safe and warm, his ordeal has only just begun."

Chapter 8

When Johnno finally awoke he was back in the bed, with the firelight glowing and lighting the cabin. But this time there were four people in the room, not just two as before. Swinging his legs over the side of his bed he slowly rose to his feet. He looked towards Freya, and then Rick – and blinked his eyes. Was it a dream? Can I make myself wake up?

"How the Hell did you do that? Rick's dead, and I left you hours ago before my flight. Have you drugged me?"

"We are so sorry about the way we surprised you, but feared you needed proof about the stories we told you." Freya spoke softly and smiled, a reassuring smile that Johnno remembered from his youth, though the lines on her face now reflected her age and years of concern, it was still his dear aunt's smile.

"Yeah, sorry buddy, I've looked after you for so many years it pained me to realise it's the only way we can prove what we claim. We can explain the 'magic trick' later, the important thing is that we bring you up to speed on what's happened, and what's planned to happen."

Freya moved towards the bed. "Your amulet, show me your amulet."

Johnno pulled the chain away from his neck and proffered the amulet, albeit reluctantly. Freya took off the ring from her right hand, and placed it by the amulet. They began to glow as if full of stars and magically linked by a strange force.

"I gave you that amulet as a child. Whenever I stroked your head I used my right hand – remember? Had I held you in my right arm your amulet would have glowed and may have frightened you – or at least peaked your curiosity at a time when I could not tell you all about myself."

This brought memories flooding back – good ones at that. In his mind's eye he could see and feel his Aunt Freya holding him, reassuring him that everything would be alright.

"And the Bell shaped charm passed on to you by the ground crew?" Johnno nodded as he saw it was safely hooked onto his chain.

"Remember him?" Johnno thought awhile, and a light was switched on in his brain. A smile crept across his face. "That was you, wasn't it?"

Freya smiled and took Johnno's head into her hands, held him close and smiled that smile he knew so well. She even smelled the same. It was a warm, pleasantly homely and lightly perfumed smell which took him back to his childhood.

"You didn't think I'd let you go on this crazy mission without one last goodbye, did you?"

Johnno smiled. "Crazy mission?"

Then the memories of operation Oxcart flashed back into his mind. He looked at Rick, with a questioning look on his face. "Where the hell do you fit into all this – whatever THIS is?" Suddenly Johnno grabbed his left shoulder and winced, as if in pain. "Christ, my arm is playing up again. Childhood incident."

Freya smiled knowingly. "The childhood incident you recall was when you slipped and fell from a tree when you were playing pirates. And it wasn't your left shoulder, it was your right."

Johnno frowned ...

"And when I took you to the local hospital you were treated by a kind doctor who gave you a red lollipop for being brave. You wore a sling for two weeks, even though you didn't want to. I even drew some healing symbols on it. Three stars, two in line and one slightly out. You even had that incorporated into a tattoo when you joined flight school as a good luck charm."

"You could have seen that when I was unconscious."

"Yes but would I know that even though it was the American Air Force where you enrolled you had 'Per Ardua Ad Astra' written underneath the American flag to recognise your British heritage. You even asked me if I minded. It was a nod to your father and your love for him."

Johnno knew that, somehow, magically, she really was his Aunt Freya. Tears began to fill his eyes and he moved slowly towards her. He hugged her. Gently at first, but then with a force created by the total love and admiration he felt for her.

Freya placed her hand on his hair and nuzzled her face into his. "There, there, min lille romfarer." she whispered. At that Johnno's tears freely flowed. After what seemed like ages they left their embrace and he was sure he saw tears in his Aunts eyes too. Rick passed Johnno a towel, allowing him to dry his eyes. Freya then took it to wipe hers.

Rick smiled. "Sorry to deceive you buddy, but it's been my job to make sure that you were ready for this. From meeting 'accidentally' when we first enlisted and all through your flight training I was there to keep you safe and keep pointing you in the right direction."

"It was you who suggested enrolling for the NASA training, wasn't it?"

Rick smiled. "Yep"

"And I suppose you fixed the crew selection to make sure we flew together."

"Yep"

"And the mission, Oxcart, I don't suppose ...."

"Yep, yep and yep again buddy."

Johnno's mind flashed back to the UFO chase, the comms blackout ... and that grey craft with its blue light. "Why didn't we hit the sucker when we mach'd up? That's what I was aiming to do. We must have been travelling at Mach 4 or 5 – we're talking nearly 4,000 miles per hour ! What else can travel at that speed?"

"We can," Freya replied "and you were drawn into the craft by an attractor beam which accelerated you into the past ... at mach 7. I think it's time for more explanation, but first let's make a drink. How do you feel about a hot chocolate?"

Johnno's mind flashed to the nights spent out in the cold as a child with his Aunt Freya.

Long walks in the forest, hours spent sledging and making snowmen or just sitting outside the cabin gazing up at the sky and its myriad of stars. There was always a hot chocolate waiting to warm them up; it was his Aunt Freya's speciality. He smiled. "Yes please. I don't suppose you have marshmallows too?"

Freya smiled, "Pink ones as I recall," walking into the kitchen.

"I owe you an explanation about what is happening, and an apology for not pre-warning you. It was something we could not do – the enemy is everywhere. And I don't mean the German army." Rick's voice was apologetic.

Johnno walked over to Rick and paused just in front of him. Rick smiled, tilting his head to one side and raising his eyebrows as he had done so many times before. He threw his arms around his puzzled friend and hugged him. Johnno instinctively hugged him back, slapping him on the back gently.

"God it's good to see you safe and sound. I thought we'd lost you."

"Not much chance of that buddy, I always was the better pilot."

Johnno grinned. "In your dreams friend, in your dreams"

Astrild threw a cloth over the log table and drew up chairs for them all to sit on. Although rustic, and slightly wobbly, they were sturdy and safe. Manni closed the compartment hatch and replaced the rug. He moved over to the log basket and placed two logs onto the fire. Sparks and embers danced and glowed as they fell into the flames.

"We need to keep warm. It will be a long night tonight with plenty of talking and many, many questions."

Johnno moved over to the table, pulled up a chair and sat down. "You can say that again friend, I have SO many questions I just hope that you have all the answers. I feel as if I'm going to wake up at any moment and find this is just a crazy dream."

"It's no dream," said Rick "but it may become a nightmare if we get things wrong."

Freya came back into the room carrying a wooden tray laden with 5 mugs. "Hot chocolate and perhaps a tot of rum to warm us on this chilly night." added Astrild, producing a small corked bottle from her apron pocket. Safely placed on the table they each picked up a drink, cradling them in their hands. The fire had begun to pick up throwing light and warmth bathing everything in its warm glow. The delicious smell of pine and hawthorn filled the room as the fire gently crackled in the hearth

"Just exactly what is going on here?" Johnno relaxed back in his chair. "And just exactly where in Hell are we?"

Manni looked at his colleagues around the table, and then at Johnno "For the people who have to live and work here it is Hell." Astrild took his hand on the table, gently squeezing it and smiling sympathetically at him. Tears formed in her eyes, reflecting the light from the fire, gently rolling down her cheeks.

Freya took the lead. "We are in Poland, in the Owl Mountains. The locals call them the Eulengebirge Mountains. Fortunately we are in a remote cabin which offers some security, but with occasional problems caused by visits from the Nazi security guards, mindful of the hate stirred up by them in the local population." She took a sip of her drink, and continued. "It is part of a Nazi complex named Der Riese, linked to the Wenceslaus mine and we are some 5 kilometres from the town of Ludwikowice Klodzie. But none of this means anything to you, does it?"

Johnno shook his head. He took a sip from his mug then, with a quizzical look on his face, frowned as he tried to take in this information and recall what had been said earlier.

He took another sip from his drink . "Poland, you say? Owl Mountains you say?" He paused and gently frowned. "Whoa! Did you say 1944?" it was as if a light had suddenly been turned on. "How did I, sorry, did WE end up in 1944? Surely that's impossible."

Rick added a note of urgency. "Freya, would you like to fill in some of the important details for my worried friend. It's been a long day and we need some rest if we are to act soon. The task details could always wait until tomorrow." Freya nodded. She told Manni and Astrild to go to bed and get some sleep. They needed to be up early to take logs down to the Nazi complex and keep their enemy off guard. Even the master race needed to keep warm in such a cold climate.

"Now to try and explain where you fit into all of this." Freya drank the dregs from her mug and placed it on the table. She smiled at Johnno and began. "The beings from Alnilam in the Orion cluster of stars have a special gift which you would call shape shifting – the ability to take the form of any creature."

Johnno smiled and then frowned. "Surely that's just in sci-fi comics – I read them – you bought them for me – as a kid."

"No, it's not just in comics, and I bought you those comics for a reason," she smiled, "it DID make you want to be a pilot and a space traveller, didn't it?" Johnno turned towards Rick and back to Freya, a faraway look in his eyes, almost as if he was mentally turning back the clock to his youth. "And now we have the scientific part. Your scientists have just discovered the body's DNA structure found as your building blocks to life. They have a way to go before they discover what it does and how it can be manipulated, but they will get there, eventually. Imagine it as a string of instructions on how your body will develop, instructions provided by your mother mainly and father too, planted in you within the womb. Well, there are many empty pages within that instruction booklet where advanced races can add their own. It's a little like an in-built computer program. One of those empty pages is actually instructions on how to copy the DNA of others and create a perfect likeness using their own body as a building block…. Shape shifting."

Johnno was enthralled. "How do you 'get in' and change the instructions to suit yourself – shape shift as you say?"

"All we need do is to make contact with the being we are looking to copy. We usually place our hands on their shoulders, from behind, and we transform into a perfect image of our unwilling host. They become unconscious and unaware, but essentially they are still alive. When they awake they have no memory of what has occurred. We can complete the transformation by just holding them, but the replication may not always be perfect. This ability is already programmed within our DNA, and we use it with great care, aware that if seen by others here on earth it could create mayhem and panic."

He sat back in his chair. A look of enlightenment mixed with total bewilderment on his face as it turned into a frown. Then the penny dropped. "Wait a minute. Then YOU must be from Alnilam, or somewhere in Orion's belt, aren't you."

Freya nodded. Rick added "We both are". Another penny dropped.

"And you are here to prevent something happening – something to do with nuclear weapons I'm guessing." Freya nodded again.

Rick smiled "Well worked out buddy," getting to his feet and walking around the table toward his friend. He looked him in the eye, and gestured towards him with his forefinger.

"And we need your help to prevent it."

"What can I do? I'm just a USAF pilot – a damn good one I might add – stuck in a time warp in the middle of a war that we have already won. The Nazis didn't even develop a nuclear weapon, did they. I know they managed to build rockets, the V1 and V2, but wasn't that all?"

"That is, or was, true. We now have an incident that could change history forever. As Federation members we are duty bound to intervene, but we cannot actively interfere. We need to 'modify' potential actions to preserve history and Germany must not develop a nuclear weapon, especially now that the Bell has re-surfaced."

"The Bell? What's the Bell?"

Freya continued .. "The Nazis have, for years, searched for mystic Aryan artefacts to help them become the master race. Hitler believes that he is a divine being, destined to lead the Master Race using supernatural powers. From the Ark of the Covenant to the staff that Moses used with supposed magical powers, they have scoured the world. Thank God they have never visited the museums in Iraq or Persia."

Rick joined in "They were advised to secretly visit India in the 1930's to the Rajasthan area, where there had been a reported nuclear war recorded in the Mahabharata, the ancient Indian manuscript. A weapon named 'brahmastra' was used - an early nuclear device created by the Pleiadians. When they dug into the desert our spies tell us that they discovered a Bell shaped object, which they took back to Germany, along with many other items, statues, ancient symbols. They named it Die Glöcke – the Bell."

"Is this Bell of any significance?" Johnno couldn't understand how a Bell could cause a nuclear blast.

"It wasn't thought to initially; they stored it away believing it was just some kind of religious artefact, perhaps a large model for a planned temple. One of the symbols on its side was copied and used – an ancient good luck symbol – and is now their swastika! But we now know that someone from the Pleiades cluster – our enemies - must have travelled back in time and offered help to the Nazi scientists – for what exact reason as yet we do not know. We tracked a time shift on our beacons placed on Iapetus, through past Phobos and finally on our last beacon located on the dark side of your Moon. If the Nazis discover its full secrets, the whole history of planet Earth will change."

Johnno looked perplexed. "How can a Bell change the Earths future?"

"This Die Glöcke is large, some ten to twelve feet tall by around 9 feet wide , and is in fact a time machine. Not only that, but inside within a locked chamber is a weapon – powered by a nuclear core and liquid metals. If they find it then we fear they could possibly reverse engineer it and create a range of nuclear devices and weapons for themselves. They are already experimenting and have been doing so for years ; they have heavy water plants in so-called neutral Norway, just a short distance via neutral Sweden to Peenemunde. Here they could load them onto their V2 rockets ... there is a V3 planned apparently."

Johnno's eyes opened wide. "They could fire these at," he paused, letting the implications sink into his brain, "England , Russia and America. We only developed Little Boy and Fat Man in 1945 – they could destroy us before then. Jeez, this IS serious."

Rick looked at Freya, almost as if asking permission to continue, then back towards Johnno "Even worse than that, using the time machine could allow them to go back into the First World War and change that conflict – perhaps even back before 1776 and change America's history forever. The United States may never have even come into being . Imagine what that would mean to the free world. We have to find and destroy the Bell, but only after we have taken the weapon away and moved it to safety, far away from Earth. It must never be allowed to be replicated or history could change and that paradox MUST be avoided at all costs. The Federation decree must be satisfied." Rick's face was deadly serious, something Johnno had never seen before. "We need someone, an inhabitant from planet Earth, who can reset the natural order of things by retrieving the weapon, and destroying the Bell. We believe that you can do that. After all, you are half Alnilamian."

Freya smiled and reached out to hold Johnno gently by his wrist. "Your father's surname was Owens. It was changed to O'Ryan to help hide his identity to that of an Irish sympathiser - and less of a threat to Germany if discovered. Can you see the link we created?"

Johnno looked as if he were far away, deep in thought wondering what this link could be. After several seconds his eyes widened, a smile crept across his face. He looked directly at Freya. "O'Ryan, I get it, yes, yes, I get it; Alnilam is in the star system of Orion, my mother was from Orion. Part of my birth right is Orion."

Freya looked at Rick, a grin across her face. "At last I can share the truth with you," her smile disappeared, "but a potentially terrible gift, one that may get you killed."

"That's the least of our worries. We have a job to do. When do we start?"

"Tomorrow we start, but tonight we sleep." Freya gestured towards the bed. "We need to

be fully prepared." She walked over towards the fire and pressed the knot on the wall; the door within the floor slowly re-opened. Rick moved slowly down the steps, offering his hand to help Freya down. She took a last look at Johnno and smiled. "A tiring and unusual day for you 'min lille romfarer' – now get some rest." The door closed gently with a hiss, the blue light left the room and everything was once again bathed in the warm glow from the fire, its embers now dying away. Johnno added another log and smiled. 'Min lille Romfarer - spaceman' was his Aunts reassuring nickname as a child. She really, really was his beloved Aunt Freya. He climbed into bed, pulling up the sheets and burying his head in the pillow. "I wonder what will tomorrow bring. Little green men I presume.." He smiled to himself and closed his eyes, fearing his thoughts would crowd out his tiredness and stop him sleeping.

He need not have worried, within moments his weariness overcame his wonderment at the day's revelations and he was sound asleep.

Chapter 9

In the distance Johnno could hear talking and people moving about, and thought it was a dream. But, as he slowly woke up and his senses fully returned, he realised that the cabin was a hive of activity with all four occupants chatting and moving around. He rubbed his eyes and propped himself up. He could smell coffee and something akin to fresh bread.

Freya smiled at him "Time to get up, we have plenty to do and it will take some planning."

He swung his legs out of bed and stood up. "Is there a bathroom I could use? I need a shower and a pee. I can't remember the last time I had a pee."

"Let me see" said Rick "I would say you last had a pee over twenty years ago".

Johnno laughed "Whoa! that IS a long time".

Manni gestured towards a door at the left of the fireplace. "No shower I'm afraid, but a sink and plenty of hot water in the jug by the sink. Oh, and there's no lock on the door, so keep whistling." Manni smiled and disappeared into the kitchen area.

Johnno poured some of the hot water into the basin and, putting his hands together, splashed water on his face. It felt good to finally wash. Looking around he found an old Gillette safety razor, and set about carefully shaving with the warm water and a little soap. His survival training in the Air Force stood him in good stead. "All I need now is a bear to attack and I can spray him away with my body odour, or frighten him with a Bell."

He took off his shirt and had a strip wash, then gathered the towel off a hook in the wall and dried himself as best he could. He looked in the small mirror to check he'd shaved cleanly, feeling around his chain and neck. Satisfied, he put his shirt back on, and then returned to his colleagues to discover what the next step of their plan entailed.

But first a cup of coffee and a piece of fresh bread was called for.

On the table was a feast to his eyes. There was fresh bread, fried eggs and bacon on platters and a steaming jug of hot coffee.

"That DOES smell good mine hosts, and boy am I hungry, my last meal was more than twenty years ago." He grinned at Rick and winked.

"Let's eat whilst we plan the day," said Astrild, pouring coffee into tin mugs around the table, "as we have little time to spare."

Johnno took some bread and added bacon to make a heart-warming sandwich. "If time is of the essence why didn't you take me back to before they found the Bell, maybe in India, and prevent them finding it?"

"We need an inhabitant of earth to satisfy the needs of the Federation. Normal earth dwellers cannot time travel yet, their DNA is not programmed to accept the forces created by the action of time displacement, and they would die if they attempted it." Freya was quite clinical in her approach.

"Whilst helping to save the early Indus civilisation from annihilation a rogue faction of theirs stole one of our time machines – the Bell as it is now known – and hid it, hoping to use it for their own gains after we had left. All this did was to speed up the Federation leaving, indignant at the way they had been treated, especially after defeating their potential invaders and new masters. The Federation have a great respect for mutual trust and pride. Hence someone from Earth must return the Bell and restore that bond of trust as it was someone from earth who stole it from them."

Johnno thought for a moment. "And that person is me? Whoa ... why didn't I die then.? I'm an inhabitant of Earth, and I've presumably time travelled to get here."

Rick glanced at Freya, again looking for a positive reaction. She nodded.

"Well Buddy, you may have been born on planet Earth but if your Aunt Freya is from Alnilam where is your mother – Freya's sister – from? You have many of her genes, way enough to protect you in time travel."

"But what if I hadn't inherited enough of those genes, I'd be .." Rick had a huge grin on his face as he cut in to the conversation. "Toast buddy .. you'd be toast. It's a good job we weren't wrong." A friendly pat on the shoulder followed as Johnno contemplated his luck.

Freya continued. "Your mother was sent back here earlier than me, in 1938, as Germany prepared for war, with the aim of feeding back information on the German war machine, and their 'Wunderwaffe' – their wonder weapons. We were concerned then about the possible interference by any rogue nation, especially if they were Pleidians.

Johnno looked stunned. "What really happened to her then?"

"Your mother Sara met and fell in love with your father whilst they were working undercover at an American air base in England. He was an agent who was being prepared for his role in the war foreseen by British Intelligence. The information they shared led them to forming a working partnership which spilled over into love. As a result of their romance their son John was born, named after his father." Freya sighed and took a deep breath.

"Please go on" .. Johnno was intrigued.

"When the Federation discovered you had been born they sent me to support and possibly replace your mother. A parachute drop and raid had been planned and there was a concern that your mother could not – would not – leave you behind whilst the raid went ahead. They were wrong."

"How wrong?" Johnno was now pushing his food around his plate totally ignoring his hunger for food. His hunger for the truth now dominated his thoughts.

"When it was discovered that V2 rockets were being manufactured in a German site in Peenemunde an RAF raid was planned. It was believed that the 'Bell' was located there, being examined and possibly retro engineered by German Scientists. The air raid, code named Hydra , was planned for August 17th 1943. There were three waves of bombers to the attack. During the first wave your mother and father, who had been parachuted into Sweden and smuggled into Peenemunde, were to enter the base to locate and destroy the Bell. It was believed to be in hanger 17 .The Nazis would believe that a bomb had fallen and would not suspect sabotage. In that way your Mother and Father had a better chance of escaping back toward neutral Sweden. The work force, mainly made up of Jewish prisoners 'recruited' as slaves had managed to forward this information initially from a German soldier who claimed to be of Jewish descent and allied to their cause. We now know this is not true and suspect he was a Pleiadian, the cause of the time shift. It was a well-orchestrated trap."

"What happened then?"

"They were guided to hanger 17 by local resistance fighters. They cut through the wire fencing surrounding the buildings and made their way over to the hanger door. They entered safely and all was initially silent. But as the resistance fighters turned to find a safe place to hide they heard a burst of gunfire. We heard no more from two very brave people." Freya's head visibly dropped as she spoke the words. After several seconds she took a deep breath and raised her head again. "You lost your parents and gained an unworthy Aunt." She took a deep breath and composed herself.

"Even the air raid was not truly a success. Many, many of the slave labourers were killed and the research facility almost untouched. Whilst the RAF hit their planned targets we realise they had been fooled, with the research moving into the worker's quarters, and vice-versa".

Rick was visibly angry. All those good men killed, and for what?"

"We lost track of the Bell until now. We now firmly believe that it is nearby in the Wenceslaus mine complex where a circular henge is being built to act as its launch pad. They believe a henge is needed to generate the power required to activate the

Bell's systems. What they don't know, luckily for us, is that the Bell can generate its own power. The construction of the useless henge is providing us with more time to complete our mission. How lucky is that?"

Freya nodded. "The Nazis have transported many slave workers here, mainly Jews and Italian prisoners of war. They are being worked non-stop, with many dying where they toil. They have kept numbers fairly low to avoid their activities being discovered, but there is an urgency that worries us. We need to act now."

Rick continued. "They brought the Bell here, in the middle of Europe, in the belief that it would be easier to defend. Allied bombers struggle to fly this far, at least until 1945 and that would be too late."

"This Pleiadian bastard, is he here as well?" Johnno asked. There was an intense look of anger and hatred in his eyes. "Can we deal with him too?"

Rick nodded. "We strongly believe so, but he is the unknown element. He could appear in the guise of any one of many characters, obvious enemy or unknown friend. Luckily Manni and Astrild are well known to the local garrison guarding the mine where we believe the Bell is being retro-engineered to create a new, perhaps even larger, version. For now we are safe, we are of some use to them. We believe the Pleiadian does not know we're here and we are not Jewish and unlikely to be taken for slave labour." Her eyes widened for a second and she pursed her lips in recognition of that simple, yet radical, statement.

"We supply logs for their fires, it is bitterly cold here in winter. Even the supreme race feels the cold. So I supply logs in exchange for German cigarettes and chocolate." Manni added. "The cigarettes we give to the local villagers, what is left of them, and the chocolate to local children as a little treat in these trying times."

Astrild smiled. "And we supply slivovitz, our local brandy. We brew it ourselves and have been steadily making it stronger. Our hope is to use it to help disable the guards. It is so strong they will never notice. It is a VERY black market," she added, raising her eyebrows and smiling with eyes wide open at her companions.

"And now for our plan of attack." Freya beckoned to everyone to move to the table.

Astrild and Manni cleared everything away whilst Rick unfolded what looked like a fold-up map, but it had the look of aluminium. He laid it on the table and waved his hand over it to smooth it down. It seemed to float onto the table top. Incredibly, as it did so, an image appeared. It appeared to be a set of plans which seemed to show details of a factory, a workplace with several distinct areas. One area was outlined in red and labelled 'Die Glöcke'. "That," said Rick, pointing to the red area "that is our prime target. All we need do now is to plan our attack. There can be no room for error. History will surely judge us should we fail in our mission."

Chapter 10

"Any news, any updates; is there *anything* to report?" The tone was urgent, but the President was worried as he talked to his chiefs of staff.

Around the large oval table were the cream of the US defence teams, all sworn to secrecy about the impending operation, and the devastating scenario should it fail. Smoke hung in the air, wisps of blue circling in the warm air, a mixture of Cuban cigars, a pipe and Marlboro cigarettes. Coffee cups and mugs adorned the table alongside ashtrays brimming with ash; the president was sipping on whisky. It had been a long meeting. The atmosphere was tense, deep concern etched on the faces of everyone present.

Errol Gilmore, the Chairman of the Joint Chiefs of Staff, was first to speak. "We have had word that the Starman has safely landed and, presumably, has been briefed on his mission. Our nefarious contact, Mr Tesman, assures us that nothing untoward can yet have happened as our current history remains unchanged."

"How the fuck will we know if it is unchanged, history happens, goddamit."

"If there is a change Mr President, for the worse, then we would simply not be here, you may not have been born, England may no longer exist ... and there would be a swastika hanging outside the White House." His tone was clinical.

An ominous silence hung in the air.

Richard Elms, the head of the CIA, added "We have made arrangements ensuring that Mr Maia goes back in support; he deemed it necessary. Even as we speak he has made his way to Groom Lake and his underground complex located within Area 51. When he arrives safely he will confirm."

"Assuming we are successful, is Apollo ready for launch?" the President added an urgent tone to his question, aimed directly at Dr Payne, head of NASA.

"We have already tested the Lunar Module functions and the preliminary flight is planned for May, giving us two months to fine tune everything. We plan a dress rehearsal of the landing, and aim to get within 8.4 nautical miles of our planned landing area. We need to ensure that nothing goes wrong on the delivery mission. One slip on the real mission and a nuclear explosion could shift the Moon's orbit with disastrous consequences." Chewing his cigar, and moving it to one side of his mouth he added "Not to say what it will do to global tensions. The whole goddam world will be watching on TV. But, yes, we will be ready Mr President – you provide the package and I promise that we will deliver."

A mixture of relief and patriotism was tangible within the room; the only thing missing was the sound of the 'Star Spangled Banner'. Heads nodded. Sweat was mopped from brows. Everyone looked at each other for reassurance. It was so silent you could hear a pin drop.

The silence was broken by John Vasey, the army Chief of staff "Thank fuck we have the best postal delivery service in the World."

The room was filled with relieved, nervous laughter and the tension was cleared for a moment.

The President rose to his feet, looking around the room at his team. Taking a deep breath and, with a hint of Churchillian grandeur, solemnly spoke. "Let's pray to God, gentlemen that all goes to plan and the package is also safely delivered. The lives of millions of US citizens, not to mention millions of our allies and the whole free world, rest solely in our hands. Let us not forget that Project Horizon must succeed, and this is surely our first step." Reaching down onto his desk he picked up his tumbler of Jack Daniels. Raising it aloft he added words that reflected the thoughts of all staff members present.

"Let us pray for our agents in Germany.
Let us pray for their total success.
God help us if we fail,
For God will surely judge us if we do."

Chapter 11

"Just how do you plan to get me into the mining complex? I realise that the caves and tunnels may be dark, but I'm sure to stand out, don't you think?" Johnno was concerned even before the mission began. "How many USAF airmen are there in Poland?"

"Let us worry about getting you in there. We do have a contact, a solid contact, a member of the village who has lost his whole family to the Nazis. He will not let us down." The tone of Rick's voice was definitive. "He will not fail us. He has already supplied the layout for our plans at great risk to himself and his friends. They would sooner die than complete anything to support their hated captors."

Manni voiced his support. "Even now they try to sabotage the tunnels and structures. They move the reinforcements before any concrete is laid to try and weaken it. They work as slowly as possible under pain of death from their barbaric SS guards. God, they even pee what they can onto the steel inserts in the hope it will make them rust more quickly."

"But that is not enough. We must get in and destroy the Bell." Freya added a note of urgency.

"Why not fly the Bell out?" Johnno added, "Do we have to destroy it?"

"It must be destroyed so it can never be used again, by anyone, especially the Nazis." Freya was insistent.

"But surely if we can fly it out, to a date so far back that it disintegrates with time, or into the future where we have just come from that will save us the effort of getting explosives down there."

Rick gazed into the distance, and then back again. "That DOES make sense of a sort. Problem is .." he frowned and stared at the map " if we go way back then we lose the pilot with it, they have no way of returning to their own time."

Freya walked around the table, stood by Rick, also deep in thought. "If we go to the future the pilot would be safe, but would the Bell be safe there?" a pensive look on her face. "No, we **must** destroy it."

"Which explosives are we using? Plastic? C2? Gelignite? Are they powerful enough?" Johnno asked, walking around the table to stand by their side.

"We have a special explosive, a liquid that spreads around the target and is absorbed. Once detonated the target explodes from the inside." Freya dug into her pocket and handed Johnno a small cylinder to inspect. "See, small enough to conceal and yet powerful enough to work."

Johnno inspected the cylinder closely. It was black, around two inches diameter, and about four inches long. He looked perplexed. "This is going to destroy the Bell?" he said, holding it up to the light for a better view. "How on God's earth can this destroy anything?"

"Don't let its size worry you, remember that your atomic bombs are based around atoms, and look what they can do."

"Made in Alnilam I presume?"

"Yes, made in conjunction with the scientific community within Orion."

"And what would the Federation say if it fell into Nazi hands and was used as one of their wonder weapons? Imagine that on a V2 headed towards London."

Freya looked towards Rick. "He's learning." And then back towards Johnno. "It can only be detonated by adding another component, one that the Germans cannot have - our eyes. If you look at the end you'll see a glass like substance, a retinal scanner. Every one's retinal scan is different, much like fingerprints. Even shape shifters and replicants cannot copy those. We just need to add your retinal reading to its memory. Once done this end must be twisted to activate the scanner, you look at the red dot in the centre, and it's done. Once activated you have around thirty minutes to make good your escape. When the cylinder detonates it does so within the atoms of whatever it is in contact with and literally explodes from the inside. Collateral damage is kept to a minimum, in that way we are sure that none of the workers will be hurt, and nothing will remain of the Bell, only fragments." Her face was resolute and full of determination. "We just need to first locate the Bell."

Rick nodded in agreement with Freya's statement. "We have contacts to get you in the complex, we have the tools to destroy it, we just need to make sure that we get you back out alive and return you to your own time. If we are successful then you will have a life to return to, if not .." Rick's voice trailed away "If not, who knows what hell we would return to."

"Then we'll just have to make certain that we do succeed. I've not travelled all this way just to fail. I've waited twenty three years for this moment, we **cannot** fail." Johnno's voice was firm, almost indignant. He banged his fist onto the table "Just get me in there and I'll do the rest.

Hey, wait a moment; will my eyes do the trick?"

"Yes – remember the scans and tests we completed at Edwards?"

"Y..e..s.." Johnno's reply was slow and deliberate.

"Well I 'borrowed' your scan results and passed them to Freya. She then added them to the scanner. Now just all five of us in this cabin can detonate the explosive. No chance of leaving future technology with our hosts. And the Federation, they're happy."

The mood in the cabin had become sombre, yet determined and business like. The plan of the complex was studied closely, looking for the safest way in, and out. Various routes were proposed, with their pros and cons discussed. The problem was the actual location of the Bell. Whilst the circular concrete henge, which would presumably act as its launch pad, was being constructed above the complex on the outside, the Bell itself was being retro-engineered deep below ground.

"What protection is there above ground?" Johnno asked, turning the map around and pointing towards the guardhouse.

Manni answered, almost business like. "Above ground is a detachment of Waffen SS, charged with overall security of the project, supporting a secondary detachment based within the mine, mostly used for relaxing. They have no compunction in killing anyone who they see as a threat, their own regular soldiers included. The guard house supports the guard towers and usually has two soldiers on duty – these will be our initial target. They *love* our Slivovitz!" Manni grinned. "There is also a small communications hut sandwiched between the two others. Small, but a key target as this is where all communication is received and transmitted."

"Do the guards or the SS detachment ever go on leave?"

"Occasionally, but not all at once," Astrild offered "they will occasionally visit Wroclaw, about 50 kilometres away. Whilst it is a Polish city the locals act as if they revere their 'liberators', whilst their underground fighters are steadily growing and amassing arms one by one. They drink for free and carouse with local women, women who would cut their throats in an instant."

"Are there any more trips planned, do we know?"

"The commander for the complex is General Hans Krammler, a notorious Nazi, fully indoctrinated with all that his 'master race' planned to do when their third Reich came to power. He is ably supported by Jakob Storrensberg, an SS Grupenführer, known for his admiration for his Führer, and his hatred for the 'lower races', as he prefers to call them. Our contact tells us that Erich Musfelldt, an SS colleague from Majdanek, is visiting his colleague Storrensberg a fellow SS Grupenführer at the complex. He has a duty to report directly back to his Führer on progress to date. And .. it is Musfelldt's birthday on Friday – let's hope that they visit Wroclaw."

"Well, let's make Friday, and the weekend our target for operation Bell. Agreed?"

"That leaves us just two days to prepare, let's get to it." Rick pulled the map towards him and placed his fingers on the lower right corner. The image of the complex disappeared, to be replaced by a series of drawings showing the Bell and its intricacies.

"First we need to ensure Johnno's retinal data will activate our own wonder weapon, and then look for a plan 'B', should anything go wrong, and that includes looking at the Bell's controls and how to open the compartment which holds the weapon."

Freya pulled a small box out of her pocket "Maybe these will help." Inside was a pair of contact lenses, tinted blue to match Johnno's eyes. "Try these for size.", offering them to Johnno. He took them out, one at a time, and clumsily inserting them into his eyes.

"Sorry, I've never done this before." He stood there, eyes watering and blinking in pain as he attempted to make them as comfortable as possible.

Freya then passed what seemed to be two small, thin black cylinders to Rick. Outwardly they had the appearance of conjoined black pencils. Rick held them in one hand and gripped the top of each, extending them lengthwise telescopically. They were now around eight inches long. He then gripped them at their centres and pulled them apart, a thin membrane screen appeared between the two edges, almost transparent it now had the appearance of a small TV screen, only completely flat. Rick busied himself touching the screen on his side, pressing a set of symbols which was located at the bottom.

Johnno looked bemused, although inside he was deeply impressed at yet another amazing piece of technology.

"Look at your watch." Rick instructed his bemused colleague. Rick smiled, and then showed Freya, and then Manni and Astrild the screen image. They nodded encouragingly. "Whoa, that's the time, is it?

"Well, can I see what you're smiling at?"

Rick turned the screen towards Rick. It had a live image of Johnno looking back at himself. "Whoa, how the ..."

"It's your lenses my friend. They include a special transmitter. In that way we can see exactly what you see."

"You can see everything?"

"Yes, everything my friend." adding with a grin on his face "Be careful when you visit the john, I'd keep your eyes closed."

Johnno smiled, swaying his head from side to side "Ha Ha Ha " he added in a loud, exaggerated voice. He then realised their true potential.

"So – so you can see exactly what I see. You guide me when I'm deep in the complex and then when I reach the Bell," then paused in thought for a moment "but how can I hear you?"

Freya walked over. "And just in case the portascreen is not working ..." she touched the ring on her right hand, twisted the 'stone' gently, and a pale translucent light began to shine just above, almost as if it was a screen made by water mist. Johnno looked on in amazement as the mist formed into an image, a 3D hologram of him in great detail, albeit just twelve inches in height. He turned his body, keeping a fixed gaze on the misty form in front of him, amazed as the image replicated his every movement.

"Now that IS cool".

"So you're never alone, I'm always there to support you". She twisted the stone in the opposite direction and the image faded away.

"Now it's my turn." Manni passed him a small piece of what looked like clear plastic. "It is shaped to fit in your ear, try it."

Johnno carefully manoeuvred the unit into his ear.

"As well as letting you hear us, we can hear you. Try it – gently touch it to activate and whisper something."

Johnno turned away, and whispered something into his hands.

Rick replied "It was a Harley Davidson Electra Glide – we called it 'Shovel', and you were a terrible passenger." They all smiled as Johnno added "No swearing under my breath then."

Freya moved towards the fire. "I will need to contact London, we need to arrange a special surprise for Saturday." She opened up the hatchway in the door, and descended into the shimmering blue haze.

"And we need to complete our visit to the complex and deliver our logs and brandy."

Manni and Astrild donned their coats, pulled on fur lined hats and readied to leave.

After checking the coast was clear through the windows they slipped the bolts on the door and quickly moved outside, pulling the door shut behind them. Rick bolted the door.

"What can we do to prepare?" Johnno was keen to get started.

"We need to know the complex layout back to front. We need to know exactly where the Bell is located, and we need to practise with your lenses and earpiece. There may be a surprise or two lurking below, we MUST be perfect in sending and receiving info."

"So it's back to flight school then."

"Sure is, partner."

Chapter 12

Manni and Astrild carefully guided their horse drawn cart down the winding path towards the Wenceslaus compound. All motor vehicles had been impounded by the German occupation forces, the majority being damaged to prevent their further use by local inhabitants. They feared 'hit and run' tactics by the local partisans which could hinder their progress within the mines.

It was mid-October and light flurries of snow had already begun, making the path slippery and potentially dangerous. As they talked a stream of water vapour left their mouths, soon lost in the chill morning air. Manni gently flicked the reins to keep the horse gently moving "This is a pleasant way to pass an Autumnal hour."

Astrild smiled "Let's hope this mission succeeds and we can do this again purely for pleasure," a wistful look in her eye. As they neared the mine they were approached by two guards. One levelled his weapon at them, the other gestured to them with his arm

"Halt – keep your wagon well back – we have an essential convoy arriving."

Manni pulled back on the reins and the horse obeyed and stopped moving.

"Can I have a pee whilst we're waiting." Manni called over to one guard. "Cold weather , and all that, you know."

The guards looked at each other, each awaiting confirmation from their colleague.

"That's OK," shouted back the soldier who had beckoned them to stop, "but stay close, my colleague is extremely nervous and very trigger happy."

Manni moved over to the side of the track and climbed a slight rise behind him. He gestured behind the tree "OK here?"

"Fine," shouted the guard, "but be quick."

Manni moved around the back of the tree, out of sight of the guards. He took a pair of small binoculars from his pocket and scanned the distant track to see what the convoy consisted of. Pushing a small button either side of the frame he zoomed in on the trucks noisily approaching the mine. His heart sank. On the trailers behind the trucks he could see long, large items covered in tarpaulins. Some were flapping loose at the top, caused by their resistance on the long journey. Manni could make out the pointed outlines of a rocket. He swiftly took photos, and managed a small video.

"Oh Gods of Orion, no. That's what these tunnels are for. They are going to launch their V2 rockets from them. They must be closer than we thought."

His musings were disturbed by the shouts from the guard who was still aiming his machine gun at them. "Hoi, what are you doing there?" speaking as he moved towards Manni.

Manni swiftly put his binoculars into his jacket pocket and unzipped his trousers. He emerged from behind the tree, making a display of zipping his trousers back up. "Sorry," he smiled "it's the cold weather." shrugging his shoulders.

The guard gestured with his machine gun, directing him to climb back on his seat.

He climbed back onto the cart, taking the reins in his hands, all the while offering a slight smile towards his two adversaries.

In the distance the sound of diesel engines steadily grew quieter as the convoy entered the compound and disappeared into the mine opening.

A walkie talkie crackled into life, with guard number 1 answering.

"Jah, Mein Kapitan." he said, his posture visibly stiffening as he did so. Turning to face his colleague he nodded and gestured, and then gestured for the cart to proceed. His face broke into a wide grin as he held the horses halter, preventing the cart from moving. Manni felt uneasy, had he guessed what he had been doing behind the tree?

"I trust your brandy is a good vintage today?"

Astrild smiled and reached behind her into a wooden case covered by an old blanket.

Handing a small bottle over to the guard. "Only the very best, it's been an excellent year."

The guard eagerly accepted, and released his grip on the halter.

Manni slapped the reins "Trot on Odin." The horse dutifully trotted onwards.

Behind them one of the guards pulled out the cork with his teeth.

"Gute gesundheit mein freund" and duly took a swig from the bottle.

"Moge der krieg bald enden Mein College." added guard number two, accepting the bottle from his colleague, and also taking a large mouthful. They replaced the cork, guard number two placing the bottle in his trench coat.

"Nur zeit fur eine zigarette?"

"Yah" They turned their backs towards the disappearing cart. They lit their cigarettes and began to chatter.

As the cart moved away Manni waited until the soldier's voices had faded into the distance. Once he felt safe he told Astrild what he had seen.

"The tunnels are not just to keep the Bell secret. They will be using them to store the V2 rockets as well. If they discover the hidden weapon then all hell will literally break loose. We have to destroy the Bell, **and** the weapon."

Astrild was taken aback, her face a picture of deep contemplation. "What if they already have it?"

"We need to deliver our goods and see if our contact can update us. The weekend cannot come soon enough, Johnno's task just got a whole lot harder."

Manni clipped at the reins and Odin dutifully trotted on. As they came to the end of the woodland lane they approached the mine complex.

A newly laid road led into the mine opening, which was now blocked off by two large gates. The road itself led east, leading to local villages and then on to Wroclaw by a circuitous route. There was deep concern about the road being spotted from above as bombers flew over on their nightly missions. There weren't many raids, and the report of a crashed aircraft a few nights before had spooked the German high command. They were still on the lookout, but were becoming satisfied that it had been a false alarm, no damage to the forest having been seen from above by their Fiesler spotter planes, and no wreckage being found. The consensus now was that a single, damaged, aircraft had jettisoned a dud bomb before attempting to fly safely home.

Two guard towers were located at either side of the main gate with a smaller entrance just to one side, allowing the comings and goings of soldiers and the burial crew taking the bodies of the dead workers outside of the complex. The bodies of dead workers were carted away, usually by handcart or horse drawn cart if there were several, and dumped in a clearing around four hundred yards away. As the bodies piled up they were torched and burned, usually every two or three weeks. Then they dig a pit somewhere in the forest and bury them, but never in the same place twice. These bodies were initially left at the side of the workings within the mine as a warning to those inside not to slacken off their work.

Many workers, slaves to all intents and purposes, were whipped by the SS guards within the mine workings, and kicked into the side where they could be finished off with a single shot from a Luger or Walther pistol. As Polish captives arrived weekly, with prisoners of war also being sent to work on one of the Führer's Wunderwaffe, the lives of individuals were of no consequence to their captors. As long as the tunnels were being hewn out by hand, with no real tell-tale signs above ground of earth moving equipment, they believed that their secret compound was safe, and impregnable.

Manni and Astrild drove up to the main gate, the smaller one being too small to allow the horse and its cargo through.

A guard walked up to the gate, and signalled to the guard tower above that all was fine. The sentry nodded, and turned away. One of the gates was swung open and Manni coaxed Odin through.

"The usual cargo my friends, wood to keep your outsides warm and slivovitz to keep your insides warm."

The guard waved him through, and gestured for him to stop. He walked around the back of the cart and pulled away the tarpaulin covering the log piles. The logs were neatly stacked forming a 'v' shape and filled the cart. He gave it a cursory inspection and pulled the tarpaulin back over.

"Guard house, over there," he growled, "and don't be long, we have work to do."

Manni led Odin and its cargo over to the guard house. The log pile was situated around the back, the guard house itself a simple log built structure, around twenty feet by fifteen, lined on the outside with planed rough wood. There were windows to three sides, allowing its occupants easy views to the guard towers, the mine entrance as well as the road. It had a wooden table in the centre, surrounded by four wooden chairs – an obvious clue as to the maximum number of soldiers usually in there at any one time. At the far end there was a large log burning stove. This kept the hut warm and had a flat surface on top for an old black kettle and metal coffee pot.

At the side nearest the mine entrance was the communications hut. It was of a similar size and housed the essential communications equipment. It was manned at all times, and also had a log burning stove on the side closest to the guard house. These stoves, plus the desire for free, strong drink had proven to be Manni and Astrild's way into the tentative trust of their German 'hosts'.

Manni climbed over onto the back of his cart and removed the tarpaulin. "You go inside and deliver the brandy to our friends inside, I'll begin to unload the logs." He passed over the wooden box containing the bottles of brandy and then began to unload the logs, restacking them neatly alongside those already there. As he did he carefully looked around to check his position. The months of repetition had allowed him to realise the safest place to approach the guard house. He had placed the horse and its cart alongside extending directly away from one side. By doing this he had created a blind spot where the guards in the towers and by the gate could not see him directly and the back wall, which faced the woodland behind, had no window.

As he unloaded the logs he sang local folk songs, allowing all and sundry to know where he was. In this manner he knew they would not look for him until he had finished his tasks.

Astrild knocked on the door awaiting permission to enter.

"Eingeben."

Astrild clicked the latch and opened the door, looking around the room as she entered. There was just one soldier present. She placed the box containing the bottles of brandy on the table; turning towards the solitary guard she asked "All alone today Herr Korporal ?"

The guard looked slightly taken aback. He then looked around the room and said quietly "Toilettenpause. Sorry, toilet break for my fellow corporal."

"Your brandy is on the table – do you have anything for me?"

The guard thought for a moment, then smiled. "Ah yes, your chocolate and cigarettes." He turned and walked over to a desk at the rear of the cabin. Alongside an array of mugs was a small package. The guard picked it up and walked back over to his guest and jokingly added "You do know I could be sent to Russia for this."

Astrild took the parcel. "It is our little secret. Are all the items here?"

"Yes, of course. You will remember me when this dreadful war ends, won't you?"

"Do not worry. You will have safety and a life back with your family. It is a Federation promise." He smiled knowingly as he appeared to be thinking of his family back home in Hanover.

Astrild turned quickly. She opened the door and went outside towards her colleague.

Back inside the guard smiled and slowly blinked his eyes, no pupils, no whites – just a blue-black shiny mass.

Eyes as smooth and as black as haematite.

Manni had almost completed the new log pile as Astrild approached. "Did you get everything?"

"Yes, it is safely received."

"So we'd better be heading home then."

Manni loaded the last log onto the top of the pile and returned to Odin. They climbed back on board and approached the gate house. The guard there acknowledged their desire to leave and opened one side of the gates. There was a cursory check under the tarpaulin, the guard lifting it with the barrel of his machine gun. He waved them through. Manni waved back and smiled as he guided Odin through the gates and up towards the path that led safely home.

Astrild shouted "Auf Wiedersehen." waved, and then under her breath she added "you Nazi bastards!"

Manni let out a small laugh "Be careful, one of those Nazi bastards is on our side." He clipped the reins and Odin began a steady canter back towards home along the narrow path.

"Tread carefully Odin, we have valuable cargo on board"

The silence of the pine forest was punctuated by bird song. The haunting call of several owls was interspersed with the steady rhythmic calls of pigeons. The smaller birds added to the chatter with their repeated, melodious tweets. It could have been a peaceful autumn day in any woodland anywhere in the world. These calls, coupled with the clatter of Odin's steady footsteps made it seem that war, and the danger presented by the mine's secrets, were a million miles away and all was well with the world. The pleasant aroma of the pine forest mixed with spruce trees only added to the delusion.

Soon they had arrived back at their cabin retreat. Manni pulled the reins gently and the cart came to a halt. He climbed down from his seat, lifting the reins high above the horse's withers and then it's head.

"You take in the package and I'll unbridle Odin."

Astrild climbed down and nodded. She hurried to the cabin door and tapped a rhythm of knocks for safe entry. The door slowly opened, Freya greeting her and beckoned her inside.

"Manni is with Odin, he won't be long."

"Do you have the package." Freya's tone was urgent.

"Yes." and she duly passed over a small parcel.

Johnno and Rick had now appeared and Freya walked over to the table, placing the package of cigarettes and chocolate in the centre.

"What's so special about cigarettes and chocolate?" Johnno seemed nonplussed.

"Not just chocolate my friend, but our safe way into the mine." Rick added as he took the parcel and began to unwrap it.

Astrild moved over to the table and spoke, her voice full of concern. "We have a problem. V2 rockets. We have seen two of them delivered today, maybe even three. We've heard that the Blizna site has been relocated to Heiderkraut and believe these have been diverted for use here"

Freya turned to face her "Are you sure?" she paused, "how can you be certain?"

"Manni took photographs and a small film record, we are sure."

Rick had finished un-wrapping the parcel. He laid the contents out upon the table. There was a serious tone to his voice. "Then we have to get this right first time, there can be no room for errors."

"Yes, but how can chocolate and cigarettes help?" Johnno was still confused.

"Not just chocolate old buddy." Rick was unwrapping a large chocolate bar. It was a Hershey bar, passed over to their contact in a previous visit. It had supposedly been part of a consignment of goods dropped by an American support flights over Poland from so called neutral bases in Switzerland. It is dropped to help keep up local morale but many had been found and confiscated by the 'Blue Police' officers, those Polish turncoats hoping for greater rewards when Germany won the war. Unbeknown to them this was exactly what US intelligence believed they would do, dropping thousands of bars over the area 'by mistake' to support their agents' story.

Rick carefully un-wrapped it, unfolding the wrapper and flattening it carefully under his hands. He repeated the sequence three more times, each time placing the wrappers together to make a larger sheet.

"Now for the magic." Rick took a book from the fire surround and placed it on the table. He opened it to reveal a hollowed out section, inside was what looked like a piece of flat glass, around five inches by three inches. He took it out and held it above the wrappers. Pressing one corner caused a light to emanate from the glass, shining down upon them. He moved it around gently from side to side, and up and down in order to make it fit the shape of the assembled wrappers. To Johnno's amazement the wrappers began to lose their folds and form into perfectly flat pieces of paper. Freya looked at them closely as they flattened, with images and text beginning to appear as if by magic. She carefully re-arranged them, moving them around until a complete image appeared. This image was then projected onto the stuccoed wall above the fire. The enlarged view was now much clearer. Manni walked over and removed the rifle, the image was clearer still.

"That's it." she said triumphantly.

"That's what?" Johnno replied.

A voice came from over by the door as Manni entered, closing the door behind him and removing his hat, banging it against his jacket causing small flecks of snow to fall on the floor.

"THAT is our way into the mine - **and** our way back out again."

Chapter 13

Freya walked over to the wall and studied the map, remarking to Johnno "The beauty of this mine is that it is actually a natural cave complex with many internal caverns. The Germans are just enlarging the original entrance and reinforcing cavern areas for their research. They believe that the natural depth will keep their secrets hidden away from allied eyes... and if there is an accident of any kind then the natural caverns will contain them."

Manni looked perplexed. "They appear to have moved the Bell from research area 1 to area 2. See, here it is highlighted in red," he pointed to the map. "that **is** worrying, does it mean they are making progress in finding its secrets I wonder."

"It is still accessible from the main tunnel, but further away from our exit point, here," Freya was pointing at what appeared to be a small crack on the left side of the map, opposite the research area caverns. "this is a narrow passage leading out into the hill above. It is narrow, but will allow us a way out, if only in single file."

Johnno studied the map, noting the fine detail in the research areas. "It seems a coincidence that the V2 rockets have just been delivered at the same time that a visit is planned by Musfelldt. I've a feeling that something bad is about to happen."

"All the more reason to put our plan into operation as soon as possible."

Johnno turned to face Freya "Yes, but how do we actually get into the research areas?"

Before she could answer the cabin door swung open. Stood there, silhouetted by the fading light from the open door stood the German Oberleutnant flanked by two soldiers, armed with MP40 machine guns.

"It was foolish of you to leave the door unlocked."

Freya flashed a menacing glance to Manni.

The Oberleutnant gestured with his luger for the 5 startled occupants to move away from the wall. Slowly they complied.

"Hands behind your heads please." he added, in a mock mannerly fashion.

Manni glanced at the rifle, now stood against the wall, weighing up his chances of success.

"I wouldn't do that, my friend, as my colleagues will cut you in half before you can get half way there."

Manni relaxed and moved over to the right hand side of the room, joining his colleagues. All stood dutifully with their hands clasped behind their heads.

The Oberleutnant moved over to the table, examining the, now plain, chocolate wrappers. With his gloved hand he swept them off the table. As he did so he moved towards the image above the fireplace.

"This looks like the mine complex. I wonder who is your contact? I'm not sure how you found this updated plan but you are clearly spies who are planning to kill innocent workers as well as dutiful and heroic soldiers from our German homeland. I even heard you mention our Grupenführers, Krammler, Storrensberg and Musfelldt. You are also assassins. As such I sentence you to death," He paused for dramatic effect, then turned back to face them, "with immediate effect. Take them outside and shoot them."

Manni faced his colleagues "Sorry my friends, it is my fault that we die."

One of the soldiers walked over to the fire, and gestured with his machine gun for the 5 occupants to go outside.

As they trooped out the Oberleutnant smiled to himself. "I should get an Iron Cross for this."

Beneath him he felt the mat on the floor ride up against his boot. He leaned down and pulled it to one side. He began to stamp his feet on the floor, to no avail. "Perhaps a secret switch.". At that he began to move his hands over the wall above the fire. As he kept feeling the wall for a hidden switch he heard a click, then the hiss of a door opening where the rug had been. He grinned as he looked down into the misty blue light.

"Perhaps even an Iron Cross **and** a promotion. I could soon be a General even."

From outside came a burst of machine gun fire, quickly followed by another, and then a final long burst. Then all was quiet. In the distance an owl hooted but no birdsong.

Back within the mine complex the gunfire was heard by the guards in the guard tower. One went to his telephone; wound the charging handle at the side, being out through to the officer's quarters located deep within the mine.

Krammler believed that he would be safe in the bowels of the mine should their true identity be discovered and bombing raids ordered to destroy the mine. It was also his belief that leaving the slave workers to eat and sleep where they worked within the shafts would also discourage attacks by partisans as well as air attacks.

An SS officer picked up the phone.

"Guard post 2 here. Shots fired in the woods, machine gun fire we believe."

The officer turned to speak to his comrades, who were sat in a cavern which had been enlarged slightly and internally concreted to create the form of a room. It was lit from above, power coming from a generator in an adjoining 'room'. Ventilation was through metal ducting fixed to the roof which ran along the mine shafts to the outside of the complex. A rough fireplace had been constructed to give a semblance of normality. This burned the wooden logs supplied by Manni and Astrild. Steel tubing had been shaped and was fed into the ventilation ducting forming a crude but effective chimney. Wooden bunk beds along one side completed the living area.

It was a small detachment of men, ten in total. Five were sat around a central table drinking slivovitz – what else – relaxing with top buttons of their jackets undone. The remaining four were on duty, ensuring that the work of the slave labourers was continuing.

"Do we have any patrols out today? There's a report of gunfire in the woods."

One officer at the head of the table removed a cigar from his lips and sat forward in his chair, resting his hands on the table. "Oberleutnant Schulze was on security patrol with two of his men. He had reported possible enemy activity outside the compound, where that crash was reported." He turned to his colleagues and laughed loudly. "It seems that he was right." Raising his glass he offered the toast "Death to all enemies of the Fatherland.".

They all raised their glasses "To the Fatherland," each drinking to the toast.

"No problem. More vermin killed." replacing the phone in the handset re-joining his colleagues at the table he picked up his own glass and raised it high in the air "and death to our enemies wherever we find them." They responded by pouring another drink and cheering.

He smiled. "And now, perhaps we can have a friendly game of cards, gentlemen?"

Chapter 14

Noticing the steps as he peered down into the blue mist the Oberleutnant prepared to descend and find the secrets hidden in this remote cabin. As he did the door opened and a soldier marched in.

"All complete?" the Oberleutnant growled.

The soldier snapped his heels together.

"Jawohl Mein Oberleutnant."

Then, from behind the soldier, Freya appeared first, and then Manni, with Astrild, Rick and Johnno appearing from behind his left shoulder. "It appears you have now found our contact." Freya glanced at the soldier, who now levelled his machine gun at his Oberleutnant. He gestured for him to come away from the floor opening.

"Your weapon, Mein Oberleutnant."

The officer stared at his underling whilst gripping and re-gripping the handle on his pistol.

"I wouldn't do that; I'll cut you in half before you can pull the trigger."

Reluctantly he placed his weapon on the table.

Triumphantly Rick added "Now we have our way in, and out, of the mine complex."

Manni gestured to the Oberleutnant to sit down, where he was quickly tied to the chair.

"You will never get into the mine. Security is strict, especially with our guest arriving. If you surrender to me now I will show you mercy."

Manni lowered his head to face his enemy. "We have already witnessed your mercy."

Schulze growled in anger "And you have killed a loyal member of the German Occupying Army; your sentence should be death – preferably by firing squad."

Manni smiled, and then performed an exaggerated bow, extending his arm in a sweeping motion towards the cabin door. Johnno and Rick were supporting an unconscious soldier, bringing him into the cabin and seating him beside his senior officer.

"Killed? No, he is merely stunned. We are not savages, but seek peace and an end to meaningless loss of life."

They made short work of tying him up as well; both soldiers were now secured to their chairs and were turned around to face the wall.

Rick turned to Johnno "Say hello to Johan, our contact within the mine." He walked forward and saluted. "Pleased to meet you, I've heard a lot about you and you volunteering to help."

Freya patted him on the back. "Well done, how did you manage to arrange this assignment?"

"I believe we have a leak somewhere. I overheard the Oberleutnant telling his superiors of his suspicions about our cabin, along with those he held for Manni and Astrild. I 'made myself available' whilst he was looking for armed support as he prepared to leave the mine. Luckily I was chosen. The alternative would have been to follow and ambush them – contrary to Federation directives."

"My fellow soldier over there is married with children. He is a former nurse who will open a celebrated nursing home after the war ends as penance for what he believes were his sins in the war, especially here with the slave labour he has witnessed. He deserves to live his life as planned."

Johnno faced Rick. "This other soldier, just how did you stun him? One moment he was standing, the next his legs buckled and he passed out."

"Just like this, old buddy." At that he pointed a small, compass sized disc at the back of the Oberleutnant. Pressing on top caused a fine beam of green light to be emitted. Almost instantaneously his head gently fell forward.

Johnno was impressed. "How ....?" Before he could ask the question Freya explained.

"It is quite simple. Your body is controlled by electrical impulses. We use this device to overload those impulses and the target becomes unconscious. We can vary the time from minutes to days. We call it a neuroliser. Its actual name is a neural pathway analyser and signal blocker." she smiled. "But neuroliser is much easier to remember and say." Her tone regained its seriousness. "Remember our Federation aims. We cannot intentionally cause death and perhaps change the future. He will also have no recollection of these events, memory is merely electrical storage, and we modify that storage."

"I don't suppose?" Johnno flashed a smile at his friend.

Rick smiled and handed a disc to Johnno. "See the dial on top? Move clockwise with your finger and the gauge lights up. One light is one rin, that's around thirty of your seconds and then it doubles up another nine times until we have around ten days. It's simple, effective and no threat to life. The victim wakes up with a slight headache - and a has a really good sleep."

The device clicked magnetically into a wrist strap; to all intents and purposes it was just an oversized watch. He passed it over to Johnno, adding "Take good care of it; it cannot fall into enemy hands. Alien weaponry, and all that."

Johnno strapped it to his wrist, looking at it admiringly.

"If you are concerned about losing it then simply touch and move the dial counter clockwise – that will set up a self-destruct timer. It uses the same times again, from 30 seconds to 10 days. Not a large explosion, it uses electromagnetic radiation to 'fry' its circuits, rendering it useless and un-repairable."

"Can I make it really self-destruct, you know, explode at all? I mean, if there is a real emergency?"

Rick glanced at Freya, looking for approval of any kind. Freya nodded.

"If you really need an explosive self-destruct you need to pull up on the central dial until it locks, and then turn counter clockwise. This then sets up an internal full power overload resulting in quite a large explosion. But be careful, you only have around sixty seconds to make your escape. It is for emergencies only, and I mean emergencies, OK?"

Johnno nodded. "I understand, real emergencies only."

Freya picked up the wrappers and threw them into the fire. They disintegrated in a sulphur yellow flash. "Manni and Rick will guide you into the complex," she said almost as an aside "we just need your disguise sorting."

Rick stood directly behind the Oberleutnant, turned to Johnno and raised his eyebrows with a knowing smile, and then placed his hands on the epaulettes of the uniform. He closed his eyes, as if in deep concentration, and took a deep breath.

The Oberleutnant's head slowly slumped further forward as if his very being was being drained out of him. Rick's own body began to change form. His height and shape took on that of his imprisoned target. Finally even the uniform he wore appeared on Rick's body. After fifteen to twenty seconds the transposition was complete. He turned to face Johnno.

"How's that buddy?"

Johnno stared back, incredulous. It was Rick's voice, but it was emanating from the Oberleutnant's body.

"Close your mouth buddy – and take a breath."

Rick then closed his eyes for a second, and spoke again. "Is that clever or what? Alien technology my friend, alien technology."

"That was fucking amazing – sorry about my language – but it was truly, truly amazing!"

"It's DNA buddy, that's all, DNA. I am now, to all intents and purposes, Oberleutnant Thomas Schulze."

"But I understood what you were saying ... in German ... I can't speak German."

"Thank your earpiece buddy; it's all done for you by your earpiece."

Manni then stood behind the seated soldier. He placed his hands on his shoulders and the amazing process was repeated. Manni smiled, cocked his head to one side and looked down at his new form. "Korporal Otto Mayer at your service."

Their transformation complete the two 'new' German soldiers manhandled their unconscious body hosts into the bedroom at the rear of the cabin, knowing they would be safe there until the operation was complete and their re-appearance would be too late to affect their task.

Freya moved towards Rick. "Now we have a guard and his superior, all we need now is a second guard who can destroy the Bell.". She gestured for Johnno to move towards Johan, who was now seated in another chair. She sighed, and took a deep breath. "Remember your mother - my sister - was also from Alnilam."

Johnno's eyes glazed over momentarily as he thought of his missing mother.

"And she passed on her DNA to you."

Johnno looked slightly bemused. Then he smiled, eyes slightly closed.

"Are you saying I can try that trick – that, that shape shifting. Is that where we're going with this?"

Freya nodded. "All you need is training and perhaps an initial boost. Johan has volunteered to be your subject. He will be taken to the nearby village for safe keeping and cared for until you return his body to him."

Johan turned to face Johnno. "My parents are Jewish and were forced to flee to America before they were rounded up and sent away to rehabilitation centres. They are better known here as concentration camps. I hid my religious background and outwardly became a fervent Nazi. Ever since I have looked to find ways of defeating Nazism." he spat on the floor.

Freya placed her hand reassuringly on Johan's shoulder. "He has arranged for several 'dead' slaves to be taken outside for cremation. Once there the local villagers collect them and take them to their scattered villages to recover. That is how we get much of our information, first hand from the slave workers who live in the tunnels."

"Hopefully my war ends here." he added, smiling back at Freya, placing his hand on hers.

"Come on Johnno, you can do it. Gott segne euch alle und viel Glück!"

Johnno looked bemused, then smiled and shrugged his shoulders.

Johan smiled. "God bless you all, and good luck."

Johnno took a deep breath and moved towards Johan, facing him and placing his hands on his shoulders.

"No, not that way," said Freya, "your transformation will be a mirror image of Johan; you must stand **behind** him for a true replication."

Johnno apologised, walking behind Johan and dutifully placing his hands on his shoulders.

"What next?"

"Now close your eyes, gently squeeze his shoulders and try to feel the blood coursing through his veins. You need to create a bond with his very being, his cells, everything that is Johan Engel."

Johnno closed his eyes; then he screwed them up, squeezing and releasing his hands. "C'mon, c'mon." he said under his breath. Eventually, with a huge sigh, he let go of Johan. He looked down at himself, inspected his arms and his hands but nothing had changed.

"You're trying too hard. You have to relax and sense his body rhythms."

Johnno placed his hands on Johan's shoulders again. "Sorry about this my friend." He tried squeezing, then shuffling his feet, opening and closing his eyes – all to no avail. "Sorry, it isn't happening. Can't I just borrow his uniform?"

Freya shook her head. "Johan is a known guard; he has the ability to travel throughout the complex unchallenged. His face is well known, yours is not. There will be extra vigilance now that Musfelldt is visiting. You *must* shape shift."

The mood in the cabin became tense. They had all assumed that Johnno would be able to shape shift and assume another identity. Their mission was possibly in jeopardy and they realised that the future history of the world could change with disastrous consequences.

Rick spoke first. "Remember when we saw the Beatles and we tried meditation?"

"Yeh, in the middle of the desert with a six pack of Budweiser, how will that help?"

"It's essentially the same, but without the Budweiser. Empty your mind and let Johan's very being seep in through your skin. You have to believe in yourself and **believe** that you can become Johan."

Johnno shuffled his feet. "OK, here goes nothing." He replaced his hands on Johan's shoulders, dutifully closing his eyes, breathed out slowly and concentrated as best he could. "I can do this, I can do this." He thought to himself. "I must do this, I must do this."

"Look – look." Astrild had noted a haze forming around Johan's body.

Johnno's hands seemed to become almost transparent as if a connection was being made. Sweat poured from his forehead. He began to shiver.

Freya moved in behind him, placing her warm hands on top of Johnno's. "Concentrate. Concentrate my little spaceman." Johnno felt a surge, almost like the static he had experienced many times in flight school. It was as if he had links direct to Johan's blood flow. His skin began to tingle as if suffering from sunburn. His scalp felt as if it was covered in goose bumps, electrical ones. He could sense his body cells almost dancing, vibrating; in his mind's eye he could see a line of spirals twisting and turning, with small dots clicking in place, extending and completing the complex patterns. "I must do this, I must do this." he heard himself repeating over and over. "I must, I must."

Suddenly all the feelings subsided. His static had disappeared. His body no longer pumped sweat. He relaxed and moved back from Johan's seated figure. Feeling more than a little deflated he sighed. "Sorry guys, I guess I need a lot more practice."

Freya smiled and held up a mirror. Johnno looked at himself, a quizzical look on his face. He looked down at Johan who was now slumped in his chair.

He looked down his body and saw he was now clothed in a German uniform. He held up both arms and inspected them closely. He had done it! He had somehow managed to transform himself and shape shift.

He grinned; "Hello Korporal Johan Engel".

There was an instantaneous cheer from everyone in the cabin. They rushed to pat him on the back and congratulate him. Freya hugged him with all her might.

"All you needed was a helping hand."

"Yes, How do I get back to Johnno when I need to – is he lost forever?"

"Simply close your eyes; release all thoughts of your host and imagine you are back in your body. Remember something unique in your memory to act as a trigger – something only you will ever recall."

He duly closed his eyes and took a deep breath in. He visualised himself looking in a mirror and seeing his own face. He recalled nights star gazing with his beloved Freya and the one night he tripped as he was looking upwards and walking in the woods. He had wanted to cry but, as a brave spaceman, he knew he could not. He tore a hole in the knee of his trousers. His body felt as if it had been drained – as if an elevator had descended from his head to his feet. He wobbled slightly, grabbing a chair back for support. Opening his eyes he looked around the room.

"Well done buddy."

Johnno looked back in the mirror and saw his own form had returned. "Good looking isn't he," he mused.

Johan began to groan in his chair. Johnno quickly placed his hands back on his shoulders and closed his eyes. This time he immediately felt a surge as Johan's very being seemed to flow into his body. He felt as if they had somehow become connected, some kind of mutual force was powering them both. This time the transformation was almost as instantaneous as he had seen with Freya and Rick. He stood back and inspected his newly returned uniform and then took another look in the mirror. He felt a surge of pride. His mother had gifted him with a priceless skill, a skill which he had now seemingly mastered.

Rick approached him, warmly shaking his hand. "And now, Korporal Johan Engel, you are ready for your mission."

Johnno clicked his heels in mock salutation and performed a Nazi salute. "Ja wohl, mein Oberleutnant."

Chapter 15

It was now late evening when the conspirators sat down to finalise details for the destruction of the Bell. In the warm glow of the log fire they sat around the table. Freya and Astrild were standing, the three chairs holding the unconscious hosts had been moved to the bedroom. They walked around the room as the conversation flowed, occasionally checking through the window for any sign of the lights of vehicles approaching, or the sound of boots on the stones in the rough track outside of the cabin. They could not afford a second surprise visit from their German neighbours.

"Our first task is to move the real Johan into the village. Under cover of darkness several of our partisan friends will collect him and transport him to a safe house." Freya was concerned for his safety. "Astrild, can you see that's done please?" Astrild nodded.

Rick returned from checking the windows. "Our main plan is clear. We enter the mine under the guise of security checks for Musfelldt's visit. Our contacts tell us he is arriving first thing in the morning to complete his own. He always tries to catch his own detachments off-guard, it gives him a sense of warped authority, but I am sure they will be ready." Rick continued. "He will tour the complex and inspect the Bell, checking on progress with the scientists working on it. He will instruct his underlings to compile a full written report and then insist on telephoning his Führer to boast of his achievements. He's an arrogant bastard."

Astrild walked over, arms crossed. "A light lunch is planned. Several local farmers have 'donated' their produce. It is mainly chicken and vegetables. That leads us to believe that he plans to travel to view Wroclaw for an overnight stay on the same evening. Contacts there advise us that the Hotel Hoppenzoll is to expect a special guest and his compliment of fellow officers."

Freya joined them by the window, once more checking outside for their safety. Looking back into the room she added "Once we hear that he has arrived safely, and a safe distance away, we have arranged for a surprise that will delay his return and, more importantly, the return of his entourage."

"But we're not allowed to kill him, are we?" Johnno looked on disappointingly.

"When he does try to return he will find that the road has been bombed and is impassable. If he tries the railway, no problem, as that will also be badly damaged. We believe that one of his goals is to see a V2 rocket launched from the back of a lorry – the Wunderwaffe new design. No launch pads, no giveaway concrete runways." Rick continued. "We need to be within the complex when Musfelldt arrives, but keeping our heads down. Once he leaves with his entourage we can start to head into the mine complex. We need to go down around two hundred metres, that's two hundred and twenty yards for you old buddy, and look for research lab 2 on the right – that's Forschungslabor 2." Rick's voice was calm, yet displaying an urgent tone now that their plan was finally coming together.

"We will all enter and locate the Bell. At that point you must find a way in and do your thing while we cover your back."

"Find my way in?" queried Johnno. "Doesn't it have a door?"

"It is a concealed door. Luckily the Bell shaped charm that Freya presented to you when she posed as ground crew is the key. All you have to do is find where to put it. This craft is so old even we don't know all its secrets."

"No problem then." Johnno said sarcastically.

"We DO know how the controls work though," added Freya optimistically, "we can view them through your lenses and tell you what to do."

"We can then leave the mine on an outside security check. Hopefully job done."

"Can I then travel home again?" Johnno sounded hopeful.

"Oh yes. And with a suitable gift for your President."

Johnno looked baffled, and then all became clear. "The hidden weapon, I presume."

"Yes" said Rick, "Then it goes back home to where it belongs."

Freya declared it was time for a good night's sleep, tomorrow would see the culmination of their long contrived plan. Astrild and Freya ambled towards the second bedroom. "Goodnight min lille romfarer." Johnno smiled, "Goodnight Aunt, and sweet dreams of home."

Manni opened a cupboard door and retrieved a corked bottle of his favourite brandy and three small shot glasses. "Shall we have a nightcap, my colleagues?" He removed the cork with his teeth and poured three generous shots. They each took a glass.

"To success." they clinked glasses and took a sip

"I propose a toast gentleman. To the end of this infernal war, and to the safe guarding of our future times." Again clinking glasses and sipping at the soothing liquid.

"To the future, may it be the one that we want and truly deserve," added Johnno poignantly as they downed the last of their drinks. Manni bade them goodnight, settling down on a chair by the fire, which was now almost dead. He threw on more logs, using a metal poker to push them in place and stir up the ashes to a steady yellow glow. Soon the bark on the new logs began to glow, and then burn, as the fire regained its strength.

"Sweet dreams my friends, and may our Gods be with us tomorrow." He pulled the blanket up to his neck complaining "This uniform is making me itch.

Rick and Johnno smiled, "Cheap German material!"

Johnno turned towards his new found friend. "How did you get involved in all this, are you from Alnilam as well?"

"Almost. I'm from the sister planet you call Mintaka. I actually work as a Federation minister, my concerns are based on planet Earth, with an overview of reporting back on your planet's progress and activities. My predecessors liaised with former non-earthly visitors, you'd be surprised how many there have been ... and still are at present. It is a constant battle between good and evil, dissuading those who see profit in earth's development and its resources."

Johnno poured a couple more drinks. Rick took a sip and continued. "Many other civilisations are thousands of years ahead of Earth in their development and their technology. See how far you have come in a little over sixty years, from a single flight in a flimsy wooden craft to leaving your planet and even planning to visit the moon. As their resources become depleted they look to neighbouring planets to replenish."

Johnno was transfixed as his friend told his story. "Aren't they too far away to reach us, I'm sure a light year is a L O N G way".

"We can use methods that you haven't yet dreamed of. For instance this Bell we are looking to destroy, it IS a time machine, OK?" Johnno knew he had travelled back in time so he knew it would be true. "Imagine setting the time where you are about to travel as the current time. Set the destination as somewhere, anywhere else. Then depart. You are there in a matter of minutes."

"Yeh, but how does the time machine work?"

"That part is complex. It's about setting up an electrical force field, one powerful enough to find the 4th dimension of time. It must spin to do this, though the inside floats in a liquid core, so no movement there." Rick realised he needed to give his friend a much simpler explanation.

"Imagine you get on a train at a station and the train moves along the track to the next station, OK?" Johnno nodded.

"Well imagine getting on the train and the station moves instead. In one direction the train travels into the future, in the other direction it goes into the past. You simply leave the train at the year you wish to visit."

"That seems relatively simple, but how do you regulate how far backwards or forwards you travel. Is it guesswork?"

"Each planet and each galaxy has a different concept in measuring time. On earth it is years, months etc. On Orion it is Klax, Klix and Reams, in the Pleiades group of planets it is, well, unpronounceable. But they are all based on the length of a day in the home planet. Within the Bell is a computer which can be reset or programmed to suit the time units on that planet. As it was last used on Earth then those settings should still be active."

"How do you actually set the date?"

"It's on the main console – like a desk – at the control system. You enter the date and time in numbers – digitally – and the system does the rest. Bingo!"

"And how do you pick the destination?"

"Above the main console is a screen produced very much like a TV image. It is programmed with thousands of maps of planets and galaxies. You just touch the screen and move the images about until you find the right general area. If you then put two fingers on the screen and move then sideways then the image magnifies, zooming in on your target. You can repeat this process until you can see within 1 metre of your intended destination. Touch the screen and a small box appears, then off you go."

"Whoa! A touch screen system. I bet that will never take off on Earth. We love our wired remotes." Rick smiled, knowingly. "And now it's time for shuteye old buddy, we have a busy time ahead of us. School's out for the day."

Johnno stood up and walked around to Rick, who was also standing behind his chair. He threw his arms around his long-time friend and hugged him tight in a manhug.

"I thought I'd lost you my friend" Johnno spoke softly, "I thought you were a goner."

Rick responded with a bear hug of his own. "I promise we'll complete this flight safely, the old team back together," walking over to the fireplace and using the poker to get a good fire burning.

He then settled in a chair opposite Manni, covering himself with a blanket pulled up to his neck. "Goodnight buddy, tomorrow we finish operation Horizon."

Johnno collapsed on to the bed in the corner of the room, the one he felt he knew personally. "Goodnight buddy, sweet dreams." He lay back and pulled his pillow in towards his head.

The room went silent apart from the constant crackling as the burning logs released their smoke sap. There was an occasional 'pop' as the wood settled and a sweet heady aroma of burning pine filled the air. The flames sent dancing shadows to all the walls, a picture of tranquillity. Outside a gentle flurry of snow was falling and the woods became silent, apart from the occasional 'hoot' of a hungry owl, eyeing up the forest floor for his latest meal.

Johnno dreamed of his childhood home, thankfully the nightmare did not return tonight.

.....

When Johnno woke in the early morning the cabin was already a hive of activity.

As his eyes opened he was startled to see a German officer sat drinking coffee. He felt at a holster on his waist band, feeling for a handgun.

"Whoa buddy, remember who I am. Who WE are."

Johnno visibly relaxed when he recalled the events of the day before and his inauguration to shape shifting. He grinned rather sheepishly when he realised what he had done. He felt the contours of his new face, and then the stubble on his chin. "Even the master race needs a shave." He climbed out of his bed and made his way to the table. Breakfast today was eggs and kabanosy, washed down by strong black coffee. Above the fireplace the plan of the mine complex was still projected, with Manni closely examining the layout in case a plan 'B' was called for.

"We could exit by the side passage, here," pointing to a small exit on the north side of the mine "should our western getaway be unavailable."

Freya examined the layout closely. "The difficulty will be in traversing the tunnel shaft from the labs where the Bell is located. We will need to silence the scientists and disable the guards placed in there. Any untoward noise and our exit could well be blocked."

Johnno put down his fork, picked up his coffee mug and moved towards the layout. He pointed to a circular pattern at the top right hand corner. "What's this, a gun emplacement?"

"That's the circular protective henge where they hopefully plan to test the Bell's functions. They will be expecting a tremendous power surge and have built this structure to contain any damage should anything go wrong.

It is surrounded by trees and not visible from above," before adding nonchalantly "wasted time which only helps our cause."

Rick had joined his friend at the fireplace. "How do they plan to move the Bell to the henge? I see no outside path, and surely that would leave it open to attack if moved outside of the complex."

Johnno scanned the plan closely and saw no exit near the labs. "There must be a way out somewhere, here," pointing to the space between the labs and the external henge structure.

"Our contact knows nothing of that, but I do see your point." Freya's eyebrows contorted slightly, "I assume he has no clearance for that area. Still, as long as we can complete our task and destroy the Bell before it is moved, then that exit is of no real relevance to us."

"Time for a shave then, as our English allies say I wouldn't like to be given 'jankers' by an irate SS officer." Manni directed him back towards the small washroom. He used a towel to lift a jug off the stone heart by the fire "Hot water, but I'm afraid you will have to use soap and no aftershave." he laughed. "Don't use all the water, the rest of this German detachment will also need to look their best.". Johnno gratefully accepted the hot water and entered a small side room for his wash and shave. Manni and Rick followed suit and emerged to don their full uniforms.

"If caught we could be shot as spies." Manni had a wry grin on his face.

Rick was fastening his belt and feeling if his uniform was straight "Yeah, but would they believe where we came from?". Manni laughed before going outside and firing up the engine of the Kubelwagen, the one used by the 'raiding party' the day before.

Rick looked in the mirror, adjusting his hat and pulling down on his jacket to remove the creases. He clicked his heels in mock arrogance, saluted Freya and Astrild. "I shall see you soon my friends. May our Gods be on our side." He marched outside to join Manni.

Freya walked over to Johnno and hugged him. She then took his face in her hands and kissed him on the forehead. "Good luck my little spaceman. We shall reminisce when all this is over. Please be careful."

"Apparently I was born to do this. I shall succeed and we WILL reminisce, don't worry."

"Your mother and father would be so proud if they could see you now. Their son, a true soldier of the universe, completing a task that they started." Johnno suddenly froze. "My wallet, where is my wallet?"

Freya smiled and shook her head. She disappeared into the washroom and returned with the wallet in hand. Johnno gratefully took it from her and opened it to find his faded black and white photograph of his parents. He held it up, showed it to Freya, and then kissed it for luck before carefully replacing it. Johnno smiled the mother of all smiles and then gave Freya the hug of all hugs. He stepped back, still holding the top of his Aunt's arms. "When will I see you again?"

"Don't worry; I shall be there to meet you as you leave the mine. I have several diversions to plan elsewhere to ensure your success. Astrild and I will be in constant contact, don't forget your ear piece ... and your lenses. I shall be with you all the way." She tenderly kissed his forehead.

He had forgotten his ear piece, it fitted so well. He gently touched it. "I'll be right there gentlemen," a comment obviously aimed at Rick and Manni.

"And we will be waiting right here" came the reply.

He thought about the lenses. "Damn, I went to the john this morning."

"You sure did buddy, you sure did." Rick laughed out loud.

Johnno left, his hands lingering in his aunt's grip until he broke away. He marched outside, closing the cabin door behind him. Manni was driving; Rick was in the rear, Johnno climbed in alongside Manni. Holding his MP40 upright by his side, he glanced at Rick and then Manni, taking a deep breath. "OK gentlemen, let's do this."

Manni put the vehicle in gear and started off down the track. They were just 100 yards down the track when Johnno grabbed Manni's arm. "Whoa, whoa, wait up a second!" The Kubelwagen came to a skidding halt. Johnno looked at Manni, then at Rick, and back again. "We've forgotten one very important fact."

Two concerned faces looked worryingly at each other, and then back at Johnno. Rick leaned forward in his seat. "We've gone over the plan step by step. Barring the Führer himself arriving we're as ready as we can be."

"What if someone speaks to me? I'm not sure if you haven't noticed, I may understand the words, but I can't actually speak German!" Manni laughed. "Is that all?" and turned to Rick. "We forgot to tell him."

"Your earpiece is the result of amazing technology. As well as communicating with us it also acts as a universal translator. It uses the electrical pulses ... it harnesses radio waves emanating from the brain and ..."

Rick struggled to explain. "All you need to know is that it can translate languages instantly. It then tells your brain how to reply in that language."

Johnno looked bemused.

Manni smiled. "Let's demonstrate"

"Wie spät ist es?"

Johnno looked at his watch. "Es ist kurz nach zehn"

Rick joined in. "jaka jest dziś pogoda?"

Johnno looked around. "łagodnie pada śnieg"

"See. No problems there. Just think it, and say it. Just don't lose your earpiece buddy, or then you really are in trouble." Johnno looked suitably impressed. He patted Manni on the shoulder

"Drive on, driver. Sorry, that should be .. weiterfahren, fahrer"

Manni restarted the engine and the trio moved on towards their planned operation.

"Should we sing Deutschland über alles to pass the time?"

Rick leaned forward and hit Johnno with his hat. "Nein"

It could have been an autumn day in New England. The leaves on the trees looked as if they were in a smouldering fire with every shade of red reflecting and radiating the sun's rays. Birdsong surrounded our trio and the damp smell of a dying summer hung in the air.

"What's the story with you and Astrild, is there more than just a working partnership?"

Manni smiled and glanced at Johnno. "Very observant my friend, what gave it away?"

"Not much really, maybe it's just the way you look at each other when you're talking"

"We have both worked alongside Freya for many years. Our job is to support her in overseeing care of the Federation of planets, you might say we are a kind of galactic police force. Having seen much death, destruction and waste in the history of our star system's development we are committed to preventing it elsewhere, allowing civilisations to develop and prosper naturally. We have seen many systems plundered by beings that just wish to strip them of their resources, almost creating slaves of them, much like the Nazis here at this time."

"You're sort of a Cosmic babysitter almost?"

"You could say that. Astrild's role is communications. She is in constant contact with the Federation and is the one who authorised your time travel to occur. We must avoid any paradoxes which could drastically alter the natural processes of development across many, many star systems. Imagine how history would have change had Herr Hitler not survived your first world war.

Or if Stalin had not come to power. Any one of the millions killed by either could have become the scientist who discovers a cure for cancer."

Johnno pondered the statement. "And that secret room back at the hut?"

"It is our command centre. It has a direct link back to our headquarters on Alnilam. We use an accelerated form of digital radio waves encased in a pulsed beam of light to send and receive messages, this makes them fast and almost undetectable. We also maintain contact, don't ask me how, with associates in 1969, keeping them up to date with progress."

Johnno looked impressed "So they know what we are doing, right now?"

"Yes, minute by minute."

"What about your personal life? Are you two actually married?"

Manni's face took on the demeanour of a man in love. His eyes sparkled; his lips formed an almost imperceptible smile. "Yes, for many years we have made a perfect team in more ways than one."

"Children?"

"We have just the one. A boy, or should I say a young man now."

"I bet you miss him."

"We do, but we hope to be reunited with him soon."

Johnno reached over and gave Manni's forearm a reassuring hug. "I'm sure you will my friend, I'm sure you will. Perhaps I could have the pleasure of meeting him one day."

Manni turned and nodded. "I hope so, I truly hope so."

"And I am sure that you will." Astrild's voice came through their ear pieces "Now take care on the mission."

Johnno noticed a single tear run down Manni's cheek as he smiled in recognition of her voice. "We will, we will my dear one." Manni replied.

Johnno felt a pang of jealousy. He'd had several girlfriends in his life but had not yet met 'the one'. He had always wanted a family, that someone to love and children to dote on. Freya had provided unconditional love and support as long as he could remember and he wanted to provide that kind of love himself for children who would grow up alongside a mother and father who loved them. He missed having a mother and father in his life and was determined that his children would not suffer that emptiness.

Rick realised he needed to change the atmosphere, they were about to confront the enemy and needed all their wits about them.

"Are we there yet" a voice came from the rear of the vehicle "I may need to stop for a wee." Johnno and Manni both burst into laughter and the tension was lifted.

They drove on in silence, the occasional sweet sound of birdsong being their only companion, as they neared their destination.

Chapter 16

As the gates to the mine complex came into view Rick addressed to his colleagues. "Remember we are German soldiers. Be confident. Be assured. In order to maintain security, soldiers and SS members have been drawn from diverse units. They do not want friendships to form, they just need blind obedience."

Manni added "Your fellow soldiers know nothing of your past. Try to keep any conversation on a professional level. Your cover as Korporal Johan Engel is safe.".

Johnno did not look too impressed, but was sure he would soon find out if, to all intents and purposes, he was Korporal Johan Engel. Manni slowed down the Kubelwagen as he approached the gates. The guard in the tower acknowledged Rick's salute and signalled for the gate to open. A second guard approached. Rick acknowledged and returned his salute. "Good morning Herr Oberleutnant, I trust you had good hunting last night"

"Excellent. We believe we may have killed several of the local so-called resistance. As a precaution we stayed over in one of their huts – rather primitive – but with a good fire and plenty of their brandy we enjoyed their hospitality."

The guard smiled a beaming smile. "Do we need to collect any bodies?"

"Not today. We have left them to rot in the forest, a feast for their fellow vermin. We have also booby-trapped their hut. Be sure to warn our patrols, I'd hate to lose any fellow officers." He paused and then grinned "Let the local peasants find the surprise waiting for them." The guard saluted as Manni put the vehicle back into gear and drove into the lion's den.

"Pull over to the left – there, see. More trucks and transport." Johnno had noticed an area to the left of the compound gates. They parked their vehicle.

Manni got out and opened the door for Rick. Johnno walked around to meet them.

"Follow my lead," Rick said earnestly "this is where it starts to get real."

As they approached the outside buildings Johnno memorised the layout. Guard hut to the right, by the towers, communications in the centre and to the left the main exterior assembly point for officers and their charges. He glanced to the mine entrance to the left. It had obviously been engineered to take in the trucks laden with their V2 rockets. To his surprise there was no blast door fitted. He could only assume that they were confident in their secret location, or totally incompetent.

From his left came a pitiful sight. Two severely malnourished mine workers were struggling to push a cart towards the gate. To one side a German guard was berating them, banging the cart with his wooden baton.

"Faster, faster, lazy swine! Open the gates for the garbage patrol," waving his baton at the guards, grinning as he duly obliged.

Rick stopped to let the cart go past. "Good work, good work," he shouted to the guard with the baton, who promptly stopped to salute him. "Carry on; the smell is getting to me." He put his hand to his nose in mock disgust. The guard continued to berate the workers. "Faster, faster, you have work to do." As the cart passed Johnno saw it was piled high with emaciated corpses clad in rags or naked. His initial fear and revulsion created an automatic reaction as he began to move forward. Manni grabbed his elbow and spoke softly. "We are here to save them. For those poor souls it is too late. Be patient my friend, we will have our revenge."

Once the cart had passed they continued over to the main hut. On entering they found it was empty. Tables and chairs were arranged in the centre of the room. On two sides were lockers where the soldiers kept their few precious belongings and a spare uniform and greatcoat. Another wall sported racks where off-duty soldiers could stack their weapons. It was ominously empty. On the far side was a makeshift kitchen. They obviously relaxed and ate in here.

"Let's have a coffee while we wait" Manni wandered over to the range where a coffee pot was on a cast iron oven top.

Rick looked at the empty weapons rack. "I was planning to add some of this to their barrels." He pulled a small container from his pocket. "Expanding metal, a favourite of mine, but it will unfortunately have to wait." He put his hands to his chin as he pondered as to why they were alone in the hut.

"Musfelldt, that's it, Musfelldt is due and all soldiers are on duty, probably lining the mine. No time for coffee. Let's mingle with the rest of our German colleagues in the mine. This could even cover our tracks as we look for Forschungslabor 2".

Johnno took a deep breath, pulled down on his uniform and adjusted his forage cap. "Let's do this." As they left the cabin they looked around them. The guards were in the tower and several SS officers had appeared and formed a mini guard of honour by the gate. At their head were two officers, looking smug yet concerned, worrying about the professionalism of their welcome.

"That must be Krammler and Storrensberg. This is the ideal time to enter the mine and mingle; out of sight and all that." Rick turned smartly to his right and led his colleagues towards the mine entrance.

As they marched towards the entrance a voice beckoned them from behind.

"Oberleutnant Schulze, this way if you please."

Rick froze in his tracks. His heart began to hammer in his chest. He glanced nervously at his colleagues. They gripped their weapons tightly ready to respond, fight and probably die. They were completely outnumbered. The shout was louder this time "Oberleutnant Schulze, this way if you please." Rick turned about to face the direction of the voice.

It was Krammler, no less.

Rick smiled. "Wish me luck," he said through gritted teach and began to march towards the assembled SS officers and Krammler himself. Manni and Johnno also performed an about-turn and escorted Rick, one on either side. Johnno's thoughts were racing "Have we been found out? Who do I shoot first?"

He gripped his weapon tightly, but the knot in his stomach was tighter still.

Rick approached Krammler and Storrensberg with a forced smile upon his face. As he reached them he stood to attention, clicked his heels smartly and saluted, an action replicated by his two colleagues. "Good morning Commander, I trust all is well and ready for our honoured guest. I was just about to enter the mine and check all is well, we don't want any surprises." Krammler's face showed no signs of recognition. His stern demeanour showed all was not well. He had been a civil engineer before the war, completing many projects for his hero, Herr Hitler. His steady rise through the ranks came as he completed many projects linked to the V1 and V2 weapon systems. As well as underground mining, where he showed a propensity for working his slaves and POW's literally to death, he had devised the new system for launching V2 rockets on the move. His latest project, designing and building the henge for trials with 'Die Glöcke' he believed was his crowning achievement. He was detached from his underlings, and ruled with a rod of iron. He took great delight in shooting his slave workforce to 'motivate' those left alive.

"Last night, you and your two … " he looked at Manni and Johnno , pointing to them with a loose glove in a gloved hand "… your two colleagues went on patrol and did not return. Can you please explain yourself?"

"We have been on the lookout for local partisans. Their activity has increased since the report of a crashed craft in the forest. As my main concern is the security of our current project, and any potential planned attacks on our distinguished visitor I immediately requisitioned these two trusted guards and set about clearing the immediate area."

"Were you successful Oberleutnant?"

"We caught site of several locals acting suspiciously. My Korporals here tracked them and soon finished them off. Their bodies fell into the river and are now presumably fish food. That is, of course, if the fish will eat the vermin." Rick flashed an arrogant smile, and used one of his gloves to brush his sleeve nonchalantly. "We then found a cabin where we presumed they may have been based. We parked our vehicle at the rear and waited inside should anyone return. They did not, but their brandy, wine and what little food they had made a welcoming meal. As it was late we decided to wait all night but no-one returned. I presume we have finished them all off. As a precaution we have left several surprises in the form of booby traps should they return. An excellent patrol I believe."

Rick sounded as confident as he could, though he could feel his buttocks clenching as he spoke.

Krammler's face remained stern. He turned to face Storrensberg, whose face was also stony and set as if that was his permanent expression. His spectacles were the standard issue for fervent Nazis, small circular wire frames which he wore as a sop to his hero Joseph Goebbels. A neatly trimmed fine moustache completed the picture, that of an arrogant Nazi with a hugely inflated ego. Johnno and Manni remained at attention, with each one preparing for the fire fight which would surely follow.

Krammler turned and slowly approached Rick, who maintained his forced smile. He could feel a small bead of sweat beginning to roll down the back of his neck. Surely this was it.

"Did you show them any mercy? Offer them immunity if they talked?"

Rick visibly stiffened his back, thrusting his chest forward. His throat felt dry, but he spoke as arrogantly as he could. "Certainly not, Kommander. WE are the master race and they must learn to live in subjugation. We will not tolerate disobedience in any form."

Krammler stared into Rick's eyes. He glanced back at Storrensberg, and then back to face Rick. His eyes widened, he raised his arms and gripped Rick by both shoulders. Suddenly his face broke into a wide grin. "Splendid, just splendid Oberleutnant! These local inbreeds need to be shown how the master race rules their country, the whole of Europe and soon the entire world will be at our feet."

"Thank you Kommander." Rick heard himself saying through a throat so dry he felt he was back in the desert on his Harley. Behind him his two colleagues relaxed the grip on their weapons, relieved that they had not been found out.

"Now go into the mine and be just as vigorous with your security checks. Any workers who you believe may cause trouble need dealing with. We must show

Gruppenführer Musfelldt the progress we have made so he can assure our glorious leader that soon he will be able to conquer the world with our Wunderwaffe."

"You can rely on me Kommander, " came a curt reply, full of authority. He took one step back and saluted. "Heil Hitler." His smart 'about face' was mirrored by Manni and Johnno. He marched steadfastly towards the mine entrance, flanked by his two, very relieved, colleagues.

Behind him Krammler stood and watched as the trio marched away.

He turned to his colleague "We need more soldiers of his calibre Jakob."

Storrensberg smiled and nodded "I agree Hans, three of my finest."

Krammler turned to watch the trio march away. As he did so he slowly blinked his eyes

Eyes as smooth and as black as haematite..

Chapter 17

The trio made continuous observations as they approached the mine opening in the knowledge that Freya would be listening in and making notes. "Gravel road into the mine, obviously to allow the trucks to enter and be armed in total secrecy," Rick noted, steadfastly keeping his gaze straight ahead. "And to leave ready for launch, but I wonder where from?"

They scanned the layout looking for a way out to any potential launch area. "To the left, here," Manni noted "there is parking for their ordinary transport but it leads to a larger clearing beyond, just on the edge of the forest."

Rick glanced sideways under the guise of addressing his Korporal. "It would certainly allow a truck to enter and manoeuvre, and be sheltered to some extent by the trees."

Johnno joined in. "If we need to prevent any launches it must be done there. We cannot seal the mine; it would trap and kill all the prisoners as well as the Germans in there. The Federation, I presume, would not be too happy about that."

"I agree. We would be better sabotaging any rockets allowing them to be destroyed after launching, preferably mid-flight." He took a deep breath. "And now we enter the doorway to Hell. Good luck my friends."

They had now reached the mine entrance, to be met by a smell; a smell which consisted of dust, diesel oil, sweat, faeces and despair. It hit all three of them like a musty curtain hanging from an open doorway to decay. As they entered their eyes slowly became accustomed to the semi-darkness within. It was lit by large light bulbs suspended close to the rough-hewn ceiling some twenty feet or so above their heads.

The mine was about thirty feet wide, the sides being mostly marked with the grooves made by the rough pickaxes used by the slaves and POW's, no time wasted reinforcing with bricks here. At either side was a small channel hewn into the floor. This was used by the slaves as a latrine during working hours, usually up to sixteen hours each day. Work only stopped at nights when the lights were put out to discourage rogue air attacks – bright lights within a dark forest presented an easy target.

As they progressed deeper within the tunnel they began to hear the sound of workers using pickaxes and shovels as they strived to widen and deepen the cave under the eyes of their SS torturers, soulless devotees of the Third Reich who held nothing but contempt for their captured work force. They reached the parked wagons, laden with their V2 rockets, shielded by large tarpaulins to keep the dust and dirt away from their electrical innards. They just fitted into the tunnel, their cargo laid on the back of each flat bed. There were three trucks, but only two had rockets on them.

Rick patted the trucks on the side as he passed them. "Wunderwaffe," he said loudly, "now we will show them how the 3rd Reich operates." A soldier on guard appeared from behind the last truck, aiming his rifle at the three approaching figures. As soon as he realised he was facing an officer he swiftly lowered his weapon and stood to attention.

"Your name, soldier"

"Korporal Erich Gruber – SIR"

"Well done Korporal. Anyone may enter here and be a saboteur. I shall commend you to your immediate superiors."

"Thank you – SIR." he replied with a grin, obviously pleased with his performance and praise proffered by an Oberleutnant.

"Now go about your business and guard our valuable cargo." At that he saluted again, turned about face and marched off behind the trucks.

The trio marched deeper into the mine, deeper into the obnoxious aura that seeped into their senses. They stopped a little further on, Rick giving the impression of checking the work completed so far. He spoke in low tones to his colleagues. "Two rockets. I would guess their initial target would be London and possibly Moscow, armed with nuclear weapons. Hitler will then threaten other allied countries; I'm not sure if he could reach New York yet, but he could if he harnessed the full power of the hidden weapon."

"What's with the third truck?" Johnno sounded concerned "Why bring an empty truck with a spare tarpaulin all this way?"

"I don't know" Rick looked perplexed, "that IS worrying. Let's hope it's nothing too sinister and we find out before it's too late."

Manni nudged Rick gently on the arm "SS approaching," he whispered under his breath. From behind the wagons, from the left hand side, there appeared a figure.

Rick turned to face him as he approached. The black uniform was covered in dust, but still had the recognisable form of evil. He was the epitome of the desired Aryan race, at least six feet tall, a physique honed by hours of exercise with a mop of wavy blond hair completing the picture. In one hand he held a whip, in the other a metal tube around two feet long with two protrusions at the end. Rick looked at the metal tube with a questioning look in his eyes, and then back at his enemy, who promptly remembered his rank and stood to attention thrusting his chest as far forward as he could.

"It's my persuader sir. It's my cattle – sorry – lazy bastard prod. The only good thing ever to come from the Jew lovers in America."

Rick smiled and did his best to look impressed. He just wanted to test the 'persuader' on the sadistic bastard holding it. "At least the Federation would surely approve," – the thought flashed through his mind.

"Good afternoon" Rick looked towards his rank on his arm "Feldwebel. I'm pleased to see it appears that everything is going well, are we still on target ?" The SS sergeant looked full of himself. He swaggered a little and slapped the prod into his left hand twice. "Yes sir. Only two deaths today, I'm sure you passed them on the way in." Rick nodded, revulsion flooding his thoughts. "We should be fully secure in the next week or so and we can then rid ourselves of the vermin who tunnel our mines like rats."

"Carry on Sergeant; we must create a good impression for our honoured guest. I shall be sure to put in a good word with your Oberführer."

He smiled a smug smile, saluted, then turned and strode away purposely. "Come on you lazy bastards. Work harder or my little friends here will help to persuade you." His arrogant voice echoed around the tunnel, an obvious show of power to impress his very impressible Oberleutnant.

Manni glanced to the left. He could see a timber door supported by wrought iron hinges. Another SS soldier exited the room and pushed the door shut behind him. He ran after his colleague. "Manfred, wait for me," eager to catch up with his colleague and inflict more pain on the slave workers.

"SS quarters obviously, that's handy to know." Rick nodded, and then turned to face his colleagues. He spoke loudly. "Let's continue with our visit. Our esteemed visitor must be impressed with our progress." As he spoke he rolled his eyes and smiled. "Must keep up the pretence." he voiced softly.

They re-formed and continued to move deeper into the tunnel, Rick trying to portray the nonchalant air of an over confident aggressor. His eyes darted from side to side as he walked, noting anything and everything that may be of use to them. Manni muttered "Into the lion's den," to which Johnno replied "let's make sure we're not their next meal."

As they made their way towards the current work area Rick moved from one side of the tunnel to the other, ostensibly checking the progress and security of the tunnel walls. He constantly muttered "good, very good," as he surveyed the scene.

The walls bore the marks and grooves of pick axes, occasionally bearing copper coloured stains which looked to have been splashed on by brushes. Rick recoiled away from them when he realised they were actually blood splashes more than likely caused by the whips used by their sadistic overlords. The channel cut into the floor also showed the signs of blood, partly worn away by the stains left by urine and faeces. There should also, no doubt, be copious vomit stains in the mix. However these slaves were fed just enough watery gruel and raw vegetables to keep them working until they dropped where they were; they had no vomit to expel. Many friends made frenzied attempts to lift their colleagues who had fallen through fatigue. If they were not back on their feet within thirty seconds they were deemed too ill to work, and support, and were dispatched by a single bullet from a Walther pistol. If both stayed down, both were lost.

Officers were issued with Lugers, but deemed the cost of one of their bullets was too high a price to pay for losing one worker, let the guards use their own weapons. The noise within the tunnel became louder and more intense. It mainly comprised of the SS guards 'cajoling' their charges to work harder, accompanied by the occasional crack of a short whip and the cry of its recipient.

To their right they saw a sign mounted on the wall near to carved doorway.

'Forschungslabor1.' Rick moved over and saw that the entrance way was blocked with rubble and stone. He turned to his colleagues. "That looks like a roof fall blocking the door." Realisation hit home. "That's why they had to create the second lab. Let's hope the Bell is in that one and the roof there is still intact."

As they moved towards the next opening, presumably 'Forschungslabor 2.' Rick suddenly stopped, his eyes narrowed in deep thought.

"What haven't we seen down here yet?"

"What do you mean?" Manni replied trying to figure out what Rick meant. "We've found the trucks and the V2 rocket."

"Yeah, the SS room and the ruined research lab 1," added Johnno. "We've even seen the poor souls who have died being carried out for disposal." He scanned the area around them.

"What about the rubble? The waste dug out by the workers. Surely with all these workings there must be somewhere to tip the spoil ... and no-one has passed us with any."

"And the workers too, we've hardly seen any. They must be really deep into the mine complex." Johnno added.

Manni looked concerned. "There must be a way out of the rear of the mine." Then, after a short pause for thought .. "THAT'S how they plan to move the Bell to the henge without being seen. That isn't on our plan, we'll have to think on our feet."

"Then there's no time to waste. Let's find 'Forschungslabor 2' and get the job done" Rick added with a deep sense of urgency. "We need to check if Freya has received all this info and realises our situation."

In their earpieces all three of them heard the reassuring tone of Freya's voice. "I have all that noted. Our plan of the mine complex has been updated. Should our mission fail we are highlighting the henge as a possible target for our allies back in London. Long range bombing attacks are, at last, being planned. If we cannot destroy it we can try and bury it for the foreseeable future or until we can mount another operation."

Johnno replied. "That may be too late. We will succeed … We *must* succeed"

"I am planning to join you within the mine if possible. Astrild will stay here and manage the communications. But first you must find the second laboratory and destroy the Bell." Freya's tone was now more urgent; more urgent than Johnno had ever heard. Her usual calm demeanour was slipping slightly. That worried him, that wasn't the Freya he remembered. The challenge had now become real, more real than he had felt before. The future of the known world was in the hands of just three men. He felt extremely proud. He felt extremely scared. Pulling down on his jacket and nervously pulling his collar away from his throat he pulled himself up to his full height.

"Let's do this, gentlemen."

The trio turned and continued their march into the unknown.

Chapter 18

As they went deeper into the mine complex the overwhelming stench of decay and despair grew and grew. Although there was lighting above them there was no real reflection off the cave walls; it was a cold light; cold enough to reflect its purpose in creating death, either here with its slave workers or planned later with the V2 rockets aimed at the allied capitals.

"There's a corner ahead, let's hope we find the lab there. Be prepared for the sight of pitiful workers. We cannot help them now but if, sorry, *when* we are successful we can try to help and even free as many as possible." Rick sounded hopeful, confident even. "Feel for them by all means, but remember our prime objective."

Freya's voice had regained its calm demeanour as she spoke through their earpieces, "Be careful and be outwardly dispassionate. We can best help them by successfully completing our mission."

As they rounded the corner the cave split into two passageways. To the left the workers were busy hammering on the cave walls as best they could.

An SS guard approached them. "Good afternoon Herr Oberleutnant. We are doing a good job, yes?"

Rick moved forward to meet him. "Have you forgotten how to salute your superior officers?" Rick was as severe as he could be. He took a long look at the soldier's insignia on his arm." Herr Unterscharführer?"

"Sorry, Herr Oberleutnant," came the reply, immediately saluting and staying rigidly to attention.

Manni shot a wry smile at Johnno. "Cheeky bastard," he thought.

"At ease now soldier, now give me a full update on work. Is Laboratory 2 in full operation?"

"Yes sir. Completed in record time, I may add." He sounded smug, but was too afraid to risk a smile. "The scientists have nearly completed their tasks and several are now at work in laboratory 3."

Johnno pointed to several slaves sat motionless several feet away. "Why are they not hard at work?"

"Lunch break" he said, with a sardonic grin. "A 10 minute rest and a whole bowl of gruel each!"

Manni swallowed deeply, not letting his apparent Teutonic demeanour fail. "You treat them too well."

"We do, and if they could only reach the bowls," he laughed loudly.

"Carry on Unterscharführer; we shall check your progress in both laboratories."

This time he remembered to salute, turned about face and marched further on to where the workers were toiling away.

Freya's voice was quizzical. "Two laboratories, why do they need two?" Manni covered his mouth to speak, rubbing as though he was feeling whiskers ready to be shaved "Have they found the weapon I wonder? If so, we are in deep trouble. We have to get in there without delay."

"I agree." came over the earpieces. "I'm tuning in to Johnno's lenses .. now." There was a slight pause before she continued as the connection was made. "Johnno, have a good look around where you are standing to give me an idea of the layout." Johnno complied, first looking back to where they had been, highlighting the laden trucks. He then glanced to the right, at the doorway. "SS quarters," he whispered "Though we're not sure how many. Six, possibly eight max we are guessing". He turned to look into the mine shafts. "We're at the point where the mine divides."

"Look to your left, opposite where the mine turns to the right".

Johnno did so, and in the distance he noticed a narrow crevice in the side wall.

"That could be our way out. The Germans don't appear to have tried to widen it as it's probably too dangerous, but remember where it is."

"OK, but wouldn't it be dangerous for us too?" Johnno tried not to sound too concerned.

"Not at all. We have our methods, don't worry, we have our methods."

As Johnno looked into the distance he noted several workers slumped, heads hung forlornly on skeletal chests. In front of them were the food bowls, tantalisingly just out of reach. "Bastards," he muttered under his breath. He could see the guards busy with the working slaves and proceeded to walk towards the hunched and seated figures. Glancing again to ensure there was no-one watching knelt down in front of them. "Too lazy to eat, are we?" he shouted theatrically. As he spoke he moved the bowls forward within their reach. "Eat up gentlemen, eat up. This war will not last forever," His voice kept low, his eyes scanning to ensure no SS members could see what he was doing.

The worker at the far end did not look as haggard, or as old, as his colleagues. He took the bowl gratefully, drank a little and then put the bowl to his colleague's lips. "He is old and I am young, he needs it more than me." He was obviously one of the local Polish villagers rounded up as extra Lapanka slave labour by the SS snatch squads. Johnno looked and smiled. This young man could only have been just into his teens. He was filthy and emaciated and dressed in bare rags for shorts. His filthy body bore the welts of the SS guards whips, his hands bore the marks and bruises only caused by working with heavy, unforgiving rock, but a fierce light shone in his eyes. Johnno saw in him the very best of man could be, and do. At that point his desire to succeed in his task became everything.

The young man spoke "I will pray for you, even though you are German. You have shown me that all men are capable of mercy."

A warning came into his earpiece, it was Rick. "Move back, quickly, the guards are reforming. Something is happening."

Johnno stood up, and checked if he had been seen. Mercifully he had not. He moved back towards his colleagues. They looked back towards the mine entrance, where a throng of soldiers was gathering. Behind them the SS guards were also gathering and chattering like demented schoolchildren.

"He's here," Rick volunteered. "It's Musfelldt, he's arrived."

"Then it's our chance to find the labs and see why they need laboratory 3. They will be distracted for a while as they all preen themselves as they hopefully bask in mutual praise."

"I agree," said Manni looking back into the mine, "Let's get in there and begin our operation." The trio regrouped and began their march towards the laboratories. As they turned the corner they moved out of sight of the mine entrance and into unknown territory.

The noise from the working slaves was incessant, but muted to some degree by their lack of fitness. They lined the sided of the mine like underfed ants clad in rags. As they hacked away at the walls the detritus was being loaded into crudely made handcarts and wheelbarrows for removal.

"See, they take the spoil out of the back, we were right," Manni noted.

"Yes, but why do they take the bodies through the front?" Johnno was perplexed.

"To show their fellow workers their fate when they fail to deliver."

Johnno grimaced, it was becoming too much to bear. He had read books about Germany's forced labour camps and the policy of Ostarbeiter, but this was now real. It wasn't in a book. They were human beings, not just words on a page, images in your mind. "Are you sure we can't kill the bastards? Surely your neurolisers could deal with everyone, and then we could destroy the Bell."

Rick replied in a sombre tone. "I'm afraid not. I would love to, but we could cause a paradox by changing the history of individuals. Who knows, one of these SS soldiers might even become leader of a national group of allies who drives for peace in the future, despite being a Nazi Oberleutnant in this infernal war," casting a glance at Manni, who, knowingly, nodded and returned his smile.

Rick patted him on the shoulder. "Small things matter Johnno. Actions have repercussions.

Now let's go and find those laboratories and do what we came to do .. sabotage that Bell."

Chapter 19

A small convoy arrived at the gates to the mine compound. At the front was a Kubelwagen, complete with four grey uniformed guards. This was followed by the staff car containing the honoured guest Gruppenführer Erich Musfelldt and his entourage. Completing the inconspicuous convoy was a further well-armed Kubelwagen with the obligatory bodyguards, sat to attention, the lead soldiers in both manning their MG34 heavy machine guns, body mounted for extra security. The gates opened and the small motorcade entered.

Hans Krammler moved towards the now stationary vehicle. "Heil Hitler," adopting the Nazi stretched arm salute, alongside the obligatory click of heels in well-polished boots.

Musfelldt stepped out, saluted and replied "Heil Hitler."

The formalities over they grasped each other's hands in a prolonged gesture of welcome.

"Welcome Erich, how was your journey through this infernal country side?"

"Cold, but the weather has been kind to us. Keeping our visit low key, much like your operations here, has helped keep us under the radar. I see that you keep an orderly house – the clearing outside, well stocked I see, at least we can be assured that the souls of our enemy will burn in hell and never reach salvation."

Krammler smiled a sardonic smile, acknowledging the compliment. "We do our best for our Führer and the Fatherland."

Jakob Storrensberg stepped forward, clicked his heels to attract attention. "Heil Hitler." Musfelldt responded, and then grasped his colleague's shoulder. "It has been a long time Jakob," then glancing back towards Krammler, "too long my friends."

Krammler smiled, then turned, gesturing his colleague to follow him towards the mine entrance. "Our beloved Führer is greatly pleased by your progress here. This work will turn the tide of the war and place the 3rd Reich where it truly belongs my friend. And don't forget, should you need any more volunteers for your mines I have plenty, though admittedly," he added with a sarcastic grin, "obviously not as many as before. Workshy bastards in the main, don't you think?"

Krammler nodded, acknowledging his colleague's comments.

"Blizna is progressing well, and Zement Ebensee will soon be complete Erich. It seems the gods are on our side. Der Riese is growing bigger every day."

Musfelldt smiled "Excellent news Hans."

"Thank you Erich; and we have even better news for you to pass on to our Führer. We have managed to open Die Glöcke and our scientists are beginning to unravel its secrets even as we speak. We have come a long way since Freiburg, have we not."

Musfelldt's face broke into a wide grin. "Wunderbar. This is truly going to be a birthday to remember. I shall contact the Führer and personally tell him the good news." Krammler smiled and nodded in appreciation.

"In fact, I believe that YOU can also inform him of your progress Hans." Musfelldt added, as though he was awarding his colleague a prize.

Krammler stopped in his tracks, and turned to face his new best friend. "You are too kind Erich, too kind. And I shall be honoured to mention your guidance in our endeavours."

They walked on for a few steps, and then Musfelldt stopped, taking Krammler to one side, whispered "and tonight?"

"Everything is arranged my friend. A party for yourself, plenty of drink, plenty of willing 'ladies' to keep us company and we even have 'recreation' arranged for your guards and your drivers."

Musfelldt grinned the mother of all grins.

"These are the rewards of being the master race. Now show me the progress we have made in creating a new Wunderwaffe, one that will end this God forsaken war and see us rightfully triumphant."

The entourage continued on their way towards the mine entrance.

Krammler turned towards Storrensberg. "Jakob, please ensure that our guest party is fed well and relaxed. Please ensure that their vehicles are fully fuelled," glancing at his friend Musfelldt he raised his eyebrows knowingly "they have an important journey ahead of them tonight."

At that they strolled towards the mine entrance as if in a mutual admiration society, all smiles, laughter and small talk full of their own importance and feeling somewhat assured of success in their venture.

Chapter 20

Deep within the mine complex our trio continued their inspection. It was difficult watching the slave workers toiling endlessly under the close scrutiny of their SS guards, but they realised they were there for the greater good. Soon they reached an opening to their right. Rick casually scrutinised the sign on the thick wooden door.

"Forschungslabor 2, this is it. Remember we need to be confident, we are the master race, after all. Bluff will see us through." Manni and Johnno nodded.

Rick lifted the thick iron latch. The door, crudely made with local timbers but proving to be an effective barrier to keep out prying eyes, slowly swung inwards. They adjusted their eyes to the harsh fluorescent lighting, much brighter than they had seen in the mine's tunnel. The room they had entered had been hewn out of solid rock. It was quite large in size, probably around fifty to sixty feet square, with the harsh fluorescent lights giving little respite to eyes accustomed to the semi light outside. There were several desks to one side and on the wall a schematic diagram of a structure, one which appeared to be the Bell itself, complete with scribbled notes and apparent random shapes. In the left centre of the room, standing on a circular steel plinth was a large metal object, highlighted by several spotlights placed around its base.

"That's it, she's there, it's the Bell.. Die Glöcke itself." Rick sounded triumphant.

Johnno moved towards it and was surprised to see that it had an opening to one side, which was wide open. He glanced inside and could make out the control console as promised with what looked like a glass screen directly above. Between them he could just make out a set of symbols etched, or printed, onto the inner wall. He called Rick over.

"They're in already, but nothing appears to be working. No flashing lights or anything."

"Let's hope that's their only success to date, opening the door."

"Can I help you Herr Oberleutnant?" a voice came out of the shadows, startling our two observers. One of the scientists working on the Bell and its secrets appeared from the rear of the room. "Should you be even here?"

Rick made a point of looking at the name badge on his challenger's lab coat. "Professor ..." Rick looked even more closely at the name badge

"Professor Muller, we have heard just how hard you, and you alone, have worked and how you have discovered the secrets of Die Glöcke."

Professor Muller smiled, and acknowledged the compliment.

"As you know we have a dignitary visiting today sent by the Führer himself and I want to make sure that your deeds are fully recognised. Gruppenführer Musfelldt is about to visit your laboratory and I need you to be fully ready for his visit. He has the ear of the Führer and will be reporting back his findings today. Are you ready, my friend?"

Muller could hardly contain himself.

"Yes, I am ready Herr Oberleutnant," stiffening his back and clicking his heels as if he was a high ranking officer.

"Since my last visit you have managed to find the opening into the Bell, is there any more progress that I can report to Gruppenführer Musfelldt. Please do not hesitate to demonstrate your full success – the Fatherland is relying on you."

Muller leaned forward, as if he was about to impart vital secrets. "My colleague, Professor Wagner , is currently next door in our next laboratory working on my latest findings. I managed to decode some of the script of the side," adding "I am quite fluent in ancient Indian language, you know." His face beamed " I was on site when we found her, in fact I was the first to recognise the immensity of our findings." Pomposity seemed to ooze from his veins. He hurried over to the side of the Bell. "See, here, the symbol resembling the hand of Fatima. I made a template and magnetised it and look," he took a small piece of metal from his lab coat, fastened to a long key ring. As he pressed it against the symbol on the side and the doorway slid shut, and then locked itself in place as if air pressure had forced it out. He smiled at his visitors, full of pride in what he had achieved. He placed the shape back into the recess and the door slowly moved in, and then slid open again. The professor stood back in triumph. He continued. "And we have almost succeeded in creating the energy field needed to power her up. Success is right within my, sorry, I mean to say, our grasp. I just knew magnetism would be the key .. no pun intended." He was now so smug he seemed close to wetting himself with excitement.

Rick tried his best to look as though he was impressed. He nodded his head in a positive fashion and patted Muller on the back. "Brilliant work my friend. I shall personally ensure that the Führer hears what you have done and will ensure that you receive the rewards that you deserve. But how do you plan to launch it?" Rick was testing to see if the henge really was its planned launch pad.

"I recommended these office partitions myself," pointing to the panelled laboratory walls, "when we are ready to move out to the launch area we can merely dismantle the panels, transport the Bell through the rear of the tunnels, and no-one outside is any the wiser." His face was a picture of smug arrogance.

"Brilliant, really brilliant. You have the mind of a genius." Rick had his confirmation.

Muller's chest could not have puffed out any more. He was to be a hero of the Fatherland!

Johnno stepped forward. "Well done professor, it is clear that we guard the best scientific minds in the world and we are proud to do so. But can I ask one question, as a mere layman to a specialist?"

"Of course Korporal, what is it?"

"Why do you need to create a new fuel source, has the old one run out?"

"No, no it hasn't run out. We've had test runs with various degrees of success. We are just concerned that it will not stand up to a real test flight. We're not sure exactly what metal it is made from, a tungsten-style alloy we believe, though some elements are still unknown at present." Putting his hand to the side of his mouth and lowering his voice "it IS alien, you know. Now, now, follow me.". At that he scurried towards the rear of his laboratory towards a tunnel opening.

Rick and his colleagues followed, ducking their heads to ensure they didn't end up with a major headache. After some twenty yards or so they entered another laboratory, slightly larger than laboratory 2. To their right was an office area built from prefabricated steel units. On the door was the sign "Commander Hans Krammler."

"So this is where he lives." Manni whispered to Johnno.

"Come, come my friends, more good news for the Führer. My greatest creation yet, and it's almost complete."

Our trio could not believe their eyes. There was a semblance of the symbols indented on the framework.. The seamless outer shape had been replaced by a carefully welded and finished exterior. There was an opening to one side. It had an indisputable form.

There, in front of them, stood a second Bell.

The trio tried their best to look impressed, but realised their plans had been shattered by this revelation.

"We have experimented and believe we have discovered the source of its power and it's control system, it is now ready for its first full trial."

He continued with the fervour of a sixteen year old schoolboy describing a successful experiment in the classroom. "We have recreated the mercury based serum, we call it Xerum 525. We also used thorium and beryllium oxides and by counter rotating ..." his words were cut short by a voice coming from the open doorway behind them.

"Enough professor, let's not bore our non-scientific friends with mere facts." Krammler and his entourage had entered the laboratory on their official guided tour. "Besides, why would Herr Oberleutnant want to know such boring details?"

The trio about faced and saluted their superior officers.

"We are just relishing our part in our Führer's master plane Herr Gruppenführer, and congratulating Professor Muller on progress to date." He turned to face Muller, patting him on the shoulder "a true hero of the Fatherland". Muller tried to look nonplussed, but his ego was now in overdrive.

Krammler turned to his guest Musfelldt and introduced him to Rick.

"Erich, may I introduce Oberleutnant Thomas Schulze." Rick saluted again, moving forwards to shake Musfelldt's outstretched hand. "He is an invaluable part of our security here at the mine, keeping our true aims a secret and ensuring our Führer's success."

Rick turned towards Manni and Johnno "And may I introduce my invaluable and trusted team, Korporals Mayer and Engel.". Manni snapped to attention, with Johnno seconds behind his colleague, realising he had a part to play. "Heil Hitler," was the joint response, along with an extended arm salute. "Both men responsible for personally dispatching with many local … " he paused, looking pensive, "… sightseers shall we call them. A credit to their country and their uniforms."

"At ease gentlemen." Musfelldt acknowledged their apparent devotion to the cause. Turning to the still beaming professor he took several steps forward towards the second Bell. "And when can we expect to trial this?" he spoke almost like a father to his son, gently placing his gloved hands on the Bell's body.

"We anticipate three to four days, a week at most." Muller tried to remain nonchalant. "The second Bell was a total surprise, a gift from our Aryan cousins. It was slightly damaged but we, as superior engineers, have managed to retro engineer it, using the functioning Bell as our model. Soon this will be fully functional as well."

Rick glanced at his colleagues; he felt a knot in his stomach tighten. He looked back towards his superiors and smiled. He was baffled. "why send a truck to collect the Bell, and then build a launch pad in the henge? Something isn't quite right here."

A voice came in his ear, it was Freya. "We must act as soon as Musfelldt and Krammler go on their birthday jaunt; we have no time to lose."

Johnno glanced at Rick and acknowledged he had received the message by raising his eyebrows slightly.

"So soon professor?" Krammler strode towards Muller "That is excellent news, excellent Professor Muller. We are at least three weeks ahead of schedule." His face beamed as he faced Musfelldt. "I trust you will shortly be able to inform our Führer of the good news Erich; just think what we will be able to do when we have manufactured a fleet of them."

"Lead me to your communications room Hans, the Führer will be delighted and can plan his next steps in the total domination of the world by our beloved Fatherland."

The party turned to leave. They strode through laboratory 2 on their way out. Rick and his colleagues dutifully followed with their minds busy trying to accommodate the unexpected changes to their plans. On reaching the entrance back to the tunnel entrance Krammler stopped, stroked his chin as if in thought then turned to face Musfelldt.

"Erich, as we are so close to trials I believe I must forego the pleasure of attending your birthday celebrations, much as I wish to attend. My duty to the Fatherland must be my priority and I must be here to direct operations."

"That would be a shame Hans, but I do admire your devotion to duty."

"All I need here is a small party to ensure the site is secure, your entourage and my SS teams can be spared. You will be eminently safe." Musfelldt looked slightly disappointed. "So be it Hans, I shall ensure that I return with champagne, and perhaps a young lady, to celebrate your success."

"May I make a suggestion Erich, one as a personal favour for devotion to duty?"

"Of course, what is it?"

"I would like to reward Oberleutnant Schulze for his devotion to duty. Could I recommend that he travel with you and leaves his Korporals behind as part of my guard detail?" He approached Rick and placed his arm on his shoulder as if in proud support "The Oberleutnant deserves some relaxation time after his devotion to duty and would make an admirable companion in my absence."

Musfelldt strode towards Rick, paused and smiled "That would be eminently acceptable." He placed his hand on Rick's other shoulder "Yes, yes my friend we shall both have a good time with my birthday celebrations."

Rick could do nothing but smile an embarrassed smile. Inside his heart sank, their carefully contrived plan was now in danger of failing.

"Thank you gentlemen, I shall be honoured to attend." Inside their earpieces came the sound of Freya "Damn!"

Krammler stood to one side and ushered his party ahead of him.

Rick followed his new 'friend', with Manni and Johnno in close pursuit, their minds in turmoil as everything seemed to be falling apart.

Krammler was the last to leave the laboratory.

He stood and watched them leave, a sardonic grin on his face.

As he did so he slowly blinked his eyes.

Eyes as smooth and as black as haematite..

Chapter 21

"Is the line secure Scharführer?"

"Yes Gruppenführer, totally secure and the line is scrambled."

Musfelldt removed his hat and took the telephone receiver from his sergeant. "Good afternoon mein Führer, Gruppenführer Musfelldt reporting from Wenceslaus mine, I have excellent news for you."

Herr Hitler was spending the weekend at his mountain retreat Berchtesgaden in Bavaria. Alongside him, as well as his mistress Eva Braun, were his trusted henchmen Josef Goebbels and Heinrich Himmler along with their families. He felt secure in his 'Eagles Nest', it was where he planned his conquest of Europe and, ultimately, the USA.

"Yes Erich, just how good is this news you have for me?

"Die Glöcke should be operational within the week," Musfelldt almost shouted down the phone line, "your excellent plans for Aryan domination are coming to fruition mein Führer."

Hitler could not contain his glee. He placed his hand over the receiver and addressed his guests, all waiting eagerly for their Führer to speak. "Seven days gentlemen, in seven days we shall have the most glorious Wunderwaffe. With it we shall literally change the history of the world, and Germany will rise from the ashes." His guests beamed back at him. "Well done mein Führer, it was your foresight and tenacity that has made this possible." voiced Goebbels.

"I fully agree, without your vision this would never have been possible." Himmler joined in with the mutual admiration society.

Taking his hand from the handset Hitler continued "Excellent news Erich. Inform me when the rockets are primed for launch and Die Glöcke is ready for our first demonstration on a bewildered world. Your work at Auschwitz and Majdanek has been exemplary in ridding us of the under classes which threaten Aryanism. How does the title Reichsführer Musfelldt sound to you as a reward for your loyalty?"

Musfelldt's posture stiffened significantly. His face beamed with pride.

"It sounds wonderful, and would be an honour, mein Führer. I shall contact you with news of our success within seven days. Enjoy your well-earned break and please pass on my best wishes to your esteemed guests. Heil Hitler."

He replaced the handset and turned to face Krammler, stood in the doorway. "The Führer is most pleased Hans, most pleased and passes on his congratulations and good wishes." He did not mention the promise of promotion over his good friend for fear of upsetting the true spearhead in the research and development of Die Glöcke.

Krammler nodded in appreciation. "And now for your birthday celebration. All is ready; my personal guards have joined your elite squad and are poised in their trucks full of anticipation." He turned to Rick, whose head was still full of muddled thoughts and ideas on how to save this disastrous situation.

"Are you sure I am not needed for security here Commander? You only have a skeleton crew, and I am sure that I would do more good here than carousing elsewhere."

"Nonsense Thomas, here is a chance to let your hair down for once. Wine and women and all that ...." Krammler was insistent. "If it helps I can let both of your trusted Korporals have free rein on the site for the weekend. You can call them and check security at any time."

Musfelldt strode over to Rick, placing his arm on his shoulder again in a rewarding manner. "See, all is secure. A reward for your loyalty and hard work. Our Führer sleeps well in his bed tonight, so go out and enjoy yourself."

Manni and Johnno were outside the communications cabin, but had overheard everything through their earpieces. Johnno turned as if to cough, cupping his hand to his mouth "This may be our way in gents, total sight freedom. Just mind your back Rick, this may be a trick"

Inside the hut Rick turned to face Musfelldt and smiled, proffering his hand for a handshake. "I accept your offer with gratitude Gruppenführer"

"Call me Erich – Thomas."

"Let us both have a fruitful weekend – Erich."

They turned and left the communications hut and strolled down to the rest of the cavalcade.

" We must drive on with care, blinds down on the windows. It has been a directive from the Führer himself after the fiasco with Reinhard Heydrich. An armed Kubelwagen is now an essential travelling companion, one to where we may switch places if we are under threat."

Rick smiled and opened the door for his new 'friend', promptly stepping in behind him.

The lead vehicle set off, followed by Musfelldt's entourage. At the rear was the truck laden with the SS guards, all looking forward to a weekend of drink and debauchery. As they drove off they broke into song .. Vorwärts! Vorwärts!

Musfelldt turned to Rick. "I see your fellow soldiers are in good spirits." Rick agreed, mindful of how he could have a conversation with such a depraved person for over an hour. "If you do not mind, Thomas, I may try to snatch some sleep as we drive. I anticipate a busy night tonight." Rick wanted to knock the lecherous smile off his face. "No problem Erich, It will be a night to remember. You rest after your busy day, I may even take a short nap. We have a busy night ahead." Musfelldt grinned "I do hope so Thomas." He relaxed, pushing his body back into the plush leather interior in an attempt to get comfortable.

Rick sighed with relief, perhaps he would go to sleep after all.

The convoy moved off into the distance. It was mid-afternoon and they should reach their destination before nightfall. The steady throb of diesel engines grew ever quieter as the woodland trees absorbed and hid their progress. The sound of birdsong and occasional cries of foxes soon became the dominant noise. The light snow had long since stopped and the afternoon had become a warm Autumn treat. The guards by the towers closed the gates and settled in for an evening's sentry duty. The lights at the front of the mine entrance had been dimmed as security against potential night bombing raids, now believed to be a distinct possibility after the crash in the forest. The location, small size and low security of the complex was its main form of defence. Why attack an abandoned mine in the middle of an old forest?

Johnno and Manni were unsure what to do next.

Did they chance attacking Krammler then destroy the Bell?

How would they destroy both Bells, could they find extra explosives on site?

How many guards were left on site?

How could they avoid or disable them all?

How could they ensure Rick would safely return?

All these thought ran through both their minds.

Krammler addressed them.

"Korporals."

They both stood to attention "Sir!"

"I want you both to have free rein over what you do tonight. Check anything and everything. If any of the so called workers annoy you please feel free to punish them.

Base yourselves in the vacant SS quarters. Help yourselves to food and drink. Should you want me I shall be in my office in laboratory 3. You have both done well; let's hope for a peaceful evening. Heil Hitler."

Manni and Johnno stood briskly to attention, clicking the heels of their highly polished boots. They raised their arms in a stiff salute "Heil Hitler." Both felt a huge sigh of relief.

Musfelldt strolled purposely into the mine entrance towards his office. As he disappeared into the distance Manni turned to his colleague. "This may just be our way to success. It seems almost too good to be true."

Johnno nodded in agreement. He suddenly realised they had not eaten since breakfast. "We need to formulate a plan. Let's use the SS quarters and decide over a coffee and bite to eat". "And don't forget to include me in your discussions, " came through their earpieces. It was Freya.

"I've sent Astrild to Wroclaw to help with the arrangements for the birthday party. She will make contact with Rick at the Hoppenzoll hotel. If all is well she will spirit him back here before the strike."

"Strike, what strike?" Johnno sounded surprised.

"The main route from Wroclaw to the mine will be bombed on Saturday night by allies in our Swiss base, hopefully preventing Musfelldt and his party from returning to the mine complex for several days. That should allow us to complete our task."

"What about the second Bell? How do we destroy that?"

"As that is deep within the complex I'm sure traditional explosives should take care of that. Remember our log deliveries? Look for the logs marked with three dots, the sign of Orion. They are hollow and contain plastic explosive and detonators. We placed them there as an extra backup. They can also be used to disable the rockets IF we can move the workers to safety. They are at the bottom of the pile for safety – I'd hate anyone to throw one on the fire." Freya laughed.

"Sounds like a plan to me." Manni was much more confident.

"I'll be back in touch later, until then be careful." Freya signed out.

The duo wandered over to the log pile at the rear of the guard hut. Glancing inside they were relieved to see no extra guards. They waved to the guards in the towers as they went to the log piles. "It will be a cold night friends, we'll put some logs in your guard house for you."

The guards waved in acknowledgement.

With some difficulty they carefully selected the three marked logs at the bottom of the pile, with Manni carrying them amongst several others picked at random. Johnno carried several logs into the guard hut putting one on the fire to boost its heat. The rest he placed alongside the fire.

"Let's keep them warm and hope they don't venture outside tonight."

They spent their time in the guard house disabling any weapons they could find, mostly small arms. Manni poured a small amount of his liquid metal into the barrels. When fired it would cause the breech to explode, injuring but not killing the user. Johnno stoked up the fire, carefully checking that none of the logs had three dots marked on them. "Can't be too careful, can we." grinning from ear to ear. He was feeling positive that they were, at last, going to complete their mission.

They then moved on into the Communications hut, Johnno placing the logs outside on the floor. From their outside position they could hear the strains of a German radio station playing songs from home. The music was faint, and distorted by the poor reception, but warned them that someone was inside. As they entered the soldier by the radio looked up casually, and then rushed to smarten himself up for his seniors.

"Relax, private, we have some logs here to keep you warm throughout this cold, damp night." The soldier visibly relaxed back into his seat. "Listening to songs from home .. " his face broke into a smile ".. I would normally be putting my children to bed about now," eyes glazing over.

Johnno put the logs over by the fire. "We all miss our dear ones in these troubled times."

Manni raised his eyes and signalled towards Johnno, nodding his head gently sideways. Johnno took the message on board and moved to the side of the hut, the radio operator's eyes followed him, spinning in his chair as he did so. As soon as his back was turned Manni took a small disc from his pocket. He examined the back of the radio, placing it strategically behind the receiver. The magnetic base allowed it to be fitted easily. It was un-noticeable in the array of wires and the black metal back piece fitted to the radio.

Johnno kept him talking. "Tell me about your children, how old are they?"

"A boy of five and my little girl is three. They live in Dresden, far away from the bombing. I hope to be with them soon," his eyes filled with tears as they focused somewhere in the distance. Johnno's blood ran cold. He realised the danger linked to Dresden. Here was an enemy, but he felt for him as a fellow human being, a father and a husband.

"Do you have relatives anywhere else?"

"I have a brother who lives in Baden-Baden, in the Black Forest. Beautiful countryside, even prettier than these woods."

"Then why not send your family there? Surely it would be easier to visit when you are granted leave."

He pondered for a while. "That sounds like an excellent idea. I may well do that, thank you Korporal, thank you very much for the suggestion. Yes, I shall tell them to visit my brother."

Whilst Johnno had kept the conversation going Manni had slipped several drops of a strong tranquiliser into the coffee mug by the radio set. Knowing this would render him unconscious for several hours it would provide a little extra insurance for their plans.

Johnno moved to shake the hand of his enemy. "I trust you will see your family again soon." The operator stood up and took the proffered hand in a vigorous handshake.

"Now back to your music, and enjoy your coffee while it's hot."

He lifted the mug as if raising a toast, first to Johnno and then Manni. "Prost!" He then took a drink as he toasted his new comrades.

Johnno nodded and smiled "Prost!"

They turned to leave the hut, stepping outside into the cool, damp evening air. "Soldiers' quarters next." Johnno was feeling good about his actions for a fellow human being.

"I saw what you did there. What would the Federation say about creating a paradox?"

"To Hell with the Federation, we just saved three lives." Johnno replied without breaking stride. He then bent down to collect his special logs, ensuring the 'ordinary' ones were on top. As they approached the soldiers' quarters just outside the mine entrance preparing themselves for the next round of checking their adversaries before acting. The ground was quite hard, with the noise from the added gravel warning the occupants of impending visitors. The rank and file soldiers believed it would give them the edge on any snap inspections made. There were dim lights just visible from the shuttered windows. They stood at the door and listened for the sound of conversation. Again a radio played music from home, unquestionably Wagner this time, Hitler's favourite composer.

Johnno again placed the logs outside for safety, only carrying in the ones for burning.

They braced themselves for more of the same; Johnno checked his pocket for his new space weapon. Should he carry it in his hand? No, it would be spotted. Best keep it hidden.

Manni opened the door full of anticipation. The room was empty. It seemed that they had, indeed, all been granted leave for this special birthday.

"Close the door." Manni made his way to the arms rack. There were a few rifles but the majority of weapons were obviously on their way to Wroclaw. Manni repeated his trick with his liquid metal phial.

Johnno looked around almost aimlessly, looking for anything that might help their quest. His eyes lit up when he spotted a Walther PPK in its holster hung by a locker. Deftly he removed it from the hanger, then realised that it was in a leg holster. He raised his trouser leg, attaching the holster by his ankle. He smoothed down his trousers, checking if it was too visible. "A souvenir of my trip to 1944."

Manni, still with his back to Johnno, spoke quietly. "Please don't use that unless your life is in mortal danger. OK?" Johnno realised he had been 'rumbled' and meekly agreed.

"And don't forget your lens cameras; I'm following your every move too." Freya sounded a gentle warning in his ear.

Johnno was suitably admonished. "Sorry, won't happen again."

"Now for the final part of our preparations," Manni moved to the doorway to leave the hut, "we venture into the mine itself."

They left the hut as they found it. Blinds drawn, door closed. The radio playing Wagner's Ride of the Valkyries – this seemed very apt. They collected the logs they had left outside and strode towards the mine entrance. Our duo strode into the mine and made their way to the SS rest quarters. On the way they pulled back the canvas on the parked trucks just to ensure that the rockets were still there.

As they entered the SS quarters and were again relieved to see that the room was empty, quietly closing the large wooden door behind them as they prepared to make final plans for their task ahead. After checking no-one was present Manni spoke with some trepidation.

"Right, Johnno, this is it. Operation Die Glöcke is now officially under way."

Chapter 22

On the top of a cast iron stove Johnno found an enamelled tin pot with freshly brewed coffee. He picked up two well used mugs, blew any dust out of them and poured a drink for each of them.

Manni carried the log pile over by the fire and began to search for the hidden plastic explosives. At the end of the first marked log he found a large wooden plug. He felt around his tunic pockets. "They always carry a knife of some sort, now where is it?" Eventually he opened the button on his breast pocket and took out a well-used pen knife. He carefully opened the blade and began to loosen the plug, looking for the almost invisible join where it had been pressed in. "Gotcha." – the plug came loose and then was prised out. Inside was a small pack of plastic explosive and separate detonators. "Timed fuses, that's good." He put them into his side tunic pocket. "One down, two to go."

He replaced the wooden plug, placing the log back onto the pile. Picking out the second marked log he repeated the process, placing the contents into his other side pocket. As he replaced the plug and placed the log back onto the pile the door suddenly swung open behind them.

"Good afternoon Korporals, I see you have made yourself at home." It was one of the SS guards, followed closely behind by his colleague. They strode over towards the stove, inspecting the coffee pot.

"Ah - Just enough left for the two of us on this damp evening," pouring two more mugs to the brim. "These Polish evenings chill you to the bone." He cupped his mug to warm his hands, his colleague smiling and doing likewise.

Johnno did his best not to panic, looking up and smiling at his erstwhile colleagues. Manni slipped his knife back into his pocket as calmly as he could; he slowly got to his feet and walked over to greet his enemy. Proffering a handshake he introduced himself. "Good evening,", he paused and looked at the soldier's insignia "Stabsgefreiter."

"Stabsgefreiter Hoffman, and my colleague Stabsgefreiter Klein," came a jovial reply.

"Let's lose the formality gentlemen." Johnno tried to sound polite, almost friendly "I am Johan and ," pointing to Manni "this is my colleague Otto."

Their SS friends beamed. Placing his hand to his chest and dipping his head in acknowledgement "I am Max, " and pointing to his colleague "and my colleague her is Oskar."

Johnno thought quickly. "Shall I brew more coffee for your SS brethren out marshalling the working scum?"

Oskar put down his mug and stepped forwards towards the fire, looking to warm his hands. "No need, we have been left in charge while our colleagues are out on a piss-up." He sounded pompously proud, then added "Though I would rather have been getting drunk and laid with our colleagues." A voice now changed to one of regret.

"Just four guards and a single radio operator on site," a voice whispered in our duo's ear, it was Freya, "almost too good to be true. Let's not forget Krammler and his scientists as well."

Manni and Johnno covered their concentration by moving towards the stove with their now half empty mugs, looking at each other in acknowledgement.

"Astrild and the birthday party have reached Wroclaw. We are now awaiting the road damage. All is clear for you to act. Good luck."

As they replaced their mugs onto the stove they turned just in time to see Oskar pick up the final marked log and place it on the top of the fire. "Let's get really warm and then perhaps a Schnapps before we settle down for the night." Manni and Johnno looked at each other in disbelief. They had just minutes to save themselves, and a hundred plus workers within the complex.

The logs began to crackle; Max looked at Manni with a quizzical look on his face. "What is the matter Korporal, you look worried."

Johnno moved towards the fire "I think we need to remove that log, it may get too hot."

As he did so both of the SS guards stood and blocked his path.

"No, let's get REALLY hot shall we."

Johnno was trying to remember where he had put his 'space' weapon. It wasn't on his wrist. Panic began to set in.

"Commander Krammler told us about the marked log; it contains a secret message does it not, a message for two traitorous Korporals." Both guards slowly took off their tunic tops revealing torsos that would grace any muscle bound body builder. They stood menacingly in his way, blocking the path to the fire. Johnno moved his head to one side of his human barrier; he could see the bark on the log beginning to turn bright yellow as the flames took hold.

"Gentlemen," he said, with a hint of panic now creeping into his voice "this room is going to get hotter than you could ever imagine." Johnno moved slowly forward towards his foe, wondering just how the hell he could get past them to the growing threat behind them. Where had he put his neuroliser?

"Oskar ... Max," he paused, glancing behind them "the log contains a bomb and we are all going to die if it burns." The guards looked at each other and laughed.

"A bomb, is that the best you can think of?" They stood their ground.

All seemed lost. Then, in Johnno's ear piece came a commanding voice.

"Johnno, move to your left – NOW."

He did so without hesitation.

Two beams of focussed light hit the SS guards and their inert bodies slowly crumpled silently to the floor, the only sound being a sigh as they hit the ground.

Johnno turned to see Manni with his weapon in his hand. He lunged forward, stepping over the collapsed figures on the floor, throwing the last of the coffee onto the fire, simultaneously grabbing the log and throwing backwards towards to safety. Johnno rushed to the 'kitchen' area desperately looking for water, eventually finding the pan used to store drinking water. Picking it up he rushed to the smoking log, turning it over he poured the entire contents along its length with a reassuring hiss. Manni grabbed a towel from the table and picked up the steaming log, feverishly looking for the outline of the plug. He took his knife back out of his pocket and levered furiously at the join.

To their relief the plug came away – to reveal an empty cavity.

They both looked bemused. It was the right log; it did have a plug fitted; but no explosives, no detonators. Johnno stood, leaning forward with his hands on his knees, wondering just what the hell had happened.

"Well done buddy, I'm glad you remembered your ray gun. How long are they out for?"

"I gave them just an hour or so. They'll need to get out of here safely if we need to use our explosives in the mine. Remember the Federation?"

Manni looked deep in thought.

"We obviously have a major problem here; Krammler somehow knows who we are and was waiting for us. He was obviously confident we would act today by only leaving a skeleton crew to tempt us to action. We fell into his trap." He looked again at the smouldering log and its empty cavity.

"Damn, I should have realised he obviously couldn't risk an explosion so close to his precious V2 rockets." His face took on a look of deep concern. His voice lowered. "There must be a spy in our organisation somewhere. Our next steps will have to be carefully planned."

A message came through their ear pieces. "I'm afraid we have a second problem." Freya's voice was emotional and strained.

"I cannot get in touch with Rick. Astrild cannot locate him ... and one of the trucks did not arrive at all."

Chapter 23

The convoy moved swiftly through the woods on towards Wroclaw. The drivers were fully aware of potential ambush by lone patriots and had orders to travel at speed. The two Kubelwagens were flanked at the front and rear by the trucks carrying the SS and regular soldiers towards their surprise weekend treat.

Rick sat uneasily next to his erstwhile companion Musfelldt. He was still worried as to how could he keep up such small talk for the best part of an hour if his colleague did not enjoy a small sleep as he had promised?

And just why had Krammler insist he join the celebration party and stay back at the mine?

"What did you do before this infernal war interrupted our lives in the homeland Thomas?" Rick had been supplied with a 'back story' and was now going to be put to the test. He did his best to look relaxed, nonchalant even.

"I was an engineer back home in Hannover. I studied at Hannover University and was fortunate in helping design Panzerkampfwagens ready for our inevitable war and the coming of our 3rd Reich. My favourite design was the PZ.111, very successful in securing France, Poland and devastating our communist enemies to the East."

"How did you begin your army career?"

"When I realised that war was inevitable I applied for a commission so I could do my bit for Germany and mein Führer. My excellent credentials allowed me to enlist and rapidly gain promotion. When Commander Krammler learned of my engineering credentials he personally requested my presence here as both security and support for the scientists as they reverse engineer our latest Wunderwaffe."

Their conversation was cut short by static on a walkie talkie held by the guard next to the driver. He turned to his superiors in the rear.

"Excuse me sirs. The truck to the rear has suffered a puncture to one of its tyres and is pulling over for repairs."

"Halt the convoy, at once." was the immediate response from Musfelldt.

"For security I shall move into the first truck in case this is some form of attack by local partisans. You will be safe here Thomas, do not worry." The guard leapt out and opened the door for his Gruppenführer. Musfelldt got out and hurried past the other Kubelwagen, stopping only briefly to tell Storrensberg of his concerns and actions. As he approached the truck the tailgate dropped open and two soldiers jumped out.

With their help, and that of soldiers inside, Musfelldt was spirited out of sight and potential danger.

The convoy restarted, minus the truck having its tyre repaired.

Rick wasn't sure how he felt.

He felt intense relief at not having to maintain conversation with an inquisitive enemy.

He also felt intense concern at being left as a 'sitting duck' should there really be an attack. He knew none was planned, but what if there were some partisans acting on their own? They would ignore the trucks and aim for the officers in the staff car.

He was also now at the rear of the convoy. He glanced behind only to see the headlights of the stranded truck fade into the distance. He desperately wanted to contact Freya and update her, perhaps ensuring no attacks were planned on his convoy, but how could he with a driver and a guard in close contact? Surely they would hear him.

Nervously he leaned forward and tapped the driver on the shoulder.

"Keep up soldier, keep up."

The driver studiously pressed the accelerator a little harder and closed the gap between them and Storrensberg's vehicle. Fortunately the rest of the journey was uneventful.

As they left the cover of the woods and moved towards the city the opportunity for ambush receded. Once again the silence of the evening was broken by the strains of German marching songs. The strains of "Vorwärts, Vorwärts" filled the air, sung as if the war was already over and won. As they entered the city and drove towards the hotel and bars the tune changed to "Alles gute geburstag an unseren Gruppenführer".

Rick allowed himself a wry smile. "Happy birthday to our Gruppenführer, Crawling bastards."

His earpiece was obviously working just fine.

The convoy pulled up outside the Hoppenzoll Hotel to be met by subservient staff, apparently overjoyed at their guests' choice of venue. Musfelldt jumped down from the rear of the truck with a beaming smile on his face. He turned to face his travelling companions.

"Thank you for your hospitality soldiers, now go and enjoy some of mine. Remember we return on Sunday morning," before adding in a sarcastic tone "and DO behave yourselves."

A large cheer erupted from inside the canvas cover as it drove away, doubtless headed for the nearest bars.

Storrensberg had rushed forward towards Musfelldt. "Another faultless journey Erich, thank you for your immaculate planning."

Rick overheard the comment as the door to his transport was opened by the guard. "Another crawling bastard." he mused to himself. Leaving his staff car he walked towards the hotel steps where his two companions had already been met by the hotel manager, bowing so deeply his face almost touched his knees. His immaculately coiffured hair was held rigidly in place by liberal helpings of hair cream. His suit had seen better days, as had his shoes, both quite shiny and well worn.

"We are SO honoured to have you stay with us," he said, rubbing his hands together, gesturing his guests to enter his establishment. Musfelldt removed his gloves, an action quickly mirrored by Storrensberg.

"We have the finest three suites in your hotel, yes?" Musfelldt's tone was imperious.

"Oh yes, yes. Full suites, with balconies AND your own private bathrooms."

"And the extras we requested?"

The manager gave a salacious smile, rubbing his hands together again whilst gently bowing and tilting his head to one side. "Certainly, officers of our dear Führer, you have, shall we say, bed warmers to help you sleep, if, indeed you do intend to sleep."

Musfelldt looked towards his fellow officers and beamed. "All is well gentlemen. I suggest that we have a shower and refresh ourselves and then meet at, say twenty hundred hours for a cocktail in the bar. You DO have a bar don't you?"

"Oh yes, yes. We have many, many drinks including German lagers, Barenjager, Slivovitz, Schnapps, champagne and ... saved especially for my friends ... Johnny Walker scotch whisky."

"Good, good. Now show us to our suites, we are weary after our long journey."

The manager beckoned for Musfelldt to follow him. "Gentlemen, this way please, follow me."

The Hoppenzoll had once been grand but had obviously seen better days. The general decor was one of Victorian grandeur, resplendent with gilt chandeliers – though only blessed with around half the light bulbs needed for brilliant lamination. The reception desk faced the entrance doors and was manned by an elderly lady, probably in her sixties and married to the manager. As the party of officers passed she curtsied, smiled generously and offered a gentle "Heil Hitler," probably in mock adulation for her country's oppressors.

Rick turned and proffered a smile; his colleagues marched past and ignored her.

The carpets, once plush, were now worn but bore the designs of a past magnificence and led to the grand double stairway, resplendent with its sweeping balustrades leading to a grand first floor balcony which overlooked the main entrance.

They all followed the manager, who was still attempting to bow and look full of his own importance. At the top on the facing wall of the balcony were paintings highlighting dignitaries from the past, with an oil painting of Frederick Augustus celebrating the last monarch of this now troubled country the largest and most prominent of them all.

Upon reaching the top of the stairs the Manager moved swiftly to his left, then half turned to face his guests. "Our Imperial corridor gentlemen." He then led them along towards the very end and stopped to open a door to his left. He then proffered the key to Rick.

"Room 117 for Herr Oberleutnant – the Miesko suite. Please enjoy." He bowed yet again, extending his arm to direct him into the room.

Rick nodded and turned to his colleagues. "Until twenty hundred hours then gentlemen." Both nodded in agreement as Rick entered the room. He stood just inside the doorway, but held the door slightly open.

The sound of a key in the door was followed by "Room 119 for Gruppenführer Storrensberg – the Boleslaw suite." There was a click of a pair of heels and he heard the door close.

Finally came the sound of a key in the final door. "For our especially honoured guest on his special day, our finest suite." Rick heard a creak as the door opened. "The Sobieski suite for our honoured birthday guest."

"Call me at nineteen ... sorry, you peasants still use the wrong time ... call me at 7.45 this evening, and DO NOT be late."

"Oh yes sir, no problem, 7.45 or should I say 19.45 hours." He smiled his most subservient smile and walked away backwards, bowing yet again as he went.

A look of disdain filled Musfelldt's face as he entered the room and slammed the door.

Rick moved away from his door opening to stand behind it whilst trying to quietly close it.

As the manager walked past he heard him mumble to himself. "German bastards! One day, one day."

Rick smiled. He knew he might have an ally there should he need one.

Chapter 24

Rick walked over the room towards the bed, removing his tunic and placing it on the chair back. He hung his pistol and holster over the arm on the side of his bed. He felt his greatest danger may come when he tried to sleep, there was no harm in being prepared. He then wandered over to the balcony doors. They were old metal doors in desperate need of a coat of paint, but opened quite easily overlooking the square below. He glanced in both directions. No sign of the army trucks, and apparently no emergency way out. He closed the doors. Looking back he could see how this had once been a jewel in the crown of hotels but was now lacking in splendour somewhat.

"At least it is clean and welcoming, and a chance for a shower. Let's hope for some hot water." He ambled over towards the bathroom. The design was rococo and elegant.

The shower was impressively large. He switched on the taps and waited, pleasantly surprised when lukewarm water came through.

"Just enough time for a quick shower." He undressed quickly. As he stepped in he heard a faint sound from his earpiece. Pressing his hand to his ear he could hear nothing. "Hello. Anyone there?" No reply. "Radio interference I presume." He shrugged his shoulders and continued with his shower.

Having dressed again, feeling more refreshed than he could have hoped for he then realised he hadn't contacted Freya or his two colleagues back at the mine. Then he wondered why they hadn't contacted him. He moved over the room, away from the door and sat at a desk by the balcony doors. It was dark outside and he realised he would be back in action shortly, having to entertain his two German 'friends'.

He touched his earpiece, quietly adding "Are you there Freya?" No reply.

"Manni, Johnno – can you give me an update please?" No reply.

"Are you there Freya? Is anyone there?"

After several seconds a faint voice replied. "It is Freya here. Can you give me an update Rick? I'm about to contact Manni and Johnno in the mine. Have you arrived safely?" Freya's voice was quiet, almost imperceptible.

"I'm at the Hoppenzoll, room 117, and due for drinks with Musfelldt. Be careful, one truck has not arrived and may be returning to Wenceslaus. Did you copy, one truck may be returning. You must alert Johnno and Manni."

Freya's voice was fading in and out. "I hear you about the trucks ...." and her voice faded away.

Just then there was a knock at the door.

"Thomas, it is time for cocktails. Are you ready?"

Rick turned to face the balcony doors while he finished the conversation, hoping that Freya could hear him even if he couldn't hear her. "Freya, I have to go now, please keep a watching brief over my conversations tonight. I may need help if I'm found out."

"OK – I have that." Freya was loud and clear this time. Rick stood up and shouted "I'm coming Erich, just putting on my jacket." He collected his jacket off the chair back and then moved over to the bed, collecting his holster. He glanced in the dressing table mirror and smoothed his hair down. He collected his hat, placing it carefully on his head, simultaneously pulling down on the back of his tunic.

"Here we go Oberleutnant Thomas Schulze , good luck." He opened the door to be greeted by a smiling Musfelldt with Storrensberg stood, grinning, slightly behind him.

"Good evening Erich." Then acknowledging his other adversary he nodded "And good evening to you Jakob"

Musfelldt smiled as he looked Rick in the eyes. His voice seemed .. creepy somewhat.

"Good evening ...... Erich, or is it Rick?"

Rick looked puzzled, and then he looked down. He had a luger aimed directly at his chest. Musfelldt pulled the trigger. Rick was forced back into his room by the power of the shot. Musfelldt moved forward and shot him again in the stomach. "Goodnight and goodbye … Rick Abrahams." Musfelldt took the 'Do Not Disturb' sign from the back of the door and hung it on the outside handle, slamming the door shut.

"And now for that birthday drink. A double celebration Jakob." They marched along the corridor and down the sweeping stairs.

Rick's body lay crumpled on the floor. His ear was flooded with calls from a frantic Freya

"Rick, Rick please answer will you?. What was that noise? Please come in. Rick, Rick please report back. Are you OK? Please reply."

A growing pool of blood seeped out from beneath his tunic, staining the aged opulent carpet a deep red. His eyes fluttered as he chain stoked his final breath.

His lifeless body could hear no more. Rick was dead.

Chapter 25

Unaware of their colleagues' fate Manni and Johnno were now ready to put their plan into action.

"OK Johnno, time to move. If there is a lorry returning we must act quickly. Are you ready?"

Johnno took a deep breath. He took hold of the two amulets on his neck reassuring himself he had the keys to success on him. He tapped his pocket to check he had his alien stun weapon, his 'neuroliser', on him and he knew where it was. Manni took the explosive cylinder from his breast pocket and passed it over.

"Remember; look directly at the glass insert at the end. This will then allow you to twist and activate the device. You then have 10 minutes or so to make your escape."

"Can I shorten the time say, in an emergency?"

"Only if it is really necessary; Once activated you can use the retinal scan again it will shorten the delay to around 5 minutes. That is barely time to escape, so, for your God's sake only use in an emergency." Manni placed his hand on Johnno's shoulder in a reassuring manner. "Good luck my friend, may our guardian angels be on our side. Ready?"

Johnno put the cylinder into the breast pocket of his tunic, and smiled as best he could. He felt a knot deep down in his stomach. His only thought now was how to succeed – he HAD to succeed

"As ready as I'll ever be, let's do this."

They dragged the SS guards' lifeless bodies to the bunk beds and lay them out as if asleep. When they awoke they would have no recollection of their experience, their memories somewhat scrambled by the effects of Manni's weapon. Opening the door they glanced in both directions as they slipped in between the parked trucks with their deadly loads still concealed by tarpaulins. Keeping their bodies low they checked that no-one was entering the mine. The coast seemed clear.

They moved deeper into the mineshaft, progress hidden by the half-light within. The sound of their boots on the gravel laden floor was the only sign of their progress within the dank tunnel. As they approached the laboratory entrance Johnno became aware of a presence in the near distance, a murmuring which suddenly became an oppressive silence. He gestured towards Manni and moved past the laboratory entrance. Manni was intrigued, yet annoyed. Where the hell was he going? Johnno's eyes had become accustomed to the half-light and he soon realised what was the source of the murmurings and mutterings. Along the length of the wall was a line of slave workers, manacled by a continuous length of chain passed through steel anklets. He felt revulsion at the sight which had greeted him. In front of him was a row of emaciated bodies, many near to death, all paralysed by fear at the sight of enemy uniforms coming to accost them. He recognised the first face he saw, it was the same worker he had helped to secure his food earlier on.

"Don't be afraid, we are not Germans. We are here to help you." The young face looked in disbelief, and then a wry smile appeared on his face.

"You speak very good Polish my friend"

Johnno nodded. "That is a long story; let's try to get you out of here."

Manni grabbed his shoulder, twisting Johnno's body in a half turn until face to face. "We cannot help these people, however sorry we feel. Remember our task, remember the Federation rules."

"As I said once before, to Hell with the Federation, these people need our help. Otherwise we'll be as bad as our enemy."

Johnno turned back round, searching for the main lock which held the chain secure. He pulled fruitlessly at the padlock, looking around for anything to remove it before picking up a rock to hit it with. He hit the padlock once, to no avail, the dull thud echoing around the mine's walls. As he raised his arm to hit it a second time Manni restrained him. He had a look of resignation on his face. "Too much noise! Move aside, let me deal with this."

Johnno was expecting Manni to produce something spectacular, perhaps another neuroliser or a magical metal melting liquid. He looked on in anticipation. Manni produced a set of keys from his pocket. He smiled at Johnno as he searched through several keys, finding one to fit and unlock the padlock. He turned to face his colleague with a look of triumph on his face.

"I took them from the SS guards' pocket in case we needed them for the laboratory. No need for 'space stuff'. Now let's free these poor souls and complete our mission." Johnno grabbed his colleague's shoulder, gently squeezing as he smiled. "Thank you my friend."

He turned to the young man in front of him whose face was now one of joy and wonderment. Johnno slowly pulled the chain through its securing bolt and then through his leg iron. He gestured for him to do the same for his neighbour and pass on the instructions. Johnno placed his finger to his lips.

"You must do this quietly my friend. Move out through the rear of the mine towards the large concrete structure, and may your God go with you."

The young man turned to his neighbour and passed on the instructions. He stood to his feet and moved towards Johnno, his eyes full of tears. He threw his arms around him, hugging with all his might. His emaciated frame radiated gratitude. "I shall never forget you, thank you, I thank you with all my heart."

Johnno hugged him back gently, feeling his frail body was too weak for a full manly hug. The young man turned to go, glancing back and smiling. Instead of making straight for the mine exit he diligently began helping others loosen their links to the deathly chain, helping them to rise and make their way out.

Manni broke his silence. "Now can we complete our mission?"

Johnno looked back at the disappearing throng of workers and then back towards his colleague.

"Yes, and thank you for caring my friend."

They made their way stealthily back towards the lab entrance, stopping as they reached the closed door. "Let's synchronise watches."

"We'll set them to twenty one hundred hours." Both men set their timepieces, noting "3 -2 -1 – now." They clicked the watches and set them moving.

"Do what we need to do, and meet back here at 21.15. That should give us time to leave the mine and be in the woods before the Bells are both destroyed." Manni took hold of Johnno's forearm. "Good luck my friend, let us hope history is still on our side."

Carefully opening the door a small way they listened for the sound of any voices inside. All was silent. They made their way inside, all the while glancing towards the rear of the lab where it led to the third laboratory and Krammler's office. They slid the lock on the door behind them for added security, plus a chair as extra reinforcement.

Manni gestured for Johnno to start to work on the Bell whilst he entered lab 3 in preparation for work on the 2nd Bell. He mouthed the words "Good luck," as he moved into the tunnel separating the two laboratories, quickly disappearing into the darkness.

Johnno moved towards the Bell. He felt a shiver throughout his body

"I think that's what we call déjà vu if I'm not mistaken." He quickly composed himself and set about his task once more. Scanning the surface, doing his best to recall where the professor had found the Bell shaped indentation, he removed the chain from his neck ready for use. It took several seconds of feeling and scanning the aged metal surface to locate the key indentation.

"Here goes nothing." murmuring under his breath whilst placing his amulet against the Bell surface. He waited for the door to slide open. Nothing happened. "Shit." He tried again, to no avail. His heart sank.

Looking closely at the amulet and its engraved symbols he realised what was the problem. "Wrong way around you idiot." He turned the amulet around and placed it within the indentation. To his relief there was a slight swishing sound as the door slid open revealing a dark interior, lit only by the hazy reflection from the lab's fluorescent tubes. "I should have bought a torch, why didn't I think of that."

He tentatively stepped inside, trying his best to focus his eyes in the semi-darkness. He approached what looked like the control console. As he did so he heard the swishing sound of the door closing; he turned around just in time to see the door close, enveloping him in total darkness. He began to feel his way around the wall, trying not to panic.

"I don't suppose they had light switches when this was built."

Having felt all the way around the walls his hands eventually found their way onto the console. He felt along the top, looking for anything that might help him in his dilemma. As he placed his hand flat on the console service he heard a pinging noise. To his surprise and relief the console screen became active, and the inside of the Bell begin to illuminate. Relieved, he looked around but could not see any visible source of illumination, it was as if the walls were glowing in an iridescent shade of blue.

The illumination steadily increased until the inside was bathed in light. The inside was bigger than he had imagined. As well as the console in front of him he could see seating behind him, for up to three people it appeared. The walls were bathed in blue and appeared totally smooth, meeting at their apex in the Bell shaped ceiling.

He turned to stare at the console, scanning everywhere for shapes, symbols, anything to jog his memory about what to do next. "The weapon, that's why I'm here, I need to locate the weapon first." He looked above the console at what looked like a flat television screen. Below that he could just make out as faint rectangular shape. It was the only shape visible on the walls at all. "This must be something to do with it." He began to feel the wall and the outline, placing both hands flat and feeling all around for any button or symbol to press. All he could make out was 3 small indentations in the centre of the rectangle. He felt deflated, how was he going to open the safe and get the weapon.

"Think Johnno, think!"

After what seemed like an eternity his face lit up.

"My lucky charm!" Johnno felt as if someone had switched on a light in his brain.

"My lucky charm - Orion's Belt with three stars."

He felt for the charms he had put back on his neck chain. Feeling at the surface of his lucky amulet he could feel three slight indentations. He slid the chain over his head and placed his amulet against the indentations in the wall. Nothing happened. Nonplussed, with a smile, he turned the amulet around. "Wrong way again, you idiot."

The small rectangular shape was a small door which moved inwards and then slid sideways to reveal a cavity in the wall. After replacing his neck chain, Johnno placed his hand inside, quickly locating a cold metallic object. He quickly retrieved it, lifting it upwards against the reflective lights on the interior walls, to try and see exactly what it was.

The weapon had a strange U shape to it, with the bottom of the U being square to its two sides. Johnno realised this bottom piece must be the handle. He gripped it lightly, turning it and examining it from all sides. The two 'barrels' appeared to have glass, or crystal, end pieces. There were symbols etched on the sides, but no apparent trigger to fire it. Overall it was about six inches wide with barrels around four inches long.

"All the fuss is about this, this pop-gun. Amazing."

He tucked the weapon inside his tunic for safety, fastening up all the buttons to ensure that he didn't let it fall out.

"And now for the explosives." He looked around the featureless interior, searching out what he believed would be a good spot to place it. He realised that a flat surface would be better and safer at holding the device in place. Eventually he settled on the console top. He was just about to take it from his tunic pocket when he heard a voice shouting outside of the Bell. It was Manni.

"Come quickly, we have a major problem."

Alarmed, Johnno looked how to open the door go to his colleagues help.

Although the walls were completely smooth Johnno remembered the symbols which had appeared on the console. He scanned them closely, their red outlines showing well against the dull grey surface of the console.

"Quickly, I need your help." Manni sounded desperate.

Johnno felt a slight surge of panic before he spotted a rectangular shape highlighted with a line to the centre of each side. "I don't suppose this door shaped ..." He placed his finger on the illuminated shape and the door slid open.

He moved to the doorway and saw Manni facing him. He was sat lifeless on a chair, head to one side, eyes closed, obviously unconscious. Johnno rushed towards him, lifting his head gently looking for signs of life. He gripped his shoulders gently in an effort to waken him. His voice became more concerned as panic began to seep in.

"Manni, Manni – speak to me – what's wrong?" He gently gripped his chin, turning his face towards his own looking for signs of life, any signs of life. He put his cheek near to his face. Good, he could feel warm breath, he was at least alive. He glanced down at his body, checking for signs of blood, gunshot wounds, anything. He found nothing. He appeared to be just unconscious

"Wake up buddy – come on what's wrong with you?"

From behind him in a darkened corner of the room came a recognisable voice, one that sounded very much like his unconscious friend Manni.

A figure stepped out from the shadows, it was … Manni.

Johnno did a double take, looking at the figure in front of him, and back at his unconscious double.

"Who the hell are you? Tell me what's wrong?"

"Nothing is wrong, now you have the weapon."

Manni's double levelled his arm and took aim. He fired his neuroliser at his wide eyed opponent.

Johnno crumpled and collapsed on the floor.

'Manni' walked over and looked at the figure now lying unconscious by the side of his colleague.

Looking down he smiled, and then he slowly blinked.

His eyes were as smooth and as black as haematite..

Chapter 26

In the distance he could hear voices, soft voices urging him to wake up.

"Am I dead?" he wondered "are the angels calling me?"

His eyelids felt as heavy as lead as he slowly tried to open them. In the dim light he could make out a figure close to him, talking calmly and reassuring him that he would be alright soon. "It IS an angel. I must be in heaven, wherever that is."

The voice grew louder and more insistent. "Come on; snap out of it, you must wake up."

Slowly his senses were returning. His mouth felt as if someone had rubbed it with sandpaper and then painted it. He did his best to salivate and get some liquid into his mouth. He tried to talk, but only garbled sounds escaped his lips. Blinking his eyes he tried to focus on the figure alongside him. His head was pounding, he felt as if he had been on one of his tequila nights with his buddy Rick and was suffering the next morning.

"Rick" – his voice somehow managed to garble his name "Rick, where the hell are we?"

"It's not Rick, it's me, Manni. Come on Johnno, you have to wake up."

He blinked his eyes furiously again to get a focus on where the figure appeared to be next to him. He tried to stand, but realised he was tied into his seat. He struggled trying to free his arms, but realised it was fruitless. His legs were also tied to the chair legs.

"Don't bother my friend, save your energy."

Johnno now was regaining full consciousness. Focussing on the figure beside him he realised it was Manni. "You shot me, you bastard, why?"

"Not me, my friend, it was Krammler. Or, should I say, someone who had replicated into Krammler, who then replicated me. I suspect it is our spy, probably a Pleiadian who has mastered our techniques. But we have a greater problem on our hands."

"What could be worse than getting caught?"

"We have been unconscious for two days or so. From all the noises and activity I hear outside in the mineshaft I suspect that the weapon has been successfully dismantled and its elements loaded onto the pair of V2 rockets.

I have just heard the sound of diesel engines starting. They are moving them outside to launch them. We have failed in our mission."

Johnno's face contorted to one of anger, the strength of which he had never before experienced. Then realisation dawned. They had been manipulated by this Pleiadian interloper who was intent on changing the outcome of the Second World War.

"We've been fooled from day one. All our progress had been manipulated by an outsider."

He suddenly remembered his friend Rick and realised that he too had been compromised. That's why he was sent on the birthday celebrations to get him out of the way.

"Freya said Rick could not be contacted." Then, with an air of resignation, added "He may even be dead, captured at the least."

"I know my friend, but that was always on the cards."

"Yes, but what would your Federation say about that. Why didn't they prevent it?" Johnno's voice was full of emotion, anger at losing his best friend. "A paradox, remember?"

"Perhaps they tried, we may never know."

Suddenly there came the sound of the door opening. "Someone is approaching, act as if you are unconscious again." Manni urgently whispered. Both men closed their eyes and let their heads roll forward. "They've come to finish us off," Manni thought, now they have the weapon installed, cursing his failure and the unnecessary loss of thousands of lives.

He braced himself for the pistol shot that would end their mission and signal destruction to an unsuspecting world. Johnno felt his body being shaken, his face gently slapped in an effort to waken him up. He felt sure he was about to be interrogated, tortured even, and was determined to maintain his semblance of being unconscious.

"Wake up. Please wake up." the voice was not German but distinctly Polish.

Manni glanced through half open eyes having expected to see a pistol waving German officer, but was stunned when he realised how wrong he was. Johnno raised both eyelids gently as if waking from a deep sleep. He peered to see who was shaking him. Both eyes suddenly opened wide in amazement. It was the young mine worker he had freed on his way to the Bell.

"What are you doing here? How did you get in? Can you free us?"

The young man smiled. "I have come to return the favour for the men who saved so many lives."

"Very admirable, but can you get us out of these chairs?" Manni sounded desperate "We somehow need to stop those rockets being launched."

"You are too late my friend. The two big rockets have been driven outside and I fear they are about to be launched at any moment."

"Find something to undo these ropes." Johnno nodded as he looked around the room. "Try the office next door, that's where Krammler keeps his uniform."

The young lad disappeared into the narrow corridor, re-appearing moments later.

"I think this will do it." In his hand was a sheathed SS dagger. He moved around the rear of Johnno's chair and began sawing at the rope which held him firm. Johnno pulled the rope tight, his hands swinging loose as the rope gave way. He freed his hands from the remnants of the rope as the young man moved to the front and cut the ropes tying him to the chair. Manni was then freed, both men now rubbing their wrists vigorously to restart the blood flow to their aching hands.

Johnno stood up and moved over to the young man. Placing both hands on his emaciated shoulders he looked his saviour in the eye. "Thank you, thank you for coming back to save us and putting your own life in danger."

The young man smiled and looked mildly embarrassed. He took in a deep breath, taking a proud posture as he reached to his full height. "It is my honour to repay the debt of life to a good man."

Johnno smiled back. "Are your workmates safe? Did they get away?"

The young man nodded. "We went through the rear of the mine workings. As we got outside a group of villagers led by a lady met us and helped us to escape into the night. She must have been sent by an angel."

Johnno turned to Manni and smiled. "An angel by the name of Freya. She was listening in all the time."

He suddenly realised she may still be listening. He touched his ear and asked earnestly "Are you there Freya? Please come in."

All he could hear was a faint crackling sound, the sound of radio interference.

"I'll move around and see if I can get some reception, the signal must be being blocked somehow," Manni disappeared towards Krammler's office "and I bet it's somewhere in here."

Johnno moved to the entrance door, slowly closing it to give them some security whilst they figured out what to do next. He slid the metal bolt across into its niche in the cave wall. He beckoned to the young man "pass me that chair." He did so, with Johnno jamming it against the door handle and the floor.

"Every little helps."

Holding the boy by his shoulders Johnno softly spoke. "I owe you my life young man, and I don't even know your name."

With a beaming smile he proudly announced

"My name is Josef, Josef Gorski."

Johnno felt his heart miss a beat.

Chapter 27

He moved forward and gave him a 'man hug', careful not to put too much pressure on his emaciated frame.

"It is a privilege to meet you, Josef Gorski." He felt his eyes fill with tears, realising that he now had another life he had to save, again.

Manni rushed back through. "I think I've sorted it. There was a radio transmitter in his office blocking our signals." He opened his hands to show several wafers of material, covered in a copper coloured pattern "Circuit boards." He ceremoniously dropped them on the floor and crushed them under his boots.

Johnno began to pace around the room. "What the hell do we do now? How do we stop the V2's from being launched? Can we warn London and Moscow?"

"Not with these radio systems I'm afraid."

"I can do that." Freya's voice came over their earpieces "But I fear it may be too late."

"Good to have you back Freya. Sorry we've been away." Manni's voice was apologetic.

Freya was also apologetic. "I was too busy trying to get Rick to safety when I should have been tracking you two. I fear we may have lost him."

Johnno's heart sank. He may have lost his best friend as well as failing in his mission. He took a deep breath. "No time for apologies, we need time to think and we don't have it."

Josef stepped forward "Can I help?"

Johnno gently rubbed Josef's hair, careful not to hurt him. "Thank you for the offer Josef, we'll let you know."

Johnno's thoughts briefly drifted to Joe Gordon at school and his ever friendly face. "I bet Joe would have a wonderful suggestion," he mused to himself, his voice seemingly adding to childhood memories replayed in his mind. He could see him at the head of their class talking to a group of rapt pupils, repeating his favourite mantra. "Make time to make things happen and you will succeed."

Johnno's eyes opened wide. " Yes , that's it, that's it; His face home to a beaming smile, seemingly from ear to ear. I have it," he paused in thought, "yes, I believe I know how to stop the rockets being launched." He held Josef by his shoulders and smiled directly at him. "Thank you Josef," before repeating the mantra.

"We must make time to make things happen." His voice was confident, triumphant almost. He remained looking directly at a bemused Josef Gorski. "Thank you Mr Gordon, thank you." The words of advice had come full circle.

Turning to face Manni Johnno's face was beaming. " 'Make time to make things happen.' We have a machine here that can do just that. It can make time to make things happen .. or change."

He turned to face the Bell. "Look – the answer to our prayers."

Manni's face broke into a grin. "Why yes, you may just be right my friend, you may just be right."

Freya's voice came over their earpieces. "The Federation does not take lightly to showing local life forms our future technologies. If you plan to use the Bell then Young Josef must be left behind."

"No way," Johnno replied, he has a future that affects many people, surely that transcends any Federation concerns."

Manni joined in "And, for once, I must agree. He has risked his life to save ours, he deserves to come with us and have his life saved. Remember his future?"

There was a pause and a silence that seemed to last forever. Eventually Freya replied "Yes, I had forgotten. OK, as you say, to Hell with the Federation, do what you have to."

Johnno smiled at his two colleagues. "Come on Josef, the adventure of a life time awaits us." His batteries recharged and confidence regained, he led them to the Bell. Leaning forward he pressed the Bell shaped amulet into the corresponding recess. With a gentle hiss the door slid open. He ushered his colleagues inside, pointing to the rear seating area. "Sit there while I try and work out what to do next."

The door slid shut enveloping our trio in darkness. "Don't worry, we'll soon have light." The inside soon took on its blue iridescent glow. "See."

Johnno scoured the symbols in front of him, looking for anything that may power the craft. "Come on, come on, do come on Johnno. Find something, anything to make this thing work." He was now worried that he couldn't actually pilot the Bell and his plans would come to nothing.

Freya's voice came over his earpiece. "Look at the console, slowly and carefully, and I'll see where the controls are, remember your lenses. I can help you."

"Sorry, I should have remembered." His sense of panic abated slightly as he began a slow and steady scan on the console.

"There, to your right, where the console slopes up into the screen area by your head. The Bell shape."

"Yes, I have it, what now?"

"Your Bell shaped amulet, place it in the recess. At the same time place the Orion star amulet in the recess where the weapon was stored."

Johnno unclipped both amulets from his neck chain and placed them where Freya directed. There followed a slight hum, followed by an array of lights appearing in front of him. Directly in front of him the glass screen sprung into life, displaying what appeared to be some form of map, highlighted in green.

"Can I remove the amulets, or do they need to stay there?"

"It's OK. You can put them back on your chain for safety, as you may need them again."

From behind him Johnno heard Manni's voice. "We may just do this Josef, we may just."

Johnno turned to his two colleagues "We're not there just yet, give me time." He turned back to face the screen. "What next?"

"I presume you just need to go back in time, but stay exactly where you are."

"That's the plan."

"Well the screen in front of you is a map. There should be a faint green light flashing. That shows where you are now." Johnno peered closely at the screen until he saw the green light.

"Got it."

"Now touch the green dot and pull it down towards the centre by keeping your finger on the screen. That will set your target area. Release and touch it once more and it should turn red."

He put his finger on the green dot and quickly pulled it downwards, but nothing happened.

"Slower, move it slower, it is a touch screen and needs time to respond. Try again."

This time he managed to drag the green dot gently to the centre of the screen, removing and replacing his finger to lock the co-ordinates in red.

"I've done that, what next?"

"Next comes the complicated part, putting in the date you wish to travel to."

"Oh good – complications."

Behind then Josef was peering, doing his best to spy on what was happening. He tried to get up from his seat but could not do so. He looked at Manni with panic in his eyes "Am I paralysed? I cannot move my legs."

"A Gravity belt, it holds you safely in place, but don't worry, I'll explain later."

Freya continued. "The Bell is calibrated to Earth time in years, months and a 24 hour time clock. You need to add the date using the 12 symbols at the very front of the console, these are the numbers. You'll need the year, the month and the time – four characters each. Once the date is successfully entered you can activate the Bell by pressing on the map symbol for a third time. If successful the dot will now change to blue. Look at the right side of the screen, see those six triangles," Johnno looked to the side

"Yes, I see them."

"Are any of them lit up?"

"No, they're all blank."

"Good. They are the system's memory, thankfully it must have been erased. As you program a date and destination into the machine it is recorded in the memory bank. In that way you can return to the exact time and place by pushing on one of those buttons. Remember that, it can be a lifesaver."

"I've got that. Now, when did you last talk to Rick?"

"Around 8 o'clock in the evening, just before he was due to meet Storrensberg and Musfelldt for cocktails. I believe he may have been badly injured, or even killed then."

"Right, 7.30 – sorry – 1930 it is then."

"You must be aware that, once you have activated the Bell, I cannot contact you using your earpieces until to return to the present time. If anything goes wrong I cannot help you. Please be careful, and good luck, my little spaceman."

Johnno smiled to himself. "I'll do my best, here goes nothing."

"Right, in computing zero is a number, so I can include that in the symbols."

He turned to face his two travelling companions. "Here we go gents, keep tight hold of your seats." Looking back towards the screen he took a deep breath. "Here goes nothing."

He spoke the numbers out loud as he touched each symbol.

"1..9..3..0 – the time - 2..2..1..0 – the date, and finally the year - 1..9..4..4"

As he pressed each symbol on the console it appeared simultaneously on the screen in front of him. He took a deep breath, focusing on the red dot. He touched it gently and waited for the Bell to drift them back in time.

The distant humming became ever more intense, so deep and strong that it rolled backwards and forwards in his stomach creating a feeling of deep nausea. It felt as if his stomach was rising up to meet his throat - he needed to retch and clear this ball which had stuck in his throat; he couldn't breathe and felt a panic growing inside.

His head felt as if there was a machine inside, vibrating through his skull and making his teeth ache as they constantly vibrated against each other.

His face was pressed against the metal sides of what felt like a steel drum. The metallic taste in his mouth was his own blood, a feeling only made worse by the cold, unforgiving steel plate pressing into his cheeks. He could smell ozone. He lifted his head away from the cold, hard floor desperately looking around to find a way out but the darkness was only broken in places by small blinking lights, not enough to see by, but easy to see. As he moved forwards he bumped into a metal slab, it felt like some form of desk. The lights were blinking even faster and the humming became more intense. He looked around for a clue as to where he was. Feeling around in the semi darkness only increased his feeling of fear, he could feel nothing, no clue as to where he was; the sweat on his forehead now ran into his eyes, stinging and dulling his limited vision, then down into his mouth. The salty taste on his lips made him believe he was at sea – or was it just his sweat?

Then the humming became louder and he felt his body slide sideways and feel as if it had become attached to the walls as if by magnets. The pressure on his chest increased until he found it hard to breathe. His face was forced onto its side, his cheeks forced against a steel plate, smooth steel panels forcing into his gums. He could taste the blood on his tongue; he was suffocating, lungs fighting to pull in gasps of precious air. He was hopelessly trapped, but where?

Thoughts in his mind were racing, echoing around a brain struggling to make sense of what was happening.

"How the Hell do I get out of here, when I don't know here 'here' is?"

This was it – he couldn't go on, he was terrified and tried to shout for help, but the words wouldn't leave his mouth. "Christ, I'm gone."

Realisation dawned. "It's my nightmare, it's back. How the hell do I stop it?"

Peering through his vibrated vision he could make out his passengers, their eyes full of fear. He knew he had made a mistake, but not how to stop. He crawled on hands and knees back over to the console, painfully lifting himself back to his feet, hands firmly grasping its sides for safety. "There must be a way to stop this." He feverishly pressed his finger on each and every symbol he could see. Eventually he pressed the 'Orion' symbol and the vibration began to subside.

Slowly, steadily the motion and vibration ceased and all was calm again.

"Sorry boys, that was some ride. I must have pressed a wrong button."

"But it shouldn't do that, something must be wrong with the Bell." Manni's voice was full of concern, though he tried to sound calm. "Perhaps it is a lost cause and the Bell is irreparably damaged."

Jakob was visibly shaking "Please don't do that again," he pleaded. "I'm scared."

Manni put a reassuring arm around his bony shoulders. "Don't worry, that was a minor hiccup," though he realised they were lucky to still be alive.

Johnno was feeling desperate. He was drenched in sweat, with bruises and cuts appearing on his arms where he was pinned against the walls of the Bell. He racked his brains, thinking back on his actions. "What did I do wrong?"

Freya's voice calmed him down. "You must have entered an incorrect date. The Bells system could not make sense of it and you suffered I'm afraid. You must enter the date as a twelve digit number."

"I did that."

Freya was perplexed. "Are you absolutely sure?"

"YES" his voice was stern, uncompromising. He went deep in thought. After several seconds a look of realisation flashed across his face. "Where exactly was the Bell used and hidden Manni?"

"India I believe, in the Rajasthan area, although we do have records of it being flown throughout the ancient Middle East area. Places such as ancient Sumeria, Iraq, Persia, Pakistan and the like."

"I wonder?"

"Wonder what?" sounded in his earpiece.

"We write figures and letters from left to right, some ancient texts wrote from right to left. It's the wrong way around, yet again .. hopefully. They may have programmed this computer specifically to suit the Indian and Asian continents."

He returned to the symbols on the keyboard.

"At least I've found the escape key," he added, trying to raise a smile.

"OK Freya, here we go again. Wish me luck." He turned and gave a reassuring look to his passengers. They did their best to look confident, giving each other one last look of hope.

Johnno started inputting the date again, in reverse order, speaking the numbers out loud to reassure himself.

"4..4..9..1 – the year - 0..1..2..2 – the month, and - 0...3..9..1.. the year."

The symbols on the screen reflected his input below.

"Get ready gents, please replace your trays and put your seats in an upright position". Josef looked quizzically at Manni.

"A very poor joke, don't worry Josef."

Grabbing the console for security he put his finger on the red dot and it changed to blue. He closed his eyes and held his breath.

The Bell gently hummed into life.

Chapter 28

The humming ceased. The vibration ceased. And all was still. The silence was deafening

"I've failed again, she's stopped and it hasn't worked." Johnno's voice was full of anguish.

After several seconds Manni shouted, almost in triumph. "No, look at the screen, the small dot. It's green again, it must have worked, it must have."

Johnno glanced at the screen and punched the air "Yes, yes, yes, yes." He moved forward to open the door. "Stop." Manni was insistent "We cannot risk Krammler seeing us, we're safe inside the Bell; we must somehow raise Rick from inside."

"I never thought of that. The Bell is soundproof I presume."

"That's a chance we'll have to take."

Both colleagues tried their best to raise Rick, but with no luck.

"Come in Rick, come on and answer, please come in." Their pleas were played out almost in stereo. "Five minutes wasted."

Josef was sat silently listening to the insistent repeated pleas of his saviours. He finally spoke. "Excuse me but isn't there a radio jamming the signal in the next room? You destroyed those sheet things two days later."

They looked at each other in amazement. Manni grinned, rubbing Josef's hair in an apologetic manner, smiling at the young lad's chutzpah.

"Of course, we forgot the signals being jammed. "We need to turn them off again. I'll have to chance being seen. Here goes nothing." He moved to the door way and gestured for Johnno to open it. "I'll need the talisman so I can get back in." Johnno reluctantly parted with his good luck charm, but passed it over.

"Don't lose it, and ...... good luck."

Manni slipped out of the opening and disappeared from view.

Johnno touched a symbol by the open door and it gently closed with a hiss. The minutes ticked by. "Come on Manni, hurry up." Johnno was now desperate.

"He will succeed." Josef's voice was calm and reassuring ."We do have God on our side."

The door slid open with a hiss and Manni jumped back inside, Johnno closing the door behind him.

Manni passed the amulet back. "Safe and sound." He had the circuit boards in his hand once more. "Same job, just a little earlier."

"See my friends; I said God was on our side."

"Let's try again." Johnno was more confident. He put his finger to his earpiece. "Come in Rick. Come in Rick." The silence in the Bell was palpable.

No one took a breath waiting for any reply, straining to hear Rick's voice.

Johnno was pacing the floor; he didn't want to lose his friend for a second time.

"What time is it?"

Manni looked at his watch. "Around 7.45 local time and too close for comfort."

"Come on Rick, answer, for God's sake answer man."

"What's the rush, I'm trying to shower." Rick's voice finally replied.

Johnno's voice was calm, yet serious. "Rick, just be quiet and just listen. Musfelldt knows who you are and is planning to kill you when he collects you for your evening out. You must get out, NOW."

All went quiet. "Do you hear me? Get out NOW!" Agonising seconds passed.

"Just fastening my trousers buddy then I'm out of here. I'll meet you back at the cabin."

Johnno smiled at his colleagues. He had made time to make it work, and it did work.

Manni put his hand on his colleague's shoulder.

"We need to plan our next step carefully; we still need to destroy both Bells."

Johnno smiled. "I know *exactly* what must be done."

Chapter 29

Rick took his holster from the side of the bed and checked that it was loaded. If he had to use it he would. As his friend had already stated "To Hell with the Federation."

He put on his uniform and hat, a quick glance in the mirror to check he looked OK.

He looked out from the balcony, but it was a sheer drop to the pavement below, too far to safely jump. "That's a no-no." Then he moved over to the door and opened it slightly listening for sounds of movement. Opening it wider he glanced along the corridor towards the rooms occupied by Musfelldt and Storrensberg. It was clear.

He left the room as quietly as he could, softly pulling the door shut behind him, locking it to help buy more time if needed, and making his way along the corridor towards the stairs. Grateful for the faded carpet which silenced his steps he hurried down the grand staircase, keeping a lookout for German soldiers who might have gone there to spend their birthday event. As he reached the bottom of the stairs he was met by the ever subservient manager, bowing yet again in order to ingratiate himself with his country's aggressors.

"Can I be of assistance, Herr Oberleutnant?"

Rick grabbed his elbow and manhandled him away from the stairs, checking around to see no-one was watching..

"Your office, where is it?"

The manager looked bemused, and slightly worried at the same time. "Why, over here Herr Oberleutnant, " trying to keep calm he led Rick towards his office, a room located along the corridor towards the rear of the entrance lobby. Rick opened the door, still holding the manager by his elbow, forcing him inside. He took one last glance outside then closed the door. The room was as 'tired' as the rest of the hotel, and just as dark as two table lamps and one wall light were the only sources of light.

"Do you have a key? I need to lock the door." Rick's urgent tones began to concern the manager. Was he about to be punished? Shot even?

He moved over towards his desk, and took the key from the top left hand drawer, offering it to Rick with a shaky hand. Sweat was coming from his brow as he feared the worst.

"Has the management let you down sir? What can I possibly do to make amends?" He entered his finest and deepest ingratiating mode, trying his best to smile and look sincere. Inside his heart was pounding like a drum. As a last resort he held his arm in mock salute "Heil Hitler?"

Rick locked the door, leaving the key in place and walked back over to his panicky host and smiled. "Don't worry my friend, you are not in trouble. I need your help." The words were in perfect Polish.

The manager looked bemused. He cleared his throat. "You need my help? What can I do?"

"In a few minutes all hell will break loose and my two colleagues will be looking for me. They will shoot me if they find me."

"Sh-sh-shoot you. Why would they want to shoot a fellow officer?"

"I am not a German officer. I am working with the allies on a secret mission and I have been found out. I need your help to escape," before adding, with a wry grin, "I heard your comment on the corridor - German bastards, one day, one day."

The manager gulped audibly. "Well, yes I ... I."

"Don't worry, I AM on your side. I am NOT trying to trick you, and I will not shoot you."

Fearing a trick that would see him shot as a partisan the manager looked Rick in the eyes, and cleared his throat. "Prove it!" Rick took the Luger from its holster and placed it onto the aged desk, within reach of the quivering manager.

The manager found a little courage, emboldened by the fact he was still alive. "Is that all your proof?"

Rick was thinking on his feet. He knew that vital seconds were ticking away before his 'hosts' came looking for him, with SS guards in tow.

Everyone who joined Orion's Federation was given a unique set of symbols, a serial number of sorts; when they finished training this set of symbols programmed into a microchip and inserted into their left forearm. This chip acted as an electronic key enabling weapon use, safe passage into secure quarters, computer passwords and so on. It became a rite of passage to have some of these images tattooed above the chip as a visible sign of rank and importance. Rick had just such a tattoo.

Deciding it was worth the risk he quickly took off his tunic and rolled up his shirt sleeve to show the tattoo. In the dim light it looked, to all intents and purposes, like those which were branded onto Hitler's hated Jews as they entered the ghettoes and concentration camps.

"Would a German officer be branded so? And would he speak Polska to his enemy?"

The manager's demeanour changed to one of joy.

"Come, come with me," leading Rick towards the rear of the room.

Rick rolled down his sleeve but was stopped from replacing his tunic. "I'll take care of that; and don't forget your pistol."

Rick rushed back for the luger, hurriedly refastening the holster around his waist.

At the rear of the room was a large wardrobe. One door was hung at an angle. It was, as far as anyone could see, a dilapidated wreck, a symbol of glory days past.

"I can't hide in there, they're sure to find me."

The manager smiled, tapping the side of his nose. He reached over to the wall light, twisting it anti-clockwise. A click was heard. The manager then moved over to the wardrobe and pulled it away from the wall. The unit, hinged on one side, swung open to reveal a passageway. "A feature added by the original builders. The owner had, shall I say, other lady friends apart from his wife." He smiled and coughed gently. "Though I have never used it, of course."

In the distance they heard the sound of voices, raised in a Teutonic rage, calling for the manager.

"Go quickly, my friend. When you reach the end of the corridor tap on the door three times. You will be met by Aleksy, a member of our underground state. Tell him that Abram wishes him well and that his wife Zofia will cook him pierogi when he next visits – have you got that? He will ensure safe passage out of the city. The rest is then up to you. If you have friends looking for you they will help them find you. May Yahweh keep you safe and look over you. Now go, quickly my friend, and may your mission end in success."

Rick shook Abram's hand, then hugged him tight. "Thank you my friend. May Yahweh keep you safe and look over you as well."

Rick disappeared down the passageway to safety.

Abram threw the tunic into the passageway behind him. "We may be able to use that one day." He quickly pushed the wardrobe back against the wall and levelled the wall light, mindful of the need for his immediate presence with his angry 'guests'. Looking around and checking everything was OK, then left his office.

He approached the two visibly irate officers, now flanked by SS troopers striding purposely towards him, he adopted the most menial and servile posture he could.

"How can I help you gentlemen? More wine perhaps, or maybe a nice scotch whisky?"

Chapter 30

"I know *exactly* what we both need to do." Manni was pleasantly surprised by Johnno's new found confidence. Johnno opened the door, checking that their laboratory was unmanned before stepping outside the security of the Bell

"You go back into Krammler's office and wait for him to return. Use your neuroliser to take him out of the picture."

"Easy. Then what?"

Johnno closed his eyes as he visualised what to do next. "We must bolt the door into the mine; that should stop any inquisitive SS guards from entering. Stay with Krammler in his office until I return, I shouldn't be long. We can then deal with him and the Bells."

"What about Josef?"

"He's with me."

Johnno turned and shepherded Josef back into the Bell. He looked at Manni as he disappeared back into Krammler's office. "Keep your head down buddy."

Manni glanced back and smiled. "Be safe my friend."

Johnno closed the door to the Bell and moved back to the console. Josef moved back to his seat wondering why he had been included in the latest planned visit.

"Where are we going, is it somewhere special?"

"A place stored deep in the memories of my mind."

Placing his amulets in their shaped recesses Johnno re-booted the console and screen. As he looked at the screen and its map he noticed a light in the corner of his eye. One of the memory locations had activated.

"Just as I hoped, I can return back to this very spot and this place in time."

Looking closely at the screen map, he recognised the outline of Europe, even with current borders. "That's a stroke of luck; the map must somehow be updating itself in real time."

Gradually he moved the map using his two fingers as he repeated the story details repeated so many times by his Aunt Freya when reminiscing about his mother and father. He had read his history books from cover to cover, trying to get nearer to their memories.

"It was Operation Hydra at Peenemunde.

They entered the complex from the South by boat into workshop 17.
17th August 1943
The first planes took off at 21.46
Mum and Dad entered the compound at 21.00"

He eventually managed to find the Baltic Sea, and the tell-tale shape of the head at Peenemunde. He'd repeatedly studied the maps since childhood. "Thank God for childish yearnings." Once he found the outline he needed to zoom in. "What did Freya say – two fingers again – that just moves the map." Try as he might he could not enlarge the image. Frustrated with himself he took a step back "think, think, what did she say?"

Then he recalled the image he'd seen in the cabin. "Perhaps if I …" he moved back to the screen and placed his fingers on the map outline, slowly sliding them apart. The map began to zoom inwards, the image becoming ever larger and more precise. He scrolled right into the map, finding Peenemunde itself on the coast.

"Buildings, buildings, I need a factory site " zooming in until he found the distinctive outlines showing a variety of buildings on the peninsula.

"I'm getting there." he felt elated. "I'm guessing this lower corner is where they landed and there, by the tree line is a structure. I'm hoping that's the unidentified apparatus I'm looking for."

"Are we going somewhere to safety?" Josef was shuffling on his seat and was becoming more concerned as time passed.

"I'm taking you somewhere safe, very safe, I promise."

Johnno touched the screen where he wanted to arrive, just below the complex by the tree line, hoping to find some form of cover in the trees. The target on the map showed a green spot. He gently pressed the map and the light turned red. He let out a grateful sigh

"Now for the date and time, the RIGHT way around this time"
Composing himself he took a deep breath and began to input the date and time.
"3..4..9..1 – the year - 8..0..7..1 – the date - 0..3..0..2 – the time.
Thirty minutes should be just about right to find and stop them"

He composed himself. "Here we go again Josef."

The red dot was pressed, slowly turning blue. The Bell hummed into action, only this time Johnno felt the whole thing sway gently along. He felt a gentle downwards pressure with a sensation similar to the G Forces he endured as a pilot.

Suddenly the pressure released and all was quiet.

"Are we there yet?" Josef's voice broke the silence.

Johnno smiled and thought to himself. "Some things never change?"

"I hope so Josef, I really do hope so."

He opened the door tentatively quickly glancing outside, unsure if he would still be in the mine, or outside where he had hoped to land. It was dark. He could hear birdsong. He could see a complex close by with lights along its perimeter. In the distance he could just discern a small round structure. "My target for tonight, I hope." He smiled to himself. His head pounded and his heart felt as if it would burst. "At last I can meet my mother and father," he paused, looking pensive, his mind imagining what could now be possible "and then fly them away to safety!" He had to be careful how he approached the allied raiding party; he'd hate to be shot by his own parents!

Josef had joined him by the open door. "What do we plan to do?"

"There is no '**WE**' young man, I know what **I** have to do."

He turned to face Josef. He put both of his arms on his shoulders and forced a gentle grin from his lips. He was worried for his young charge, and fearful of losing him, affecting the future of so many young lives, including his own.

"You need to stay here where you will be safe. The console is still switched on so please don't touch anything whilst I'm away."

"I'm not stupid." Josef sounded slightly hurt by the comment.

"I know, I'm sorry, but I really need to keep you safe. If I haven't returned within one hour then, and only then, you can do something." He guided Josef towards the console and its screen. "Can you see this small light, just here inside the triangle?" he said, pointing to the right of the screen." Josef nodded. "If I'm not back within the hour press this and it will take you back to Manni. Tell him what happened and tell him I'm sorry."

Josef nodded again. Slightly worried that he may lose his saviour, but attempting to put a brave face on for him. "I pray for your safe return."

Johnno gave him a hug. "You are a brave young man Josef; I see a great future ahead of you." He opened the door again and, taking one last look backwards he winked at Josef, closing the door behind him.

Josef sat back on his seat. "I must not touch anything." settling back to wait for Johnno's safe return. "One hour, how long is one hour?" he murmured, wondering how he could gauge one hour when he did not possess a watch. Something Johnno had not reckoned on.

The inside of the Bell was bathed in a shimmering blue light. It was quite warm and totally silent. Josef felt tired, it had been a long day. He settled down on the floor in front of the bench seat, gathered his hands around his legs, resting his head onto his knees. "I shall be ready for you my friend. Please stay safe whatever you have planned." He struggled to keep his eyes open. Sleep seemed a welcome respite from the day's activities.

He could feel his eyelids closing and struggled to keep them open.

Soon he was deep in slumber, the first peaceful sleep he'd had in years.

Chapter 31

Johnno had arrived safely. He crept out of the Bell immediately crouching down for safety. It was late evening and the light was fading but was still good enough to find his target. He was also aware it was good enough to be spotted by any guards on duty within the compound. He kept low to the ground as he moved forward.

"I'm guessing that they approached from the South West, keeping the structure between themselves and the living quarters, the experimental station with most sentries being away in the North East corner."

His combat training came flooding back to him. Keeping low he scurried towards a spot where he felt he must come across the raiding party. As he approached the structure he could start to make out its shape. It had a dome on the top, and was circular in shape. Around it was a low fence presumably left simple to hide its probable importance. Creeping forward he eventually reached the fence, noticing wire and what looked like a ceramic insulator just inside.

"Crafty bastards, it might look innocuous but it's wired with a ring main."

A searchlight began to sweep the area emanating from on top of the factory workshops in the centre of the compound. Johnno flattened his body to the ground, not daring to look up until it had passed and semi-darkness began to return. He settled down, hopeful that this was the path the raiding party would take. After what seemed like endless minutes he heard the sounds of twigs breaking and boots walking in slightly damp grass. Keeping low he edged forward to make sure it wasn't a sentry patrolling the grounds. In the distance he could just make out the outlines of several bodies, all crouching low the same as himself. He moved forward, silently, to intercept them.

As he did so he felt something cold press on the back of his neck. It was unmistakeably a gun barrel. He froze in terror, waiting for the click of a trigger and the end of his quest.

"Stand up, you German bastard, with your hands on your head."

He slowly rose to his feet, hands clasped around the back of his head. He glanced at his captor. It was obviously one of the raiding team, dressed in green, face blacked out, holding a Lee Enfield rifle to his face.

Realisation dawned. He was still wearing a German army uniform.

"Please, I am not German; I am here to save your lives."

"So that's why you wear a German uniform." His captor raised his rifle to Johnno's face.

"Codename Hydra! Operation Crossbow! I have valuable information for your English team leaders John and Sarah." His voice was calm, but inside he was desperate. He pleaded with his eyes wide open.

"Please let me talk to them." The gun was lowered slightly. "I may just shoot you, how do I know it's not a trap?"

"You don't. But your leaders will know it isn't." His captor was intrigued. How could he know the team leaders? He only found out himself when they arrived twenty four hours ago.

Keeping his rifle aimed at Johnno's head his captor leaned forward and deftly removed the luger from its holster. He gestured with his rifle for Johnno to move forward, pushing the barrel into his back as he walked away.

"Keep quiet and keep your head down. One move and you're a dead German."

The two men moved slowly forward, Johnno being especially careful not to make any sudden moves which would result in his death. After a couple of minutes they approached a group of several people, all crouched low and keeping very still and quiet. Johnno could make out four people, all similarly dressed in dark clothing with faces blackened to help with their camouflage. As they approached his captor held Johnno's collar, forcing him to stop, before whispering a warning.

"Quarrel."

"Snake." The reply.

Now assured of their safety his captor once again prodded Johnno in the back with his rifle barrel, forcing him to move forward into the group of waiting figures.

A female voice spoke. "Why have you brought a German soldier to us, has he surrendered?"

"He says he is not German. He speaks impeccable English and he has mentioned both Hydra and Crossbow."

She moved towards him, pointing her handgun to his face, asking quietly "If you are not German, then where are you from?"

Johnno looked at her face. It was camouflaged and half covered by a black woollen cap, but it was unmistakeably his mother. Freya's photographs had not given her justice.

"My name is John, John O'Ryan, and I am from England. Freya says 'Hello' "

Her eyes widened. Was this some trick? How had German intelligence found this out?

Another figure stepped out of the background. Johnno scrutinised his face closely. Although his only faded photograph was black and white, this was his father.

"Just who the hell are you, soldier?"

"Can I please show you something I have in my wallet?" Turning his head towards his captor, "Your friend here has my gun." His captor nodded and patted his waistband where the luger had been placed.

The woman gestured with her handgun. "Show us … slowly, no sudden moves."

Johnno slowly lowered his hands from behind his neck and reached down into his trouser pocket removing his wallet. As he went to open it she took it from his grasp and passed it back to her male colleague. He opened the wallet. "Now what"

"Take out the photograph"

Each divider was checked until he found the photograph and removed it. He looked stunned; "Where did you get this?" Passing it to the woman.

Her eyes opened wide. "What kind of a trick is this?"

"It is no trick. Aunt Freya passed it on to me as a child."

"Anyone could have found this. Your SS techniques do not fool me." She pulled back the trigger on her handgun "Any last words?"

"Birthmark."

She looked stunned. "Birthmark, what do you mean, birthmark?"

"A birthmark. Your son John was born with a birthmark was he not?"

The couple both seemed intrigued.

The woman spoke. "It was in the shape of a circle, just above his left ankle"

Johnno smiled and shook his head. "It is not a full circle; it's almost a crescent moon shape. And it's not on my ankle - it's here." Johnno raised his right sleeve, "where it always was."

"Where is it.? I can't see anything."

"Shit! I forgot that I've shape shifted."

"Shape shifted? How can you shape shift?"

"Freya and Rick showed me. Apparently it's in my DNA thanks to you, mother. Manni and Astrild helped too."

Johnno was struggling to find evidence ; any evidence to reinforce his claim and save his life.

".. It was inside the hut where the portal is located .. close to the Wenceslaus mine complex."

Sara's face remained as a mask, with no emotions visible at all. Johnno believed his gamble had failed and he was about to die. Suddenly his distant memories kicked in and he recalled a childhood conversation he'd had with his Aunt Freya.

Aunt Freya told me. "If you say the word 'Tutu', then I would laugh and say 'Me too'."

Agonising Seconds passed.

Sara's face broke out into a beaming smile as she slowly lowered her handgun.

"But how is this? We have left you at home, a child."

Johnno stepped forward. "I know about Orion, Alnilam and the Pleidians, Freya told me. I know you are my mother and father and I know that you are both in danger."

Instinctively Johnno moved forward and put his arms around his mother and hugged her, burying his head in her hair "Mother" was all he could say, the words almost sticking in his dried throat. Both wept gently.

"My son, my grown up son."

His father stepped forward, a smile replacing the look of intrigue. He grabbed Johnno by the hand and pulled him towards him, hugging him close to hide his tears of joy. After seconds, seconds that seemed like hours, Johnno pulled back and looked earnestly at his new found parents. His voice echoed his concerns about what he knew would happen next if he didn't prevent them from carrying out their plan.

"We need to leave here. I know that you are due to enter the structure at twenty one hundred hours, but you cannot. It is not safe." He did not have the courage to tell them that they faced death if they continued. He had found them and was now desperate to keep them in his life.

John and Sara looked perplexed. The rest of the group were stunned, and did not understand any of the conversation.

"We must hurry" a voice came from the rear, it is 8.45 already. I have been brought back from the future to destroy Die Glöcke and its contents. It is hidden in the Wenceslaus mine. Two V2 rockets are going to be modified and turned into terrible weapons, and for some reason I am the only one capable of stopping it."

His captor interjected. "I did see him emerge from a Bell shaped structure; I thought it was just another secret instrument these German bastards are developing."

Sara turned to John. "Die Glöcke, the Germans DO have it. Our intelligence was correct."

"Yes they do, and I have used it to come back and save you, but we must hurry. Please come with me," he glanced back in the direction of the Bell, "there is a weapon inside that can destroy your target and you can come with me to safety." Johnno's voice was now one of desperation.

His new found parents looked at each other, exchanging knowing glances. John put his arms around Sara as they both faced their newly discovered son.

"I'm sorry, my son, but we cannot come with you. Our destiny is planned and cannot be altered."

"Planned? Planned? How can it be planned? I'm here to save your lives, you must come with me. You must." Johnno was now pleading.

Sara stepped forward, reaching out to hold Johnno by both hands. "Freya will have told you about the dangers of a paradox. Whatever happens when we enter the structure is, for you, a part of history. It is a history that cannot be changed."

His father stepped forward. "If we were to come with you then written history will change. It may just be our two lives, but small things do matter."

Johnno could almost hear Freya saying those self-same words.

Sara continued. "And that change on history could affect what happens here, what happens with the outcome of this war, and the lives of millions of people; yourself included."

He knew they were right, but how could he lose the parents he had just found?

"Presumably you must know about the Federation and their rules."

Johnno nodded- a wry smile on his face. "But..." his words were cut short as the sound of footsteps was heard behind them.

"Everybody down." his father instructed, aiming his weapon in the direction of the footsteps, anticipating the arrival of a German sentry.

Johnno recognised the small figure approaching them.

"Don't shoot, I know who this is."

Emerging from the evening darkness came a solitary figure.

"Josef, I told you to wait for me in the Bell, you almost got shot."

"Yes, I know, but I lost track of time and came looking to see if you needed my help again."

Johnno turned to face his parents.

"Josef is a slave worker who saved my life. I'm trying to save his, and not doing a very good job by the looks of it."

The partisan who had captured Johnno stepped forward. "We plan to smuggle our inside informants, two janitors, to safety in Sweden. Perhaps young Josef could come with us. That would keep him safe."

Johnno smiled, realising this would complete the circle on Josef's life on his way to becoming Joe Gordon.

"I know about the paradox, and I know for certain that Josef is destined to leave us here for Sweden. That I know is true. Please trust me." Sara smiled and nodded.

"You must leave without delay." Johnno put his arms around Josef's shoulders in a reassuring hug. "You go with these men and they will take you to safety."

Josef looked crestfallen. "But I will never see you again, you saved MY life."

"We will meet again, I promise, when this war is over we will meet again. Please trust me, we will , in times of peace."

He put his arms around Johnno's waist, tears in his eyes. "Thank you my friend, I will never forget you."

"Nor I you Josef, nor I you."

From the distance came the sound of a bird call. "The janitors are signalling, we must go – now." Two of the figures turned to move, gesturing for Josef to join them.

They each grabbed Sara and John, forearm to forearm. "Good luck my friends. The bombers will be here soon and we must leave before they do, as must you."

They slipped away into the fading light, Josef taking one last look back at his saviour and waving.

"And now we must go." Johnno came crashing back to earth as his parents signalled their intention to leave him.

Sara hugged her son for all she was worth. "Thank you for this time young John, it will live in my memory forever."

Johnno fought back the tears, but lost the battle as they began to roll down his cheeks, realising that his mother's memories would be short.

"And we are both proud to have such a brave son to leave as our legacy," added his father, his arms enveloping his wife and child.

Johnno could feel his heart beating.

The elation he felt in finding his parents.

The loss he now felt as he had to bid them goodbye.

His father was the first to speak as he stepped back from the group hug. "You still have a mission to complete. So do we, and history will judge us if we fail."

His mother stepped back as well. "So go and complete your mission and we will complete ours."

Johnno smiled, then, almost as an afterthought he spoke. "Whatever happens don't let your men target Von Braun, or everything will change."

His mother smiled and understood; as she moved away Johnno grasped her hand gently in reassurance, and then felt it slide away as she quietly left. The pair moved away towards their target, taking one last look back at their son and waving.

"We will meet again, one day, I promise. You still have a vital mission to complete ... please remember to give our love and thanks to Freya, she's done a wonderful job in raising our son."

They turned and they were gone, disappearing into the darkness like ghosts in the night.

Johnno could feel the silence in his body. He felt empty inside. He knew his parents were going to their deaths, but realised that he had to accept this as their fate, as part of the cost for having lived a full and happy life. The tears just flowed as he made his way back towards the Bell; every step was tortuous to take knowing he'd had to leave his parents behind. He entered the Bell and sat down to compose himself.

After resting for several minutes he smiled, realising his good fortune. "I've had the privilege of meeting my parents, even briefly, years after I lost them. I told them I loved them. Who would not wish that?" His mother's final words rang in his ears, he had a mission to complete.

Using his sleeves he wiped the tears from his eyes and cheeks and moved back towards the console. He powered it up and looked to the right hand side of the screen, there were now two memory icons lit. He pressed the first, knowing it would take him back to the mine where Manni was waiting.

The map changed on the screen. He pressed the green dot to select his destination, watching it turn red. He pressed and held it and watched it turn blue. The gentle humming began as the Bell moved into action. After several seconds all was silent.

Johnno took a deep breath and composed himself in preparation for continuing his mission. He opened the door to be met by Manni, inspecting his explosive charges.

"Didn't it work this time?"

Johnno realised he had arrived back at the same instant he had left and was pleasantly surprised. He was getting the hang of this contraption.

Manni stepped inside and looked bemused. It wasn't a large interior and he couldn't see Josef, or where he could possibly be.

"Where's Josef, did you leave him behind? Is he hiding in the mine?"

"That's a long story, he's safe now, but now we have a mission to complete, let's get to it. Time really is of the essence." He glanced around the room. "Where are we up to with Krammler?"

A huge grin appeared on Manni's face "Krammler is 'asleep' in his office; he will be for hours. I have two charges to take care of this Bell; I presume you still have the explosive that Freya gave you."

"I hope so too, welcome back Johnno." The soothing sound of Freya's voice was very welcoming to both sets of ears.

"It's good to be back Freya. Yes, I have the charge safely tucked in my pocket, and I'll be glad to get out of this body and these damned itchy uniforms as soon as we can."

"Where are you now?"

"We are still in laboratory two. Krammler has been dealt with and will be out of action for several hours. We are about to place the charges and get out of here. Is Rick safe? Please tell us he is."

"Yes. The local partisans have him and Astrild hidden. They will be helping them return to us and the cabin. You did a good job saving his life, using the Bell was a master stroke. I'm very proud of you both."

Johnno tried to play down his role in saving his friend's life. "He would have done exactly the same for me or Manni."

Manni gave a nod of acknowledgment and showed the two charges in his hand. "I'll fit these to the second Bell. We'll have to move Krammler and make sure the professors aren't around, we have to ensure their immediate safety."

"You do that while Johnno sets the charges in his Bell. I think we are nearly there. I'll prepare your escape from the mine."

"Have the soldiers returned, the ones with the truck breakdown?"

"Don't worry about them; they should have been delayed by a road blockage. Several trees unfortunately fell and blocked their path. It should be hours before they return. I shall be out of contact for a while, but don't worry."

"OK Freya. I'll report back when the charges are set and ready."

Johnno moved back into the Bell, checking the compartment which originally held the hidden weapon. He believed that, by going back in time, it should still be there and ready for retrieval. To his relief it was back where he first found it. He let out a huge sigh of relief. "The weapon is still here Manni; I'll retrieve it for the second time." Safely tucked inside his tunic he retrieved the explosive device given to him a lifetime ago in the cabin.

He began looking around the console for somewhere to place it. He needed a flat surface to make sure the contact was good for the explosion, as well as ensuring a good magnetic contact

"Maybe in here," his hand felt inside the hidden compartment "that should work"

"Better here I believe."

Johnno recognised a German voice. He took his luger from his holster as secretly as he could and slowly turned to face whoever was speaking to him. To his amazement it was Krammler! To make matters worse he had Manni stood at his side, and was pointing his weapon at Manni's head.

"I would put that gun down if you want to save your friend's life" he pushed the barrel against Manni's head, forcing it over to one side.

"Sorry Johnno, I was sure he was out for the count."

"The gun, now! " Krammler gestured towards the console. Johnno reluctantly placed the luger on the top. "A sensible move my friend." Krammler lifted his other hand, showing Johnno the disc within it. "I found this in his pocket, I wonder what it does?" He pointed it at his captive and pressed the button on top. A fine burst of green light hit Manni who then crumpled to the ground unconscious.

Krammler looked amused. "A fine weapon, I can make use of this." He put it back into his pocket.

"Now come over here and move your friend away from the door," gesturing at Johnno with his pistol, he stood back allowing him to pick his friend off the floor.

"Drag him into my office. He can be dealt with if and when he wakes up."

Johnno was concerned. How much power from the neuroliser had he given Manni? Can you give too much and kill someone? What if he never wakes up? As he moved around to grab his shoulders from behind he purposely took a poor grip, holding him by the neck.

"Moron! Grab his shoulders. No wonder you are losing the war."

It was enough of a 'mistake' to feel Manni's pulse in his neck. It was there, he was alive.

He grabbed underneath the rear of his friend's arms and slowly dragged him along the short corridor to the rear office. Krammler followed closely, occasionally gesturing with his pistol and urging him to hurry up.

When they finally reached the office to his amazement he saw another Commander Krammler unconscious in his chair as Manni had told him.

"Amazing, isn't it? I am asleep there and here as well. Put your friend on the floor by the desk."

Johnno's mind was racing. He took deliberately slow movements to give him time to think. Two of them! This one must be a replicant. Shit, he must be the mole who has watched our every move. Why couldn't Freya contact him now? She could surely listen in and suggest something. He wondered if she could be listening in. Please be listening in. He stood up and tried his best to look amazed. He looked at the sleeping Krammler, and then to his captor holding a gun on him, then back again. Perhaps Freya could see the action through his lenses and organise a rescue.

Krammler stood to one side, keeping his pistol aimed at his captive. He gestured for Johnno to move towards the passageway. As he did so he placed the retrieved alien weapon onto the desk, in front of the sleeping Krammler. Out of his pocket he took a metal container, opened it and retrieved a syringe and a phial of liquid. "This phial is the antidote that will save your friend's life," placing the phial on the desk near to his unconscious friend. "And this is my leverage."

At that he deftly lifted the syringe and squirted a few drips from the tip, glancing to ensure he had done so, a dramatic gesture to ensure Johnno was watching. He leaned down, never breaking eye contact with his adversary, injecting the liquid into the back of Manni's hand.

"You look curious, almost worried. You should be. This is an experimental drug based on scopolamine, created by my good friend Josef, Josef Mengele; you have heard of him, his office is at Buchenwald?"

Johnno's eyes gave the game away.

"Good, then you know how potent it is. It paralyses the body slowly, making all muscles cease to work. Eventually, after three or four minutes the lungs cease to function and the 'patient' dies. Wonderful stuff, just enough time to interrogate someone and promise their death will be reversed. Priceless!"

Krammler pointed towards the passageway back to the Bell.

"Go through there, quickly, I have one more task to complete and, if you return me safely to this exact time and date you will be able to administer the antidote to your friend, no doubt saving his life." Krammler had the look on his face of the cat that got the cream. He gestured again with his weapon. Johnno moved ahead, slowly, wondering if he could turn and take his captor by surprise. He was expecting to feel the pain of a bullet in his back at any time. The replicant had what he wanted; he didn't need a live prisoner. He realised these were foolish thoughts, hoping there would be another way.

As they reached the laboratory he half turned to face his captor, who was still levelling his weapon at him.

"I have a trip planned and you will be taking it with me"

"Back to the Pleiades I presume?"

Krammler smiled, yet looked slightly bemused.

"No, we are going on a trip to the future and you will pilot me there."

Johnno realised that his trips must have been noted by this replicant and his proficiency at flying may be his saving grace.

"The future you say? Where to? And when?"

"All in good time. Now get into Die Glöcke and no tricks. If I have to kill you then I shall fly this contraption myself and your friend dies in four, sorry, three minutes. He is dying as we speak … "

Johnno entered the Bell. Krammler moved in behind him and stood by the bench.

"Now if you please put in our co-ordinates."

Johnno turned to face his captor.

"As I said before, where are we going to and when?"

"The scientists inform me that they will have a small working nuclear warhead for our V2 rockets by March 1945, created by using the weapon you 'lost'. I left it on my desk in the laboratory where it will be found and our glorious scientists will soon be able to unlock its secrets and use its power to devastate the world into capitulation." He had the smugness of a Nazi full of his own importance and self-belief.

"He plays the part of a moronic Nazi bastard well," thought Johnno.

"We'll visit March 1945 and collect those nuclear devices. We shall then return and I shall present my Wunderwaffe to the Führer – personally. Our first two rockets here will be delivered to Moscow and London as a warning. We can then ship the devices to all our bases over Europe. I may even present some to Emperor Hirohito. I'm sure he'd love to send a message to his American friends."

'Krammler' acted and sounded like a megalomaniac, almost a parody of Herr Hitler when delivering his motivational, war creating, speeches.

The penny dropped. "The third truck! It's there to transport the Bell with the devices! This must have been planned all along." Johnno felt that he and his team had been 'played'. Their plan had been known about, perhaps even back when he climbed into his cockpit on that eventful test flight.

"Now, if you please," Krammler jabbed his gun in Johnno's ribs, "time to put in our co-ordinates."

Johnno's mind was racing. He took a deep breath and hovered over the console.

"No tricks or you shall die, here .. now, alongside your friend." The gun was again forced into his back.

He leaned over and pointed to the screen

"The green light shows we are here, so DO NOT change it."

"What time and date do you want?"

"Let's say March 31st, 1945 at noon"

"OK" Johnno looked down at the figures on the console. "Could you please move back a little? You are making me nervous with that gun, and I'd hate to get it wrong."

Krammler moved back and to one side. "I can still see what you are doing, so be very careful."

Johnno now had the breathing space he needed.

"And read out the figures as you enter them. No tricks or you die."

Johnno read out the figures, but not as he correctly inputted. He knew he needed to go with his enemy and collect any devices manufactured, but needed to be sure that this Krammler, whoever he really was, would not be able to operate the Bell.

The war that Johnno knew ended in May 1945. If those devices became available for launching with V2 rockets the outcome would be disaster with indiscriminate deaths for hundreds of thousands of innocent people. Many more could die if the 3rd Reich was successful.

He 'spoke' the words in his mind "5..4..9..1..3..0..1..3..0..0..2..1.."

But spoke aloud

"1..2..0..0..3..1..0..3..1..9..4..5.."

"Now activate the coloured buttons on the screen"

He pressed the screen. It went from green to red and then red to blue.

There was a gentle hum and the Bell began to gently vibrate. Then all was still.

Krammler was alarmed. He sensed he had been fooled. Aiming his gun at Johnno he instructed him to do it properly, "I am not a fool, complete the flight."

"But we are here. It is 1945. It is March. It is twelve noon – sorry, twelve hundred hours."

He pushed the gun barrel into Johnno's back. "Open the door." The door slid open.

Pushing Johnno outside, he saw that the office was empty. He pushed him towards his office door to be met by an incredulous Jakob Storrensberg.

"Hans, is that you?"

"Quickly-tell me the date, the year, the time - what is it Jakob?"

Storrensberg was totally bemused. "It is March 31st 1945 around noon. Why do you ask? Where have you been all winter? We thought you must have been killed when we had the infiltration at the mine last October."

Searching for a credible story he stammered "I was called away by the Führer on a special project. Do not ask, I cannot tell you anything."

Storrensberg looked at Johnno, being held at gunpoint.

"What is he doing here? Was he on this project with you?".

"Ignore him for now. Do we have the nuclear devices? Have they been manufactured yet?"

Storrensberg pushed out his chest, looking full of his own importance. "We have four, ready to be shipped to our rocket bases in France for

immediate launch. Several more should follow in the next two months or so. They are quite complicated you know."

"Excellent work Jakob, now fetch them for me. Our beloved Führer has demanded that I deliver them personally."

Storrensberg looked concerned. "But ..."

"But nothing Jakob, this is an order direct from our Führer." Krammler was using all his strategies to exert power over his colleague. "Do you want to explain to him – personally - why he could not have them?"

Jakob relented. "I shall fetch them." He disappeared into lab 3 via Musfelldt's office, returning moments later with four small boxes.

"The devices are inside. The boxes are quite heavy as they are lead lined. Please handle them with care."

Pointing at Johnno Krammler ordered "Give them to my soldier to carry."

Johnno took them and was surprised at their weight.

"I shall inform the Führer personally of your input Jakob, I may even recommend a promotion. Well done. Now how do they function?"

Storrensberg went into technical mode. "Well, Erich, as you know the average speed of our V2 weapons is around four thousand two hundred kilometres per hour. We use a basic timing mechanism that only activates when the rocket begins its descent. We then time the device to explode, multiplying by many times the force that our normal charges can deliver." He thrust his chest forward "My idea Erich. The rocket is timed to explode above the target, greatly magnifying its lethal effect. Our enemies will soon see the power of our 3rd Reich and sue for peace."

"Wonderful work Jakob, I see a promotion here."

Storrensberg then moved forward and took one box off Johnno. He carefully opened it, presenting it to his inquisitor with a flourish. "Another of my brilliant ideas Erich." Inside the box was a polished steel ball, some one hundred millimetres or so in diameter, resting in a cushioned housing. "The letter 'L' had been engraved on the surface. London! This one is planned for London." He was almost jumping for joy. "We have two for London and two for Moscow."

"What about America? They are the main danger are they not?" Krammler seemed disappointed.

"We have that covered too Hans. Our sources tell us they are developing a similar weapon, but obviously much smaller, somewhere in Manhattan apparently. We have been assured that they are at least nine months away from a viable weapon. WE are currently engineering two devices for our Japanese allies, as well as one more of our own. We can target the East and West coast in a co-ordinated attack. We destroy New York; they can finish off Pearl Harbour and move on to California." Still beaming he added "We can have these large devices ready by the end of the month, September November at thc vcry latest."

Krammler did his best to look impressed, placing his right arm on his colleague's shoulder, "I foresee an Iron Cross AND a promotion, Brigadeführer Storrensberg."

Storrensberg was bursting with pride. "Thank you Hans," he said with a beaming smile. "Heil Hitler."

"Now return to your scientists and pass on the Führer's thanks for a job well done. Their work is greatly admired." Storrensberg bowed slightly and turned to leave the room. Krammler took his neuroliser from his pocket and fired at Storrensberg as he entered the corridor. His body slowly crumpled to the floor.

"No sense in taking chances," adding "I love this weapon." He gestured for Johnno to re-enter the Bell.

"Put those boxes on the floor by the seat, and take us back to 1944."

He carefully laid the boxes on the floor ,preparing for his next move. He smiled to himself, but ensured the smile had gone when he stood up and moved to the console. It was to be now or never.

"Take us back to 1944, 22nd October at 7.30 pm precisely. And no tricks or your friend dies."

Johnno was elated inside. "He knows nothing about the machine's memory" he thought, now for the second part of his plan. Krammler adopted the same position in the Bell's interior, just behind Johnno and to one side where he could watch the input on the console icons.

"I'm ready soldier; do not try to fool me."

"I cannot afford to, can I? my friend's life is at risk .. though, in his heart he knew that Krammler would kill them both as soon as he safely returned."

Johnno input the date numbers exactly as requested, speaking out aloud.

" 1..9..4..4..2..2..1..0..1..9..3..0.. ". Krammler stood at his shoulder, checking his actions

Johnno moved in ready to press the screen. As he did so he moved his legs inside the sides of the console, gently pressing his knees against them. He took hold of the console body with his left hand, out of sight of his captor, as he moved his right arm to press the screen and activate his commands.

"NOW if you please, activate NOW." Krammler ordered.

"OK, here we go." Johnno pressed the button to red, and then again as it activated to blue, instinctively he grabbed the console with his right hand.

The Bell began to shake violently. It was Johnno's dream all over again, but this time he was prepared for it.

He heard Krammler cry out as he was thrown against the inside of the Bell. As he did so he cracked his head and fell dazed to the floor. The shaking was constant. Johnno could feel his teeth vibrating as he clenched his jaws together. Keeping hold of the console he turned his head to see how his enemy was coping. The vibrations had thrown him against the inside wall, his gun had slipped from his hand and had slid across the floor to the rear seats. Carefully Johnno took one hand off the console and reached into his pocket for his neuroliser. He wasn't sure of its setting, but didn't really care. Minutes or hours he could use them all. Now he had it secure in his grasp he searched the console screen for the Orion symbol, his 'escape' button. He pressed it using the knuckles on his free hand and slowly, steadily the vibrations ceased and all was still.

Johnno released his grip with his hand and knees, turned to face his enemy lying prostrate on the floor, and fired his neuroliser. As the green beam hit him square in the chest he let out a sigh, his head rolling to one side. He wiped his brow with his sleeve, and took in a deep breath. He examined the settings on his weapon. He calculated that he would be unconscious for eight hours at least. He felt confident that they could now finish the job in hand now the spy in the camp had been eliminated.

"How's that for a curved ball master race, master Pleiadian, master ... whatever."

Johnno then pressed the correct memory button, one that returned them to the exact date and time they had left.

"Green, red, blue and here we go." There was a gentle hum and then silence. They had returned, only this time Johnno had four devices in his safe keeping; four devices which could change the history of the known world.

Having gathered the pistol from the floor, and the neuroliser from Krammler's pocket believing it would be safe to leave his enemy and look for Manni. He checked that the boxes were intact and safe. The boxes were not locked but held closed by a metal latch clip. "At least we can get at the contents should we need to." With one last look inside he left the Bell, leaving the door open in case a swift escape became necessary. He crossed the laboratory and listened at the door. All seemed quiet.

Opening the door slowly he quickly checked outside to see if anyone was approaching through the mine. No-one was visible. Swiftly he closed and re-bolted the door, swinging a chair around as extra strength again. He smiled as he did so "Do you come here often, apart from all the times I have tried to pick you up." He rushed through to the inner office where he hoped to find Manni alive having just had the injection. He picked up the phial from the desk and, checking that the syringe was completely empty, he recharged it with the antidote. Suddenly a thought occurred. "What if this isn't the antidote?"

He realised he had no option but to use it. He pulled up Manni's sleeve as far as he could. "Please, please be the antidote." He injected the contents into his unconscious colleague.

Initially nothing happened. Johnno took his colleague by the shoulders and gently shook him. "Come on Manni, wake up and speak to me." After seconds that felt like hours to Johnno his colleague took a deep breath and began to mumble incoherently. He opened his colleague's eyelids, feeling relieved as he saw them moving randomly, rolling around their sockets. He was alive.

Johnno slumped back slightly, and let out a huge sigh as he realised he had been in time to save him. "Strike two, master race."

Bending down towards his friend he tried to further rouse him, but it was clear he had to come around in his own time. Johnno got up and collected the alien weapon from the front of the desk where Krammler had left it. He tucked it inside his shirt, fastening the buttons to keep it safe. He buttoned his tunic, patting his 'parcel', reassuring himself. "You're going nowhere unless I go with you." He then moved around the back of the desk where the real Krammler was lying unconscious. In front of him there was a typewriter and a note he had started to write recording progress to date.

"For Mein Führer, no doubt." Suddenly Johnno's eyes opened wide. More innovations.

"That's it, I know how to dispose of the Bell and our spy in the camp."

Grabbing Krammler's chair he swung it away from the desk, its castors squeaking on the stone floor. Leaning over he began to read the start of the missive. "Mein Führer, it is with great pleasure I tell you that your brilliant plan in recovering Die Glöcke has come to fruition." Johnno pulled the sheet of paper from the carriage , rolled it into a ball, and flicked it onto his forearm , ending in the waste basket at the side of the desk. "That must be a three pointer."

He opened the desk drawers searching for a piece of paper, eventually locating some. "Oh yes, headed notepaper from Gruppenführer Hans Krammler himself. Very ironic."

The paper was quickly inserted into the typewriter and rolled around to line it up for typing.

"Ten words a minute I'm afraid" and he began to type.

Commander Gorden - Stan
This unconscious officer is posing as Hans Krammler.
He should have arrived possibly with operation 'Paperclip'
Please contact Groom Lake and tell them that the craft
In which he has arrived is officially known as Die Glöcke.
He belongs in the 'basement' level 4 at Area 51
They will know how to deal with an shape-shifter.
DO NOT remove his gloves
Lieutenant John O'Ryan USAF

He was about to remove the sheet of paper when he remembered his initial planned flight that bought him here.

PS let Commander Joe Pazzaro know that I am safe.

He pulled out the sheet of paper and quickly scan read it.

" That should do it. I wonder if they know that Area 51 is an open secret since 'Blue Book?"

Manni was beginning to regain consciousness. Behind him on a small filing cabinet Johnno found a carafe of water. He poured some into a glass and moved around to his friend who was now sitting up, his back to the desk. He bent down on his haunches, offering the glass to his mouth

"Here, drink this, you need to rehydrate."

Manni took a sip, then another. He took the glass off Johnno and poured the contents onto his head. "Nectar, pure nectar."

Realisation suddenly dawned "Krammler, there are two of them, one must be …

"A replicant, I know. I have him unconscious in the Bell. He couldn't read backwards." Johnno laughed.

"What?"

"It doesn't matter, but I do need your help with the first Bell. I have a plan to dispose of it AND our alien Krammler. He was the spy in our camp."

"He knew everything, didn't he?"

"Yes-everything. But now we're on the home stretch. Can you stand yet?"

"I think so, help me get up." Manni got to his feet and needed some support to get moving. "I have a major headache."

"We both will have one if we don't complete our assignment. Are you there Freya? Can you hear us? Freya, come in please." Johnno waited. "No joy Manni, she must be out of range or busy with Rick"

"Did I hear my name called?"

Both Johnno and Manni's faces lit up. They looked at each other in amazement

"Rick, Rick old buddy, you're safe. How are you? Where are you?"

"Thanks to you I am safe. I'm about a mile from the cabin. I need to check on our sleeping partners in the cabin and collect a weapon. What's your status?"

"It is a long story but we are in laboratory two, about to deal with Bell number one."

"Number one? What do you mean, number one?" Adding incredulously, "is there is a second Bell?"

"Afraid so buddy. The second was retro-engineered from the first. But don't worry, we've found them both and we're dealing with them."

"Was it a set-up, me going to the birthday party?"

"Very much so, but it has backfired on them. We have an almost empty mine, the workers have all escaped, and we have the shape-shifter who was pulling our strings. We are about to dispose of the first Bell, and I have a plan for the second as well."

Manni joined in. "We're looking to escape from here via the outlet on the North West side of the mine. Could you meet us there and provide firing cover if needed?"

"No problem. I'll be in touch. Well done and good luck with your plans."

Johnno was elated; finally it all seemed to be going their way and his best friend was alive.

"Right, Manni, here's my plan. We have two Bells to dispose of and I'm worried about using our plastic explosives, they're too indiscriminate."

"So ... I think I have the perfect solution"

"OK buddy, what is this perfect solution?"

Chapter 32

Johnno led Manni back to the Bell.

"I have the shape-shifter unconscious inside and I've collected four nuclear devices that were going to be used with V2 rockets."

"Where the? ... how the? "

"It's a long story Manni, but remember, I am a time machine pilot."

Johnno entered the Bell and passed the boxes back to Manni. "Be careful my friend, don't drop them whatever you do." Manni placed them safely on the floor by the internal corridor.

Having checked to ensure that the inside of the Bell was completely empty Johnno began to relay his ideas.

"We cannot send the devices to the future as they will be detonated as the Bell loses velocity as it lands."

"So…"

"And we cannot leave them here; our mission is to prevent their use in this conflict."

Manni tilted his head and gave a look of agreement.

"So we need to find a way to send them back in time, I mean WAY back in time."

"OK I see that as a possibility, but what about the two Bells. How do we deal with those?"

"I plan to send first our Bell forward in time to a secure US base along with our shape shifting friend. If we can eventually get him to Area 51 he will be held securely by experts. Then hopefully, when we return safely, we can give them the full story."

"Hmm, yes that sounds feasible. When and where?"

"I have a colleague who trained with Rick and myself in flight school. His name is Stan Gorden. I used to joke about his name being the same as my teacher in school. Anyway, he is now commanding a base deep in the countryside in Pennsylvania. It's out of the way and less likely to cause a stir when it finally lands. Less chance of a photograph as well."

"That sounds good. Can you pilot the Bell remotely?

"Nope." Johnno scratched his head. "I'll need to program the co-ordinates and, somehow, get out. If I travel to the future I may not be able to get back and help finish our task. I wonder if it's possible?" He re-entered the Bell and activated the console. Manni was half in and half out, watching his colleague closely. "I'll not come in, I may get trapped."

"See, I can use my talismans to activate the console, and then put them back around my neck. So that bit works." He turned to eye up the door mechanism. "Now how do I delay you closing?"

"Pass me your key." Manni's voice was full of confidence. "Surely if I press the key into its symbol outside here," he pointed to the Bell recess, "wouldn't that fool the Bell into keeping the door open, if only for a second or two?"

"That should give me time to jump out before I get trapped inside. Yes! We're cooking on gas now Manni."

Manni pressed the talisman into the recess and the door was held open. " Now try closing it by using the internal recess."

Johnno took a deep breath. "Here goes". He pressed the internal Bell symbol. The door started to close, and then faltered. Johnno jumped out as the door hissed shut behind him. He turned to see the door closed. He felt both of his buttocks before declaring with a grin. "They're both there."

Manni shrugged his shoulders and grinned. "See, I am now an official space engineer."

"Let's do this Manni." Johnno was keen to put his plan into action.

Manni re-opened the door allowing Johnno to step inside. He checked to see that 'Krammler' was still unconscious. "Here Manni, help me lift him on the seat. I wouldn't feel good if he broke his neck in flight, even if he deserves it." Manni stepped back outside. Johnno glanced in his direction. His hands were beginning to sweat and his pulse started racing, realising he'd only get one shot at this. He took the typed note and pinned it to Krammler's uniform, reading it aloud for one last time. "Please trust me Stan – please." Moving back into the console he immediately fixed his gaze on the screen. He began to move the screen image about looking for Stan Gorden's base. His fingers moved at speed across the screen, the image constantly changing as he did so. His face was a picture of concentration.

"Can't get this wrong or we'll scare someone shitless"

Eventually he recognised the outline of America on screen.

He zoomed in to find the state of Pennsylvania.

"It's a good job I took Geography at high school."

"Now then, where are you?" Peering into the screen, straining his eyes as he searched for his target.

"Got you." he locked the target into place. His hands moved back to the console.

"Are you still there Manni?"

"Ready and waiting my friend. Please be careful, I do not wish to finish our mission alone while you return home."

Johnno glanced in his direction and smiled. "Trust me, I don't want you to work alone either."

The console then became his focus for concentration. "Let's see. We

need a winter month for darkness. We need late afternoon when there should be less people about and Stan took command in 1965. Right to left .. , remember?" Reminding himself not to recreate his nightmare. Taking a deep breath and wiping his brow he turned to Manni again.

"Here goes nothing."

He carefully typed in the figures.

"0..4..6..1 – the time - 2..1..9..0 – the date, and -- 5..6..9..1 the year."

He turned to Manni. "Is the key in the door?"

"Yes."

"Are you ready for me?"

"Yes."

"Are you sure?" Johnno could feel his buttocks clenching as he readied himself.

"As ready as I'll ever be."

Johnno turned and took one last look at Krammler's replicant, still unconscious.

He turned back to look at Manni, his eyes imploring him to keep the door open.

"Are you sure you're ready?"

"Yes, more ready than I will ever be. Let's do this." Manni's tone was insistent, yet friendly.

Johnno turned to face the door, checking that the console was still in reach.

He pressed the green target button. It turned red.

He took a deep breath and pressed it again. It turned blue.

As he jumped for the door exit he slipped, landing on his knees just short of the door.

"Oh shit, the door's got me." The door began to slowly close, trapping Johnno in its path, half in and half out of the Bell. Manni realised he couldn't release the key from its socket, that would only give more power to the door as it tried to close. Johnno wriggled as best he could, but realised it was probably a losing battle; he'd end up travelling to the future along with the Bell and probably dying.

"Move away Manni, no need for two of us to die."

"Turn sideways my friend, you're thinner that way." Manni's voice was full of urgency.

Johnno gripped the door and frame just managing to turn sideways, momentarily releasing him from the door pressure. Manni reached in and grabbed Johnno by his uniform shoulder strap, pulling him clear just as the door hissed shut. Johnno landed on top of his friend, face to face with their incredulous eyes facing each other.

Behind them the Bell hummed, its image slowly faded, then disappeared from sight.

Johnno hugged Manni tight. "That was bloody close . Thanks buddy; my legs nearly left my body in 1944."

Manni wiped the sweat from his forehead. He was still shaking with the adrenalin rush.

"I don't often swear my friend, but 'shit', that was close."

"Too close, and we may have to do it all over again. Next time I'll put gum on my shoes."

The room fell silent, except for Johnno's deep breathing.

They both crawled over towards the wall ,resting their backs against it. Both were grinning with the realisation that part of their task was finally complete. Elated at their success.

"I wish we had champagne." Manni laughed.

"One down and one to go."

"Where and when did you send the Bell to as its destination?"

"I sent it to the ninth of December 1965 at around 4.40 in the afternoon.

A small out of the way base by the name of Kecksburg, Pennsylvania."

Chapter 33

Meanwhile, back in Washington, a concerned president was having a hurriedly arranged conversation with his chief of staff of the United States Air Force, Commander Tom Gerarty, in the Oval office. The President pressed the 'mute' button on his red phone for a semblance of secrecy

"Tom, I've got Joe Pazzaro on the red line here, we've lost our Blackbird on a test flight – what do you think we should be doing?" The President looked pensive as though deep in thought. He climbed out of his chair and walked around his desk, sitting on the end near his seated colleague.

"Remember the message we received in '65 Mr President, the Kecksburg incident. It didn't make any sense then, but by God it does now. We must assume that our missing pilots are still safe somehow and in the process of trying to get back home. We still have Gruppenführer Krammler under wraps. We've kept a lid on it until now."

"We still need to keep a lid on this; we don't want the public thinking that our enemies have the ability to use our air space undetected. Nor do we want them thinking we are at war with aliens."

"Joe – tighten up and implement a full blackout. Remind our staff of the official secrets act and their duty."

"Tom, we'll keep eyes and ears on our Russian friends and their allies. Tell our sites in the UK and Germany that we need round the clock surveillance. If anyone whispers 'why?' they'll be stationed in Elmendorf before they've finished the sentence."

Both Commanders gave an affirmative reply.

Commander Gerarty put on his peaked cap, saluted the president, and moved to leave the room.

"I'm depending on you, Tom. As soon as we have any further updates I'll get right back to you." The commander smiled uneasily and left the oval office, closing the door behind him.

"Joe, do the pilots have family that we can contact and update? We'll need to remind them of the need for total secrecy."

"No Mr. President. Both pilots were single men with no living parents. We must be grateful for small mercies."

The president pressed the 'mute' button and placed the phone to his ear. He straightened his tie and gently coughed to clear his throat, a trait he had when delivering untruths for the good of his country.

"No more news at present, but I will keep you informed. May God be with you Joe." replacing the receiver.

All alone in his Oval Office he knew what he needed to do. He moved back to his chair. Once sat down he tapped his fingers on the desk then tapped a lever on the inside of his desk leg – a small compartment swung open. Inside was a small metal object, much like a cigarette case. It appeared to be made of silver, and was smooth on both faces. He pressed on one side and the top swung open. Inside were a range of buttons with strange symbols on them. There was a small round mesh at one end, and the inside of the lid seemed to be coated in a blue plastic film.

He pressed five of the buttons in a seemingly random sequence. The object clicked, and a small image appeared on the inside of the opened lid. A face appeared.

The president moved the receiver towards his mouth, and lowered his voice.

"Richard, it's the President here."

"Good news I hope Mr President?"

"Phase 2 is complete. Secrecy is assured."

"Thank you Mr President – 1969 looks as though it may be a very good year."

The president closed the receiver, clicking it shut. He replaced it into the desk compartment and shut it firmly, ensuring the lever was back in place. He leaned back in his chair, muttering to himself. "God help those boys, and God help me ... and God help humanity if this fails."

He looked around his office, musing over decisions he had to make as President. He realised he had become somewhat detached from everyday life. Whilst he realised that there were no families who would be concerned at the loss of two good men he knew how he would feel if the fate of two of his staff was in limbo.

"We've sat on this for four L O N G years I have to give out some good news sometime, goddamit."

He picked up his red phone "Get me back in touch with Commander Joe Pazzaro please – asap." He replaced the receiver, tapping his fingers impatiently on the desk in front of him. There was a buzzing noise from the handset. He reached forward and lifted the telephone off the hook.

"Hello, are you still there Joe?"

"Yes Mr President, I'm still here. Problems?"

"Joe, take a seat, I have some really good news for you."

Chapter 34

Manni and Johnno now had to contemplate their next move, the safe disposal of the four devices as well as the second Bell.

"Can we send the devices so far into the future that they will harm no-one?"

Manni shook his head. "We don't fully know what's in the future, and these time machines can only go a limited distance before they land automatically. We could destroy lives, create a war, and tip the balance in the natural order of things. They should be destroyed here, or in some past where we know that cannot injure anyone. A tall order my friend."

Johnno's head rolled back, his eyes closed, deep in thought.

"Think, think Johnno my boy. What would Mr Gordon do?" He tried to remember at school the magical history lessons he gave, and the daily supply of amazing facts he delivered with a sense of wonderment.

"We could send it back into the Sahara desert."

"Nomads, we might kill nomads."

"Perhaps the Gobi desert?"

"Mongol tribes, linked to the history of developing Asia."

"Mars?"

"Don't even think about it."

Johnno turned his head and faced his colleague. "You certainly know your history my friend."

"Thank to Astrild; she researches all areas of development on all planets with life forms on them," adding with a smile, "she is bloody good as you would say."

Johnno tapped his ear piece. "Are you there Freya? Can you help us at all?"

An ominous silence.

"She must still be busy or out of range." Johnno was dismayed. "We can't fail now; there must be sometime, somewhere that we can utilise." He got to his feet and began to pace around the room, rubbing his neck in the hope of stimulating his brain. He turned to face Manni, his face breaking into a forced grin.

"I could do with that pee right now."

Manni laughed. "Go out into the forest my friend; no one will see you there, only the trees, and they won't tell." Johnno stopped dead in his tracks; a germ of an idea came into his mind. His eyes lit up, a broad smile spread across his face.

"That's it, thank you Mr Gordon. Thank you Manni."

Manni was bemused. "What did Mr Gordon tell you? …… What did I say?"

"He was an exceptional teacher. He would tell us amazing facts and stories which had a class full of young children gazing in awe at these mysterious tales. And there was one in particular ... Come on, we need to take these boxes next door to the second Bell." He collected two of the boxes containing the bombs and made his way into the next laboratory. Manni got to his feet collecting the second two and rushed after his colleague.

As he entered Krammler's office Johnno looked to make sure that his enemy was still unconscious. The chair was empty. "Where the fuck has he gone? He was unconscious. Are you sure he was still here when you last checked?"

"Yes, he was there."

"Are you sure? He shouldn't have come around yet and walked out of here."

The noise of a squeaking chair was heard in the last office.

They both rushed to the door. Manni tried the handle with no luck. He rattled it and pushed, still no joy. From inside the room came a quaking voice, attempting to be brave.

"It's no use, we're locked in and I have a gun pointing at you right now."

Manni turned to Johnno and whispered "That's Professor Muller. He must have found the real Krammler and dragged him through there for safety.

Johnno feigned concern. "It's Korporal Engel here. Is Commander Krammler safe? We feared he was dying."

"He's safe, and you can't fool me. I saw what you did with Die Glöcke, my baby, and now you want to kill me so I can't create any more."

"We had to do that, it was unsafe, the console was in danger of exploding."

All was silent for ten seconds

"Did you hear me, it was unsafe."

"It could not be. I was assured by Professor Maia that both consoles were perfect. I have spent my time using their designs to begin manufacturing my latest one."

"Professor Maia?" Johnno and Manni looked quizzically at each other. "Who the hell is this Professor Maia?" Realisation soon dawned on him.

"He must be the shape shifter we sent back in the first Bell."

A look of fear came over his face.

"What did he mean-his latest one? Shit. There can't be a third, can there?"

Manni Joined in. "It's Korporal Mayer here Professor. Before he took ill commander Krammler told us of his concerns about a Mr. Maia and his credentials. He asked us to check all the Bells. The first one was in danger of exploding. That's why we sent it away for safety."

Muller seemed uncertain what to do next. He had taken the unconscious Krammler into laboratory three, and had spent a great deal of time trying to wake him, with no joy so far, his leader only mumbling incoherently. He realised that, although he wasn't a soldier, he was committed to the Fatherland.

..... But he didn't want to die.

He was alone in his laboratory, surrounded by engineering and electronics equipment, his only escape being the rear exit leading to the newly built henge. Could he run outside and get help?

He knew the majority of soldiers were away for the birthday celebrations. Should he leave the Commander behind and just escape? What about the glory he would miss by not being presented to the Führer?

This Bell was intended as a gift for the Führer himself. What if he needed it to relocate and set up his 4th Reich? He must somehow complete and save his work and present it to the Führer himself. In his own tortured mind he saw himself as a potential saviour for his homeland.

He would meet his Führer in person. Surely he would be on a par with Albert Speer.

.... But he didn't want to die.

Manni continued. "Listen, Professor ... Matthew ...when the Commander regains consciousness he will back up our story. You keep him safe in there with you while we check the controls on this Bell. If all is OK we shall let you know. Is that OK with you?"

Manni talked aside to Johnno. "If we then assume that he leaves the lab at the rear towards the henge and makes his way to the guards at the front we probably have 10 minutes maximum to dispatch Bell number two. Hell, he may even just hide there until we've gone. I don't see him as a hero, do you? Our special explosive should destroy the inner workings with little damage elsewhere. It will never travel, no matter what they do to it, and a replacement should take months to fabricate"

Muller had listened intently to their offer, sweat was now pouring from his brow and he wasn't sure what to do. He knew he couldn't let them in, just in case they were lying.

He realised that if he agreed to their plan he may have time to escape and get help.

But what if they weren't lying? What if the console was faulty and he was trying to replicate and design a new one? Could that kill him? Or, even worse could it kill the Führer? He was a scientist after all, not a soldier.

Taking Krammler's Luger from its holster he nervously scanned his laboratory for anything to help him. On the worktop lay the console he was trying to recreate. There were cans of chemicals they were preparing to use as the fuel for the last Bell, thorium and beryllium oxides, dangerous but not explosive in themselves. The Bell's inner core had already been filled with Xerum 525 and the empty drums stored to one side. These drums had a skull and crossbones image posted on them, and the word 'hochexplosiv' stencilled alongside.

"Well, Matthew, are you OK with our arrangements?"

He was nervously looking anywhere around his lab for ideas.

"I'm just checking that Hans is alright, please give me a moment."

Cautiously he rolled one of the Xerum drums toward the barricaded door. He placed it flat against the door with the stencilled warning facing inwards. Feeling slightly safer he answered.

"I have a machine gun as well as a pistol, I am well armed."

"We mean you no harm, only to possibly save your life." Manni looked at Johnno and winked.

"I also have a drum of explosive liquid that I have placed against the door. If you force your way in it will explode and kill you both."

"He is bluffing," Manni whispered, "he does not want to die for the Fatherland, he wants to be a famous scientist, not a martyr."

"That's fine Matthew, a sensible precaution. We will only try to enter if you invite us in. We'll now inspect the Bell and report back to you. If we are unsure we will ask for your help. OK?"

"OK". Muller let out a huge sigh and relaxed slightly. "I shall not talk to you in case I distract you"

"He's going out of the back as we thought. Ten minutes Johnno, let's go."

Muller tucked the pistol into his waistband and crept out towards the rear of his laboratory, convinced he was about to save his Führer's pet project and become a hero of the Third Reich.

After giving Muller time to escape they both tried the door again with no joy.

"Check Krammler's desk, there must be some keys in there."

Manni pulled out the centre drawer, grinning as he displayed a set of keys on a ring.

After two attempts they unlocked the door. They pushed gently, just in case the door was booby trapped. It screeched open ... safely. In the centre of the room, by a side wall, was the second Bell.

"Right Johnno, this time we need to make sure that you get out safely BEFORE the Bell seals itself"

"I have a better idea. Do you have your special explosive ready?"

Manni nodded, taking the small canister from his pocket.

"Right, follow me" Johnno put his talisman against the body of the Bell and the door slid open.

"So far, so good. Come on."

Manni looked at Johnno quizzically and shrugged his shoulders.

"Come on, we're doing what Josef suggested."

Manni entered the cabin, to be directed towards the rear wall. There were no gravity seats in this model, just grab handles on the wall for passengers to hold onto. Johnno slid the door shut and began to peer at the screen. The console unit was obviously an original unit and not back engineered. He turned to Manni.

"Our shape-shifter has a lot to answer for, but we must thank him at present. Now hold on."

He turned around and placed his talismans in their correct recesses. The console hummed into life, the screen activating displaying a green dot to signify their location. Using his fingers in his well-practised actions he zoomed in the screen until the green dot was as large as it could be.

"Let's say twenty feet to the right, sorry, east, and down slightly."

He moved the dot over and pressed it gently, seeing it turn red. "Now for our destination and time."

"Could you give me some ideas as to when and where we are visiting?"

"All in good time my friend-and I mean **good** time." After taking a quick look at his watch he began to enter the co-ordinate figures into the keypad. As he was quite adept at this he did not call the figures out loud, just humming as he input each figure. "Right, that's it," turning to face Manni, "hang on tight my friend, we are going to complete another part of our mission."

Manni replaced the explosive charges into his pocket and hung on to two of the grab handles. Turning back to face the console Johnno gave the red light a final press and the Bell hummed into action. After several seconds the humming stopped.

Johnno moved towards the door. "Come on, no time to waste."

They emerged into laboratory three, next door to where they had started.

"What the ?" Manni looked stunned.

"We are next door, there is your third Bell under construction, and I believe that Muller has just left through ..." he looked around the room until he saw the door at the far side of the room, "there."

Manni smiled. "You are a genius my friend."

"And you are about to place those charges and help complete our latest task, go to it."

Manni moved quickly towards the Bell. Its door was open as the console had not yet been fitted. Johnno checked the drum by the door.

"Xerum 525. Does that mean anything to you?"

Manni's voice emanated from the hollow Bell. "Yes, it's their version of the real liquid we used as fuel. We call it Bramium. It is volatile but only when used between the skins of the Bell."

"How did they find out about it?"

Manni stepped out of the Bell's door. "I don't know. It is sealed within the Bell and cannot be replaced. If it leaks into the atmosphere it evaporates. There must be an inside source, hopefully the shape shifter we dispatched in Bell one."

"Have you fixed the charges?"

"Yes. I've placed them inside the recess where the console is fixed. Once they have been detonated they will never find any evidence of what has happened."

"How large of an explosion will there be? Remember we have around," he glanced at his watch, "seven minutes or so before Muller returns, possibly with reinforcements.

"There will be no explosion my friend. I have set the charge level to its lowest. It will send an electromagnetic shockwave through the body of the Bell, immobilising the Bramium, setting it solid. This Bell will never time travel anywhere."

Manni moved over to where Krammler was still sitting unconscious. He checked his pulse. "He is OK, we just need to protect him from any heat generated." Manni turned his chair around so he faced the wall. He lifted up a small filing cabinet and placed it on the desk, shielding him from any possible injury. He carefully looked to see if he was fully shielded, only moving away when he was satisfied. Krammler was dribbling as he was slowly coming round.

Manni looked towards Johnno.

"The Federation my friend, we must remember the Federation."

Johnno nodded in agreement.

"Even our enemies have rights. Now just let me set our return destination." They re-entered the Bell. Using the memory tab he set their destination for the exact time and location they left.

"Set for one minute and hop aboard our brand new time shuttle."

Manni returned to the charges and set the timer for one minute. He ran from the incomplete Bell towards his colleague and safety.

"Watch you don't trip up." A sarcastic voice came from inside Bell number two.

Manni entered to be met by a smiling colleague.

"Sorry, I couldn't resist that. Now hold tight"

Manni grabbed the hand rails. Johnno closed the Bell door and moved back towards the console. He pressed the memory button and prepared for travel. Nothing happened.

He pressed it again, still nothing happened.

"We have thirty seconds my friend, can we please leave ... NOW"

Johnno glanced back at Manni. "I'm trying"

Manni pointed to the screen. "Red, it's still red"

Johnno looked up. "Shit. It's not the same" He quickly pressed the red dot on the screen, it slowly turned blue. Taking a deep breath he pressed the memory button again. The Bell hummed into life, and then fell silent. Johnno turned to Manni and leaned back on the console.

"I think I need more than a pee."

"So do I my friend, so do I."

Johnno opened the door and they gratefully exited the Bell. They were back in laboratory 2.

"Now for the final Bell, are you ready for this one?"

Manni put his hand on Johnno's shoulder. "Well done my friend. Josef said to make time for things to happen, an intelligent young man indeed."

"Who, thankfully, becomes an intelligent and very inspirational adult." Johnno had a smug smile on his face..

Chapter 35

"Korporal Weber, Korporal Weber, please report your position'"

In the gloom of the evening a voice crackled over the communications receiver in the rear of the German truck; the last truck in the convoy that had broken down on its way to Wroclaw. Outside in the gathering darkness were several soldiers intent on fixing the apparent puncture in one of the front wheels. Trying to jack up the truck had caused problems in the soft road surface which had been hastily laid in secrecy as a supply route in and out of the mine complex. As a result the truck was perched at the edge of the road leaning precariously towards the soft verge from where it would need a half track to secure its safe recovery.

Several soldiers had ventured into the woods foraging for large fallen tree trunks which could be used as a raft to support the heavy jack as it dug into the soft road surface.

"Fucking Opel shit."

At the front of the broken truck Obergefreiter Neumann had stripped to the waist and was trying to right the truck so he could replace the damaged tyre. Around him were his colleagues urging him on.

"Come on Franz, we have women to fuck and beer to drink."

"If this had been my Famo truck we would be OK. But, no, the fucking generals who know better give us this shit to help us look inconspicuous. I mean, fucking inconspicuous in this shit hole of Poland."

As he spoke Korporal Bergman arrived, dragging a large tree trunk from a fallen conifer. "Where shall I put this Franz?"

Franz smiled "I could tell you." Then, gesturing at the front axle "Put it under here, beneath the suspension and when I say lift, you lift with all of your might."

Neumann placed some of the large branches under the engine and guided the trunk on top, raising it as high as possible. Pointing to one of his fellow rifleman Neumann Bellowed "Bergman-when the truck is raised you put these branches underneath and the jack on top, OK?"

Bergman nodded.

"And you lazy bastards" he smiled at the rest of the troop, you help lift with this tree trunk. We still have women to fuck, remember?"

"Now lift".

The troops gathered around the trunk and put their shoulders to work, raising the front of the truck.

"Now Bergman, quickly."

The young soldier spread the branches onto the road surface whilst Neumann took over the role of placing the jack in position, fixing it tightly under the front suspension. Lowering his arm slowly he ordered his colleagues to gently lower the trunk. The truck settled on the road surface. "Hold it there; keep the trunk under for extra support"

He began to pump and raise the jack, lifting the wheel off the floor just enough to remove the wheel. He quickly undid the wheel nuts and removed the damaged tyre, casting it aside and putting the spare onto its lugs. "Rubber shit. If we had my half-track we would all be drunk by now!"

The replacement wheel was quickly secured in place. "Wait until I get in the cabin and start her up." Neumann gingerly climbed into the cab, not wishing to move its centre of gravity and tip even further off the side of the road.

"Remove the jack, slowly." The truck's weight caused the soldiers on the supporting tree lever to gently buckle at the knees. Putting the truck into gear he prepared to move to the relative safety at the centre of the road.

"Now lower the tree, slowly, let the tyres grip a little."

As the tree was gently lowered the front wheel made contact with the road. Neumann gingerly pressed on the gas pedal, at the same time slowly turning the steering wheel. Slowly, steadily the truck began to move forward towards the safety of the road's centre. The tree trunk was hastily withdrawn as all the soldiers began shouting and whooping for joy.

Neumann had a smile of satisfaction on his face. "Two hours late, but now for some good beer and even better women." He leaned out of the cab window "All aboard comrades, heaven awaits."

The soldiers rushed around the back of the truck eager to get back inside and onwards with their planned evening of pleasure, courtesy of their esteemed visitor, Commander Krammler. One by one they climbed aboard and took their places on the bench seats. The last one aboard was Korporal Weber.

Amongst the babble and chatter of the newly boarded soldiers came a faint crackle of a radio receiver. The trucks were fitted with modified DMG3K radio systems. Although the range was excellent the reception very much depended on weather conditions.

"I repeat Korporal Weber, Korporal Weber, please report your position."

He rushed towards the receiver, lifting the handset. "Korporal Weber here."

"Where the fuck have you been Weber, we've been trying to raise you for over an hour."

The Korporal looked around at his colleagues, concerned that he had put them all in trouble by leaving his post.

"Our truck broke down. We were concerned that it may have been a partisan trap. We deployed a secure ring to ensure no surprise attacks occurred. I took my place in that ring whilst Obergefreiter Neumann repaired the damage."

He looked to his colleagues for support, gesturing with his eyes for sympathy. After all it was him who collected the fallen pine tree used to lift the truck. Several of his colleagues gave him the 'thumbs up'.

"How far are you from the mine?"

He frowned. "About twenty to twenty five kilometres I would guess."

"There has been an incident. There have been reports of an attack on the mine complex. You must return immediately. Seek out Commander Krammler and ensure his safety."

A collective sigh of disappointment reverberated within the truck as several soldiers swore out aloud.

"We have tried to return but the road has been damaged by an errant air strike. You must return at once and kill anyone you find there. Do you understand? You must kill on sight – our mission here is at risk."

The mood in the truck had gone from euphoria to abject disappointment. Their planned weekend of debauchery had been snatched from their grasp.

"Commander Krammler here," the radio took over as a more authoritative tone as a new voice cut in, "tell your colleagues in your troop there will be an Iron Cross presented by the Führer himself for every soldier when the spies have been caught, or shot, and a two week furlough back home with their families as an extra reward." Weber felt his back stiffen with pride as he gave his reply.

"Yes sir, understood, sir. They are as good as dead."

The mood in the rear of the truck lightened visibly. The thoughts of a visit back home to family and a decoration from the Führer overcame their disappointment of a lost weekend.

Neumann had put his tunic back on, along with his forage cap and was feeling pleased with his mechanical expertise. A whole weekend of pleasure beckoned. This feeling was soon cut short.

Neumann climbed into the cab alongside him. "Turn the truck around."

"Are you fucking crazy?"

"These are the personal orders from Commander Krammler himself. Head back to the mine, I'll explain on the way".

Neumann put the truck into reverse and carefully performed a ten point turn, watched over by his worried colleagues, wary of going over the road verge again. He'd spent enough time repairing trucks for one day. As he drove slowly forward they all jumped aboard ready for a search and kill operation ahead.

Behind them in the stranded convoy Musfelldt spoke to Storrensberg. "Jakob, ensure that their holiday is spent on the eastern front, somewhere near Moscow." He looked around furtively at the soldiers waiting in the convoy. "The same goes for our current travel partners, they must also be given the same holiday. We cannot have news leaking out about our failure to defend our latest Wunderwaffe and organising a party instead."

"Understood Erich. What shall we do about our esteemed colleague Commander Krammler?"

"He must be dealt with as well. You understand? I never did trust him. False information, and there's something about his eyes. He seems to have his own agenda. Yes … he must meet with an accident. This *must* be our secret."

Storrensberg nodded and touched the side of his nose.

"Our secret Erich, our secret."

Chapter 36

Inside Laboratory 2 the mood had become almost jovial as Johnno and Manni set about the task of destroying their original target, Die Glöcke.

Johnno was at the console about to put in his chosen co-ordinates he would use to destroy the Bell. Manni was busy looking how to set the devices to detonate when they were safely transported away, having scoured the laboratory for something to secure them on their journey. He had settled on some canvas strapping used to secure the goods delivered when in transit.

"At last my camping skills are being put to good use, I used to visit Freya when you were a child; do you recall?"

Johnno looked perplexed. "I can't say I do, sorry."

"Can you remember the man who delivered your favourite sledge on your birthday?"

Johnno turned to his colleague. "That was YOU?"

"Yes"

Johnno dug into his memory bank. "But you, you look the same now as you did then."

"Yes; it's a long way from Orion, but a short time if you know the tricks."

Johnno grinned and shook his head. "Well I'll be."

Just then there came a sound similar to rapid gunfire from the laboratory next door.

Johnno swung around, looking for his neuroliser, now safely strapped back on his wrist.

Manni grabbed his arm. "The charges, remember. Their Bell is now ... Kaput as they say."

Breathing a sigh of relief Johnno looked slightly embarrassed and, with a sheepish grin, added "Amazing the tricks that time travel plays with your memory."

Their conversation was cut short as their earpieces crackled into life.

"Manni, please come in. Johnno please come in."

It was Astrild, sounding desperate.

"Manni here. You can start to relax. We are about to deal with our final target and all is going to plan." As he spoke he gave a casual 'thumbs up' to his colleague.

"We have a slight problem. The broken down truck actually broke down on the wrong side of the road barrier we created. They have repaired the damage and are heading back to the mine."

"We should be finished here in around … " he looked to Johnno for confirmation, who held up five fingers, "five minutes. Then we are out of here. We have asked Rick to be ready by the West cavern exit."

"They have been instructed by Musfelldt and Krammler to kill on sight. You are in extreme danger. You need to complete your mission and get out of there."

"Krammler. But surely he's …" Johnno was bemused. "What does Freya say?"

"I cannot raise her. I cannot raise her at the cabin and I have not been able to contact her for hours. I am hoping that she is just out of range somewhere, hopefully."

Astrild's voice was full of concern.

"She will be safe somewhere, planning our final moves. Don't worry."

Johnno joined in. "Freya is a survivor and will soon meet us as we leave this hell hole."

"I'll join Rick at the Western cavern. Be careful. Be safe. Ka amo Te"

Johnno looked bemused. Manni smiled embarrassingly "I love you, in Orion."

Johnno smiled and turned back to his screen.

"Right, I have the map on screen and am finding ...... ah, here it is, Siberia. Are the charges in place?"

"All locked down and ready to set."

"Good. Now I need to find ... got it ... Tunguska." He secured his target with a gentle press and the location dot turned green.

"Now for the date and time" Johnno's concentration moved down to the console keyboard. "I'm looking at 1908, the 30th June and early morning, say 6.00 a.m." He fed the data into the keyboard.

"Right, set the devices for, say thirty seconds. They should detonate as the pressure of their travel affects them. If not then thirty seconds should ensure we get them safely away from here."

As he spoke Manni mouthed "Raise your arms," slipping one of the canvas tie straps around Johnno's waist. Johnno looked bemused "Do I need a new belt?"

"Just an added precaution" He tested and pulled the tie strap and his colleague was yanked towards him. "That should do it, we can't afford any more slips this time, not with just 30 seconds on the clock."

Johnno moved back to the console. He pressed the location dot and it duly turned red.

"Set the charges for thirty seconds and get out."

Manni primed the four devices and left the Bell. "Thirty seconds and counting."

Johnno pressed the screen for the final time; the dot turned a vivid blue.

"Get me out!"

Manni pulled frantically at the canvas strap. Johnno was pulled off his feet and out of the Bell, landing in a heap on the floor, his saviour lying below him. Behind them the door hissed shut. There was a gentle humming noise and the Bell shimmered and then disappeared from view. They looked at each other incredulously, almost in disbelief at what they had achieved.

"YES my friend, we have done it. Yes, Yes, Yes; Look out Tunguska, hell is on the way."

They quickly got to their feet and hugged each other, beaming smiles on their faces. Manni walked over to the empty space where the Bell had been and turned to face his colleague. He raised his arms in the air, and slowly turned on the spot.

"Well done my reluctant colleague, our task is almost complete."

A voice in their ear pieces brought them back to reality; Astrild's worried tones had been replaced by ones full of urgency. She was obviously concerned for the safety of her husband and colleague.

"Manni, Johnno, the enemy truck is just some twenty minutes or so away. You need to leave at once. Do you hear, you must leave at once."

"We are on our way. Repeat. We are on our way. Mission complete."

Both men took one last look at the empty space where the Bell had been.

"Come on, my friend, it's time to leave. We have the weapon, the Bells are destroyed and your future on Earth should now be secure. It's time we went home."

Johnno patted his colleague on the shoulder. "Thanks to you my friend, thanks to you. Now let's leave this God forsaken place."

They quickly made for the door back into the mine area, stopping briefly to listen for activity outside. Manni slightly opened it, taking a brief glance in both directions to check that the coast was clear. They stepped outside, closing the door behind them. Manni took a small pen like item out of his pocket. He pulled it apart in the centre, and rejoined it much like a fountain pen. Johnno was intrigued, another space weapon? The door was made of heavy wooden boards secured by thick metal hinges and a metal latch. There was no way of locking it from the outside, but Manni had other ideas.

"Watch this, my friend". He pointed the 'pen' where the latch secured the door. A brilliant white beam came out of the tip and began to melt the metal. He carefully moved along the latch, melting the steel parts together. He looked back at Johnno.

"It's a form of plasma welding, very efficient." He repeated the process where the door hinges hung onto their lugs. With a smile of satisfaction Manni announced "Get through that if you can, Professor Muller."

As they prepared to move over to the far side of the mine to seek out the western exit they glanced back and saw the trucks laden with the V2 rockets.

Both stopped dead in their tracks.

Manni looked his colleague in the eyes "Are you thinking what I'm thinking?"

"Unfortunately, yes. If they are launched even without any special warheads they will kill many people, most probably civilians."

"We could use the charges we brought with us. I still have them in my pockets, we could place them in the controls somewhere."

"Surely that would kill any operators when it is launched. Have we forgotten your Federation rulebook ?"

Manni had a look of resignation on his face. "You're right. But what can we do, we only have minutes to decide."

"Come on Johnno, think, think."

The silence within the mine was almost deafening as both minds set to finding a solution. How to destroy the rockets without potentially killing anyone?

Johnno spoke out aloud. "Come on Johnno, we studied these at White Sands. There must be a way, there must be." He was visualising the captured rockets he'd studied in his courses with the USAF. "Alcohol, oxygen, turbines, combustion, can we disturb these actions?" Suddenly a look of realisation crept across his face. "That's it, simple really. We just need to disarm the warhead. It can then land with little damage, just a major car crash hopefully. Manni, your neurolisers, they disturb electric currents don't they?"

"Yes, but what good is that?"

"If I remember correctly the warhead has an electric fuse, actioned only when the rocket hits the target. Could your weapon's radiation fry the warhead circuits as well, rendering them useless?" Johnno continued, sounding ever more enthusiastic "And, better still, the damage would not be obvious, they'd never know the rockets were useless when they actually launch them."

"Theoretically it would work, I suppose. We'd have to use full power, and set it to electrically self-destruct in order to generate enough force to damage the circuits inside the rocket as well as its own." Manni's face broke into a broad smile. "But we'll never know if we don't try. Lead on my friend, lead on."

They moved towards the trucks "You DO know where the fuse is, don't you?"

"In the nose cone if I remember correctly. And our job is made easier as they are both almost flat on the truck beds. I never was any good at mountain climbing."

They made their way stealthily back towards the trucks, keeping a look out for any SS guards who could still be stationed in their quarters awaiting their arrival. Johnno climbed up onto the bonnet of the first truck. Manni opened the window from the inside so Johnno could use the open space on the door as a step up onto the roof of the cab. The tarpaulin was still slightly loose as a result of its long journey. He quickly undid the securing ropes, exposing the cone and warhead. Looking to the second truck in order to check Manni's progress he was surprised to see no-one there.

He checked all around only to see his colleague in the semi-darkness just moving towards the SS quarters doorway.

Manni waved his plasma pen and grinned. "Extra security. Two doors locked are better than one".

Turning back to the task in hand Johnno took his neuroliser from its base on his wrist. He placed it against the nose cone tip, painted in a lurid yellow colour. It clicked into place as the magnetic base took effect.

"Yes." he said enthusiastically. "Made for the job."

"Now I need to turn this … " he paused to remember his instruction from what seemed like an age ago, "counter clockwise then ..."

From behind and below him came the sound of a strange voice

"Excuse me Korporal, may we help you?"

Johnno looked back to see the two SS guards stood at the side of the truck smiling up at him. He mumbled to himself "Shit, where have they come from? Manni must have messed up somehow with the time, they should still be unconscious." He was unsure if they knew that Manni was around somewhere, perhaps able to help him somehow. He glanced around, but he wasn't to be seen. Why hadn't he warned him? Why didn't he neurolise the guards? Why hadn't he welded the doors shut?

"I am just checking the current capacity and resistance on the warhead circuit as ordered by Gruppenführer Musfelldt," in the belief that bullshitting would buy him some time.

The two guards looked at each other and grinned. "Ah, you mean the Gruppenführer Musfelldt who has just sent us up here as he left Wroclaw on his way to rejoin Commander Krammler. The same Commander who informed us that there were spies in the mine intent on destroying our rockets."

"Shit." Johnno mumbled to himself again "They seem to know everything."

"Korporal ... I mean, Johnno, you need to come down here." One of the guards beckoned him down, gesturing with his pistol. He needed to buy time. Where the hell was Manni? Why didn't he fire? He even knows my name. Johnno's thoughts were racing. He needed to buy time.

"I just need the final reading on my meter. I won't be a minute."

"Correct, you will **not** be a minute, you will come down **now**."

The second guard stood on the door runner, reached up for Johnno's leg and pulled him down from the cab roof. He bounced off the bonnet and then hit the floor hard, feeling his teeth crack together and causing his gums to bleed. His eyes watered. He rubbed them, opening them wide in an attempt to get his focus back. Although he was dazed he instinctively felt for the neuroliser on his wrist, only to realise it was still attached to the warhead. He wiped the blood from his mouth and tried to get to his feet, only to be met by a boot to the stomach, sending him reeling forward past the front of the truck.

"Where is your friend Manni? We'd like to talk to him as well.... Johnno." Both soldiers were grinning, glancing at each other in anticipation of the intended capture of two enemy spies.

He was now on all fours, blood still pouring from his mouth and gasping for air as the pain in his stomach was making him retch

"Your friend, Manni, where is he please?" The guard moved forward aiming to kick Johnno's prostrate figure again. As he swung his foot forward Johnno's self-defence training kicked in.

Grabbing the foot as it swung he twisted it as hard as he could, pushing at the same time. The guard spun violently, hitting his head on the truck door and crashing to the floor. He slowly got back to his feet and turned to face his aggressor. He felt his forehead, discovering a cut above his left eye. He wiped the blood with the back of his hand, and grinned as he turned to his colleague. "He wants to fight me Oskar" turning to face his opponent, still on the floor, he lifted his hand and waved his forefinger just as a teacher admonishing a pupil "that was a bad move Johnno, I shall make sure that you suffer as you've never suffered before."

His colleague grinned. "Leave some for me, Max, you can't have all the fun."

Johnno knew it would just be a matter of time before he was beaten unconscious, possibly to death. The two muscle bound morons derived pleasure from inflicting pain, something he had witnessed with the slave workers and their abysmal lives in the mine. He found it hard to believe that Manni had deserted him. He had the means to disable both guards and save him from possible death. Maybe he'd encountered them earlier and was dead already?

Realising the inevitability of what was about to happen he rose slowly to his feet, still feeling the pain from his opponent's boot to his stomach. Adopting a boxing stance he stood and faced his enemy.

"Right, which of you morons wants to die first?"

Both guards laughed out loud. Oskar stood to one side, gesturing for his colleague to step forward. "After you Max, and can you please leave some for me?" Max nodded in thanks, stepped forward and mirrored Johnno's stance.

"Prepare to die – slowly … very slowly."

Max had been a professional boxer before the war and had been working as a bouncer in the Blue Angels, a Berlin nightclub owned by a prominent gangster. He was used to beating opponents to a pulp and had already had one murder charge dropped by a judge who had been 'charmed' by the club owner. He was looking forward to fighting someone who might offer some resistance, however futile. He was sure that he had 'lost his edge' by beating the pathetic defenceless slaves who laboured for them day and night.

Johnno saw the look of fury in his eyes. He took a deep breath, spat out a mouthful of blood towards his opponent's feet, and prepared for the fight of his life.

Chapter 37

"Gentlemen - do not move, or we will shoot. Hands in the air … NOW please." The voice came from behind the SS guards.

Bemused, they both turned around to be confronted by the tower guards from the mine entrance, both aiming their rifles directly at them.

"Don't be fucking stupid soldiers. We are interrogating a spy here."

"I said they would claim that, didn't I?"

Manni's voice came from behind them, followed by Manni himself. Johnno relaxed his stance and, joining in the subterfuge, pointed to the tip of the V2. "Look, I found them trying to plant an explosive device on the rocket, we could all be killed."

"He's talking fucking nonsense. HE was the one trying to blow up the missiles, not us, you idiots."

The SS thugs started to walk towards the guards covering them. The guard steadied their stance. "We said do not move or we WILL shoot."

"Take them back to their quarters and I will prove they are the spies that Commander warned you about." Manni gestured towards the entrance to their quarters. "If you are worried keep all of us covered and we will show you these are the two spies you were told to kill on sight." The tower guards were unsure what to do and looked at each other for reassurance.

"Commander Krammler did say there were two spies, perhaps we should shoot all four to be safe."

Manni's voice was indignant. "And kill two officers working directly under orders from the Führer? Do you really want to serve the rest of your on the Eastern Front?"

They again looked at each other for reassurance.

Manni gestured towards their quarters. "Come on, I have proof of their treachery," raising his arms to match the stance of the SS guards. Johnno struggled to keep himself upright, but also raised his arms.

"He is telling the truth, let's check their quarters." Johnno sounded confident but had no idea what Manni's plan actually entailed. He wiped the blood from his mouth again.

"In there, and no tricks," the tower guards gestured with their rifles, "and put your hands on your head." Feeling more confident they continued. "We cannot lose can we? We can kill all four of you in a fire fight if needs be and be hailed as heroes of the 3rd Reich, can't we Heinrich?"

"I suppose so, Klaus."

Max spoke, growling in anger. "You are fucking morons, you WILL end up on the Eastern front, and we will ensure you lead any attacks made there."

Reluctantly the SS guards made their way toward their quarters, preceded by Johnno and Manni, followed closely by the tower guards rifles aimed nervously ahead of them. They entered the room, the guards gesturing for all four suspects to stand by the rear wall.

"Where is your proof soldier?" one of the tower guards addressed Manni.

Manni gestured with his head towards the log pile.

"Look at the logs they have bought in. We have discovered some have been marked with 3 dots on the end for easy identification."

"Cover them, I'll check." one of the guards moved over towards the log pile. After a quick inspection he selected two, lifting them out, looking at his colleague and nodding "He's right, these two are marked as he says."

The SS guards looked baffled. "We haven't done that you idiot, they must have been here before." Max was venomous with anger.

"Now look closely, there is an insert pressed in the end. Prise it out with a knife or something. Here, " Manni lowered one arm and took his penknife from his pocket, passing it to the guard still covering them, "use this."

The guard backed up slowly towards his colleague, keeping his rifle levelled at his four suspects, and passed him the knife.

The second guard placed his rifle against the wall. "Keep them covered Klaus." He placed the log, end down, on the floor. He opened a blade and dug it into the end of the log and tried to turn the supposed insert. To his amazement it began to turn.

"Now lever it out." instructed Manni.

Heinrich looked up towards Manni, and then back to the log, levering the insert free.

"Look inside," Manni shouted enthusiastically, "it's an explosive device they've smuggled in here. They were just waiting for a chance to use it. Now is an ideal time while most of the mine's detachment are missing."

Johnno grinned. What a clever, conniving friend he had in Manni. How could he have doubted him earlier on?

Heinrich pulled out the cylinder, showing it to his colleague.

"He's right, those SS bastards are the spies."

"You fucking idiots. Think what you are doing," SS guard Klaus roared at them, "they are the spies, shoot them."

Both tower guards raised their rifles, aiming them directly at their hated SS guards.

"Come over here soldiers," Johnno and Manni were invited to their side, "while we decide how to deal with these SS vermin." Lowering their arms they joined their new 'allies', the tower guards.

"What do you suggest we do with them?" The tower guards looked towards their two new allies for guidance.

Manni smiled. "I could use a secret Aryan technique to disable them, one that our Führer has discovered himself. We could then try them as spies and they will be shot. You, on the other hand, will get a medal and a promotion from the Führer himself. I know him well. He actually devised our mission here."

Both guards beamed with pride.

Johnno smiled. "Even more of a cheeky bastard"

"Tell them to turn their backs to us." Manni addressed the guards.

"You heard him, turn around and face the wall."

Slowly they turned to face the wall, fearful of the fate that awaited them. Would this be a bullet to the back of the head?

Klaus half turned to face his guards, ranting with anger "You are still fucking idiots. THEY are the spies."

Heinrich, now full of courage and a new found confidence, replied.

"I said turn your backs to us, vermin; we do not want to see your faces."

Manni looked at him and winked. "Well done Heinrich, spoken just like the fuehrer's envoy. Now keep them covered." Both guards stiffened their stance, anticipating the click of a pistol being cocked.

Manni moved towards the guards, deftly removing his neuroliser from his wrist. It was still set from around two hours ago, the setting he used on Krammler. He twisted to his right and made a show of raising his left hand, hovering over the head of his captive. He mumbled several incoherent words then placed his fingers on his neck, apparently squeezing his carotid artery. With his right hand he activated his neuroliser, keeping the beam hidden from view.

Klaus duly sank to the floor, unconscious.

Heinrich's eyes were shut tight, awaiting the inevitable bullet to the head. He heard the groan as his colleague buckled at the knees, chancing to open his eyes as he fell to the floor. His eyes looked questioningly at his captor. His colleague was down, yet no shot was fired. Manni winked at him

The tower guards looked at each other in amazement, beaming smiles on their faces.

"Now for the other SS swine." Heinrich was full of confidence "do it … now."

"Yes, now" echoed Klaus, brimming with the confidence that only a future recipient of the Iron Cross could raise.

Oskar turned to face Manni again.

"Turn your head, or you will die Oskar." He slowly, deliberately, turned his head to face the wall, awaiting the same fate as his colleague.

Realising what Manni had actually done Johnno turned to the guards, beckoning towards Manni "Do you mind if I try this skill taught to me by the Führer himself? Then, perhaps, we could teach you if I'm successful."

"Why certainly Korporal, please be our guest."

Manni grinned. "Please shake my hand my friend and use your powers wisely." The neuroliser was deftly passed between them. Johnno mirrored Manni's actions, mumbling "Hubble bubble, toil and trouble under his breath."

"Ever the showman." thought Manni.

Heinrich sank to the floor. Johnno turned around and took a bow. "Wunderbar, truly wunderbar." Both guards were duly impressed.

Manni gestured to Johnno pointing to his wrist. The returning truck must surely be on their doorstep and about to arrive. Johnno raised his eyes in agreement.

"And now we shall show you the Aryan technique as we said, taught to us by the Führer himself."

Both guards looked like children promised toys on Christmas morning. They looked at each other and grinned.

"What do we do?" Klaus was the first to speak.

"Put your rifles, here, against the wall." Johnno took the weapons and leaned them securely by the door, ever mindful they may be needed for their, as yet, unplanned escape.

"We'll use the SS guards. They may be unconscious but we can inflict further pain on them."

The guards looked at each other, full of the joys of inflicting further pain on the spies they had arrested. "We never did like the high-handed bastards." Manni gestured for them to stand behind the unconscious figures on the floor. Like a pair of schoolchildren they followed instructions, each one standing behind a dormant target.

"You are too high; can you reach down to their necks?"

Klaus tried to reach down by bending at the waist, but rose up again shaking his head.

"Could we kneel behind them?" he asked.

"Brilliant idea Klaus, well deduced." Manni nodded and smiled in agreement, looking like a successful school teacher with his special needs pupils. Both guards took their place directly behind their prey, looking back at Manni for guidance.

"Now place your left hand over their heads, so your hand is touching their necks. OK? Face the wall and concentrate, this is the difficult part."

As they turned their heads towards their victims Manni retrieved his neuroliser from Johnno and checked the settings. Still OK for two hours or so.

"Now repeat after me ... gort says klaatu barada nikto … while gently squeezing their necks."

Both men repeated the phrase, as best they could, in harmony. "Gort says klaatu barada nikto" echoed around the room

"Again my friends, you are nearly there."

Gort says klaatu barada nikto," was spoken in reverential tones, echoing once more around the room .

Johnno was smiling as he looked towards Manni. He shook his head in mock disbelief.

Manni fired twice and both guards slumped to the floor.

"At least the SS bastards broke their fall."

"The greatest sci-fi film of all time?" posed Johnno

"This has a real ring of truth," replied Manni, smiling, "just ask Gort if you don't believe me." He grabbed Johnno by the arm "Now to get out of here – fast."

"What took you so long to get the guards?"

"I heard the commotion and realised that I had to plant the evidence first, sorry to worry you."

They headed for the door. "Do we need these?" Johnno pointed at the rifles.

"No, we have rockets to disable and a weapon to deliver, but we could …. " Manni unclipped the magazines from each weapon, and used the bolt action to remove the live round. He dropped the useless weapons on the ground. "We don't want them shooting each other, do we?" Johnno nodded and approached the SS guards. He pulled them over to their left side, searching for a weapon. Each had a Walther pistol in a holster. He removed both, released the magazine clips and removed the live rounds.

They took one last look behind them. The unconscious guards were away from any danger. There were no weapons to tempt them when they awoke. All they had in their defence was a magical Aryan charm as a means of backing up their stories. They exited the room, closing the heavy wooden door behind them. Manni took out his laser style pen and welded the hinges and lock just as he had done with the laboratory door.

Keeping cover behind the trucks they moved cautiously back towards the rockets, fearful of the imminent arrival of the returning soldiers.

Johnno climbed up onto the bonnet of the truck once more. As he reached the nose cone he saw his neuroliser was still safely in place. Manni climbed up alongside him. "Just checking where it goes my friend I see, as near to the tip as possible. Wait here. I'll go ahead and attach mine."

Johnno smiled. "Wait here? What else could I do?" He looked down at the rocket from his high vantage point. This was a messenger of death, but it was still a thing of beauty and simplicity.

How could such a weapon of war be built? Whose twisted mind devised such a killing machine? Sadly it was the very same person who was responsible for him being here today, Werner Von Braun. The same person responsible for the Saturn rockets, the Gemini program and the Apollo program that he himself wanted desperately to be a part of.

Why does it so often take conflict to progress?

His thoughts were interrupted by the sound of a whistle in the distance.

Manni was atop the second rocket with his neuroliser securely fastened in place.

"We must time this well my friend." Manni's voice echoed in the still air of the mine.

"Ready when you are."

"Right, turn the dial counter clockwise as far as it will go."

Johnno's concentration returned to the job in hand. He gripped the dial and turned until it clicked and would turn no more. "That's done. Remind me what's next."

"We are looking for an almost immediate action, just minutes at most. But we need to find cover should anything go wrong." Johnno nodded. He looked behind him back into the mine. There was an empty trailer to pass and, perhaps, fifty yards or so to the relative safety of the western exit tunnel.

"Two minutes should be enough, will it set that low?"

"No problem. See the centre of the dial; it should now be glowing red as a warning."

Focussing his tired eyes on the dial took a while. He was still hurting from the kicks he received in his fight with Oskar. Eventually he saw a red glow in the centre. "Got it."

"Now each press on the centre, above the red light, adds one ces, sorry, around thirty of your seconds to the timer. So we need four presses. OK?"

"Affirmative."

"Before we start we need to synchronise our presses, OK?"

"Affirmative"

"I'll count down from five, then give it four presses. Here we go partner."

"Affirmative."

"Five, four, three, two, one ... Press one, Press two, Press three, Press four and go!"

Manni climbed off the truck bonnet and made his way towards Johnno and the rear of the mine, and safety. Johnno slid off the truck bonnet and fell to the floor. His legs buckled underneath him, the boot to his ribs obviously causing more damage than he had realised. He was struggling to breathe. He was struggling to get to his feet.

As Manni approached the exit tunnel he turned to see if Johnno had caught up with him, but he was nowhere to be seen. Desperation began to set in. The charges were set, he had no time to return and stop them. "Where are you? You must get here my friend, now!"

In the semi darkness he saw a figure struggling to get to his feet as he passed the empty truck. Johnno was obviously in trouble.

Without a thought for his own safety Manni rushed back to the crumpled figure.

"Leave me, I'm struggling to breathe."

"Leave you, and face the wrath of Freya, no way my friend."

Manni crouched down, took Johnno's arm and placed it across his shoulder. "Come on my friend, not far to go."

He lifted Johnno to his feet, supporting him as best he could. Somehow they struggled back to the western exit, collapsing in a neat heap behind the cave wall. And not a moment too soon.

The charges went off almost simultaneously.

The cave was filled with a series of electrical discharges, very much like mini lightning bolts. The air was filled with a smell of ozone. The whole cave complex seemed to shake as if hit by a mini earthquake. Small rocks and shingle fell freely from the mine's roof and walls, some falling on our prone figures. A choking dust rushed out from the Western exit, covering everything in a fine layer of dust.

Eventually all was calm and quiet again, save for the occasional noise of falling shingle somewhere in the depths of the mine. Both men were covered in dust. Manni was the first to get up, shaking his clothes free from the yellow dust that had engulfed them. He coughed several times, compounding it with a sneeze.

"I guess it worked," peering back at the missiles which, thankfully, had not exploded. One unforeseen problem was the damage to the lighting. Several lights had also blown putting the mine into a dangerously dark state.

Johnno struggled to his feet, leaning against the cave wall for support. "Freya told me never to play with fireworks, and, boy was she right."

"Stay here my friend, I'll go back and see if we were successful." Manni disappeared back towards the trucks and their missiles, the dust now settling making it slightly easier to see where he was going. Deftly he climbed onto the first truck and examined the nose cone. The neuroliser was still attached, but now obviously 'dead'. No lights were visible on the controls, it most certainly had used an EMF to fry it's circuits and, hopefully, those within the rocket. He removed it and examined it closely. He was amazed at the engineering obviously used in its construction. It looked undamaged, yet its circuits were obviously beyond repair and it was now useless.

"That's a testament to engineers back on Mintaka."

On checking the second rocket he found the neuroliser there with the same result, obviously 'dead' but seemingly undamaged. As he placed this into his tunic pocket alongside the first one a thought flashed through his mind. "Best keep these for security, alien technology and all that. I may even be able to use these somewhere in the future." He touched his earpiece and spoke. "Well that seems to have worked. Let's pray that these weapons land as scrap metal. Heil Hitler." He jumped down from the truck, glancing back towards the mine entrance as he made his way back to the exit. There was still no sign of any soldiers arriving. "So far, so good."

The floor of the mine was covered in a fine layer of dust, leaving footprints as he made his way back to the Western exit and safety. Small stones crunched beneath his feet, reminding him of the shingle beaches on his home planet where he would play as a child. He thought of Astrild. Perhaps he should contact her.

"Are you there Astrild? Can you hear me?"

Static was the only sound he heard

"The charge probably disturbed reception," he thought to himself, "I'll contact her when we're safely through the Western exit."

Eventually, through the semi darkness he saw Johnno leaning against the cave wall, brushing the dust from his hair and trying his best to stay upright.

"We did it my friend, we did it. The rockets did not explode and I have good reason to believe that the circuits are fried just as we had hoped."

Johnno's face seemed full of despair and disappointment.

"What is wrong my friend? The Bells are destroyed, the rockets are useless and we have the weapon safely on your person." He looked quizzically at his friend "We DO have the weapon safe, don't we?"

"Yes, that's no problem, but I believe this might be a problem, " pointing behind him towards the cave exit. Manni stepped to one side to look.

It was full to the ceiling with rocks and boulders. Manni's shoulders visibly dropped. "It was the vibrations. It must have been the vibrations. I never considered that. I am so sorry my friend. I should have known better."

Johnno slid to the floor, putting his hands on his knees he rested against the cave wall. "So near, and yet so far."

In the distance they heard the sound of trucks approaching the mine entrance.

Johnno looked up at Manni "This just gets better and better. We should have left when we had the chance."

"No, my friend, we did what was right. Now we need a miracle, but miracles can, and do happen."

Chapter 38

From within the dark woodland track the returning truck saw the guard towers come into view as its headlights hit home. A rising pall of dust was flowing out of the mine entrance, sparsely lit by the reduced lighting inside.

Franz Neumann was coaxing his truck to arrive safely home, having no spare tyre should there be another incident. He peered into the distance and brought his truck to a grinding halt. The dust rising from the mine entrance gave an eerie look to the scene, the dim lights highlighting the yellow, almost luminous, fog.

"Commander Krammler was right. There has been an incursion, no guards appear to be posted on the towers. We must proceed with the utmost care."

Some five minutes or so earlier the truck had been flagged down by the commander as the truck neared home. He had approached the truck from the direction of the henge, flagging it down using a torch in either hand. Neumann slowed the truck to a steady stop, leapt from the cab and saluted his commanding officer.

"Are you alright sir, you look unsteady on your feet."

Krammler did his best to feign fatigue, speaking as though he was struggling to breathe.

"I'm fine now soldier but proceed with care; there has been an attack on the mine and I'm sure I heard explosions. I just managed to escape through the laboratory exits."

Neumann turned to re-enter his cab, grabbing the door to help him step up into his seat.

"Do not go just yet, I fear there may be more explosives set to detonate. Your lives are in peril. Wait for five minutes or so just to be safe."

Inside the truck the soldiers were straining to hear the conversation. "There has been an attack and explosions; it appears that the Commander may be the only survivor." "Polish bastards, the slaves must have somehow done this. Let's teach them a lesson they never forget." The sound of rifle bolts and machine guns being primed for use reverberated through the still night air.

"Can we help you sir?" Neumann had jumped back down from his cab and was concerned about his superior officer. "Do you wish to return with us at your back? Just say the word and we're with you." He snapped to attention.

"Thank you soldier, I wish the 3rd Reich had many more like you."

Neumann's back stiffened even more in pride.

"No. I shall re-enter by the henge and the laboratories, I may be of more use if I can help you with a simple pincer movement. Do you have a spare weapon I can use?"

"MP40 for the Commander – NOW." Neumann barked out the order.

Korporal Weber jumped from the rear of the truck and ran around to his superior officer, proffering his machine gun.

"Sir." he barked.

"Thank you Korporal. I shall put it to good use."

"Shall I contact Gruppenführer Musfelldt with an update?"

"No need Korporal, I have already informed them and they are on their way back. I trust you will have flushed out the insurgents before your Gruppenführer returns with his detachment."

"Yes sir, we are all determined not to let you down, aren't we men?" The rear of the truck erupted with sound as every soldier showed their support.

"How many men do you need sir? We have several aces in our troop."

"None- thank you. If I can flush them out from the rear with gunfire you should be able to trap them as they try to escape. Set up a crossfire. Now wait here for five minutes whilst I get into position; then give them hell."

Neumann and Weber both saluted. "Good luck sir, we wish the 3rd Reich had more officers as brave and dedicated as you sir. We will follow you anywhere." Neumann was excellent at using 'bullshit' to further his career.

Krammler smiled, acknowledging their praise. "Thank you soldiers. Now go, do your duty for the Fatherland." He turned and retreated down the path leading to the henge, keeping low in order to present a smaller target. As he turned the corner, out of sight of the truck, he stopped and hid behind a bush. After three or four minutes he heard the truck restart, slowly making its way towards the mine entrance and its compound, its dimmed headlights picking out the pine trees that lined the road, giving them an ethereal look.

Krammler smiled and stepped out from behind the bush. "I knew they couldn't wait. Idiots."

He maintained his position as he watched the truck lights disappear into the distance, its diesel engine throbbing into eventual silence. Stepping forward he checked again to ensure they had gone out of sight.

He blinked his eyes.

Eyes as smooth and as black as haematite.

Chapter 39

Neumann slowly edged the truck forwards towards the gates to the mine, anxiously peering in the semi darkness for any signs of life. It rolled to a gentle halt.

In the rear of the truck the soldiers began to quietly exit , keeping a quiet, conscious lookout for signs of an ambush. Neumann exited his cab and moved around to the rear of the truck to join his colleagues where they assembled as a fighting troop.

"We need to wait for a sign from the Commander as he drives any potential enemy rebels towards us." Feldwebel Bauer, a battle hardened veteran had taken charge. He was the troop's lucky mascot, having fought successfully at Sedan in 1940, defeating partisans and the British in Crete in 1941, the second battle of Kharkov in 1942. He exuded confidence and was very much a father figure, supporting and cajoling his younger squad members in pursuit of excellence. His presence within this top secret project was seen as both a reward for his devotion to duty as well as his ability to thrive under pressure.

His troop listened eagerly for instructions; instructions that could lead to success, and a well -earned rest at home with much loved and much missed families.

"Neumann, take three men and move to the left side of the guard tower. Bergmann, you take your three to the right, and keep low, no sense in providing an easy target. I'll take centre ground with my group. When anyone exits the entrance just wait for my word and we can cut them down before they reach any cover. Understood? "

The soldiers kept low and stealthily moved into position, keeping their weapons aimed at the mine entrance. As the dust was now settling the lights left undamaged by the electrical charges provided just enough light to illuminate several feet at the entrance.

Bauer leaned into the cab and turned out the lights, he didn't want any un-necessary evidence of their presence as they waited outside. He took a last look to his troops on both sides, gesturing for them to keep as low as possible. He then settled himself down, waiting for the imminent signal, probably gunfire, from within the mine which would result in a victorious gunfight. He could almost smell his wife's perfume, and see joy on his children's faces as he scooped them up in his arms.

He could even hear them calling "Papa" as he entered the door.

Chapter 40

Deep within the mine, by the blocked western exit, Johnno was finding it harder to get his breath, propped up against the cave wall, as the pain in his ribs seemed to get worse by the minute. Every breath causing a severe pain deep within his chest. His breathing was becoming more laboured as he felt as if a knife was stabbing him each time he breathed in. He was close to passing out with the pain.

Manni was talking via his ear piece, telling Rick and his team waiting outside of their predicament. "The exit is blocked, mostly rubble. We need rockphaser. I repeat, we need rockphaser – NOW please. We believe the enemy is about to enter the mine and time is of the essence."

"Understood. We should be 'live' in five minutes or so."

Outside the collapsed exit Rick was aware of the situation and had already considered rockphaser. As he organised his partisan force and prepared to return to the cabin he heard a familiar voice behind him.

"I believe this might help." He turned to face the approaching figure, instinctively raising his weapon to face the direction of the voice. From out of the darkness a figure approached. Rick shone a torch, picking out the body at first, and then highlighting the face. It was Freya, carrying a canvas style bag over her shoulder. It was around four feet in length, and quite bulky, though it seemed to have little weight to it.

Rick's face lit up. "Boy are we glad to see you, we feared the worst."

"Sorry I've been out of touch, I had to delay the returning birthday boy after he discovered you had become a party pooper."

Rick grinned. "That was one party I was only too glad to miss. But, how did you know about rockphaser? I've only just found out."

Freya smiled. "It was just anticipation. I bought this down from the cabin last week and hid it in the undergrowth, just in case. Knowing the geology of this area, and the problems enlarging the mine I … "

Rick cut in. ".. Am always ready for anything." eagerly reaching over as Freya passed him the shoulder bag. "Is it charged?"

"Fully charged, and ready to go."

Rick opened the bag and began assembly of the rockphaser.

Inside the mine Manni gestured to his colleague. "Open your jacket and let me see your injuries."

"Do we have time for this?"

"Yes, plenty …. I think." Manni did his best to sound confident.

Johnno undid his tunic, displaying a dusty, dirty shirt underneath. Manni began to feel Johnno's ribs. All went well until he pressed low on the right hand side, causing his patient to wince with pain. "Ah, that's the problem."

"No shit, doctor." Johnno tried his best to smile as he fought the immediate pain.

"We can fix that for now. One broken rib, no bleeding, just pain."

"Well noted doctor, stating the obvious." Johnno's demeanour changed. "Sorry I let you down."

"You haven't, and all I need is my standard field kit."

Manni reached inside his shirt by his waist and pulled out a small pouch attached to a belt which had been placed around his waist, underneath his clothing.

"So that's where you keep your money."

"Amongst other things." Manni by slid his fingers along the top opening the pouch. Reaching inside he pulled out a small, pre-packed field dressing. His first action was to squeeze the sealed pack between his fingers, ensuring every part of the package had been squashed.

"Pull up your shirt." Johnno did so, with some discomfort as it was tucked in beneath his waist band. The lower right side was red and inflamed and showing signs of bruising already. Manni opened the dressing pack, tearing off a strip which had sealed it in its sterile pack. Leaning over, he adopted his best doctor's approach, to place the dressing on Johnno's inflamed rib cage. "This will hurt … " Johnno winced as Manni firmly applied the dressing, "… for ten seconds or so, then you will see how good a doctor I really am."

Johnno slumped back against the cave wall. The pain was intense but within seconds he felt it subsiding. It was as if a magic cloth was wiping his rib cage and washing away the pain. He could breathe easily again.

"Better?"

"How the hell did you do that? I feel … normal, no, in fact I feel great."

"Pain is sent by electrical nerve impulses to your brain. The dressing merely switches off those impulses. You weren't bleeding so it was quite easy."

Johnno struggled to get back to his feet, tucking his shirt back into his trousers, marvelling at his pain relief with a simple dressing. Then reality returned. In the distance the sound of electrical discharges continued to break the silence. A strong smell of ozone permeated throughout the semi darkness, made all the more noticeable as the dust had all but settled leaving a fine layer all over the mine floor.

"But we are still stuck down here with a returning garrison about to enter the mine and wipe us out."

"You still have the weapon secure?"

Johnno felt inside his shirt and, to his horror, it had disappeared. He looked again – no joy. He began to panic and began to search all around him on the floor for the weapon, his only real reason to be here.

"Shit, it's gone. Where the fuck have I dropped it?" His voice was full of anger and despair. "It could be anywhere."

Manni tried to sound confident and reassure his friend. "You had it when we left the laboratory, right?"

He cast his mind back. He remembered consciously feeling for it as they left the laboratory, ostensibly to escape from the mine. "Yes, I'm sure I did."

"So it is either here or somewhere near the rockets. You look around here and I'll go back and look. Be methodical, do not panic. We WILL find it." Although inside Manni was panicking, if only a little.

"Let's hope I haven't welded the door shut and locked it in the guard room," he mumbled under his breath as he made his way back to the trucks.

Johnno was searching frantically on the floor of the mine when a voice came through his ear piece. "Freya here, are you both safe?"

For Johnno this was the voice of an angel. "Freya, you're alive, we were worried to death about you."

"I've been busy and I'm here with Rick. We're hoping to get you out soon. Is the weapon safe?"

"Well yes … and no. It is no longer in the Bell, but we have been in a fight and, well, we cannot locate it at the present, but I'm sure we will." He was crossing his fingers as he spoke.

"You have destroyed both Bells and damaged the third in progress, which is excellent. But you MUST find the weapon. That is the main reason for you mission."

Johnno was crestfallen, how could he let down his beloved Freya? How could he have been so stupid and lose the one thing that mattered most with his mission. A thought crossed his mind.

"Freya, I could use a spare pair of eyes. Can you view the mine through my lenses and help me look?"

There was a pause of several seconds. "Sorry, I can only see the dust and some static."

Johnno resigned himself to the fact he had failed on his mission.

From the semi-darkness a figure approached. Johnno felt on his wrist for his neuroliser, only to realise he no longer had it. He looked around for a rock, anything he could fight back with if necessary.

"It's me, Manni." A familiar figure approached a huge grin on his face, and waving the missing weapon in his right arm. Johnno ran and grabbed his friend in a mighty bear hug. "You son of a gun. Where was it?"

Manni was full of emotion. Beaming with success he grabbed Johnno by his shoulders, his face so full of a smile it was all Johnno could see of his friend.

"Your fight with the SS ape, when you were kicked. I thought that was when you may have lost it and I was right. It was on the floor and had been pushed underneath the front of the truck. Here," he proffered the weapon to his, now ecstatic, friend.

Johnno took the weapon and kissed it for luck.

"Manni, my friend, you have saved my life, and my sanity."

Manni smiled and nodded. "My friend I hope we have saved many, many lives. Now keep it safe."

Johnno placed it back within his shirt, ensuring he had fastened as many buttons as he could. He then made a point of fastening his tunic buttons, finally checking it was safely stored by patting his chest where the weapon was located. He instinctively grabbed Manni with a man-hug. He couldn't speak, but tears filled his eyes, leaving dust trails on his cheeks.

Manni stepped back from the hug, looked him in the face and smiled. "I know my friend, I know. Now for that miracle."

Outside of the collapsed west exit Rick had been busy. He unpacked the canvas bag to reveal a collection of components, each with the metallic look of aluminium or titanium. Carefully locating each component part he expertly began the process of assembly. Three legs were located within a circular ring, creating a tripod mounting, around eighteen inches in height, and with a span of three feet or so. Next he took out a mounting plate, clicking it into place on the top of the circular ring. Then came what looked like a long tubular gun barrel, some six inches or so in diameter, into which he located two rear components, quadrant shaped, creating a double handled grip to the rear. His final act was to remove a container which had the look of a thermos flask.

Donning a pair of gloves which came with the package he slowly unscrewed the lid of the flask and took out what looked like a glass rod. It's glowing green iridescence lighting up, and reflecting from, his face.

The three resistance fighters who had volunteered to help rescue Rick's colleagues were watching intently. They had seen nothing like this before and were completely intrigued as Rick went through his assembly routine. As they became bathed in the green glow from the rod they examined their clothing as small specks of light seemed to dance around them.

Rick then lifted open a small hinged flap at the rear of the barrel, where he inserted the glowing green rod. He clicked the hinge shut, the darkness returned and Rick breathed a sigh of relief. He turned to his partisan support. "The battery."

All three smiled and nodded as they heard a word that they recognised.

Freya patted him on the shoulder. "Well done, how long do we need to wait?"

Rick turned to Freya and spoke with a slight hesitancy.

"The usual, three or four minutes. Let's hope that is fast enough."

He tapped his earpiece in the hope of gaining a better reception and faced the collapsed entrance, hopefully his colleague's exit.

"Manni, please get ready for rockphaser. Do you hear? Get ready for rockphaser. About to charge and fire."

"We're ready when you are, please hurry, the enemy is literally at the front door, and I bet they're pissed off at losing their furlough."

Johnno was baffled. He realised that it would take hours to painstakingly remove the rubble from within the collapsed exit tunnel, hours they did not have. He strained his ears listening for any approaching German soldiers, who were intent on wreaking revenge for the destruction of the Bell and the loss of their leave. He was concerned that, in order to save their lives and deliver the weapon, they may have to return fire on any advancing enemy.

What weapons would they use?

He still had a pistol, but they would be coming with machine guns and grenades.

No-one had informed **them** about the Federation and its rules. To come so far and be so close to success, and then be killed seemed meaningless. He couldn't 'make any more time' to change this situation. His days of flying the Bells was over.

"Firing , Manni."

Johnno heard the words in his earpiece at the same time as Manni. He glanced at his friend with a questioning look. What the hell did 'firing' mean? Manni held his friend by the arm, gently urging him back away from the inner entrance. "We need to move away my friend, and by several feet."

He did as he was told, still wondering what was happening, glancing behind him as he did so. Outside the mine Rick had donned a pair of glasses which housed dark red lenses. "Turn away please Freya." He then turned to his three partisans, speaking and gesturing for them to look away as best he could. They were a little baffled why, but duly did so when Freya did so.

His major concern was in not letting them actually see his rockphaser in action, Alien technology and all that.

The two triggers located in the rear quadrants at the rear of the barrel were gently pressed. There followed a high pitched whirring noise, immediately followed by a circular ring of light emanating from the front of the cylinder. As it met the rubble in the collapsed exit it highlighted a ring of around three feet in diameter.

"Not quite large enough for a quick exit." Rick adjusted a dial at the rear, expanding the ring annulus to around six feet in diameter. "Much better... Firing full charge Manni...Homing in on your radio frequency...

NOW."

Rick pushed the triggers in to their full extent and the circular imprint began to glow even brighter. As it did so the rocks and rubble began to disintegrate and disappear. Slowly, steadily it moved deeper into the blocked tunnel, removing rubble and original cave sides as it went, the only visible sign of the rock disappearing was a white vapour, it was as if steam was being used to cut through rock.

Inside the mine Johnno was still baffled. He looked towards Manni sat with an inane grin on his face. "That miracle you wished for, my friend, is on the way."

Johnno turned to the sound of rubble falling. He strained his eyes to see the opening to the western exit suddenly appear in front of his eyes.

"There, my friend, is your miracle."

Johnno looked stunned. He gingerly moved forward to the tunnel entrance, feeling the cave walls where they had been cut by the rockphaser. He then moved and felt the other side, turning to Manni in wonderment.

"They're smooth, as smooth as glass. How ... What ... I don't."

"I'll explain later, we need to move, and fast. You go ahead and I'll follow."

Johnno rushed forward towards the new exit, he didn't really have to crouch a great deal as the tunnel was quite tall. As he disappeared further in the tunnel it became darker, harder to discern a safe path, and he slowed his pace down. "No point in breaking my neck now."

It took around a minute to exit the mine, but it seemed like a lifetime in the darkness.

Then …

He could smell fresh air.

He could smell the dampness of a pine forest.

He could smell safety!

As he left the confines of the cave he stopped, rubbing his eyes gently as they became accustomed to the lack of light in the chill night air.

"Hey buddy." It was Rick's voice. He turned to face it and saw a dark figure which he instinctively knew was his best friend. He rushed towards him, almost tripping over the tripod stand of the rockphaser. They hugged as only best friends could, Johnno pulling his head back to see his friend's face. "It's good to see you my friend, thanks for saving my life."

Rick smiled, talking through tears of joy. "And thank you for creating the time needed to save mine."

"What about me?" Another voice emanated from the darkness. It was Freya's turn for a reunion.

Johnno gave Rick one last pat on the back and moved over to his beloved Freya. As he went to hug and kiss her they bumped heads. "Don't knock me out now," she whispered, "it's been a long journey to this point. Well done my little soldier." Johnno stood back and looked deep in thought for a moment, lost in this moment in time. As he stood trying to make sense of everything their reunion was cut short by Manni's arrival.

"We need to move, quite quickly in fact. I've set the charges to block this exit again, and we have just two minutes or so to move on."

Rick signalled to his partisans, asking them to pick up the rock phaser.

He collected the canvas bag as two of the partisans lifted the rockphaser and hurriedly began to leave.

It was difficult to move quickly and safely through the woods, their only source of light being the moon, though almost full there were still many dark areas and roots they could easily fall over. They dare not use torches until they were well clear of the mine for fear of being discovered. They were around two hundred yards from the exit when the first charge exploded, quickly followed by a second. Manni looked back but could see little in the darkness. A look of satisfaction crept slowly across his face. They were out. They were safe, at least for the time being, and they were on the road to completing their mission.

"Stop here and dismantle the rockphaser, we should be safe and out of sight by now." Rick was keen to safely store the weapon of salvation.

Johnno looked back to see if any lights were visible, evidence of anyone following in their tracks, but all was clear. Manni moved to help dismantle and stow the weapon, showing the partisan helpers how it came apart and was stored in the canvas style bag.

Johnno couldn't wait any longer; he had to know about this latest piece of alien kit. "How the hell does this thing work? I mean, it melted rock for Christ sake."

"A question too far my friend, it would take too long to explain how it works and vapourises solid rock. When you get back home check your history. The Egyptians and their sarcophagi, the stones at Baalbek, Peruvian stone walls, and I can go on. How do you think Geronimo managed to evade capture in Arizona for years?"

"So you've been here before," came the jovial reply from Johnno.

"Many times my friend, many times. We look after our own."

Their conversation was cut short. "The weapon is packed, we need to move back to the safety of the cabin." Manni's voice had more than a hint of urgency in it.

"You lead the way Rick," Freya stepped to one side, "and I'll keep a lookout for anyone following".

At last it seemed safe enough to use torches. Rick opened his rucksack and passed a small torch to each one present. Johnno examined it closely but couldn't find the switch. Rick leaned over and touched the base, the torch immediately coming to life. "It's a touch control. One turns on, two touches brighter, three touches off. OK?"

The partisans had been watching closely, each turning on their torches with the resultant pool of light highlighting the way ahead. Rick turned towards them. "Listen, my friends, it is better if you move back to your homes for safety. There will be many Germans checking the local villages looking for an excuse to arrest and kill anyone who may have helped us tonight. You must think of yourself and your families now." They looked at each other and acknowledged that this was good advice.

"Let us know if we can help you again. Anything we can do to make these oppressive bastards leave our land, you just let us know." All three seemed fervent in their desires for peace, and nodded in agreement.

Rick smiled and took his hand. "It is our pleasure and duty to help you. But please, you must keep all details of tonight's operation a secret, it should help save lives and shorten this terrible war."

"It is our secret, we shall tell no-one."

There was a round of handshakes and well wishes and the trio departed, the lights from their torches slowly blending in with the night and its shadows and all was quiet again.

"What about their torches, alien technology and all that?" Johnno voiced his concerns.

"They are using a rechargeable system powering special light diodes. Once their cells have discharged they have no way to charge them. They will just be discarded as useless."

"Right, let's make our way back home." Manni turned to lead the way, his torch highlighting the way ahead.

Johnno glanced back at Freya. She smiled and waved back, then gestured for them to go ahead. "I have things to attend to. Go in safety and I'll meet up with you soon."

"The final steps buddy, the final steps." Rick's voice reflected the success of their mission to date.

Johnno smiled "It's a long way from Groom Lake old friend, let's hope we can soon return and have another cool beer on the 375."

"I'll drink to that buddy, I'll drink to that."

Chapter 41

At the front of the mine Bauer was becoming impatient. Glancing at his watch, the luminous fingers told him that they had been waiting almost fifteen minutes. He tapped the dial to check it was working properly. He realised it was a dumb move as his watch had never failed him. He looked to both sides, shrugging his shoulders to show that he was as baffled as they were, waiting so long for the signal from their Commander.

Suddenly from inside of the mine came the sound of an explosion, muffled slightly as it came from the depths. A pall of dust blew. Then there came another. More dust blew out from the mine entrance.

"Commander Krammler's signal at last."

Bauer pulled back the bolt on his machine gun and slowly got to his feet. "Right men, this could be it, be ready to open fire as soon as you see anyone, and I mean anyone, trying to escape." From all around him came the sound of rifles and machine guns being cocked ready for firing.

Suddenly, from behind them, came a distant sound of engines approaching. Bauer turned his head in the direction of the sound and gestured for his men to keep quiet.

"Are they behind us Korporal?" one of his troops cautiously, nervously, asked.

"I'm not sure, we'll take no chances." He signalled to the soldiers on both flanks to stay down. Pointing his two fingers to his eyes, and then towards the mine entrance.

"With me." He stood up and started to move towards the rear of the truck, his troop at his heels. He listened again; the vehicles were coming along the track they had used. He motioned for his men to crouch down, and they aimed their weapons towards the oncoming noise.

"On my command."

The engine noise grew louder. "Stupid bastards. Drive into my trap, why don't you?" He was looking forward to killing local partisans for target practice. "Dumb Polskies, they never learn." As the vehicles came into sight the soldiers raised their weapons ready to fire.

Standing up in the approaching Kubelwagen was Gruppenführer Musfelldt himself, looking as arrogant as a conquering hero returning to the scene of his latest success.

"Hold your fire." Bauer shouted as loud as he could and getting to his feet "Hold your fire, they're ours."

The Kubelwagen swung around by the side of the truck. Bauer rushed to his commander, standing to a stiff salute. His small troop echoed his movement.

"Situation report Feldwebel." barked Musfelldt. A soldier rushed around to open the door, allowing his commander to exit. "I trust the assailants are all dead by now."

Bauer's heart sank. He was used to success but had yet to taste it here. "We have them surrounded sir. Once they leave the mine we shall have them"

"How many are there inside Feldwebel?"

This was going from bad to worse.

"We're not sure sir"

"Not sure! Not good enough."

Desperately trying to salvage his position, especially in front of the troops he had been leading to a supposed easy victory, he offered. "We did save Commander Krammler sir. He has re-entered through the henge area and is presently flushing out the enemy." Musfelldt whacked the side of his boots with his riding crop and looked deep in thought. "Krammler, you say. Who was with him?"

"No one, sir, and he refused our help. He went back in alone."

Musfelldt strode purposefully, menacingly, towards Bauer, tapping him on his shoulder with his crop. Bauer swallowed hard, trying to ignore the closeness of his commanding officer, straining every sinew to remain the calm and composed soldier he believed himself to be.

"And just how long ago was this, Feldwebel Bauer?" Musfelldt had lowered the tone of his voice, but sounded both officious and threatening at the same time.

"Around twenty minutes or so, sir."

Musfelldt stepped back and raised the stakes by raising his voice. "Twenty minutes! You have waited twenty minutes while the enemy has possibly escaped, or even set traps for us when we enter. What kind of a soldier are you? - you idiot. Get in there, now, and you will lead from the front."

"Yes sir." he snapped to attention. Concerned that he had lost the confidence of his men he turned and began to run towards the mine. His experience told him he could be running straight into a trap. It may be crossfire, it could be explosives left as booby traps, but he was determined to regain the respect of his men, and of his Gruppenführer.

"Behind me men and shoot on sight." The troops all rose to their feet and fell in behind their sergeant.

Gruppenführer Musfelldt, in his wisdom and desire for self-preservation, waited outside of the mine. After several minutes Bauer appeared at the mine entrance, walking confidently towards Musfelldt.

"All clear, … sir."

"I heard no shots."

"There is no-one in there, sir. Everyone has disappeared. Even the guards we left on duty."

"Well, let's find them sergeant. This isn't science fiction, they can't just disappear."

Musfelldt signalled to the three armed guards in his Kubelwagen to follow. "Guard my rear, we don't want surprise attacks." They marched into the mine, passing the trucks laden with the V2 rockets. A soldier appeared from behind the trucks, which were being examined for signs of sabotage "No damage that we can see, sir."

A second soldier appeared from between the trucks. "The SS guard room sir. We can't get in sir. It's, well, it's welded shut."

Musfelldt turned to Schultz. "Well, Bauer?" Bauer turned to one of his troop. "Get me a sledgehammer, I'll open it," desperately hoping that it wasn't booby trapped. There were plenty of sledgehammers lying around and one was quickly passed to him..

"Stand back everyone, it may be booby trapped."

Musfelldt was the first to move, standing behind the body of a truck. His colleagues sought what shelter they could.

Having located the welds the Korporal was convinced he could break through them. He swung the hammer, aiming directly at the latch lock first and then the hinges. After seven or eight mighty swings, which just about robbed him of all his strength, the door finally came loose. Still desperate to regain the confidence of his leader and his men he ordered them to stay back. He swung the door open tentatively, eagerly searching for any signs of trip wires. Once assured he was clear he opened the door.

"All clear sir." Musfelldt rushed around in the hope of finding his enemy trapped. As they entered the room they saw the four guards lying flat out on the floor.

"Are they dead ?"

Bauer felt their necks, looking for signs of life. Each had a faint pulse.

"They're still alive sir, just."

"Good, they can walk to the stockade when they wake up and answer for their stupidity."

As they exited back into the mine a soldier ran over to them, pointing back towards the laboratory door. "The door to the laboratory, that is welded shut also, we can't get in."

Bauer followed Musfelldt towards the lab door, picking up his discarded sledgehammer on the way. He swiftly repeated the successful process in removing the welded door to the laboratory, confident that it would not be booby trapped. He did, however, make a performance of demanding that everyone stay back while he checked for explosives, thus, apparently risking his life again.

Musfelldt pushed past him as he finally opened the door. His heart sank when he saw that the first Bell was missing. Perhaps it had been moved to safety? He rushed through the passageway into the laboratory next door, to be confronted by a second empty space. He was now fearful of the punishment that his Führer would impart, especially after his reassuring phone call made just a couple of days before. He made his way towards the final, unfinished, Bell. This was to be made available as a gift for his Führer, his final chance to ingratiate himself into the Führer's inner circle.

He found his way blocked. The door was locked. Were the assailants still inside? He decided to call their bluff. He drew his Luger from its holder. Bauer was stood directly behind him, and was gestured to move forwards towards the door. Once he was safely behind his sergeant he announced, with great authority in his voice.

"It is Gruppenführer Musfelldt here. We have you surrounded. I have soldiers inside the mine and outside by the henge covering all the exits. Surrender now and I will spare your life."

Silence.

He raised his voice to its full tone of authority in an endeavour to be as threatening as he could be. "I repeat, it is Gruppenführer Musfelldt here. We have you surrounded. I have soldiers inside the mine and outside by the henge covering all the exits. Surrender now and I will spare your life."

Ten seconds or so passed slowly. Then a feeble voice came from behind the door. "I also have a gun, and a bomb. How do I know it is you and not the spies who stole my prized Bell?"

Musfelldt stood back from the door, just in case. "Professor Muller, Maximilian, we spoke just the other day to you about the progress on the Bell. Remember? Is Professor Wagner with you? I appointed him also."

"No. I haven't seen Wilhelm since Gruppenführer Musfelldt left for Krakow."

"And the Commander, have you seen him lately?"

"Not since he left me to go for help."

Bauer stepped forward. "He told us less than thirty minutes ago that he was coming back to the laboratory to flush out the spies. Is he not there?"

"No, I am all alone," then, realising he may have weakened his position, adding "but I do have a big gun and a bomb by the door."

Musfelldt took another step backwards, but kept his Luger aimed towards the door and the voice. The tone of his voice changed. "Maximilian, if that bomb goes off it will kill you as well, and destroy your work of art, Die Glöcke. We could easily have rushed you from behind, but we need you and Die Glöcke safe. Remember, the Führer is depending on you personally to create his Wunderwaffe."

Muller weighed up his options. They could have rushed him from the henge side.

He **does** want to finish his final masterpiece.

The voices don't sound like those he heard from the two earlier attackers.

Plus, he didn't really want to die. "Death is for heroes, I am a scientist."

After seconds that seemed to last forever he gave his answer.

"OK. I shall open the door but I shall keep my hand on the trigger for the bomb." He realised the stupidity of that remark, but believed it would give him the edge if they were really the enemy. From behind the door the metallic sound of a large metal drum could be heard as it was rolled away from the door. Muller turned the key in the door and stepped back as quickly as he could, still aiming his purloined Luger at the door.

"We're coming in Maximilian. Please do not shoot." Bauer noticed a hint of fear in the Gruppenführer's voice.

Musfelldt beckoned for Bauer to enter first, no sense in losing an officer when a sergeant would hardly be missed. Muller immediately recognised Bauer and let out a huge sigh of relief.

Musfelldt rushed in, safely tucked behind his sergeant, his eyes immediately scanning the laboratory for a sight of the final Bell. It was there, apparently untouched, safe and sound. He realised this final Bell was his saviour, but the loss of the two others could be the end of his career. He may even face a firing squad. He immediately went on a charm offensive to save what he could from such a bad situation. He turned to the Professor, proffering his hand for a handshake.

"Well done Maximilian, the Führer will hear about this. How you single-handedly saved his personal Die Glöcke, fighting off insurgents in the process."

Muller beamed. "It was nothing Gruppenführer; I love the Fatherland and would die for my Führer in defending his Wunderwaffe"

Musfelldt put his arm around Muller's shoulders and guided him away from Bauer, towards the remaining Bell. He lowered his voice as if imparting a secret to a dear friend. "I shall not tell the Führer how you managed to lose two of his Wunderwaffe that will be our secret, will it not Maximilian? We don't want you to die in front of a firing squad, do we?"

Muller swallowed hard. A look of fear crossed his face. His heart missed a beat.

"Yes Gruppenführer … our secret."

Musfelldt's defence mechanism went into over drive.

"You may call me Erich, Maximilian"

Muller beamed with pride.

"Thank you ...... Erich."

"Now you forget all this and get back to perfecting your masterpiece. I shall let you personally deliver it to the Führer when it is complete. A great honour, is it not Maximilian?"

"Indeed, Erich, I shall not let you down."

"For the Führer and the Fatherland!"

Muller stood to attention and saluted. Using his most authoritative voice he echoed the sentiment.

"For the Führer and the Fatherland"

Musfelldt snapped an officious salute in return, and set off to find his colleague Storrensberg.

Believing that he had secured Muller's silence Musfelldt moved away, back towards his Feldwebel and the completion of the search in the mine. He led the way back into the mine shaft "Follow me sergeant, we have spies to find and deal with."

The mine had been a hive of activity, the remaining soldiers seeking out insurgents who had obviously been long gone.

Musfelldt stopped dead in his tracks. He looked around him, swivelling on his heels to get a good luck at the mine from entrance towards the rear.

"Do you notice anything sergeant?"

Schultz looked around, wondering what he should have seen, but hadn't. He was stumped.

"The mine is unusually quiet Commander, but it is night time."

"The workers, all the workers, where in hell's name are they? Even their foul smell has gone"

Realisation dawned. The mine was empty. The workers must have escaped. He barked orders at his troop.

"Scour the mine complex, now, and check the henge to the rear."

Several soldiers scurried around towards the rear of the mine, knowing in their hearts that no-one was there; they had already looked but were afraid to tell their commander.

"Sergeant, sergeant, over here." The jubilant tones of one of his troop beckoned him towards the V2 rockets. Schultz raced over, with Musfelldt following a safe distance behind.

"I found this hidden inside the bottom of the rocket. I think it may be a bomb"

Musfelldt stopped dead in his tracks again. "Check it out sergeant."

The soldier was holding a device of some kind in his hand. Unbeknown to him it was one of the neurolisers that had been used to damage the electrical circuits in the nose cone. When Manni had returned to look for the missing weapon he had placed the defunct devices within the base of the rockets as a 'red herring'. He believed that was the first place anyone would look and they would then stop looking in the belief they had been successful.

In an effort to restore his credentials Bauer knew he had to act quickly. He didn't have a clue what it was, but realised neither would his 'superior' officer.

"It is probably a bomb. Just wait while I try to disarm it." On examining it he saw the tell-tale signs of an overloaded circuit, flash marks on the casing. Inside he breathed a sigh of relief. He then fiddled with non-existent controls on the top for several minutes, grimacing and twisting the device as if he knew exactly what he was doing, before declaring "It is now safe." He closed his eyes and quietly prayed that he was right, gambling on there being one in each rocket. "Search the second rocket, NOW, we must act quickly"

He was, of course, right. Manni had placed one device in each rocket. "Here sergeant…." a second soldier held a device at arm's length, delivering it to his saviour. Bauer duly 'disarmed' this device also. Placing the defunct devices in his tunic pocket he called out "We're safe now Commander. I shall destroy them later; at least I have saved our valuable rockets."

Musfelldt appeared impressed, but more relieved believing he had another piece of 'ammunition' that he could himself use to impress his Führer when he called, helping him climb out of the hell hole he had let himself get into by listening to the missing Commander Krammler.

"Well done sergeant. Are you not glad that I led you back into this hell hole? The Führer will hear of your gallantry this evening." Bauer beamed with pride, the missing night of entertainment was now a distant memory, he was proud to be a soldier of the Fatherland once more.

"Has anyone seen any sign of the slave workers?" Musfelldt's request was one of urgency and authority. How could they just disappear?

"Over here Commander, something you need to see." One of the soldiers was calling from the rear of the mine, his voice sounding as if he had discovered the night's secrets.

Musfelldt turned smartly on his heels, a path appeared between the soldiers as if by magic as he strode purposely towards the direction of the voice. As he reached the now collapsed west exit the soldier pointed to the sealed exit. He stood smartly to attention. "The exit Gruppenführer, it has totally collapsed, perhaps our spies caused this."

Musfelldt's face twisted into a sardonic smile, his mind going into overdrive as he fought to salvage his reputation. "Our assailants obviously heard us return and, fearing the inevitable fire fight that would follow, chanced to escape down this shaft with the slaves. I can only assume that they booby trapped it in the hope of killing us as we pursued them. They obviously detonated it too soon and were killed in a trap of their own doing."

Bauer immediately stepped forward. "Would you like me to dig for survivors, sir?"

"No. They have been trapped like rats in a cage and deserve to lie there and rot. Perhaps Commander Krammler was with them. He may even have been a traitor. If so, he has died like a rat as well. Sweep the mine one last time whilst I go and inform the Führer, via Gruppenführer Storrensberg of course, of our glorious success in fighting off a surprise attack by a determined enemy. Well done men, you have saved the missiles and our secret project. The Führer will hear of your courage."

A cheer rang around the mine shaft, several soldiers even throwing their caps in the air. Their cheers echoed and put the first joyful sounds ever heard in this dungeon of a workplace.

Musfelldt smiled and saluted. "Carry on Feldwebel Bauer. Be assured that you will be mentioned in despatches." Bauer returned his salute, and rejoined his colleagues in performing a final sweep of the caves.

Musfelldt marched towards the mine entrance with the air of a man who had successfully repelled an enemy attack whilst leading from the front. In reality he realised that he needed the support of his men and probably Storrensberg if he was to keep up the pretence of success whilst he had actually lost two secret devices and all of his slave workers.

"I shall ask Josef for more volunteers from his newly formed Hungarian section of Der Riese. Or I may contact our mutual friends at Mittelbau-Dora as we have so much in common. Two or three hundred should be enough to complete the tunnel, and can be here in a day or so. I shall then request more V2 weapons so we may fight a rear guard action for the Führer as we complete his new Wunderwaffe."

As he strode out of the mine his confidence soared. His steps became more confident. He now believed he could pull this charade off.

"Secret weapons need time to be developed. The V1 took two full years, the V2 needed six, the V3 is on the drawing board as we speak. Whilst we have been here just for one year. This time next year we will be fully operational and the war will be won."

As he neared the gates the final part of the birthday party returned, the trucks pulling up with soldiers rushing in towards him. "Search the mine soldiers, we have seen off the enemy, look for survivors," before adding sarcastically, "IF there are any."

Storrensberg approached with a look of deep concern on his face. As he drew level Musfelldt put his arm around his colleague's shoulder and gently turned him around, redirecting him back towards the huts outside. "Jakob, my friend, follow me into the communications hut. We must have a comforting slivovitz to warm ourselves on this cold evening."

Storrensberg smiled, it seemed that all was well and he also was not in trouble.

"That sounds good Erich-that sounds very good."

They strolled towards the Communication hut as if on a victory parade.

Musfelldt leaned into towards his friend, adding

"And then we have an important message to send to our Führer."

Chapter 42

The sight of the cabin looming out of the darkness filled Johnno's entire being with hope, and thanks. Hope that they could actually safeguard the future he inhabited and thanks for their survival in the present. He turned to his friends beside him, feeling his eyes beginning to water again. He rubbed them, gently this time, as he fought to keep them dry. He had never been one for crying, but realised there must be a reason for his eyes filling up with tears.

"There she is, our refuge in a weary world"

Rick nodded. "Soon we shall be ourselves again, in more ways than one, and we can toast ourselves and our colleagues, as well as the success of our mission." Johnno grabbed Rick by the shoulder, gently squeezing in a sign of acknowledgement and affection. A voice came from just behind them "And I can be Manni again, and shave off this awful stubble from this awful face." Johnno instinctively felt the stubble on his own chin and smiled, "Amen to that my friend."

As they approached the cabin Rick motioned for his two colleagues to keep quiet. He directed them to approach each side whilst he entered the cabin door at the front. He placed his fingers to his lips, whispering "No sense in taking chances now. Let's be sure all is well inside before we enter."

Johnno moved towards the left and Manni towards the right. They turned off their torches and approached quietly. Rick cautiously crept to the cabin door, pausing outside to listen for any signs of activity. He slowly pressed down the latch whilst gently pushing against the door. He was relieved to find it locked. He reached over to the cabin wall where a cabin sign was fixed. "Sanktuarium." He murmured softly to himself and smiled. The sign was hinged and pulled away from the wall to reveal a cavity, complete with a key. He retrieved it and then quietly inserted it into the lock, turning it as gently as he could. He winced as the lock opened with a final dull click

He cupped his hand to his mouth.

"I'm about to enter, any signs of activity?"

Johnno looked through the closed bedroom window but could see nothing. "Johnno here. It seems clear, all still in darkness."

Manni had glanced through the window into the living area, but could just see the light barely flickering from the fireplace. He moved to the rear and looked through into the bedroom. As his eyes became accustomed to the darkness the dark silhouettes of three seated figures could just be made out through a small gap in the rudimentary curtains. He decided to take a chance and turned on his torch, first shining it towards the floor. "Just checking the rear bedroom, give me a moment." He struggled to place the torch beam through the gap as well as actually seeing what was inside. Eventually the light fell on the silhouettes. It was their prisoners, the donors for their replicant selves. "I see three unconscious captives here who, may I say, are not as good looking as we do."

Johnno smiled, Rick rolled his eyes and shook his head.

Rick slowly opened the door, entering with his neuroliser in hand, just in case. Glancing around the living area he could see it was only barely lit up by the glowing embers of the dying fire. "Living area all clear." He quickly moved around each room in the cabin, his torch being held above his weapon, highlighting each room in turn.

Finally he could relax, clicking his weapon back onto his wrist. "We have an all clear gentlemen, please come inside, all clear.."

Johnno entered first, closely followed by Manni. The trio looked at each other, barely able to believe what they had managed to do. Instinctively they moved and met in a group hug, beaming smiles being the order of the day.

"We did it my friends, we fucking did it." Manni was jubilant.

"Not quite finished yet," added Johnno, with a voice of caution "I can't help feeling that something bad is still going to happen." Rick grabbed Johnno's head with both hands , smiled and stared him face to face. "You always were the cautious one, even back home in the good ole' USA ... back home in the future, where you will shortly return my friend. Nothing bad will happen."

A smile slowly appeared on Johnno's face. "Yeah, I suppose you're right," before adding, "when can I have my own body back?"

Rick's face broke out into a broad grin. "Right now. Come on my friends, it's time to change for dinner."

Johnno shook his head in mock disbelief. "And you said I was the one with the bad jokes."

Rick led them into the bedroom where their donors still sat unconscious. "Remember the procedure Johnno? Stand behind, hold their shoulders and empty your mind. Feel their blood coursing in your veins, their essence leaving your body."

"You go first, and remind me."

Rick nodded and stood behind the Oberleutnant. Gripping both shoulders he took in a deep breath, closing both eyes, raising his head in the air just slightly. Slowly, steadily, Rick's whole body began to change and meld into a new shape. Within thirty seconds or so the 'real' Rick was back. He breathed out, turning to face Johnno, smiling as he did so. He adopted a pose, both arms outstretched as if in welcome. "Hi buddy, your old friend is back."

"Now my turn." Manni stood behind the Korporal, placing both hands on his shoulders. He seemed to take a much deeper breath, but closed his eyes the same. Slowly Manni's shape returned until he too was back to his old self. "MUCH better looking, don't you agree?"

Johnno moved behind Johan, their 'man on the inside'. His mind raced with thoughts of failure. "What if I cannot get myself back? What if Johan is forever trapped here in limbo? Will I die if he wakes?"

"I don't know if I can do this ...."

Rick cut in "Yes you can. You had doubts about flying the Intruder. Remember? And then thought you'd fail when you tried the Phantom." Johnno nodded, his mind wandering back to his days at flight school. "And don't forget about Blackbird and NASA? Come on buddy, you *can* do this."

He nodded again in agreement. "You're right, I CAN do this." Moving around behind Johan, he carefully and deliberately placed his hands on his donor's shoulders. Closing his eyes he took in a deep breath, lifted his face towards the ceiling, doing his best to mimic the actions of his colleagues. "Must relax, must relax," the thought reverberated through his brain. He felt a tingle throughout his body and a sense of being part of something else. It was almost an 'out of body' experience. He felt cold, then hot, then slightly dizzy. In the distance he could just make out voices reassuring him, telling him that he could do it.

The symbiotic feeling began to drain away; he could feel himself losing the 'connection'.

Then he felt a pair of hands on his shoulders, a reassuring feeling adding a wave of warmth throughout his body, he suddenly became aware of his very essence. He could 'see' spirals floating towards him. He became aware of his heart beat filling his body with a steady beat. He felt a wave of heat pass from his toes, slowly moving upwards towards his head. And then it was gone. His body felt as if it was in a chiller. His muscles relaxed. Sweat was pouring from his forehead, gently stinging his eyes as he struggled to open them.

"Sorry buddy, I just can't do this."

"Can't do what?"

"This replicate thing."

The room filled with laughter. Why would they laugh at him? He wasn't from Orion. He didn't have any magical powers. Manni placed a mirror in front of his face.

"Welcome back John O'Ryan, welcome back."

He struggled to focus, but could then see someone he recognised in the mirror. Himself! "I did it. YES … I did it." His voice sounded triumphant. He looked towards his friends, now recognisable as the real Rick and Manni. "I fucking well did it."

"With just a little bit of help from me." Rick bowed his head "I gave you a jump start, just the same as when you had that old '57 Cadillac and that wouldn't work either, remember?" He pulled his friend towards him, providing a 'man hug' "That's what friends do; we look out for each other." He smiled, giving his buddy a final congratulatory slap on the back.

"What next?" Johnno was keen to move on and complete their mission

"We need to wake Johan, and prepare his back story. Then we need to prepare and vacate the cabin."

"Then can we wash and shave and have something to eat? I'm starving."

"Typical, always thinking of your Belly!"

Manni re-entered the living area and moved towards the log pile at the side of the fireplace. "I'll stoke up the fire and get some fresh coffee on the go."

Astrild had been waiting in the living area. When she heard the congratulatory shouts she entered the bedroom. It was her task to wake Johan fully from his torpid state.. He felt weak, but was ecstatic to hear about the success of the mission.

"Have some food with us and then make your way to the village for safety. The pipeline to Switzerland is still open – please take it, and quickly. You will not be safe if you return to the mine and are recognised."

"I shall take some food with me if you don't mind. The sooner I start my journey the sooner I can rejoin our allied forces and be of some use in this damned war."

Astrild packed some food whilst Johan brushed down his uniform, placed his hat in his lapel, hiding it all under a khaki coloured trench coat

"Those clothes have never looked as good my friend."

He sat, thankfully gulping down the coffee to vanquish the thirst forced on him by his spell in 'hibernation'. After a couple of minutes or so he got to his feet. With regret he finally bid a farewell to his new allies.

"I have lost my family to these bastard Nazis, but have found a new one with my lifelong friends."

Johnno shook his hand warmly. "We are your new family Johan, and we will always be there for you should you need us."

Johan's face was full of pride. "Thank you," was all he could manage to say, the words emerging from a soul full of gratitude

"We must thank YOU for putting your life at risk, we're forever grateful."

Johan smiled. "Look me up after the war is over, I plan to open a garage repairing cars ... any kind ... apart from Volkswagens, of course," a huge grin on his face.

"May your God be with you my friend." At that he left, quietly closing the door behind him.

Rick gently put his hand on Johnno's shoulder. "Don't worry – he makes it, and does open that garage. He opens a successful Volvo car dealership in Gothenburg."

Johnno smiled, "If only I could see into the future ... if only." Turning away he made his way to the bedroom where he could finally wash and shave, removing the grime and dirt ingrained with sweat that covered him. But, hard as he tried, he still couldn't relax.

He felt something still wasn't quite right, but wasn't quite sure exactly what was still troubling him. He racked his brains, re-running old memories; unfortunately his recent injury and concussion were pushing his recent memories to the back of his mind. Still, tomorrow he should be able to return home and complete the final part of his mission.

Hopefully.

Chapter 43

The smell of eggs and bacon worked better than an alarm clock.

He was back to being a child again with his favourite Aunt, preparing a hearty breakfast before embarking on another day full of adventure. He could see the pine clad forests complete with a topping of early morning mist. The stream swirled and glugged around its rock base, so crystal clear you could see the minnows darting between the shelter of pebbles and moss covered rocks dumped there by long gone glaciers. A smile crept across his face as he began to fully waken. His mouth salivated at the expectation of a morning feast. His eyes finally flickered open, he took in a deep breath as the world came flooding back after his first real sleep in days.

"That smells good Aunt Freya, where to today?"

"Back home we hope, and I'm not your Aunt Freya, sunshine." Rick was standing by the table in the middle of the room, loading it up with breakfast for the day. He glanced through the open bedroom door "Freya isn't back yet, I assume she bedded down somewhere for the night. Are you ready for breakfast yet?"

"Am I ready, and some…"

He climbed out of bed, slowly getting to his feet, swaying gently as he did so. He felt as though he was suffering from a hangover. He flashed a smile towards his friend. "Tequila legs!"

Rick leaned in by the door. "Don't worry, that's quite normal when you first replicate. Go and have a pee, splash your face with some cold water and your eggs will be done by the time you return." Standing over the bowl he poured in some water from the jug, splashing his face with the cold water seemed to re-boot his brain. Towelling himself dry he glanced in the mirror, smiling at his own face once more. "John O'Ryan, what a tale you will have to tell your grandchildren; and I bet they won't believe you. Shit, even I have trouble believing you."

He meandered back into the main room, to be welcomed by all three of his colleagues, their beaming faces smiling back at him. "Let's eat my friends, our task is nearly over."

"This is like old times back in ... back in ... the future at Edwards." Johnno couldn't resist laughing at his inane comment. Even Rick saw the funny side. "An early morning breakfast; Followed by a training flight in an azure sky; And finally, in the evening a drive in the desert followed by an ice cold beer." His eyes seemed to glaze over momentarily as this memory was crystal clear.

"That sounds like an idyllic life, and soon you will be back there enjoying it all over again." Manni sounded a little jealous.

"Hopefully my friend."

"Do you have anyone special back there? Someone who misses you." Astrild added a motherly tone.

"No, I'm afraid not yet. Flying has been my life until now, but perhaps I need to find someone to share my life with." Manni took hold of Astrild's hand. "I can thoroughly recommend it my friend."

The conversation over breakfast allowed Johnno to gently slip back into reality. A world where people ate together, smiled together, and did not worry about being killed for an obscure belief or twisted ideal. He felt as if he was with family again. Pushing his empty plate away his face was one of ecstasy. "Is there a farm nearby? If there is I need to visit them and thank them for their glorious produce."

"No farm my friend, all home grown." Manni laughed. "We stopped eating animals and their offspring many years ago, we manufacture our food ourselves, down there," pointing to where the hidden chamber lay under the rug.

"You make it?"

"Yes in our food processor. We tell it what food taste we want, and it's appearance and it is produced synthetically. All the taste, all the goodness and nothing is killed in the process. Only the coffee is real my friend."

Johnno smiled. "Alien technology and all that, put to a really good use, brilliant." Leaning back in his chair he looked back at Rick "Speaking of technology, how the hell did that UFO go so fast and then disappear? Super rockets?"

"It's quite simple really. We've developed an anti-gravity device that stops our craft falling to ground, it actually repels gravity and produces thrust; it wants to stay airborne with little energy used." He took a sip from his coffee and continued. "Then add a motor which is powered by light. Basically the beam propels us forward, up to the speed of light. When we have missions on planets such as Earth that is all we need."

"And how did it just disappear?"

"Stealth technology, very much like the US is just now developing. Oh, and autonomous androids to pilot them. They're not affected by sudden stops, or accelerating to light speed in seconds. That's the kind that we encountered when our aircraft was approached and taken." Realisation seemed to dawn as Rick put his mug back on the table. "Speaking of our aircraft we need to collect it and get you back so you can deliver your parcel. You still have our very important parcel, don't you?"

Johnno patted his chest. "I've taped it to my body, there's no way it will get lost again." His face frowned as Rick's last sentence sunk in. "Did you say collect our aircraft?"

"Yes, we have it hidden in a nearby clearing, and we need to get you aboard and home a s a p. Jackets on buddy, let's go and find a blackbird hiding in the forest, one that doesn't whistle."

"Is it time to go?"

"Time to go buddy"

Johnno put on his jacket and gathered his boots still not daring to believe it was nearly all over. He couldn't help smiling as Rick donned his Aviator glasses as usual, perched above his head, as if he was going out on a routine mission.

"Just who do I give the package to when I get home?"

"When WE get home buddy, we have to pass it on directly to the President, in person."

"THE President?"

"Yep; THE President himself. He's been kept up to date on your progress thanks to Astrild here."

"Does that mean we are going to the White House?" Johnno couldn't contain his excitement.

"Yep."

A faraway look came into Johnno's eyes. He wiped away a tear before it could be seen. He thought how proud his parents would be, and his beloved Aunt Freya. Perhaps she would even be there with him.

"A scarf?"

Johnno snapped back to reality. "Pardon?"

"A scarf, do you need a scarf?" Astrild proffered one.

"No thanks, I'm fine." Johnno thought a scarf would not look good with his flight suit.

Soon all four had donned jackets ready to brave the cold weather.

"At least it's dry and sunny, just the kind of day for a pleasing flight home." Johnno was elated. "Home … that has a certain 'ring' about it, doesn't it."

Rick's final act was to collect a rucksack which was sat below the coat hangers. He swung it onto his back, Astrild helping him get the second strap over his shoulder. Manni locked the cabin and replaced the key as they set out on the final leg of their mission. To all intents and purposes it looked as if four friends were off for a walk in the woods without a care in the world.

The sky was a radiant blue with only an odd wispy white cloud smeared across its face. The trees allowed a dappled sunlight to force its way through the canopy producing an almost fairy tale quality to the paths through towards the clearing. The birds were busy with their morning song, reinforcing territories and impressing their mates. The horrors of war and their battles to save the alien weapon now seemed a million miles away. Within fifteen minutes or so the trees began to thin out as they approached a clearing, covered only in a verdant green of grass, moss and dying wildflowers. The sun shone brilliantly, reflecting the vivid greens and browns of the floor where it fell.

Rick stopped as they left the forest cover extending both arms in front of him as if presenting something amazing.

"There she is buddy, your taxi ride home."

Johnno smiled in embarrassment as he could see nothing at all.

"Yes. OK - where?"

Rick allowed himself a self-satisfied grin. "You can't see her?"

Johnno shook his head. "OK , what's this trick about? I can't see a thing."

"Then let me bring her back to you."

Rick took the rucksack from his back and opened the top straps. The back and front fell away simultaneously, revealing a device that Johnno took to be what looked like a radio communications system. He then pulled up a round aerial located in the top and switched the unit on. After several seconds a rotating image appeared on a front screen, one which resembled an aircraft. Johnno was intrigued and walked over to his friend to have a look at the image.

The outline looked familiar, very familiar.

He frowned , eyes trying their best to focus. "Is that an outline of an aircraft?

"Not just any aircraft buddy, this is our aircraft .. your ride home."

Rick then pressed down four switches, one after the other. The aerial began to turn as the unit hummed into life. Slowly, incredibly the outline of something huge began to shimmer and radiate, gradually forming an image in front of them. The area was bathed in a bluish green glow, almost too bright to be looked at safely. Johnno shielded his eyes as the light intensified. And then it was gone. Removing his hand from his eyes Johnno blinked as he tried to focus on what was now sat in front of him. It was a Blackbird aircraft. Looking at the image on the fuselage he recognised it as OD1N, his chosen insignia. It was HIS Blackbird.

"How the fuck did you do that?" and, realising what he had said he turned to face his colleagues. "Sorry Astrild. But where did she come from? How did you , I mean just how …"

Rick was closing up his rucksack as he spoke. "You recognise the three dimensions in life my friend. Well the fourth dimension is time." He pulled the straps tight as he secured his device. "As you know we can control time to an extent. All I did was place your … sorry, our aircraft one day in the future, where it remained permanently unseen until now. As each day passed it was forwarded just one day ahead. Pretty nifty, huh."

"I am impressed buddy, I am SO impressed. But you've forgotten one thing; don't we need a runway to take off?"

"We've added a little extra technology which will allow you to lift off vertically. Once airborne it is programmed to disappear as you travel back to your future, to be lost in the ethos of space time forever." Rick passed the rucksack to Manni. "Take good care of this, I'll see you some time in the future my friend." They shook hands, and then hugged.

Johnno gave Astrild a hug, and kissed both cheeks. "Thank you for everything, I mean, everything. We owe our success to yourself and Manni."

"You are most welcome. Let's hope we meet again one day, hopefully somewhere peaceful."

He then moved over to Manni, offering a hand to shake. Manni knocked it to one side and hugged him. Johnno couldn't look at his colleague, but spoke as they hugged,

"Thank you for saving my life, I am indebted to you."

"No my friend, it is I, and everyone on Earth, who is indebted to you. Have a safe journey and a good landing. I believe the saying is 'Fair wind and following seas. Your seas here being the seas of time itself." Smiling, he gave one last reassuring nod of his head, then turned and made his way towards his Blackbird, and home.

He breathed in deeply, savouring the heady aroma of the damp trees in the forest. He could sense the fallen leaves crumple beneath his feet as he made his way to his aircraft. He paused and smiled to himself when he realised there was even a ladder there, propped against the fuselage, allowing him to climb into his cockpit. He reached up and touched the side, warmed gently by the heat of the day, its black outline as sleek as ever. "Welcome back Johnno, Odin's taxi to the future awaits." As he lifted his leg to the first rung of the ladder his silent musings were cut short as he heard Rick's alarmed voice shout out.

On turning he saw a look of panic on his colleague's face.

"Freya's in trouble!"

Johnno turned and hurried back to see Rick holding his earpiece, instinctively touching his own ,concerned as he heard a gentle sound of alarm in Freya's voice.

"Sorry to trouble you but I have problems here." Her voice sounded strange.

"We are about to return with the weapon, aboard my beautiful craft dedicated to your namesake, queen of the heavens. Do you need to come with us?"

"Yes, I see her, she's beautiful, but I have a problem back at the cabin."

Rick's voice broke in. "What is it Freya? We're about to leave with the package"

"German soldiers are approaching the cabin. I fear we've been compromised. I am in danger."

"We must go back" Rick's voice was loaded with urgency as he turned to face his friend.

"We have technology to secure back there. It must not fall into the hands of the Germans or this mission will just be a waste of time. You take off buddy, I'm sure I'll get to see you soon."

"No way my friend. We started together and we'll end it together. Besides, it appears that my favourite Aunt is in danger back there."

Rick accepted the inevitable and gripped his friend's arm in gratitude. "We'll leave your Blackbird here, she will she safe for a day or so. No-one comes here and it's not on a flight path to anywhere. If not … " He moved over to the aircraft fuselage and placed a small explosive device low on the fuselage. "Just a little insurance buddy. If we go, she goes too." He handed the remote detonator to Johnno.

"Keep this safe. It has a range of a mile or so, easily within reach of the cabin. Let's hope we don't need to use it. I much prefer the 60's in the good old USA to the 40's in Poland".

"It's safe with me." Johnno placed the detonator in the map pocket of his flight suit, zipping it firmly shut. "Now let's go and see if we can save Freya."

Manni and Astrild collected the weapons they had lain on the floor and turned back to the track which had almost brought them to safety. Rick touched his earpiece. "We're on our way Freya, approaching from the rear of the cabin."

"Don't worry, I won't neurolise you. But please hurry or I fear our mission will be compromised."

Johnno was deeply concerned. His mind raced as he tried to put all the pieces of this mission in their correct place. "How did they find out about the cabin?

Have the two sleeping captives finally awoken? Was his beloved Freya in danger?" He couldn't lose his beloved Aunt, not after all they had gone through. All four colleagues instinctively broke into a trot, carefully avoiding the detritus on the forest floor.

As they approached the cabin Rick gestured for them to leave the path, holding his finger to his lips to remind them of the need for silence. They began the precarious approach to the rear of the cabin; ever vigilant listening for the sounds of any traffic or the Teutonic tones of the enemies as they also approached the cabin. Rick gestured for Manni and Astrild to approach from the right.

"You're with me buddy," Rick led Johnno towards the left.

"Remember the Federation; we don't want casualties if we can help it. Neuroliser use only."

Manni and Astrild nodded, and slipped away to the right, crouching low as they went, ensuring their neurolisers were set to a stun mode. Johnno grabbed Rick by the arm, stopping him from moving forward. He looked concerned. "We have no neurolisers, remember, we used them on the rockets." Rick smiled, putting his hand into his jacket pocket. "Will these help?" In his hand were two more weapons.

"I always carry at least one spare, remember, you never know when you'll need it."

Johnno grinned as his mind flashed back to warm desert nights and ice cold beers.

"Just the trick." He took one from his friend's hand. "Is it set?"

"Set on stun. Now let's see what's troubling Freya."

"Nothing untoward here." Manni reported back as a low whispering message into Rick's earpiece. As Rick approached the bedroom window he quickly glanced in, pulling his head back sharply. "It is difficult to see in the dark." He pulled down his aviator glasses, leaving his partner bemused. "Night vision my friend, special issue. Alien technology and all that. Rick winked. He glanced back in, first quickly and then a slow steady look.

"Our German friends are still there, apparently still in a deep sleep. Everything looks OK."

He touched his earpiece. "Freya, we are coming in, everything looks OK out here."

Silence

"Did you hear Freya? We are coming in, all is clear out here"

Silence

Rick tried to give a reassuring look to Johnno. "Perhaps her ear piece has failed."

They moved around to the front of the cabin, where Manni and Astrild were waiting, pressed back against the front wall. They nodded. Rick held up his hand .. three fingers, two fingers, one finger ... then mouthed "Go."

Rick entered first moving to the left, Manni next, moving to the right in a well-rehearsed drill.

In front of them was Freya, a weapon aimed at the door, with a look of fear on her face.

"Don't fire, it's us." Johnno ran in allowing her a full view of his face. A look of relief flashed over her face as she visibly relaxed, lowering her weapon.

"Thank God it's you. I don't know who to trust anymore." She stepped forward reaching for her beloved nephew's reassuring arms.

Astrild was the last to enter, closing and bolting the door behind her.

"What happened, where's the danger?" Rick was quickly checking out each room as he spoke. "Where are the Germans who are approaching?"

Freya stepped back from Johnno, gently squeezing his forearms as she did so. "We have a traitor somewhere. I'm afraid to say it's Johan, our so-called informant. I believe he's really Maia, the Pleiadian replicant."

"What makes you say that?" Rick moved around the table to face her.

"As I was about to leave the cabin and join you I ran one last sweep on the German radio wave bands just to check everything had calmed down at the mine. Commander Krammler has ordered a detachment of his men to check out the cabin for the bodies of his two missing soldiers." She lowered her eyes slightly, "apparently Korporal Engel told them that he had escaped whilst his colleagues were captured and tortured."

"No, not Johan." Manni was stunned. "He's Jewish, he's their natural enemy."

Freya turned to face him. "He says he's Jewish, do we have proof?"

Manni pondered. "I suppose not. But why help us then betray us?

Freya shrugged her shoulders. "Who knows why? But we have been

compromised. They are on their way now. I was worried that Maia had replicated one of you and was here to finish the job, and kill us all."

"We must act quickly if we are to deliver the package with you my friend. Can you find your way back to your aircraft alone?" Rick was quickly changing his plans.

"I suppose so."

"Good. We'll delay the German patrol long enough for you to escape and for us … " he glanced at Manni and Astrild "…for us to remove or destroy the technology here."

"I have a better idea." Freya stepped forward. "Give me the package and I'll return it for you. That will allow both you and Johnno to return in your aircraft whilst we destroy the technology. They will not suspect me as Johan as given them your descriptions. By the time they find the clearing you will be long gone."

"Sounds feasible, what do you think Johnno?"

Johnno was hesitant. "I'm not sure. How will you deliver the package Freya? Remember it has to be taken back to the future, to my future."

"I have ways and means. Don't worry, I'll meet you again in 1969 and I can deliver it personally."

Johnno seemed reluctant. He looked to his best friend for guidance.

"Would it work, I thought there had to be human input only on the final delivery. Will it be OK if - sorry Aunt Freya - if an alien delivered it?"

Rick seemed unsure. "I suppose so, but we have no time to waste, we'll have to go with it. It seems the best chance to save the package at present."

Johnno unzipped the front of his flying suit, unbuttoning his shirt. He winced as he pulled on the tape which held the weapon to his body. Holding it in his hand he examined it, turning it over and smoothing his hand along the central grip. "All this trouble for you, one small weapon."

Astrild's calm voice replied. "One small weapon which could change the history of a planet in a heartbeat."

Johnno acknowledged Freya's concerns. He looked towards his Aunt Freya, the calm look on his face hiding his demeanour. He slowly took off his talisman from his neck, gripping it in his right hand alongside the weapon, a look of resignation on his face. He paused.

"Am I still your little soldier, my dear Aunt?"

"Of course"

He stretched out his hand to pass over the weapon. Freya reached out and, as she did so, he looked to the ring on her left hand. It was dull and lifeless.

Johnno smiled. "I thought as much.". A look of anxiety spread over Freya's face. Johnno raised the weapon, aiming it towards Freya. As he gently pressed the trigger, a vivid yellow light shot out from the barrel. Her knees buckled, her eyes slowly closed as she slid to the floor.

Rick was open mouthed. He turned to face his friend, a look of complete surprise and amazement on his face. "What the hell just happened?"

"I neurolised her, that's just what happened."

Chapter 44

The room fell silent, everyone stunned by Johnno's actions. Rick gave his partner a quizzical look, his best friend who he had trusted with his life.

His best friend who, without hesitation, had just shot his favourite Aunt ... his trusted mentor.

Instinctively Rick, Manni and Astrild reached for their weapons before they too were shot.

Johnno raised his hands in the air. "I'm not mad. I'm not the rogue replicant, and **that** is not Freya," Calmly placing his weapons on the table.

"And I guarantee that there are no Germans approaching, that was just a ruse to get us back to the cabin with our package." He turned to face Manni. "Unlock the door and listen. Can you hear a vehicle approaching? Can you hear German voices? Surely they would have been here by now."

Manni looked towards Rick, who nodded towards the door, adding "Send up a watcher.", whilst still keeping Johnno covered with his neuroliser.

Manni slowly unbolted the door, opening it just enough to hear outside. After several seconds he opened it further, before stepping through and glancing towards the path and the mine. Astrild joined him as they both warily ventured towards the path, crouching down as they approached. She handed him a watcher. This was a small flying drone, about four inches in diameter, covered in a non-reflective black paint. Manni carefully placed it on the ground, and stepped back towards Astrild. Four small puffs of air came out of the bottom edges as it rose into the air and then darted off in the direction of the mine.

Inside Rick moved over to the screen by the fire, switching it on. A set of four images immediately appeared on the screen, displayed in four corners, showing the path towards the mine complex, sent back by the watcher. It moved at tremendous speed, darting between branches and keeping low enough to view the path as well as both sides and the path where it had just travelled. Within minutes it had reached where the path led directly to the mine and stopped dead, hovering and rotating ensuring a full 360 degrees view was visible. The guards could be seen in their towers, one casually smoking, oblivious to the fact he was being filmed.

Rick inspected the screen closely, and then turned towards his colleagues outside. "Call it back; there is no-one approaching, friend or foe." Astrild had also been watching on her remote control, reassured that Johnno's claim had been verified. Soon the watcher returned, landing on exactly the same spot from where it had begun its journey.

Fully reassured they re-entered the cabin. "All clear, no sign of any Germans. No sign of anyone actually."

Rick gestured towards the screen on the wall and nodded in agreement.

Johnno turned to face Rick, his arms still raised. "Ask yourself the question, would the Germans have announced on an open radio band what their intentions were?"

Rick glanced at Manni, who shrugged his shoulders. "I suppose not."

"And how did she know that Johan had supposedly betrayed us, he has no reason to. Didn't he lose family at Storrensberg's camp? I'm more inclined to believe he tried to kill Storrensberg than betray us."

"Why do you believe that this is not Freya?" Astrild stepped forward "What makes you so sure?"

Johnno slowly lowered his arms, and sat down in a chair by the table. "My first inkling came when we were trapped in the mine waiting for Rick to help us escape. I asked Freya, who had been missing for hours, if she could see help find the weapon I'd dropped."

"So? She did say that the dust was affecting her vision."

"Did you actually see her use her ring to see?"

"No, I was assembling and setting up the rockphaser."

"I thought so. She couldn't see because she didn't know about the ring but, more importantly, when I had the fight with the SS guard he hit me so hard that my eyes watered. When I rubbed them the lenses came out and fell on the floor somewhere." He looked directly at Rick " I didn't want to tell you I'd lost them, alien technology and all that. Sorry."

Rick slowly lowered his weapon; he desperately wanted to believe his friend, if this was indeed his friend. Manni did likewise, but kept his finger on the button should he suddenly need to act. He glanced at Astrild, who looked down at her hand, still holding her weapon in readiness also.

"When we reached the aircraft I asked her again to 'view' through my eyes and see the aircraft, dedicated to her namesake, queen of the heavens"

"So?"

"That finally convinced me that it could not be Freya. If she could actually see my craft she would notice it was dedicated to Odin and not Frigga. Freya spent years telling me all the tales of Norse mythology. The real Freya would not make such a simple error."

"Have you thought that her vision may have been impaired? !"

"More proof came right here. I was never her 'little soldier'; right from being a little boy and just able to walk I was always 'min lille romfarer', 'my little spaceman'. We both hated fighting and wars, she would NEVER wish me to be a soldier. Jeez, we even bumped heads when we kissed. We've greeted each other with a kiss to the cheeks for all our lives- 'left, right, kiss goodnight'. The real Freya would automatically kiss me as she always did." Rick relaxed and sat down at the table, it seemed to be making sense to him, especially information that only he was privy to.

"The final proof came when she reached over and asked me to pass over the package."

Astrild stepped forward, still holding her weapon concealed in the palm of her hand "And this proof was...?"

"The real Freya has her ring on her right hand, NOT on her left. As a child she always avoided hugging me with it in case it hurt. I now realise it was also to protect the ring and its amazing powers."

Rick leaned over Freya's inert body to inspect her hands. The ring was on her left hand.

"Remember, when you warned me about replication. You must stand **behind** your subject. Either this idiot was unaware of that, or Freya made sure she had her back covered somehow."

Manni stepped forward, kneeling down to examine 'her'. "If this isn't Freya, who is it then?"

"Presumably the spy in our midst, the same one who nearly had me killed in my hotel room."

"Will Freya now be found? Can she find her way back here?" Johnno's voice was full of concern as he suddenly realised his real Aunt was missing.

"She would regain her own persona if her replicant gave her up, or was dead. We have an unconscious replicant here my friends, one we can question when he wakes up. You were lucky old buddy, lucky you didn't kill 'her'. At least we can get answers when 'she' awakes."

Johnno leaned over and picked up the weapon. "I guessed it worked the same as your neurolisers. I twisted the left dial clockwise. That was right, wasn't it?" Manni reached over and examined the weapon. He smiled at Rick, "Two dials."

Johnno was perplexed. "Two dials, what does that mean?"

"It means, my friend, that if you had used the right hand dial you would have vapourised our replicant friend and the Federation would have been deeply unhappy." The smile on his face gave the game away, he repeated "Really deeply unhappy."

"So all we need do is wait for 'her' to wake up, and tell us where Freya is." Johnno sounded as positive as he could, desperately hoping he would get a positive reply.

"Wake up, yes. But Pleidians are notorious for dying for their cause, knowing full well that the Federation is on their side and protects them. This could prove tricky my friend, very tricky. But we do know that Freya is still alive. Replicants cannot subsume dead bodies, their targets must be alive, and stay alive."

Rick turned 'Freya' onto her back, and pulled her over toward a chair by the table where Manni helped to lift her onto the seat still, apparently, deeply unconscious.

Manni turned to Astrild, "Keep an eye on her. We'll get a message back informing our council that the weapon is safe and will be delivered shortly. But we have a minor problem to solve first." Turning to Johnno "You must return with it and trust us to safely deliver Freya to you as soon as she is safely delivered to us."

Rick placed a comforting hand on his best friend's shoulder "Manni's right. The weapon is the priority and we will find Freya for you." Manni moved aside the rug whilst Astrild activated the trap door. Light shone out of the 'cellar' like a supersized torch, highlighting the timber ceiling.

They slowly descended the steps and prepared to contact their council.

Johnno gestured towards the side bedroom "I'll check our visitors are still unconscious, I'd hate them to wake up and add to this confusion."

"No problem. I'll unset the package to make it safe, and then we can get you back to your aircraft and your flight home."

Johnno approached the sleeping captives, placing two fingers gently on their necks, checking their carotid pulses to ensure they were still alive and safe. He was amazed. "A pulse rate of ….. twenty four – they're almost in a coma."

The examination was cut short as he heard the sounds of a scuffle behind him. He turned to face the door in order to see, or hear more, of what was going on. He could hear Rick's voice calling him back in, but it sounded strange, almost metallic as he repeated his request again.

He entered the room and stopped dead in his tracks – in front of him stood two identical figures, both were, to all intents and purposes, his best friend Rick.

"What the …..?"

Both Ricks turned towards him and smiled. Both spoke totally in unison.

"I bet this is a surprise." They looked towards each other. "Which one of us is real?

Johnno rubbed his eyes, completely stunned by what he saw, and heard.

Manni slowly appeared from the trapdoor. "Oh shit – we have a replicant shifter on our hands."

"Correct. Both 'Ricks' spoke in unison."

Johnno was totally baffled. "What the fuck is a replicant shifter?"

"A figure that replicates another, whilst also fully controlling their host's body A sort of super shifter." Manni slowly moved towards the weapon on the table.

As he did so both Ricks spoke again. "Correct my friend, and do not

attempt to use the weapon, you may just kill your colleague instead of me."

Johnno's mind was racing, how the hell could he save Rick when he may well attack the wrong one and kill him instead?

"I see you are perplexed, but all will become clear as you help me return home with the weapon that you kindly retrieved for me. First of all take the weapon from the table. Remember, if you take a chance you may well kill your colleague," before adding with a wry grin, "of course you could kill both of us and complete your mission, but I'm sure you value the life of your best friend."

Johnno moved slowly past the two figures, and gingerly took the weapon from the table.

"Now set it to strong stun – the left dial – all the way around." Johnno placed his hand on the left dial and slowly turned it.

"OK, now what?"

The two 'Ricks' turned and gestured to Manni and Astrild. "You two – come up the steps and stand against the wall by the door where I can see you both."

Johnno stepped back as his two colleagues moved towards the wall. They stopped, still facing the wall.

"Turn around." They both slowly complied. "Now Johnno you will stun them both. Oh, and if you get it wrong and they die, it will be totally your fault if they do." Both 'Ricks' laughed in in unison. Johnno was reticent. Should he take a chance and stun both figures? Yes, he could do that if he was quick enough.

"I see what you are thinking, but please do not try that. You see when I was stunned the first time it weakened my anatomy. We shape shifters are a delicate bunch you see. If either of us was stunned just one more time I'm afraid we would both die. And it's goodbye Rick."

"He could be bluffing and I can take them both out." Johnno's mind was racing. But if he is telling the truth he realised he could kill his best friend; he couldn't take the chance, he had to play along until a real opportunity came to rescue Rick. He was sure it would, or was he?

Manni spoke softly. "Just do it Johnno, we'll be OK, we trust you." He took a hold of Astrild's hand. "You'll think of something to stop him taking the weapon, trust in yourself."

"Freya is waiting for you to save her, just do it." Astrild's voice was reassuring.

He slowly turned to face them both and paused for several seconds. From behind him a pair of urgent voices rang out.

"Hurry up, or I will see to them myself and remember, I care not for the Federation, or it's supposed values."

His mouth was dry, he felt he had failed his friends and struggled to talk. One word just crept out of his lips, "Sorry."

At that he fired the weapon to stun both of his friends. He took careful aim at their midriffs, hopefully to cause least pain. As their bodies crumpled and fell to the floor behind him two voices sounded in unison.

"Well done, and now for part two of my plan. My return to my future."

Johnno was angry, but realised he had to keep calm for Rick's sake if he was to save him.

"What next, kill me?"

"That was a very good attempt, my friend. I could easily have done that when I took over Commander Krammler's body. Yes that was me. Now who DID you send forward to … Kecksburg, wasn't it? Herr Hitler will miss his commander, I fear"

Johnno realised he'd been tricked by a master trickster.

"No, with you gone your real friend might just have the chance to break free from my will and all may be lost. However if I keep you alive your friend remains subdued – he fears losing you as well. Isn't friendship wonderful? And it is also a weakness for your pathetic war-mongering civilisation in general."

Johnno kept looking at both entities, searching for something that would tell him who the real Rick was. Both Ricks gestured towards the cabin door. "Outside, we ... sorry ... I, have an appointment to keep in the future."

He realised that the shape shifter meant to kill both him and Rick as soon as he felt he was safe. He had to think of something before that happened … he just had to.

Johnno stepped outside of the cabin, the two entities followed close behind, closing the cabin door as they left.

"I'm sure when our two German friends awake they will be able to deal with your two colleagues. Perhaps they might strike lucky and get a job in the mine." The entities added sarcastically. "They may even end up alongside your missing Freya."

"Freya's in the mine?" Johnno's mind recoiled at the thought. "But surely she can't be, we freed all the slave workers and she wasn't there." He was baffled by the comment, but made a mental note.

"Now keep walking towards the clearing where you have your craft hidden. And taking your time will do you no good whatsoever." For the first time their tone sounded menacing.

His mind was in turmoil. He knew he had to keep calm and save his friend. As he walked in front of the two entities he slowly raised his arm and as casually as he could, felt the outline of the remote detonator in his pocket. If the idea was to steal his Blackbird at least he could destroy it in flight.

"Arms where we can see them please, no tricks."

Johnno turned to face his captors as he walked. "My ribs hurt remember, when one of you saved me from a good kicking in the mine." Johnno hoped the 'real' Rick would reply.

"Yes, one of us did," was the joint reply. "A good attempt, but not good enough. Now keep walking."

Johnno continued to keep talking, desperate to slow down their progress. "Why do you want to change the history of a whole world, possibly condemning millions to die?"

"Simple. I present the weapon to my good friend Albert and demonstrate its obvious future potential. He has the total trust of Herr Hitler, who grants me a personal audience – which I obviously insist is in complete secrecy, just the two of us. I show him my shape shifting skills also, and offer to act as a body double, for his personal safety of course."

He turned to face the entities and stopped walking, more time to think. Flattery, that may slow them down "Why, as a body double surely you put your own life at risk when you have the universe free to travel in?"

"That's your problem earthling, thinking small. At the right time the 'body double' is killed, leaving me as Herr Hitler himself to lead his Third Reich to victory. Russia, America and Britain destroyed by nuclear weapons. Japan takes Asia and China with conventional weapons, and then I take Japan as well. Soon I control a whole planet and I am no longer a nomad and I fulfil my true destiny."

"You're as mad as Hitler, you'll make a good couple."

"Maybe so, but **I** am infinitely more powerful. Now please keep moving as one of us has an important appointment to keep."

The forest was calm and tranquil, Johnno's thoughts were not. Each step towards the clearing was surely one step closer to their deaths. He realised that this paled into insignificance if the weapon and its secrets were gifted to the enemy. He may even have no future to return to anyway if that were the case. "Think Johnno, think. What would Freya say? What would Rick do? I can't attack them, I have to outsmart them. But how? … how can I do that?"

All too soon they reached the clearing, and Johnno's Blackbird came into view.

"She is beautiful, it is just a pity you will never live to fly her again. Now keep moving, just the other side of your aircraft." Johnno turned to check that both Ricks were still guiding him in the vain hope that the real Rick had somehow broken free, unfortunately they were both still there. He knew that somewhere deep inside one of these shifters was the real Rick, but how could he reach that deep memory?

As Johnno reached his aircraft he patted the fuselage. "Goodbye Odin, I'm sorry that we can't fly again and touch the face of God." He then ducked under her fuselage and kept moving slowly forward. The two replicants followed him until they were all in the clearing on the far side of the Blackbird

"Very poetic, I'm sure, poetic but pathetic." was the joint reply. "Now stop there."

Johnno expected to feel a pain in his back as he anticipated being neurolised, or worse, but nothing happened.

The entities approached him. "We realised what a good hiding place this was when we spotted your craft, albeit one day in the future. Thank you, or should I thank your departed colleagues?"

"You cannot fly my craft, so why come here?"

"Because of this ..." both entities produced a small device which they aimed ahead of them. They emitted a dull melodic sound which seemed to bounce back towards them. Slowly, but surely, an image appeared in front of them. It was as if a million points of light slowly began to glow and spread sideways, joining and forming the outline of a craft. As the image became more of a solid three dimensional structure Johnno realised it was a small flying craft of some kind. After twenty seconds or so it had fully emerged in all its splendour.

It was a dull grey colour, with two apparent cockpits placed back to back on top of its hull, similar to the layout of his craft. Around twelve feet across its wingtips and perhaps twenty feet long, it was essentially pear shaped, obviously increasing its aerodynamics. The hull itself showed no signs of joints or rivets, but an occasional dark patch presumably caused by the heat of high speed travel. Around its perimeter was what looked like a band of opaque glass, around three to four inches wide, which Johnno took to be the means of propulsion, the harnessing of light that Rick had mentioned.

Illegible markings were displayed beneath each cockpit, resembling cuneiform writing and mathematical shapes.

"She is a small craft, but worthy enough for our journey today."

Realising he had to play for time Johnno began to inspect the craft.

How ...?"

We call it stealth. We use … " the entities paused "no, it is of no matter, you would begin to discover this in eighty years or so. My Aryan friends will have it as a gift from their new leader."

Johnno hid his anger, deciding to try some flattery in order to gain time. "She is beautiful I must admit." He began to walk around the craft taking everything in. He looked underneath and realised the craft was actually hovering twelve inches or so from the ground. He glanced towards the entities.

"It is just anti-gravity my friend. You will – sorry - you would have discovered this technology in one hundred years or so. My new friends will have this within days."

He glanced within the cockpits. The layout here seemed familiar, a contoured seat complete with full body restraints, whilst the control panel reminding him of the one he had operated in the Bell, a totally flat surface with icons and shapes as controls. All the time he was feeling the contours in apparent admiration. "Boy, would I love to fly one of these."

"No more time for flattery, or stalling, it is now time for us to leave. Please move away from my craft, and be ready to pass over the weapon."

Johnno stepped back from the craft, his mind racing as he prepared to possibly die. "Think, think … " His brain was in overdrive.

The entities moved forward and touched a small symbol on the side of the craft. Immediately both cockpits slowly opened. The craft lowered itself to the floor as the entities both climbed onto the 'wing' of the craft and gently lowering themselves inside.

Johnno's latest thought flashed through his mind.

"Perhaps whoever receives the weapon is the shifter."

The entities settled themselves in the cramped cockpits, donning their flight helmets and fastening their seat harnesses in unison.

"And now for the weapon, if you please."

Johnno readied himself to, hopefully, deal with the shape shifter. To his dismay a small hatch opened on the wing side nearest to him. The entities smiled. "Hoping to use the weapon on me and save your friend? I think not. Place it within the compartment please. Then I can be on my way and eject your friend to the elements."

Johnno smiled, at last he realised what to do, a possible way to save his friend. Rick was about to die regardless.

He moved slowly forward holding the weapon in front of him. As he approached the compartment he suddenly stopped and looked at the nearest entity with a look of resignation to his fate.

"You have won, may your soul rot in hell, or whatever you call hell."

Both entities smiled, a smug smile accompanied by a nod of the head - the smile of success.

Johnno stepped back one pace and shouted at the top of his voice.

"Activate Shutter!"

Within milliseconds the rear canopy blew off, its occupant shot skywards in his ejector seat. It quickly reached a height of five hundred feet or so, then stabilised as small jets appeared from underneath. Slowly it began to descend.

Johnno smiled and whispered "Well done Rick". He dropped the weapon to the floor, pulling out a Walther pistol that he had taken as a souvenir when in the mine. He aimed it at the shifter, who was still transfixed at what had just happened. His body began to glow gently as it mutated slowly regaining the form of Mr. Maia.

"Well done my friend, but you have still lost. Your Aunt Freya will still burn in hell and never reach salvation."

Johnno re-gripped the pistol, still aiming at Maia. "That's your second mistake, now I know Freya may be released if she has been replicated."

Maia stared Johnno down ....

... with eyes as smooth and as black as haematite.

He grinned. "Perhaps, but you cannot shoot me; your Federation will not allow it."

Johnno fired the pistol, hitting Maia in the shoulder with a satisfying thud. His face was one of amazement. Placing his hand over the wound he examined the green blood seeping through his fingers.

Johnno fired again, this bullet hitting him in the other shoulder "To hell with the Federation I say. It's Not my Federation. I'm from earth, remember?"

Maia struggled to close the canopy lid as he tried to make his escape.

Johnno fired again, this bullet ricocheting off the closing canopy. He immediately aimed at the closing compartment on the wing of the craft, several bullets entering with a satisfying thud before the compartment eventually closed, the following shots again bouncing off the fuselage. Inside Maia was struggling with the controls. The intense pain in both shoulders made manoeuvring within the confined space of the cockpit almost impossible. As he released the pressure on his shoulder the intense pain flooded back into his body, blood now oozing freely from both wounds. His vision was becoming blurred as he desperately searched for the right control icons to press, blood now seeping and pooling onto the panel itself.

Slowly, silently the craft began to rise into the air.

A noise behind him caused Johnno to spin around, gun poised to shoot in defence. It was Rick, who rushed forward to hug his friend in the biggest of all man hugs. "Thanks buddy. I could see your pain but couldn't break free from his control. How did you know I'd eject?"

"Air Force Training buddy, Air Force Training. Just like Pavlov's dog. You know those controls inside out, and how to eject … alien technology and all that."

Rick stepped back and looked skyward to see Maia's craft slowly climbing towards the cover of the clouds. "You shot the bastard, didn't you?"

Johnno smiled. "Two shots, actually. Just enough to slow him down, but not kill him."

"You remembered the Federation at last. Well done."

"Well, not exactly. How high would you say he was now?"

Rick looked up again. "Around one or two thousand feet, give or take, he IS moving very slowly."

"That's far enough to keep us safe I believe". Johnno reached into his pocket and took out the remote detonator provided by Rick earlier in the day.

"What ...?"

"When I passed under our Blackbird and caressed the fuselage I simply removed the explosive charge in the hope I could somehow make use of it, perhaps even to kill us all if needs be. Then, when I admired the shifter's craft I attached it underneath. See ...." Johnno flicked open the protective cover and pressed the switch.

"Oops!"

High above them there came a brilliant flash of light. A shockwave emanated in all directions as the craft disintegrated. Seconds later there came a sound like thunder .The myriad of trees saw their final autumn leaves blown away as their trunks absorbed the aftermath of the blast. Then all was quiet. The birds ceased their incessant songs of joy. The only sound left was the wind blowing through the trees into the distance with hurricane force, and soon even that was gone.

"As I said to Maia, to Hell with the Federation."

Johnno reached down and picked up the weapon, securing it once again within his jacket. He patted it immediately – just to be sure.

Rick's voice was full of concern. "Yeah, to hell with the federation, but what about Freya? We never found out where she is, he never even gave us a clue."

Johnno smiled. "Oh yes he did. We need to go and collect Manni and Astrild, who should only be nursing a mild headache at best. And then we go and find Freya. No time to waste buddy, let's hope we're not too late."

Johnno patted his friend on the shoulder, a reassuring smile on his face.

They both turned and began to jog back down the path to the cabin to check on Manni and Astrild, and then hopefully onwards to save Freya as well.

Chapter 45

"Is there **any** news, any updates, do we have **anything** to report?"

The tone was urgent, but the President was attempting not to look too worried as he talked to his chiefs of staff.

Around the large oval table were the cream of the US defence teams, all sworn to secrecy about the impending operation, and the devastating scenario should it fail. Smoke hung in the air, a mixture of Cuban cigars and Marlboro cigarettes. Coffee cups and mugs adorned the table; the president was sipping on whisky. It had been a long meeting. The atmosphere was tense, deep concern etched on the faces of everyone present.

Errol Gilmore, the Chairman of the Joint Chiefs of Staff, spoke. "We have had word that the Starman has safely landed and is fully immersed with his mission. Apparently there were three other weapons which were of interest and these have been successfully neutralised. One of those we have in storage, successfully collected from Kecksburg. History, as yet, remains unchanged sir."

"How the fuck will we know if it is unchanged, history happens, goddamit."

"If there is a change Mr President, for the worse, then we would simply not be here, you may not have been born, England may no longer exist, Russia might be a vassal state ... and there would be a swastika hanging outside the White House."

An ominous silence hung in the air.

Suddenly the door to the office swung open and in walked a studious looking Chief of Staff, Tom Gerarty. He moved over to the president whilst reading a faxed report, clutched tightly in his hand.

"Sorry I'm late Mr President but we have a strange occurrence to report."

The president looked up, as did all the other staff in the room.

"Go on Tom, but good news only if you please."

"It is good news, I think, Mr President." Gerarty looked pensive.

The President smiled. "Go on, we could all use some good news right now."

"It's Tesman, Mr Maia's colleague, he's ...... disappeared."

The President was not a fan of Tesman, only accepting him into the team at the insistence of the CIA, who felt it was the best way to keep an eye on him. His name had regularly been mentioned by the authors of 'Blue Book' as a potential go-between with their newly discovered alien friends.

"Disappeared? Where?- and more to the point , how?"

"Well, that's it Mr President, he just, sort of .... faded away and disappeared before the eyes of his minders within this morning."

"What do you men , faded away? People don't just fade away. Where was this?"

"As we approached the secure 'visitor' site on level 4 in area 51."

"His colleague, Maia, has he returned?"

"Not to my knowledge, all contact has been lost."

"Good. I never did trust the bastard. His eyes, you know, something about them." He swung his chair back around to face the team; their smiles mirrored that on the face of the president himself. "So we're one step closer to success gentlemen. Assuming we are successful, is Apollo ready for launch?" the President added an urgent tone to his question, aimed directly at Dr Payne, head of NASA.

"We have already tested the Lunar Module functions and the preliminary flight is planned for May, giving us two months to fine tune everything. We plan a dress rehearsal of the landing, and aim to get within 8 or 9 nautical miles of our planned landing area. We need to ensure that nothing goes wrong on the delivery mission. One slip on the real mission and a nuclear explosion could shift the Moon's orbit, with disastrous consequences."

Chewing his cigar, and moving it to one side of his mouth he added "Not to say what it will do to global tensions. The whole goddam world will be watching on TV." Removing his cigar "But, yes, we will be ready Mr President – you provide the package and we will deliver."

A mixture of relief and patriotism was tangible within the room; the only thing missing was the sound of the 'Star Spangled Banner'. Heads nodded. Sweat was mopped from brows. Everyone looked at each other for reassurance. It was so silent you could hear a pin drop.

The silence was broken by John Vasey, the army Chief of staff.

"Thank fuck we have the best postal delivery service in the World".

Everyone laughed and the tension was cleared for a while.

The President got to his feet, looking around the room at his team. Taking a deep breath and, with a hint of Churchillian grandeur, solemnly spoke. "Let's pray to God, gentlemen that all goes to plan and the package is also safely delivered. The lives of millions of US citizens, not to mention millions of our allies and the whole free world, rest solely in our hands. Let us not forget that Project Horizon must succeed, and this is surely our first step." He reached down onto his desk and picked up his tumbler of Jack Daniels.

Raising it aloft he added words that reflected the thoughts of all staff members present.

"Let us pray for our agents in Germany.
Let us pray for their total success.
God help us if we fail.
God will surely judge us if we do."

Chapter 46

The smell was unbearable and it was almost impossible to breathe, the duct tape pressed firmly against her mouth only exacerbating the pressure on her chest allowing only shallow intakes of air through her nose. She moved her head from side to side to create some space for air to enter. She tried to move her arms so she could push, but they were bound tightly behind her. She kicked out with her legs, but these too were bound at the ankles. She tried to shout out, but the tape and whatever lay on her helped to muffle any noise she could make. She relaxed back, exhausted by her apparent wasted efforts to escape.

As Freya began to regain consciousness her mind swirled with questions.

"Where am I? How long have I been here? Why can't I breathe properly?"

Her brain told her to remain calm, panic would only increase her suffering and pain. "Come on Freya, think, you must think girl, how did I get here? ... wherever 'here' is."

She tried to think back, attempting to clear the fog in her brain. Her eyes began to focus on the narrow shafts of light that fought their way through whatever held her down and kept her prisoner. Realising she must have been neurolised, all trainees for the Federation undergo this procedure in training, she desperately tried to remember when it could have happened. Memories began to return bit by bit.. She recalled the mission and greeting Johnno as it began.

"There was a birthday party? A troop convoy to ... to ... where?

Rick was shot dead! Her heart raced. Dead? But I arranged to have him collected safely by the resistance. How can he be dead?

More 'fog' cleared. She relaxed. Johnno had saved him. "Good, I remember that". The cabin, what about the cabin?

The communications unit in the hidden compartment. Who did she talk to? Who contacted her? .... She was leaving to help arrange Rick's return. It was like an electric shock to her system as the memory finally pieced itself together and kicked in.

"Maia! I was asked to meet Maia and feedback details of progress. I met him in the clearing. He activated the stealth on his craft. He was polite. He said he knew little but I had fed back details daily to him. I thought that was strange." She dug deep into the depths of her returning memories. He needed to witness any progress on the cabin screen as soon as possible, the President himself had authorised his visit. The memories began to fade as weariness returned.

"Concentrate Freya, you must concentrate!" She could see him gesturing for her to lead the way, and as she stepped forward the sharp pain she felt between her shoulder blades, the feeling of nausea as she slipped into nothingness.

"The bastard; he neurolised me. Maia is the traitor!"

Anger flooded through her body as she struggled to free herself. Whatever was keeping her trapped was moving with her and making it even more difficult for her to breathe. The shafts of light were still there, giving her some form of hope. "Is it the sky or am I locked into a building somewhere, perhaps even the mine. What's keeping me down? Why does it move with me?"

She had no sense of day or night and no idea how long she had been there. It could have been hours, or days, or even weeks. She rationalised. "I don't feel hungry. Well, not really hungry, so it is more likely hours than days."

Had she had been missed? "What if Maia had been a replicant and she was his target?" I may never be missed. Her heart sank. She attempted to rally her thoughts.

"No, I'm sure that 'min lille romfarer' will know in his heart any replicant isn't me. He will surely see through any replicant ... I hope. No, I'm sure he will … eventually."

She tried in vain to move and release herself, but the effort just tired her weary body. The neuroliser had weakened her, she needed time to recover. She could no longer muster the strength to struggle; breathing had become a struggle in itself. She was fighting to stay awake but her eyes slowly closed and the world began to drift away. The shafts of light started to disappear and darkness returned. She gently slipped back into unconsciousness, her lifeless body trapped by an unknown force gently pressing down onto her and keeping her prisoner.

Surely the release of death could not be too far away.

Chapter 47

Johnno felt it seemed to take forever as he ran back towards the cabin. He felt every bump and hollow on the path as he concentrated on not falling, it would be stupidity to injure himself now. Freya's life was possibly in the balance and his mission was in danger of failure. Stumbling on a fallen branch he remonstrated himself "Careful you fool, careful. It's just like the fitness runs that Freya made me do as a boy, and I didn't fall then."

"Whoa, careful buddy, we're almost there". Rick's calm voice masked his true feelings, he too knew Freya's life was at risk and there was no time to waste.

In the distance two figures appeared out of the trees, headed straight in their direction. Johnno and Rick stopped dead in their tracks, fearful it may be part of an enemy patrol. They approached slowly, seemingly just as cautious and concerned who they would be meeting. Two recognisable figures came into view, now warily walking towards them.

"Is that you ... Manni and Astrild?" Rick's voice was full of disbelief "it can't be."

"Oh yes it can, and it is." Johnno sounded triumphant "Come on". He set off again as fast as he could. Fearful that they might not have been recognised and may be neurolised in 'friendly fire' Rick shouted out as loud as he could. "Manni, Astrild, it's us, Rick and Johnno."

There was a mutual session of hugging and back slapping as they finally met. Manni faced Johnno and held him by the shoulders "I thought we were goners when you zapped us."

Rick was standing with his arm around Astrild, with a grin that seemed to stretch from ear to ear. "Yeah, buddy, so did I"

"I told you he was an idiot. When he told me to turn the left dial all the way round I did so ... all the way around to the lowest setting. I realised that he must have been listening to our conversation when he was so-called unconscious, and the lowest setting only lasted minutes, so that's what I did." He smiled and shrugged his shoulders. "That, and the fact I'm a wonderful actor."

"You had us all fooled as well."

Johnno's mood changed quickly. "Right, we need to go and find Freya, before it's too late."

"You know where she is?" Astrild's voice rose slightly as her hopes for Freya's survival suddenly increased.

"I think so ...." Johnno hinted at some uncertainty. "Maia must have been present in the mines when we first visited in the guise of our German hosts. I now realise that he was the spy who had replicated Krammler. When he mentioned the clearing where bodies of the poor dead workers were dumped he remarked 'the souls of our enemies will burn in hell and never reach salvation'."

Rick frowned and looked deep in thought, but slowly a dawn of realisation came over him, the frown melting into a smile. "I see, yes, when he was boasting in the cockpit just before take-off."

"That's right buddy. He said the same phrase word for word. Freya has been hidden in the mound of bodies ready for disposal and burying. I'm guessing that task has been held back by the events of the last couple of days, and she should still be there."

Manni looked towards Astrild, their faces full of concern. "We've tried contacting her with no luck; all we get is static on her wavelength."

"Maia will have taken her earpiece and used it himself to listen in on our conversations as he replicated Freya. **That's** how he kept being at the right place at the right time. We have no way of contacting her; she's all alone, hopefully alive, in the clearing. Maia obviously had no respect for the Federation, he was about to kill us both by his craft." He drew in a long breath "Could he have killed Freya?"

Johnno's heart sunk. Rick grasped his shoulder. "Not unless it was a last dying act. Remember she had to be alive when he took over her body, let's hope she still is."

Johnno looked Rick in the eye, doing his best to sound upbeat. "Remember the old saying, the opera ain't over 'till the fat lady sings; well it ain't over; we have no time to waste, let's go and save her."

Rick smiled and looked towards Manni and Astrild. "Johnno's right, we haven't come this far to give up now." Johnno's face took on a steely grin. A steely, but very relieved grin.

"We'll need some 'watchers', and camouflage jackets from the cabin." Rick sounded confident and upbeat. "We can get there before it's too dark and begin our search. There can't be too many poor souls left lying there. Let's do this. Let's go and find Freya then we can finish our mission."

The four of them turned to retrace their steps to the cabin, hearts and souls lifted with Rick's words. They were infinitely more confident that she could be found, alive, and brought back to the relative safety of the cabin.

On reaching the cabin they separated and set about their tasks as quickly as they could. Manni and Astrild descended into the hidden compartment and re-emerged with two watchers and controls, placing them on the table as they checked the remote controls were functioning OK. "I'll set them to infra-red just in case it's too dark when we get there." Manni adjusted the watchers accordingly whilst Astrild confirmed the remote screen was set to receive. Rick collected the warm camouflage jackets from a pine wardrobe in the main bedroom.

"Remember the caps in the pockets," before tentatively adding, "and we may need the black stick for our faces."

Johnno checked on the two remaining captives, relieved to find them still alive but still deeply unconscious. He checked their pulses again. He called out to Rick "Twenty four beats per second. Is that OK?".

"No problem. When they get to forty five plus it means they're coming round. We've plenty of time."

As he was about to leave the room Johnno turned back and searched through their pockets. He found what he wanted, another Walther pistol. He ejected the magazine from the grip, and inserted it into his own souvenir pistol. He now had extra bullets should he need them. If it was to be a matter of life or death for his beloved Freya then he would kill anyone who got in his way. As he emerged from the bedroom he found his colleagues already jacketed. Rick held out Johnno's jacket to help him put it on before adding a dark knitted woollen hat. Manni passed him a stick of face black. "Just in case it's dark when we get there"

Johnno was puzzled. "I thought you said it was an 'easy hour' when you delivered the logs. Why should it be dark?"

Rick answered. "We need to be unseen, unheard. I'm afraid old Odin is quite noisy, especially when pulling the cart. We'll have to go on foot, mindful at all times of German patrols. The attack in the mine has made them rather nervous."

Johnno nodded. "I suppose so."

Rick handed him a replacement neuroliser. "Fasten this to your wrist and let's hope we don't need to use it." His voice adopted a sombre tone. "We may only have one chance of safely retrieving Freya. Let's be careful and let's work as a team."

Manni and Astrild led the way and disappeared through the cabin door. As Rick was about to follow Johnno held him gently by the arm, holding him back. "Thanks for this buddy; I know you're taking a big gamble for me and for Freya. You should be sending me back with the weapon, job done."

Rick smiled and patted his friend's hand. "You wouldn't go back, knowing her life was in danger," pausing for a second he added, " and nor would I. Let's do this and then we can get back to old 'shovel' and an ice cold beer.

They turned and exited the cabin. Rick stopped about five yards from the cabin and smiled. "Just in case our friends do waken up, or someone comes snooping."

By his side were the remnants of a wooden gate attached to a dilapidated row of fencing. He waved his left arm over the top of the gate post and a cone of grey light appeared from the ground up, surrounding the cabin as if it were in the safety of a glass globe. Slowly it seemed to fade away and become totally transparent.

"Energy shield. No way in or out."

Johnno looked impressed. "Alien technology and all that?"

"Something like that"

They set off down the path at a quick pace, in single file, mindful of possible German patrols, especially after their efforts of the previous days. It had begun to snow, only in flurries, but the pleasant autumnal air had been replaced by the onset of winter, which seemed to arrive early within these high pine and hardwood forests. The path had become slightly treacherous forcing them to be more careful with each step as they moved closer to their goal. It was beginning to become quite dark, the grey snow clouds beginning to blot out any remnants of afternoon sunlight that tried in vain to enter through the canopy of pine trees. The sun was low in the sky and fighting a losing battle in trying to light up the forest floor.

Eventually they reached the bend in the path where the mine and its compound could be seen. They all huddled down; taking what cover they could from the tree trunks and bushes that still had leaves upon them. The compound lights were on, showing the layout to which they had all become familiar. The guards were in their towers and the gates firmly locked. An occasional figure could be seen hurrying across between the huts and the mine entrance.

Rick turned and whispered "They must be confident that the weather is protecting them from possible probing air raids. It's a pity we can't get a message back to the RAF."

"Surely that would put any new prisoners at risk as well." Johnno sounded concerned "Besides, they have no functioning Bell left to develop. Let's hope they believe their tunnel is big enough for its planned use and no more poor souls are rounded up and worked to death."

Manni leaned over, pointing to his right. "The clearing is over in this direction, keep low and follow me." It was difficult to move quickly and safely on the slippery, leaf-laden floor. Rick slipped and landed on a tree branch, which promptly snapped , sending a resonating 'crack' through the still evening air. "Shit!"

All four of them immediately ducked down, seeking whatever cover they could find. The guards in the towers, particularly jumpy after events of late, quickly switched on their searchlights, scanning the darkening forest with their powerful beams. Other guards rushed from their quarters, quickly donning jackets as they ran towards the compound gate, rifles and machine guns at the ready. The searchlight beams were illuminating the general area where the four lay hidden as best they could, but there was only just enough light to reduce their efficiency. As the guards began to unlock the gates there came a strange sound from behind Rick. He turned to see Johnno cup his hands to his mouth and make a howling, barking noise. He poised, and made the sounds again. It sounded like a dog's bark, but occasionally higher pitched and longer, almost like a scream. In the compound the soldiers stopped and looked at each other. The barking sound came again. The guards in the tower turned back their search lights, and then turned them off. They looked down at their half-dressed colleagues.

"Foxes," they shouted, before laughing and adding "probably fighting over any meat and bones left out there by our removals teams."

As they retreated back to the warmth of their mess huts one of the soldiers looked up. "I hope they get a Bellyful."

All was quiet again.

Rick turned to Johnno and whispered "Well done buddy, where the hell did you learn that?"

"Aunt Freya. Let's call it human technology and all that."

They patiently waited for another five minutes or so, with Johnno adding the occasional fox sound to help reassure the enemy that all was well, then began to move forwards again towards their goal.

Eventually the tree cover disappeared as they approached the clearing. Manni was the first to arrive to find ... nothing. He looked around, checking his bearings to make sure he was at the right place.

He was. Any bodies which had been dumped there had gone.

Soon his colleagues arrived to find Manni stood in an empty clearing. He turned to Astrild. "Send up the watchers, she may have escaped and be hiding somewhere."

Both watchers were prepared and sent up, set to scour the area in a spiral pattern ensuring that no patch of land was missed. Manni stood alongside her as they both scanned the screen looking for the faintest patch of light that would indicate a heat source and, potentially, someone alive.

"What's that, there?" Manni pointed to a faint spot of light on the screen. They both strained to see a faint luminous point on the right of the screen. Astrild set the watcher to 'hover'; after several seconds the light began to move across the screen in irregular steps.

"It's just a rabbit."

Astrild set the watcher back on its searching, spiral path. They approached the mine complex where several soldiers could be seen walking around the compound. Astrild set it to hover, although silent in operation she was fearful it may still be spotted. After several minutes they knew that no-one was there, hiding or not. They realised that it was a lost cause, calling back the watchers.

The trio looked on as Johnno began to rush around the barren area, kicking the snow with his feet in the desperate hope of finding a clue which could lead to his beloved Aunt. From the corner of his eye he was sure he saw a faint light, a glow beneath the white tablecloth of snow. He moved erratically until it re-appeared just in front of him. It wasn't too bright, but there it was, a definite glow just in front of him. He fell to the ground and began to search frantically for something, anything, to give him hope. The ground was quite hard and scorched with tufts of grass here and there just visible through the freshly fallen snow. His friends looked on sympathetically as he scrabbled around on his knees, frantic for evidence she was still alive.

"What's this?" feeling something metallic under his fingers. His fingers were now becoming numb as he scraped away the snow to reveal his find. He lifted it towards his face; it was a ring, a large ring. Taking a torch from his pocket, being careful not to shine it and give away their position, he cupped the ring in his fingers and switched on the torch.

It was Freya's ring, he was sure, and it was faintly glowing. He reached into the top of his jacket to pull the amulet and chain clear of his clothing and placed it by the ring. It began to glow much brighter, glimmering as though it contained a myriad of tiny stars.

Johnno couldn't contain his excitement. He turned to face his friends, holding the prized evidence in front of him, desperately seeking their reassurance that, somehow, Freya was still alive. His voice was full of hope. Hope and desperation combined.

"Look, look, Freya's ring. She would NEVER have lost this. She WAS here, I was right, but where can she have gone to? Who's taken her?" His voice dropped to one of forlorn hope as he glanced around at the empty clearing. "Where are any of the poor souls from the mine?"

Manni was the first to reply.

"Sorry Johnno, they're all gone."

"They can't be. Why? How?"

"I don't know. They always left them a while before removing them. We must have spooked them and they've been moved early."

"Removing them? Where? Let's go and find them."

Manni glanced at Rick, and over to Astrild. His face was solemn.

"Where do they remove them?" Johnno's voice was insistent.

Manni looked towards Rick again. Rick raised his head in acknowledgement. He knew how difficult it was for Manni to continue. He moved over towards his friend and placed his arm on his shoulder.

"They remove them to burn them, and hide the evidence of their atrocities."

Johnno's voice was filled with anguish, anger and despair. "They can't do that, I know she's alive, I just do. She left this ring as a sign, a message of some kind." He could not be consoled. The thought of his dear Freya being dead was too much to take in. "She can't be dead, she just can't be. We're talking about Freya here."

"I'm sorry buddy, we were too late I'm afraid. She must have left the ring in the hope that you would find it and feel some kind of comfort."

Then the tears started. Johnno fell to his knees. "I'm sorry I let you down dear Freya, I am so, so sorry."

"No-one has let her down buddy. Maia gave us all the run around, none of us was any the wiser. He even used her ear piece; he was well prepared to screw us all at any cost. We never saw this coming, and you did zap the bastard."

His friends kept vigil while he said a sad goodbye to his Aunt, eventually helping him stand and begin their slow return to the safety of the cabin where they could take full stock of what had happened.

Chapter 48

Johnno cut a forlorn figure, sat at the table just staring at the ring he held in his hand. He moved it gently between his fingers, with fond memories stirring of his childhood when his dear Aunt would let him hold it and try it for size. They always laughed when it just fell off his fingers as it was way too big. She would always make sure it was safely placed back on her finger when they finished playing.

"One day I will show you its secrets and the stars in the sky will be yours." A faint smile broke across his face as the cherished memories played back in his mind.

"One day the stars in the sky will be yours."

He frowned, and then turned to see Rick smiling at him. Could he read his mind? "What did you say?"

"One day the stars in the sky will be yours."

Johnno was stunned. How could Rick be in on one of his personal memories?

"Don't worry buddy, I'm not a mind reader. I saw you looking fondly at the ring and I recalled what all mothers tell their children back on Alnilam. I just guessed that's what Freya said to you." Johnno smiled and was lost in thought, cherishing the idea that his dear Aunt had treated him much the same as a mother would do.

Rick placed his hand on his friend's shoulder. "Come on, I think it's time that the stars were all yours." Johnno looked slightly puzzled as Rick pulled back the rug allowing the trapdoor to slide open.

"Come on, Starman, Freya's legacy awaits."

He turned to see Manni gesturing for him to follow his friend into the chamber.

Johnno stood and pushed his seat back, still slightly wary of what Rick was about to show him. He carefully followed his friend down into the chamber, recalling the first time he had done so when hiding in there just days ago. The door above him slid shut, and he was back bathed in a translucent light which seemed to come from everywhere, and nowhere, all at once. He looked around, wondering just what was so interesting and why Rick had led him there. It was still mildly claustrophobic, with no evidence as to why it was of obvious importance. Rick broke the silence.

"Can you see the symbols on this sidewall?"

Although he had seen them before, he realised he hadn't taken much notice of them; he had been more concerned about being trapped in the cell and not knowing why at the time.

"Look closely, do you recognise any of them?"

Johnno moved over to the back wall and peered closely at the symbols. He felt along with his fingers but everything felt quite smooth, as well as soft to the touch .He remembered his first encounter and his amazement as he encountered a pliable metal, something he knew could not exist. His eyes followed the shape of the circle, examining each symbol closely until he spotted a shape he recognised. He turned to Rick, pointing at his discovery. "It's the shape of my talisman. It's the key we used for the Bells." He sounded startled, almost ecstatic with his discovery.

Rick nodded and gestured towards the symbol.

"Perhaps it still is a key of sorts. Go on, try it."

Johnno felt inside his shirt, pulling gently at the chain which kept his talisman safe. He looked towards Rick for reassurance, and then placed it against the symbol on the wall. To his amazement the circle of symbols slowly rotated clockwise. The 'wall' then slowly began to fade and disappear like fog in the morning sunshine. In front of him now was a large room, some twenty feet or so square, seemingly too large to fit under the cabin. He gingerly stepped inside, his brain struggling to take in all he saw.

"Whoa, where are we? Are we still under the cabin? We can't be, can we?"

"Still under the cabin buddy."

To his left was an array of machinery which he took to be the controls of some equipment. There were small bright lights rapidly blinking on and off, with flat surfaces looking like keyboards of some fashion, full of strange symbols, much like those he found in the Bell, along the top of the console style table. Large screens covered the back of the console top and, set on the wall above them, were small pieces of equipment. Johnno recognised neurolisers and watchers among them. Small lights flashed on their faces as they were presumably being recharged ready for use.

Ahead of him the wall was fully covered in what seemed like a non-reflective glass, he struggled to see his own reflection as he moved towards it. It was soft to the touch, almost like a plastic 'sandwich' holding a gel substance inside. To his right the wall seemed to be made of the same substance he had seen in the ante chamber. It was a dull metallic grey, with no features on it at all.

"Is this some kind of workshop? An operations centre?" Johnno's eyes were everywhere, trying to take in this impossible space.

"Sort of, but it's more like a transit hub." Suddenly an alarm sounded and a row of lights began to flash in sequence above the blank wall to the right. "And we have incoming. Step back towards me buddy."

Johnno took several steps back towards the left hand side of the room. The lights began to flash rapidly and the wall took on a glowing hue, a hue which began to pulsate in sequence with the lights. He looked on amazed as the wall began to seemingly dissolve, much the same as the ante room, but here it took on the look of a three dimensional tunnel. In the distance something appeared from the inky blackness and seemingly walked towards them. As the entity grew closer Johnno could just perceive a human form, coming towards them, growing ever larger. Finally a figure stepped out of the 'tunnel' – it was Astrild!

She stepped forward and hugged Johnno. "It's good to see you up and about my friend, and I'm sure you have a million questions, questions which I presume Rick is about to answer."

"Close your mouth buddy. The last time I saw you that excited was the first time we had a personal visit to the Gemini project in training."

The 'tunnel' behind Astrild seemed to circle in on itself as it closed, the lights ceased to flash and the alarm fell silent. All was deathly quiet. After what seemed like an age Johnno spoke.

"That, whatever 'that' was, was amazing." He looked to Astrild "Where did you appear from? Was it another room? Was it the forest? I mean, that was mind blowing."

Astrild stepped forward "I'm just back from reporting to the Federation committee, informing them of the success to date of our special mission, but also of our sad loss."

"Isn't that on ...?"

"Yes, back in the Rigel complex."

"But that's over 1,000 light years away."

"1,344 to be precise."

Johnno turned and found a chair to sit on, stunned by the apparently impossible news just given to him. Astrild smiled at Rick as she moved to re-enter the cabin and join Manni 'upstairs'. "It's time he knew, and it's a second option for him now."

Rick sat down alongside his friend. "Time for some home truths buddy"

"Am I going to like this?" Johnno prepared himself for more, apparently amazing, revelations.

"As a race we have been visiting Earth for thousands of years. We developed as an advanced civilisation some time before your ancestors and went through the same traumas that your planet is suffering, endless wars and the need for superiority. Our Federation eventually came into being, along with the development of a code for life throughout the universe. As such we are dedicated to helping races survive and develop in a peaceful manner. But even we got it wrong occasionally. We added our RNA and DNA into early mankind and were often regarded as Gods. It went to our heads and we caused many problems before we recognised that **we** might be the problem. One of our early emissaries, name of An, led the council of the Annunaki who all fell into the crime of being worshipped as Gods by the peoples they helped. When we tried to make amends and remove them they caused a huge flood in the ensuing battles and many lives were lost. Not our finest hour."

"I take it that the battles listed in the Mahabharata weren't your finest hour either."

Rick looked pensive. "Err, no, that's why we're here today. But, thanks to you, we may be able to finally close that chapter."

"Is there any good news?"

"Plenty. We have helped civilisations develop agriculture, irrigation and form working societies where there were only hunting parties keen to keep the best for themselves and starve their enemies. Quetzalcoatl was tremendously successful in helping the Americas develop." Rick smiled as he was lost deep in thought. "He was an amazing character with a huge bushy beard. He even had a coat made from feathers to try and explain to his followers that was how he could fly. Priceless."

"Did you visit Egypt and help with the pyramids? A new book by an author called Von Daniken seems to think so."

"There's Egypt, Sumeria, Greece, Turkey, Japan. We're even mentioned in the Bible. I'm sure one day the truth will out, but until then it's our secret."

"Do you fly in space ships? We're seeing a lot of them lately."

"We did so extensively in our early days. Now they're flown by machine entities, you'd call them robots, programmed to perform tasks of exploration. To cover Earth we have a permanent base on the far side of the moon, one on Mars and one on Triton in Neptune's orbit. Although they're fast, especially when we first used wormholes, cleverly identified by your scientists Einstein and Rosen, we now use portals. Astrild just appeared through one."

"Okay. Spaceships I understand, but what's a portal?"

"It's a series of tunnels linking parts of the universe and even areas within planets. It's complicated but we basically choose a destination and tell our portal, or doorway, and it opens a path to the destination. We use the invisible parts of space, you will eventually call it 'dark space' and use its dark energy to power our travel and protect our bodies in transit. A trip back to Riga takes about two minutes. Pretty cool, huh?"

Johnno was impressed. He saw a potential answer to their problems on how to complete the mission quickly and easily. "So can you take me to the moon with our package?"

"Sorry, no. It's complicated, but the package must be delivered via your President and his official couriers. That's all arranged back home, all you need do is deliver the package to the President. It's a form of what you'd call horse-trading buddy."

Johnno got to his feet and looked over the console table, gently moving his fingers across the tops of the keypads. "I take it this is where you programme your visits, just like we did in the Bell."

Rick walked over to his friend, grinning. "Nope, better than that. New Alien technology and all that." He took Johnno over to the far glass wall and pressed an icon on the right hand side. The panel lit up in a series of columns, each displaying an array of ten large symbols illuminated by a bright blue light. He gestured for his friend to join him.

"We've done this before; time for my talisman to go into action again?"

"No, it's easier than that. Look for the shape of your talisman, see … there," pointing to a symbol just below the top of the displayed shapes. "Now put Freya's ring against it and gently press."

Johnno moved over, taking the ring from his pocket and placing it against the symbol, pressing gently against it. The surface of the screen took on the shape of the ring as it gently gave way, seemingly absorbing it completely. He pulled his hand back and looked at Rick with concern.

"Don't worry, you'll get it back," pointing to the large wall panel adding, "just look at this."

From behind the icon where the ring had been inserted there came a series of electrical impulses which resembled fine bolts of lightning. They raced and tracked wildly to be met by a myriad of blue pulsating points which had appeared on the screen, each one linked to each other by a fine array of lines, giving the appearance of a gigantic geometric spider's web. Within seconds the screen had the appearance of a crazy paved set of pathways with each pulsating point linked to each. Johnno immediately thought of the freeways, roads and intersections he had viewed whilst flying over Los Angeles and San Francisco.

In the centre was a larger light which pulsated as a bright, luminous, green colour, to the bottom left a dimmer red one shone slightly less brightly.

"Very impressive I'm sure, but what exactly am I looking at ?"

"Today, old buddy, the stars in the skies are yours. Go on, take a closer look."

He stepped nearer to the display of dots, closely scrutinising them. "Sorry, I can't make sense of this. What is it exactly?"

Rick stood alongside him and placed two fingers either side of the central red light. As he pulled his fingers apart the image increased in size making them infinitely more visible and recognisable. Johnno pointed to a set of small illuminated dots.

"It's Orion's belt," he couldn't contain his surprise, "there's Alnitak, and Alnilam and Minteka." He pointed excitedly towards the top. "Betelgeuse, with Rigel at the bottom. It's a star map!"

"Not just a star map, it shows all the portal pathways across our part of the galaxy." Rick put his fingers on the edge of the enlarged screen and pulled them together, closing the map back down to its original display "Now buddy click on the bottom left red light, pull it up to the centre and then open it like I did."

Johnno excitedly pressed his finger on the light, reinvigorated as he experimented with new technology again. Once there he stretched the display open to highlight a star with eight planets circling it, the third one out being the red light. "It's Earth, and our solar system!"

"Drag to make it larger." Rick was encouraging him to experiment.

He did so. As the image of Earth grew larger so did the pathways linking it back to Orion and all the other thousands of planets and constellations. Johnno dragged the image larger until it was covering the centre of the screen. As the image grew larger new lines appeared linking sites across the face of the Earth from North and South America to Europe, onto Asia and one aimed directly at the centre of Australia. Johnno looked closely at points on the map.

He pointed to South America, and turned to face Rick.

"Sacsayhuamán – we built it around the Inca civilisation. The one to the right is Teotihuacán in Mexico, and further down is Nazca. We even have one in Monument Valley in good old Arizona and in Utah we were good friends with the Anasazi people."

Johnno scoured the images on the screen, pointing to Egypt first.

"The sphinx, we built that around 12,000 years ago. Just above it is Cappadocia in Turkey, we knew it as Derinkuyu."

"This is awesome. And these are all portal pathways?"

"Yep. Pretty damned amazing or what? Each line shows a portal pathway we can use, with each illuminated dot of light being a destination. All you need to do is press your own portal to start, see." Rick pressed the illuminated dot on Earth "And then press where you want to travel to." Rick squeezed the star map back down until everything was again visible. He then pressed on the base in Orion. Immediately pathways were lit up, gently flashing to show direct and indirect routes available between the two portals. "Some of the portal destinations have developed civilisations, some are yet to develop and some just harbour animal and plant life. We can even develop 'dead' planets by a process of terraforming. It's been many thousands of years in the making, and we plan to share it with your very own Earth when the time is right."

Johnno turned to face his friend. "So it's a long way off then?"

Rick merely raised his eyebrows and smiled. "Maybe, but your mission helps bring it that bit closer."

Johnno stepped back. His beloved Freya had kept her promise, the stars were all his. "Could I use it one day?"

"Yes, if needs be. Your DNA has been modified by way of your parents. You've inherited your mother's genes. Yes, you could do it."

"I would like to visit where Freya was born, and pay my respects to her there in her real home."

"She always said that home was where you were."

Johnno smiled in a mixture of pride and embarrassment.

"Let's complete the mission buddy, and we'll see what we can do. Now collect your ring and keep it safe."

Johnno moved back to the screen on the right of the display, and looked to Rick for guidance on what to do next.

"Just put your finger onto the symbol where the ring is located and gently push again." As he pressed the ring seemed to move in a little further and then push itself back out of the screen, dropping safely into his hands. Immediately all the lines began to fade off the screen, the myriad of dots disappeared and the screen returned to the look of matt glass.

He tossed the ring several inches into the air, before catching it and replacing it in his top pocket, giving it a gentle pat to ensure it was safely bedded in. He extended his arm towards the rear of the room where they had entered "You go first you my friend; and thank you for sharing this with me. I feel closer than ever to Freya now and it has given me some solace."

Rick moved back to his friend and smiled. They hugged a hug of deep friendship before stepping out of the room into the small ante chamber.

Rick placed his hand high in the right hand corner and pressed a small, hardly discernible plate in the roof space. It gave way slightly under his fingers, and then returned as would a switch. The wall to the chamber began to re-appear and re-assemble just as if someone had filled a glass container with grey smoke. In seconds it was complete, and the chamber was hiding its secret once again. They climbed back up into the cabin space where Manni and Astrild were waiting, sat at the table drinking coffee. The door to the hidden chamber hissed shut, Rick replacing the rug.

There was an ominous silence; no-one knew what to say next. Yesterday had been the worst day possible.

Today some of the Federation's secrets had been shared in an attempt to give some sense of purpose to their mission and its loss.

Johnno spoke first. "That was amazing, Freya would be so grateful that you shared it with me." His voice almost broke with emotion, and the room was full with a discernible solemn tension. Pulling out a chair from the table he closed his eyes and took in a deep breath. "Damn, that coffee smells good." He paused and looked at his colleagues one by one.

"And we have a mission to complete. Freya would give me hell if I packed in now!"

Chapter 49

Johnno knelt down and placed a small wooden cross in the ground just behind the cabin. It had been carved from a piece of tree branch he'd found, cutting off just enough to whittle the shape of a rudimentary cross. He used a small piece of stone as a hammer as the snow had made the ground quite hard. "It's not much of a memorial dear Aunt, but I swear I'll return in the future and find this spot once again; I'll have something more fitting then, perhaps I could plant some cornflowers or twinflowers, your favourite.". He looked towards the heavens as if looking for her soul. "I'm sorry I couldn't get to you in time, but I will complete the mission. Wherever you are now, perhaps at Frigga's side, you can look down on me and I'll make you proud again."

He felt a hand on his shoulder. He spoke without looking up. "She was special, you know. She took me in and gave me a wonderful life, not just honouring the promise she made to my parents, she went way above that. I can see her now holding my shoulders on my first bike ride, boy did we laugh that day, especially when she told me that she'd never ridden one. The sparkle in her eyes when I did something special for her, baking cookies or even just making her a coffee. I remember lying on the warm ground staring up at the millions of stars when she'd point out galaxies and planets. It was even better when she bought me a telescope for Christmas; I never knew how she could afford to look after me, but look after me she certainly did. We spent hours scouring the skies; planets, comets, asteroids ... and the Northern Lights made chills run down my spine." He paused and wiped the tears from his cheeks and then gently laughed. "And now I know why she was so interested in me knowing the outline of Orion's belt and learning the names of all of the stars around it."

"You've lost a wonderful Aunt and I've lost a wonderful friend .... But you've never lost those memories; you did briefly find your parents, and that must have been a special moment for you."

Johnno closed his eyes recalling the meeting near Peenemunde. He wanted to savour every moment, recall every second of the all too short a time he had with them.

"Do you think I'll ever see them again? Would that be possible, alien technology and all that?"

"Who knows buddy, perhaps the first law of thermodynamics works with spirit energy as well, we are all controlled by electrical impulses."

"You sound just like the NASA instructor at flight school."

Rick grinned, and then his thoughts drifted back to the job in hand. "Time to go buddy. Remember we have a special package to deliver."

Johnno rubbed his eyes and wiped away the tears that had rolled down his cheeks, then stood up alongside Rick. "She was my hero you know."

"I know .... but we must remember that her sacrifice will save the lives of millions."

Johnno forced a smile. "There is that, a hero and a saviour."

The two friends made their way back around to the front of the cabin, the freshly fallen snow crunching beneath their boots. The forest was still and calm, the snow absorbing any errant sounds.

There was no bird song.

It seemed as if they too were mourning a lost, gentle soul.

Having said their goodbyes again Johnno and Rick set out for the clearing where the Blackbird was waiting to take them back to 1969. Manni and Astrild remained at the cabin preparing to close it down as a base for operations, and to close the portal down until further notice. To all intents and purposes it was to remain a deserted cabin, a potential haven for any fleeing partisans or weary travellers in the future. Once they had used the portal to travel back to their home it would remain hidden and closed down until reactivated by a visit sometime in the future.

They both moved swiftly towards their craft, careful not to slip on the snow covered ground. The only signs that anyone had been there before were the small imprints made by birds foraging for nuts and seeds on the ground, and the ominous signs of a fox circling around their perimeter looking to make them into his meal for the day.

"I never asked before, how do we get airborne? We have no runway."

"Remember anti-gravity? We've fitted pads under the wings to let us take to the air vertically. As soon as we begin forward motion they're programmed to fall away and self-destruct."

"About that forward motion, how do we go forward, sorry, back to 1969?"

"Remember the new fuel we were supposedly testing? That was a gift from visiting friends in Area 51 in exchange for safe return of the package, fully sanctioned by the Federation. Once airborne you open the throttle, the pads keep us in a holding pattern until the engines are at maximum throttle, the new fuel kicks in, the pads fall away and hopefully we're on our way back home. That's all I can really tell you."

He looked at Johnno, who was nodding as if in agreement. They both spoke as one voice.

"Alien technology and all that."

Johnno grinned "So the Federation have given the OK; and to think how I've pissed them off".

As they reached the clearing the Blackbird came into sight. Although covered in a fine dusting of snow, which had obviously helped keep her hidden from above, her outline was unmistakeable.

"I may have said this once before but Jeez, Johnno, she still looks beautiful."

Both pilots moved around their craft to give it a pre-flight inspection. They felt the body for damage, tested the ailerons for movement and the inside of the engines for any debris. Apart from snow on the bottom of the intakes they were clear. No damage to the turbine blades.

Johnno congratulated Rick. "I'm not sure how you brought her down in one piece, and undamaged, but she appears ready to fly, as good as she ever was."

"The hardest part was getting you down in one piece, you're much more delicate." Rick had a sarcastic tone in his voice. "We had to separate you from your beloved Blackbird as that was the more difficult to land safely." He looked Johnno up and down, and then said with a grin "You were made to bounce a little."

"Thanks a million buddy." His eyes narrowed as if in thought "So you came down with her? How the hell did you land?"

"Manni set up a tractor beam and she just glided in her, like a baby into its mother's arms."

"And me?"

"I thought about just dropping you," Rick laughed, "but luckily for you Astrild set up a tractor beam to bring you safely down as well." He gestured towards the snow covered craft.

"Come on buddy, let's fire her up and go home."

"Roger to that buddy, Roger to that."

Rick placed the small ladder against the fuselage and made his way towards his rear cockpit. The snow slid down the polished glass dome as he lifted it ready to enter. He manipulated himself into the tight space, fastening himself into his seat securely.

"Whatever you do, DO NOT shout 'Activate Shutter', or you're all on your own." Rick was laughing as he recalled his great escape.

Johnno followed close behind, opening his cockpit and climbing into his seat. "Jeez, I forgot just how snug the fit is in here." He manoeuvred himself downwards, donning his helmet and then fastening himself in securely. "What about the ladder?"

"That will fall away as we begin to climb; it's not hooked in, no problem."

They began the pre-flight checks. The displays in front of them all sprang into life with lights reassuringly coming on to signal everything was still functional.

"Altitude indicator checks out. Compass check. Power supply OK. Fuel OK." Johnno had a sudden thought. "The anti-gravity devices on the wings, how do we control them?"

Rick's voice was reassuring. "I've got them buddy, you just tell me when we're ready to take off and I'll do the rest."

Johnno sank back into his seat, assured that all pre-flight checks were OK. His mind drifted back to the last time he entered the cockpit for the test flights just days ago, yet years apart. His whole world had changed in such a short time, the time he had spent making sure that the history of the rest of world did not. He felt around his neck and gently pulled out his talisman, a lasting remnant of his Aunt's presence, and gently kissed it. As he placed it safely back inside his shirt he patted his breast pocket, reassuring himself that Freya's ring was safe and sound. Finally he felt to make sure that the alien weapon was safely tucked inside his shirt **and** his flight suit; there was no way that was being placed in a pocket for safety – if he could feel it against his body he knew for certain it was safe. He knew that losing it once was careless, twice would be unforgiveable.

He settled back into his well-practised flight routine.

"Right, I'm about to power the engines and warm them ready for flight."

"Roger that"

Just as he was about feed in the power he heard some static in his ear. He listened carefully but could not discern what was being said.

"What was that Rick? Please repeat"

"Repeat what?"

"Repeat your message."

The static re-appeared. Johnno was baffled. He could hear Rick clearly, but another message was trying to get through.

"Shit, I've left my ear piece in."

"Are we Go for engine start?" Rick's voice drowned out the static.

"Not yet Rick, I forgot to remove my earpiece, it needs to come out, sorry." As Johnno removed his helmet the static cleared into an obvious voice message.

"Manni here, a German truck is approaching and I fear we have been discovered."

Johnno spoke into his helmet microphone.

"Rick, put in your earpiece, I think Manni and Astrild are in trouble."

Rick took off his helmet, reached into his flight suit retrieving his ear piece.

"Come in Manni, we hear you, is there a problem?"

"A German truck is approaching; I fear we've been found out. You must get away now. I repeat, get away now. We'll hold them back here."

"Send up a watcher and hit them with an EMF charge, that should hold them"

"We've tried that with no joy, it is still approaching at speed."

"Try again, there's no way it can keep going, unless ..."

Johnno joined in. "Unless what?"

"Unless the EMF is being blocked, and only another alien technology can do that. We must have another alien interloper on our trail."

"They're here and …. they've driven right past. They must know where you are and they're on the way. Get away now if you can. I repeat, they are on their way, you must get away now."

"We can't do that. They're just minutes away, and it will take at least ten minutes to warm the engines through in this weather. If we try and take off we'll be sitting ducks." Johnno's voice was calm but insistent. "We need to get down, find some cover and see what we're up against."

Both pilots took off their helmets, pushed themselves up and out of the cockpits and, ignoring the ladder, jumped down to the ground.

"Here, you'll need this," Rick handed a neuroliser over to his friend, "set to mid stun, we'll need a day or more to make sure we've dealt with them."

Looking around the clearing there was not much room for cover. Johnno made for the trees by the side of the path and gestured for Rick to move to the other side. They had been taught emergency measures at flight school for downed pilots. "I've got this side, you're over there. We'll hit them before they know it as they leave the truck. Good luck buddy."

Rick patted his colleague on the shoulder and they both ducked down as low as they could and made their way over to the limited cover of the trees.

Johnno checked the setting on his weapon. "Is it clockwise or counter clockwise?" He looked closely at the dial. "Oh shit, I'll put it somewhere in the middle, that should stop them."

Rick was more concerned that any alien within the truck would not be a fan of the Federation and have a more deadly weapon than theirs. At full power alien weapons had the ability to vaporise anything from people to steel. Realisation dawned only too quickly.

"That's why they bypassed the cabin; they're here to destroy the Blackbird. Then the package won't matter as Johnno can't return and deliver it."

He readied himself for the shot of his life; he had to disable any replicant or shape shifter as soon as they left the truck's cabin. If he didn't then the mission would be over.

They heard the truck approaching before it came into view. Rick lifted his body slightly and looked over to where Johnno was hiding. They nodded as if both knew this would be the deciding confrontation which could seal their fate, or see them finally succeed. The truck appeared and drove forward towards the clearing, seemingly oblivious to the diesel engine's throaty throb giving away its position.

"Cocky bastards." Johnno strained his eyes ready to pick out his targets.

The truck came to a halt in full view of the Blackbird, everything went silent again as the throbbing engine was switched off. Johnno raised his body slightly to get a better view of the truck's tailgate, waiting for it to swing down as the soldiers appeared. Rick moved to his left as he aimed his weapon towards the truck and its driver, waiting for the cab door to open when he could take his first shot

Nothing happened. No-one appeared.

Johnno could feel the sweat move down his forehead as the anticipation of battle swallowed him up. His mouth was dry.

"Come out you bastards, let's get this over with," he spoke under his breath. Still nothing happened. It was an impasse.

Should they approach the truck? Was it an elaborate trap? Were more soldiers following as reinforcements and they were just waiting for them? They hadn't heard from Manni, so there should not be more of them. Was this to be a waiting game, the loser being the first to break cover?

Suddenly a message came from Manni into our colleagues' earpieces.

"It's Manni here. We're located directly behind you on the pathway. We have your positions and we can give covering fire."

Rick touched his earpiece, cupping his hands around his mouth.

"Well done, we may need all the help we can get. I see a driver and possibly one passenger. We cannot confirm how many soldiers are on board."

Johnno cut in. "The tailgate is up, the canvas is down. It may be full with as many as twelve of them. Take care approaching our positions."

"Roger that. We'll move as close as we can. I'm on Rick's side to the rear, Astrild is with you Johnno. Let us know when to move in."

The impasse continued for several minutes, the tension grew.

"Rick here, I see movement on the driver's side. The cab window is opening. I'm taking aim." The cab window was slowly wound down, but Rick was unable to get a clear shot at the driver, who was obviously leaning back into his cabin. Rick shuffled a little more to his left to get a better view.

"There's something coming out of the cab window. It's a weapon I think. I'm taking a shot" As he was about to fire Manni's voice rang in his ear "Don't do that. I see a shape with some cloth attached to it." He strained his eyes to view it clearly. "It looks like a wheel brace with a white cloth hanging from it. Unless I'm mistaken I think they want to surrender." Manni was incredulous.

"I can't believe it, it IS a white flag; the bastards want to surrender."

Rick was ultra-cautious. "Manni, move forward towards the cab door and I'll do the same. Keep me covered, let's not get too confident. Johnno, you and Astrild check the rear to check for an ambush. Let's do this my friends." Manni edged his way forwards as directed towards the cab door, decorated with a white flag of sorts. Rick moved forwards cautiously, his weapon trained on what he could see of the driver.

Johnno and Astrild were just as cautious at the rear of the truck, keeping both weapons trained on the canvas, fully expecting it to open and reveal a series of machine gun barrels. As they made the final approach Johnno motioned for Astrild to lift the canvas with him and make their 'attack'.

With his weapon in his right hand he counted with his left. Three fingers-Two fingers-One finger.

They swung open the canvas to reveal ... nothing. The rear of the truck was empty. Feeling more than a little relieved he relayed the message to Rick and Manni. "The truck is empty, no-one here and no weapons loaded. It's all clear. We're moving forward to check the passenger door."

Keeping their bodies flat to the truck body they edged their way forward, trying to view the passenger through the overtaking mirror mounted on the door. On the other side Rick had reached the driver's door, with Manni just feet away, covering his colleague. He reached for the door handle; weapon trained on the driver, pressed and swung it open.

"Don't shoot, please don't shoot." The driver leaned forward out of the relative darkness of the cabin.

Rick was amazed. His eyes opened wide and a broad smile erupted on his face. Smiling back at him was Johan, their contact within the mine. He had saved their lives back at the cabin and was here yet again.

"Johan, Good to see you. You scared the beejeezus out of us there AND you nearly got shot"

"It's good to see you too my friend." His voice emanated from a dry mouth.

On the passenger side Johnno could hear voices and was unsure if his colleagues were safe, or had been ambushed. He reached up for the handle to the door, nodding to Astrild and gesturing to keep him covered. He took a deep breath and swung open the door, aiming his weapon at the passenger.

A smiling face greeted him.

"Hello, min lille romfarer."

Chapter 50

Johnno couldn't believe his eyes, his dearest wish seemed to have come true and his beloved Freya had returned from the dead. But was it a trick? Was it another replicant? Was it another shape shifter? His brain was in meltdown. He listened out for a sound of warning from Rick, or even the distinctive sound of a neuroliser being fired. He wasn't sure if he should raise his own and fire, just to be sure; just to be certain that it wasn't some elaborate final trap.

"What are you waiting for? Give your favourite Aunt a hug." Rick's voice was reassuring and welcoming. Johnno glanced across the cabin to see Rick smiling and nodding his head in the reassuring way he always did. Johnno looked back at 'Freya', gazing deep into her eyes, desperately searching for a hint of the sparkle that had welcomed him every morning as a child.

She reached down, gesturing for Johnno to help her out of the cab. He placed his arms under hers and gently lifted her down.

As soon as he smelled her hair and her distinctive light perfume he was transported back to his childhood. In his mind's eye they were back in the forest playing games, enjoying picnics ... enjoying life. His eyes filled with tears.

It WAS his Freya. They just stood and looked at each other, and hugged, then hugged again.

"I thought I'd lost you … forever."

"You nearly did ... but I'm safe now and back to look after you again."

Johnno didn't want to let go for fear of losing her again. Desperate for answers he struggled to speak. "Just how? What?" He was lost for words.

She stepped back and turned to see Johan and Rick coming around the front of the truck towards them. She smiled and moved towards Johan, hugging his waist, gently kissing his cheek. "This is my saviour. When I thought all hope had gone he found me and rescued me."

Johan looked slightly embarrassed. "I was in the right place at the right time, and luck was on our side." Johnno grabbed him by the hand. "I just can't thank you enough." Again he was lost for words.

Freya moved over to Manni and Astrild, who both enveloped her in a group hug. As they separated Astrild grabbed Freya's hands and gave her a hug of her own.

"We all thought …. "

"I know, but today wasn't the day for me to die." Turning to face Johnno again, her face full of pride. "Today I help min lille romfarer to complete his mission."

"What happened to you? We were certain that we'd find you in that awful clearing. Where did you go?"

"I was ambushed by a so called Federation agent, name of Maia. I was totally fooled. I must be losing my touch." She closed her eyes as she continued, visualising every move. "I turned my back on him and he neurolised me. Next thing I remember is regaining consciousness but being unable to move, trapped by something I couldn't see. After trying to escape somehow I must have blacked out again. This is where Johan, dear Johan, comes in."

Still feeling mildly embarrassed Johan continued. "The Russian army is fast approaching from the East. The New York Post has headlined details of what is happening at Auschwitz –Birkenau. Orders have come from Hitler himself to remove all traces of the way that slave labourers are used and then dealt with when they die. He does not want the world to know about his concentration camps and his methodical system the Germans use to 'cleanse' humanity. Musfelldt ordered his men to clean up the cremation site in the woods and dispose of any bodies elsewhere. They always relied on the wildlife to remove the bones, bears foxes and the like, but there was no time to waste. Normally they would use the slaves to do their dirty work but, thanks to you gentlemen, there are no healthy slaves left to do their bidding."

"How did you end up with the task?" Johnno had seen many newsreels highlighting the Nazi's inhumanity, and couldn't countenance the thought of all those wasted lives, killed merely for a warped and twisted belief. "I thought that you had gone back to your village for sanctuary."

"I went back to the mine to collect the last of my mementoes, a watch and a ring my parents gave to me when they realised their lives were in danger. I couldn't leave without them," patting his breast pocket, accompanied by a slightly embarrassed smile. "When I heard the news and realised what was happening I volunteered to dispose of the bodies. There was so much panic in the mine that no-one realised I had 'come back from the dead'. I knew that none of the soldiers wanted the task, so I was left to it. I am in contact with several resistance groups in the area and could inform them what I had done. My aim was simply to remove the poor souls and bury them somewhere safe in the woods. I'd note their tattoo numbers and make a note of where they actually lay. After this infernal war is over they can then be laid to rest with dignity alongside their names. The resistance were to meet and help me."

Johnno placed his hand on Johan's shoulder. "Good man."

"I arrived at the site and carefully lifted the corpses into the truck. The poor souls were so emaciated I had little difficulty lifting and carrying them." He paused to wipe his eyes, and take a deep breath.

Freya continued the story for him. "I was aware of something happening as I began to regain consciousness. As the poor souls were lifted from me I felt the pressure on my chest release and I could finally breathe easily again. Only then did I realise where I was, and assumed that I too was being taken away for disposal. I couldn't release my hands, but managed to squeeze the ring from my finger and hide it beneath my body. I knew you would come looking for me and, hopefully, find it." She smiled at Johnno, holding both his hands and kissing them gently. "I just wanted you to have something to remember me by."

Johan continued. "The last 'body' I found was Freya, bound and gagged, I just wanted to get her away as quickly as possible before anyone of my German comrades appeared. I realised that she was still alive, but was barely conscious, so I lifted her gently into the truck with the other poor souls, and removed the tape from her mouth. I gave her a sip of water from my bottle, but she could barely speak. I lifted the tailgate and drove away as quickly as I could, deep into the forest."

"My mouth was so dry and I felt so weak that I couldn't tell Johan about my ring left on the ground, but that was obviously a blessing in disguise."

"Whilst my resistance friends laid the poor souls to rest I helped Freya recover and here we are today"

"Are you really OK?" Johnno sounded worried.

"Yes. It was just the after-effects of the neuroliser that weakened me. Time and water to drink soon cured that. Thank the gods that Maia didn't know how to use that weapon effectively. We should be grateful that he was, indeed, an idiot."

Rick glanced at Johnno and smiled. "Great minds, and all that."

Freya's face suddenly took on a look of deep concern. She looked straight at Johnno. Her voice was full of angst.

"Maia, he's still out there somewhere. His mission is to stop you. You have to be careful."

"He's certainly out there somewhere. In fact he's everywhere out there." Rick's humour eluded Freya, who looked totally bemused.

Johnno hugged her and smiled. "Don't worry about Maia. He's been dealt with. We'll fill you in with all the details later."

"We need to get you back with your package," Manni was back on task, "and the sooner the better."

Johnno turned to Johan. "What will you do now? Is it safe to return to camp?"

"I believe that the end of the war is in sight. I can do far more good working with the resistance. If I don't return they will presume that I've been killed somehow, but they won't risk looking for me. They hate these woods. I'll be OK my friend, don't worry."

"What about our two captives back in the cabin?"

Manni's voice was calm and reassuring. "No worries, my friend. I will use Johan's truck here to drive them deep into the forest. When they finally come round and realise where they are we'll be long gone and the cabin will, to all intents and purposes, be an empty cabin again. We've filled their pockets with Pervitin, and sprinkled some on their uniforms. Their superiors will, hopefully, believe that any story they tell will have been created during a drug fuelled stupor."

He suddenly stepped back, cupping his hand over his ear. He had maintained a radio contact with communications back within the cabin. He listened intently. "Apparently Maia had a partner. A certain Mr. Tesman. They were both in the control tower when you started the mission."

"Is he here now?" Freya was worried he had come to finish their mission and kill her beloved nephew.

"No, he disappeared as he was being escorted back to area 51."

"What do you mean, he disappeared? Where were his escorts? What were they doing? Did he do a runner?" Johnno was also worried that his mission was about to take another nasty turn.

"No, apparently he literally just disappeared in front of their eyes. Well, according to his escorts he had the look of a TV screen when it loses its signal. He just appeared to break apart and then he was gone." Manni looked towards Rick and Freya.

"It looks like he's using a phaser"

"What the fuck, sorry Aunt Freya, what the hell is a phaser?"

"Remember when I explained about time travel, and how stations move?"

"Yep"

"Well that's only possible because there are is the extra dimension of time."

"O ....K....."

"Well, actually, there are more than four dimensions and a phaser allows the wearer to slip out of one dimension into the next. They literally disappear from our world into another."

"So can he appear here? Should we be worried?"

Freya joined in the conversation. "Thankfully, no. A great deal of power is needed to use this weapon. There must be a base unit somewhere which generates this power, which is usually only active over a few miles at most, and that generates a dimension for him to use. He can travel to a chosen spot within reason, but can only return through this dimensional pathway back to the power source. Once his body phaser is activated he is transported safely back to his base within ten seconds or so. BUT, and here's the only good piece of news, it cannot traverse time."

"That sounds positive, why the concern then, surely we're safe here."

"Here, yes. But when you return he becomes a threat once more."

"I bet the base unit is in our 'guest quarters' back in Area 51." Manni sounded confident. "Tesman disappeared near there. I bet I'm right."

"Guest quarters, what are the guest quarters?"

"A misleading title for secrets that the US government wish to keep safe. Its way down beneath ground level, up to fourteen levels actually. It's where your US keeps their alien visitors who first arrived, sorry, who WILL arrive in 1947, beginning at Roswell. Many have arrived since, some benevolent but many now pissed off at being kept in cages like a zoo. They have repeatedly been promised freedom and integration, but your government is afraid to let the public know the truth." Manni's eyes widened as a thought crossed his mind. "Tesman probably realises that their primary mission has failed with the demise of Maia. If he somehow gets his hands on the weapon now who knows what he'll use it for. He's got plenty of allies down there."

"Then we'll just have to ensure that it passes on to the President, and then onto our lunar outpost as planned." Rick's voice was calm, but full of authority. Johnno was puzzled. "But if the phaser only has a range of miles, its base is within Area 51, how will he be able to get to use it in the White House, that's hundreds of miles away."

"The presentation isn't planned for the White House. The President is keen to endorse our activities at Groom Lake and plans to receive the package there. Less publicity you see. He doesn't want to let Joe Public in on the act. Who can say 'no' to the President?"

Johnno turned to Freya, reached out and held both her hands. "Don't worry, we've gotten this far, and we'll see it through to the end. The package *will* be delivered."

She smiled as she hugged him. "I know, but please be very careful, this Tesman seems as if he will stop at nothing to prevent the return of the weapon."

The group all fell silent, mindful of what they needed to do next to make their mission a success.

Rick spoke first. "Right buddy, back to our Blackbird, we have a flight to complete. Third time lucky, huh."

Johan climbed back into the truck "Anyone for a lift to the cabin? I've plenty of room. I always wanted to drive a taxi."

After a final flurry of handshakes and hugs the group set out to complete their final actions before leaving the cabin and transporting to safety. Johnno hugged Freya, keeping hold as if his life depended on it. He eventually stepped back, still holding on to her hands. "Will I see you again? I've lost you once; I couldn't stand to do it again."

"Of course you will. I'll be there to see you hand over the package. I promise, now go and complete your mission."

As Johnno and Rick made their way back to the Blackbird they heard the throb of the truck's engine slowly fade into the distance. Johnno took one last glance back to see the tail lights disappear and fade as they drove away.

"I didn't know the President was coming to Groom Lake, a big deal, huh? Do you think I could get his autograph?"

Rick smiled. "No, but you're welcome to mine."

"Yeah, right. Mind you I've just thought of something. Our fancy cigar box in Blackbird, do you mind if I borrow it?"

Rick glanced at his friend, a quizzical look on his face. "Not at all, providing you donate your cigar to me as your loyal and dutiful friend."

"I was just thinking if we are to present the weapon to the President wouldn't it look much better, more official even, if it was in a fancy hardwood presentation box?"

"I agree buddy, PLUS there will be less chance of shooting him by mistake. Wouldn't THAT be a photo opportunity?"

"What do you mean, shoot the president?"

"Just joking buddy .... I've seen you on the range, he's TOTALLY safe."

Their mood was lightened as they began their pre-flight checks once again. Johnno started the engines to warm them through. Plenty of fuel on board, even the gauges for the experimental fuel registered 80%. All readings were A.O.K, they were ready to take their flight back to the future and complete the mission. After twenty minutes or so Johnno felt confident enough to take off and return to the world he left many days ago.

"All ready for take-off , activate your anti-gravity pads when ready."

"Here we go buddy, hold on to your seat."

The plane vibrated slightly as it left the ground, and began to gently rise into the air. There was no disturbance as it did so, even the snow remained on the fuselage. They rose above the tree line and hovered.

"Whoa, this is some way to start a flight. Why can't all aircraft have this vertical take-off or landing built in? We need to make a recommendation to Bell aircraft when we get home. No need for runways, just up and away."

"You may have to wait a while for that one buddy." Rick strained his neck to get the best view possible from all sides of his cockpit canopy. "Just checking for bogies, buddy, anyone would have a hell of a job explaining this when they got back to base."

Johnno checked his radar screen. "All clear here, the nearest pings are around 5 miles away at around 30,000 feet – hopefully some of our boys delivering presents to Herr Hitler."

"Roger that." Rick continued to control the ascent. "Five thousand feet should get us clear and ready to leave, high enough to fly but well below bomber ceiling."

"Still clear on the radar, radar tracking moving to our North."

The aircraft picked up speed as it steadily rose up high into the air. After several minutes they were ready.

"Five thousand feet attained. Feed in the power slowly and I'll hold us here."

"Roger that. Compass setting? Are we travelling back to the time we left?"

"Just head due East buddy, due East will do just fine. And no, we don't want to create a paradox."

"What kind of paradox?"

"If you recall both Maia and Tesman were in the control tower when we left. We now know that Maia is dead and Tesman hiding somewhere. If we arrive back at the exact time we left there would be a paradox – would they still be there? Would Maia still be alive or dead?"

"Whoa ... heavy stuff buddy."

"So we'll aim for seven days later and claim we had engine trouble. The public will buy that, while the President is in on our mission."

"What about Joe, our own Joe Pazzaro? Does he know?"

"The President, he was the first to be approached as Blackbird is one of his pet projects. Joe only found out after we'd started. Politics is a dirty game. Now let's go home buddy, we've a package to deliver."

As Johnno slowly fed in the power the aircraft began to judder, its nose moving up and down as it strained to escape. Three quarters power ... full power and the vibrations became more intense. Johnno was concerned that his aircraft would break up under the pressure. "I trust that Russian titanium is good quality." Rick's voice finally came through Johnno's headphones.

"3-2-1 Pads are away!" The pads went into freefall, landing in the forest below. Within seconds they were nothing more than a pile of ash on the snow covered ground, to be eventually blown away by the wind and rain.

Johnno had taken off from an aircraft carrier and thought he was fully prepared for the acceleration, but this was something else. His body was forced back into his seat with such a force he felt he was back at NASA on the centrifuge. Eventually he relaxed as his muscle memory kicked back in and he was flying his beloved aircraft once more.

Johnno struggled to speak, his chest still feeling as if a huge weight was resting on it "Jeez, this is some ride."

"Sure is buddy, now hit the experimental fuel button and hold on tight – we're in for a REAL ride."

Johnno strained to reach forward and flick the fuel switch; the pressure surge immediately returned. He strained to see out of his cockpit, still wary of meeting air traffic. To his right, in the distance, he could see the con trails of the bombers on their way to deliver their deadly payload, resembling a swarm of bees on their way to a cornfield full of wild flowers.

"Why am I worrying, they couldn't even see us at this speed."

In the distance Joe Pazzaro was glancing out of his cockpit window and swore he could see something unidentified below their flight path. He pointed them out to his co-pilot "Look over there; it must be the 'Foo fighters' everyone is talking about." His crew glanced over to see a momentary flash in the distance. He then got back to the job in hand and carried on with his mission. "Keep your eyes open for enemy fighters boys; we're in the Kraut's back yard."

Johnno glanced to see what speed he was actually flying at. The dial seemed to be jammed fully open. The sky outside suddenly dimmed and went completely black, not a cloud, star or planet in sight. A haze seemed to appear around his cockpit, a blue haze with the appearance of thin fog. His eyes were drawn outside to his wings, which seemed to glow with a crackling light, arcing out as if there was an electrical short circuit somewhere. He had read books about strange phenomenon, and thought that this looked very much like St. Elmo's fire.

In the distance he could just make out a spiral of light, a slowly revolving vortex of light resembling the inside of an ice cream cone as its diameter seemed to narrow and taper in the distance. The cone was surrounded by clouds and, as they moved further into its pathway they became fully enveloped, immediately becoming noticeably darker. Lightning began to fork all around them, briefly illuminating the cloud cover, only to be replaced immediately by darkness

In his headphones came Rick's jubilant voice "1969 here we come, we're finally on our way home."

In an instant they had passed through the vortex and came out of the other side into a clear blue sky. "Throttle back buddy, no need to overshoot and visit Peru."

Johnno throttled back as his plane reverted to its normal flight and speed. Glancing down he immediately recognised the outline of America's East coast through the thin veil of summer clouds. His voice was full of emotion and almost breaking up as relief flooded back throughout his tired and aching body.

"We did it, we fucking well did it."

"We sure did buddy, now set us back on course for home; we have a president to meet and a package to deliver."

"Roger that."

Chapter 51

It had been a quiet couple of days in the control tower at Groom Lake. Well, quiet compared to the events of last week when the US lost one of its prized new breed of stealth aircraft. The loss had been 'hushed up' in the hope that wreckage would eventually be found, both crew members having successfully bailed out and survived whilst waiting for their rescue.

That was the hope, anyway. Today all that was to change as they prepared for a presidential visit.

Commander Pazzaro was keen to ensure that everything was ship shape for the visit, knowing just how important it was, especially if his latest information was up to date. Outside on the tarmac aircraft had been lined up in neat rows, highlighting the special nature of the operations flown from this base. The mid-day heat had generated a heat haze which became more obvious as the lines of aircraft and their ground crews retreated into the distance. This haze gave the appearance of a mirage with wavy mirror images of craft and personnel giving the look of an impressionist painting.

Around him in his control tower staff were busy ensuring everything was in order. All un-necessary rubbish removed, no stray pieces of paper to litter the desks, and no visitors allowed – he'd learned his lesson by trusting the CIA and letting Maia and Mr Tesman be present when his two valued crew members disappeared, along with their top secret aircraft. The commander was standing, almost motionless, scanning the skies for a sign, any sign, that the mission he'd been involved with had been a success. He had his customary cigar stub being chewed and moved relentlessly around his mouth, a trait which showed just how tense he was.

"Tell me as soon as you get a radar signal, especially from the North West," he reminded the operator yet again, his eyes not moving from the binoculars he was scanning the horizon with.

"Yes sir," came the reply from the radar station. The operator was unsure why they were still scanning the skies, especially from one major direction, especially as their guest from the White House had already flown in the day before and was safely ensconced in his bomb proof quarters below. He looked around to his colleague sat next to him, shrugging his shoulders slightly, with a mildly quizzical look on his face. His colleague 'replied' by opening his eyes slightly wider, as if to say "I don't know what we're doing either."

Suddenly there came an almost inaudible 'ping' from the screen. The operator immediately looked back towards his screen, peering intently at the cause of the warning. Suddenly, in the top left hand side of his screen, a visible green dot appeared as if from nowhere, moving rapidly towards them. He was visibly stunned by the sudden appearance of an aircraft approaching, especially at the speed with which it appeared.

"We have a reading sir, coming from the North West. It just ...."

"Yes, it just what?" Pazzaro was still scanning the skies but as yet could see nothing.

"It just appeared from nowhere sir, from nowhere. It's about one hundred miles out, heading at around 300^0, but coming in hot, real hot."

"Get him to identify himself son, the sooner the better."

"Groom lake calling unidentified aircraft, please come in."

All that came from the speakers was static. The whole room was now in readiness for defensive measures as this unknown aircraft approached. Every technician was now looking towards the speakers, hoping and praying to hear a friendly voice. The room was completely filled with an almost deafening silence.

"Groom Lake calling unidentified aircraft - please come in. State your call sign." Even more static, which seemed much louder as each person strained their ears, hoping for a friendly voice. Then the aircraft's secret identification code appeared alongside the green blip.

"Sir, it's our missing aircraft, I think she's back, I don't know how but I think she's back." His voice sounded incredulous. How could an aircraft go missing for a week?

Pazzaro punched the air. "They did it, they Goddam did it."

"Groom lake calling aircraft O D 1 N, please respond."

"I repeat, Groom Lake calling aircraft O D 1 N please respond."

The speakers burst into life.

"Aircraft call sign O D 1 N here, permission to land please? I repeat - permission to land ?"

After a brief pause the room erupted with cheers and whoops and cries of 'YES' as they prepared to welcome home their missing heroes. The loudspeaker crackled into life once again.

"Sorry we're late Commander, we had to collect a package."

Pazzaro's face beamed with delight. Not only were his crew safe but they had been successful with their mission. He turned to face his staff, his much respected demeanour causing his men to fall silent again, albeit with smiles all over their faces.

He addressed them with a tone of seriousness in his voice, though the smile on his face really gave away his feelings of delight.

"Gentlemen, I have no need to remind you of our obligations to keep this matter completely top secret. All I can say is that our pilots were on a secret mission and are almost safely home."

As one, very relieved, voice came the reply "Yes sir!"

Pazzaro was beaming, allowing his binoculars to rest on his chest. He strode purposely towards the exit, pausing as he reached the door. He turned slowly, and sounding like a father who was welcoming home his family, addressed his team.

"Now bring them safely home boys, take him straight in to hangar 6. Finally I have some good news to pass on to the president."

Again, as one voice, came the reply to their much revered commander.

"Yes sir"

"Doesn't Groom look GOOD?" Johnno was approaching the runway and feeling as if he was finally coming home, before adding as if an afterthought "and nothing has changed, history is still the same."

"Sure thing buddy, we did it. Nothing has changed, I just hope someone has taken care of old 'shovel' for me. I think we deserve a ride and a beer."

"Oh yes … Count me in buddy, count me in."

The Blackbird appeared, as if by magic, through the wavering heat haze at the end of the runway and made a text book landing. At the end Johnno taxied his craft back around towards the security hangars close to the control tower, guided by a jubilant ground crew member and his ecstatically waving paddles, leaving a wake of sand and dust behind them. They entered the open hangar doorway, as they came to a halt Johnno cut the power to the engines; the vibrations of flight replaced by the still euphoria of a safe landing. Even their aircraft seemed to relax as it came to a halt, the suspension of its landing gear sighing as it came to rest.

Finally they could relax a little and begin to savour the success of their mission. All that was left was the delivery of the package, the small weapon that almost created a large change in the modern history of the world. Ground crew rushed towards them, eager to get them safely back in base and keen to forward their own congratulations on their victorious return. A ladder was quickly placed against the fuselage as the cockpits slowly opened revealing the two heroic, but travel weary, pilots. Johnno was careful to remember his cigar box and its important contents, passing it down to ground crew, and retrieving it immediately his feet touched the ground.

Ceremoniously he kneeled down and kissed the ground, before getting back to his feet and welcoming his co-pilot as he left the bottom of the ladder. He threw his arms around his life-saving and life affirming friend and gave him the hug of all hugs.

Around them the number of ground crew was steadily rising, all eager to see their heroes' return, all eager to shake the hands of their pilots, part of their family. There were cheers and much back-slapping as everyone tried to get in on the act. All our pilots could do was stand there and smile, as they were overwhelmed and hailed as conquering heroes.

"Can't you give us a clue where you've been sirs?" a voice came from the back of the entourage of staff, it was Chuck, the ground crew member who had wished him good luck as they left on their mission.

"Was it the Russkis? We thought we'd lost you."

Johnno winked at him. "If I told you I'd still have to kill you."

"We couldn't have that sir. It's good to have you back."

From the rear of the hangar a figure approached, it was Commander Pazzaro, accompanied by his adjutant. As he came near a natural path appeared through the throng of ground crew, allowing the returning heroes to finally be visible. Both Johnno and Rick stood to attention and saluted their commanding officer. Pazzaro did likewise, but then stepped forward to shake both their hands.

"You have completed a superb job gentleman. You have the package secure?"

Johnno took the cigar box, which had been firmly entrenched under his arm, and offered it to his commander.

Pazzaro smiled. "You keep it son, it will be your privilege to present it to the president yourself, both of you in fact have an audience arranged with him in our security suite."

Johnno's pride took a major boost. His mind raced. "The commander called me 'son' AND I am about to meet the president."

Pazzaro gestured for them to join him as he walked back towards his office and the planned meeting with the president. A shout came from behind them from one of the ground crew.

"What shall we do with your aircraft sirs? She does look a little scorched to say the least."

Rick turned, examining the tell-tale marks of superfast flight along her fuselage.

"Oh just top up the gas and oil, and check the tyres."

As they walked across the hangar floor a thought crossed his mind. "Excuse me commander, how did you know we would be returning today?"

"Damnest thing that ... we had a message from the CIA, one of their operatives informed us that you would be coming home at around mid-day today. They said her call sign was Freya, apparently she arrived a week ago."

Johnno smiled and looked back towards Rick. He looked back at the commander and was sure he winked as well.

They continued on their way out of the hanger towards the security suite. As they walked Rick noticed a large plane in the distance, surrounded by a ring of armed guards.

"The Boeing, over there, is that ...?"

"Air Force One son, its first ever visit."

Johnno was impressed and felt quite proud inside. The president had flown in specially to meet them, though he was a little disappointed at not being able to visit the White House. The two guards snapped to attention as they approached the entrance to the main buildings.

"At ease gentlemen."

The trio entered. The cool of the building was a welcome relief from the burning sun and the hot tarmac pathway. It took a while for their eyes to become accustomed to the gentle lights of the corridor away from the relentless glare of the sun.

"We know about Tesman and Maia," Pazzaro added almost nonchalantly as he led the weary pilots along the corridor past several non-descript doors towards a lift at the far end, again guarded by a pair of armed soldiers. "They were passed as secure by the CIA and offered as valuable liaison," you could sense the disbelief in his voice, "dumb bastards." The lift doors opened, welcoming them inside as they approached. Pazzaro leaned forward and, taking a key from his trouser pocket, opened a locked compartment on the lift's control panel. He pressed a green button, speaking into a voice panel at the same time. "Commander Pazzaro descending to USAF suites." He released the button and securely locked the compartment. The lift began its slow descent

"Security, gentlemen, security. Thanks to you we no longer have to worry about Maia, but Tesman is another matter. We are aware of his ability to phase, hence the heightened security and our deep cover here."

"I have to ask why here and not the White House?" Rick seemed baffled by the decisions made by the top brass.

"He couldn't get himself there so why take the risk?" Johnno added to the argument.

"I fully agree but who can over-rule the president? Once he became aware of our 'guests' on levels 6 and 14 he decided that he would be their go-between, hoping to secure world peace. If nothing else he realised that their advanced technology would be a great help to America's defence of the free world. And then, when he then learned about Lunex, our plan to build an underground base on the moon, he was hooked."

Pazzaro rolled his eyes. "Little did we know someone had already built one, several thousands of years ago."

Rick smiled. "And that's where I came in. Some of your guests on level 14 are actually from Orion, placed there to help ensure that a kind of truce is maintained between our 'children' on Earth and your guests. Once we learned of the plan to travel back and help Hitler, an act which goes against all the beliefs of the Federation, we had to act. Thanks to you Johnno we're almost home and dry."

"Almost? But what's to stop Tesman trying to get this?" Johnno looked down to the cigar box under his arm. "Surely we're within range of his base unit. It IS below us somewhere, isn't it?"

The lift came to a halt, the doors opened automatically, revealing two more armed guards awaiting them. They snapped to attention, Pazzaro acknowledging them. "Stand down soldiers." They entered an air-conditioned corridor. The floor seemed to be a highly polished marble, the walls decorated and lined with paintings. It seemed surreal on an air force base, and more reminiscent of a lobby within a Howard Johnson hotel. Pazzaro set off along the corridor, continuing the discussion. "We've noticed a marked power surge in 14, occurring when Tesman seemingly activates the main unit of his contraption. We're constantly monitoring now in the hope that we get some kind of warning that he's on his way."

"Why not just cut all power to level 14?" Johnno's question seemed reasonable.

Pazzaro looked towards Rick. "Over to you."

"We can't do that. Many of the occupants rely on special atmospheres generated within sealed areas. Not everyone breathes oxygen I'm afraid. Cutting off the power would seal their fate, causing the deaths of many of them. The Federation would look upon that as a rebellious act and cut all ties with its contacts on Earth – and that would prove disastrous, especially in the current tense climate. We only just managed to convince Khrushchev to back down in '62."

Johnno stopped dead in his tracks. "That was you?"

"We let slip to Mr Khrushchev that there may be some future technology hidden in Turkey. We convinced our American allies to remove its missiles from there and leave the bases too. Fortunately our American allies had already retrieved this technology and, I am assured, have destroyed it. Russia moved in, and are still searching for it. Good luck with that."

About half way along the corridor Pazzaro stopped alongside a non-descript door, again flanked by two armed guards. Johnno glanced at the door and, although he could see a definite outline, no door handle was visible, just a numeric keypad.

Pazzaro lowered his voice. "We know that Tesman has phased into our buildings and examined the plans of its layout, we caught him with our surveillance cameras. He's taken photographs of the dining area, where the president will dine with his guests after you have passed the package on to him. We believe that is where Tesman will make his move, and we'll be ready for him." Leaning forward he deftly pressed six of the keypad figures. The door hissed and slowly opened.

"Here is your guest suite gentlemen. You have your own rooms complete with a welcoming ensuite shower. These guards will come in with you and stay in the ante room for your safety." Pointing to Johnno's cigar box he added "I suggest you place that in the room safe, pick your own combination, we can't afford to lose it now." Turning to walk away he stopped and turned back to face Johnno and smiled. "And don't forget to bring it with you when I collect you for your presidential meeting. We can't afford to fall at the last hurdle." He turned and made his way along the corridor. Without breaking stride he called out. "You just have time for a shower and change of clothing gentlemen. You are due to meet the president in one hour."

The two guards ushered them into the room, taking up positions in the hallway, the ante chamber to the suite. Johnno moved towards the right hand door, saluting playfully as Rick moved towards the one on the left. Johnno laughed, speaking in a mock 'posh' voice "See you for cocktails in one hour."

"I'd sooner have an ice cold Budweiser."

"Me too," added one of the guards.

Johnno entered his room. Although it had no windows it was well lit by diffused lights set within panels in the wall. The furniture was modern but sparse, obviously aimed at short stay visitors who needed security. Laid out on the bed was his dress uniform, freshly ironed, and a pair of boots polished to within an inch of their life. Ambling over towards the shower room he discovered the safe hidden within the wardrobe and placed his package inside. He set the four digit code."1 9 4 4 – that's a number I'll never forget." The package now safe he entered the shower room, walking over to the mirror he placed his hands either side and stared at his reflection, taking a long look at the weary face looking back at him. "God I look tired, and I need a shave."

Closing his eyes he reflected on the last few days of his previously uneventful life. Had he really travelled back in time? Battled embittered Nazis? Had he really met his long gone parents? Had he really lost Rick and Freya and then saved them both? Had he really had a part in preserving the history of the world?

Me? A little kid who wanted to be a spaceman, doing all that with his best friend? His best friend who had informed him that part of him was really from outer space?

"This would make a wonderful story for my children, one day. If only I was allowed to write it. … if ever I have kids."

He smiled when he realised which toiletries had been provided, Safeguard soap and a familiar blue bottle. He picked it up, removed its lid, and took a deep breath. "Aqua Velva the smell of home." He removed his shirt, turning to one side slightly he realised that the bruises to his ribs were now a beautiful shade of purple and blue.

"He was one big bastard that guard. I wonder if he's still alive today?"

After shaving he turned on the shower. Waiting for a moment he let it warm through and was momentarily lost in thought, realising he may be in for an eventful afternoon and evening. The hot shower felt like honey on his skin. He recalled his last shower on the base, unaware of where life was about to lead him. He leaned against the cubicle wall, finally able to relax and forget the burden placed on him. The hot, welcoming cascade of water seemed to wash his worries away. He stood motionless, finally able to drop his guard and relax for a while.

Reality suddenly kicked back in.

"Shit, I wonder if I need to make a speech?"

Chapter 52

It had been a while since he had worn a full dress uniform. Having showered and shaved he now felt ready to gear up for his afternoon appointment.

The guard tapped gently on the door. "Five minutes lieutenant, then it's time to go sir."

"Nearly there" He'd lost some weight on his adventures, but that suited him well. "A little bit of slack around my belly will do me no harm."

He checked himself in the mirror, carefully smoothing and pulling down his jacket. Turning to the side he checked his profile, patting his stomach gently. He put on his hat, carefully adjusting the fit. Finally he collected his special box from the wall safe and turned to leave the room.

Outside Rick was waiting to greet him alongside the two guards who would escort them to their VIP meeting. "Well, buddy; this is it, the final part of our operation. Today's the day we get our lives back."

Johnno made a point of looking his colleague up and down. "Jeez, do I look as good as you do?"

"You look even better my friend, much better."

The two guards snapped to attention as Commander Pazzaro approached them, who was also wearing his full dress uniform. Rick and Johnno stood to attention and saluted as well, the gesture returned by their commander. Pazzaro was pulling gently at his collar, as if relieving the pressure on his neck. "I can't let you young bucks take all the glory, though I'm sure something must have shrunk in the wash."

"Probably, sir." Rick raised his eyebrows in mock surprise.

Pazzaro about turned, ready to walk back along the corridor, ordering one of the guard escorts to walk ahead of them, the other to cover their backs.

"No time to waste gentlemen. It's almost 1600 hours, time to meet your president. I'm sure he is just as proud of you as I am."

Rick swore he could see a small tear glistening in his Commander's eye.

"Just serving our flag sir, serving the flag."

Pazzaro acknowledged the comment and nodded. Then turned and led them along the corridor towards the conference room, the final, almost miscellaneous, door at the end. The two guards took their positions outside, one each side of the door. Pazzaro used the keypad and entered with his two revered pilots the room burst into life as everyone present stood and applauded the two returning heroes. He stood back, allowing them their moment in the limelight.

Johnno and Rick both looked mildly embarrassed, allowing a slight smile to appear on their faces; a smile that grew broader the longer the applause continued. They did not recognise anyone there, but were impressed by the abundance of stars on their well-groomed lapels.

On each side, stood against the walls, were figures in dark suits complimented by the obligatory crew cut hairstyle, obviously the president's security guards. There were four each side, plus two at the rear.

One by one they broke protocol and joined in with the applause, their mask like demeanour breaking into broad smiles. They may have been unaware why these two pilots were being greeted as conquering heroes, but, as ex-service men themselves, could recognise a successful secret mission when they saw it. Eventually the applause died down as the assembled personnel began to take their seats again. The security guards resumed their traditional stance, expressionless faces, hands crossed by their crotch, permanently on the lookout for possible trouble.

The room itself was surprisingly compact as far as military conference rooms are concerned. There was the obligatory central oval table where the guests were seated, and a lectern at the far end, already adorned with the presidential seal. The president had brought along his confidantes, the staff on whose recommendations he acted and had been supporting him throughout this operation, all sat along one side of the oval table.

Nearest the lectern in his role as Head of joint chief of staff was Errol Gilmore. Next to him was Tom Gerarty, then Richard Elms, John Vasey, and finally Dr Payne.

Tom Gerarty slowly rose from his seat gesturing towards Pazzaro.

"Take a seat Joe. And that goes for you too gentlemen. This is a proud day for the United States Air Force, may I thank you for your efforts during this dangerous operation." Murmurs of approval were heard amongst his colleagues, accompanied by the ritual slapping of hands on the table top.

Our trio took their seats, Johnno nearest the lectern in readiness for his presentation of the package to the president. Rick was seated next to him, with their commander towards the rear, allowing his men to bask in the glory of their successful exploits.

They removed their hats and placed them on the table by their name tags.

Johnno's mind was racing. "Oh yes, name tags as well, what would Freya think?" Glancing at Rick, he raised his eyebrows as if in mock disbelief. Rick winked back.

Tom Gerarty slowly got to his feet and strode towards the front corner of the room. As the door opened he stood to attention, saluting whoever was entering.

It was 1600 hours precisely.

"Gentlemen, the President of the United States of America."

Chapter 53

In a small control room somewhere on site two guards were sat monitoring TV screens and a control unit measuring the power input and output within the many levels of Groom Lake complex. Their specific job was to monitor activity on level 14.

As soon as Tesman's role and unique ability to phase and teleport had been discovered a search had been implemented where possible to find the primary power source, the one generating the dimensional gap he utilised. They were unable to gain full access to level 14 due to the belligerence and potential unrest it would cause with those guests who were 'dissatisfied'.

The guards had a small transistor radio, strictly forbidden on duty, but were unconcerned as everyone who was anyone was guarding their VIP guest.

"Are you sure we're OK down here, we can't be caught."; guard one was uneasy with the radio being on.

Guard two didn't look up, too intent on listening to the game.

"Nah, don't worry, we're literally way off their radar." From the radio speaker came the sound of an umpire calling 'strike two'. He grabbed the radio and shouted into the speaker "Come on Sing-Sing, we can do this, I got ten bucks on the Dodgers to win."

"Then I'll have ten bucks on the Braves."

"I'll take that bet, sucker."

Guard two, Bill took a ten dollar bill from his money clip and placed on the desk.

Guard one, Dave, did not look up, but acknowledged the bet.

"Thank you for that donation Billy boy, I'll collect it later."

"No chance, the Braves went one up in one – they gotta win."

"Dream on Billy boy, dream on."

Behind them the control unit showed a spike in power, barely perceptible, but definitely a sign of something large being powered up. An alarm beeped simultaneously, causing Bill to turn and look. The power spike on the gauge had returned to normal, everything seemed to be OK. He looked up to check on the CCTV monitors, cameras were dotted throughout level 14, but nothing seemed untoward, no unusual or suspicious activity. Several of the corridors were in darkness, specially kept that way for the 'Greys' who disliked bright lights due to the structure of their eyes. Activity within the other corridors seemed normal, as did the structures in which those guests who did not use oxygen as their main source for breathing.

He reset the audible alarm and turned around to his colleague.

"Everything looks OK here Dave; it must just be the transformers kicking in. Some of our guests do need to breathe occasionally," he added with a hint of sarcasm in his voice.

Many of the guards, and ground crew, on site were none too keen on the idea of alien guests within their compound. Their abiding fear was what would happen if the guests really got pissed off with their lot.

"If the alarm sound again we'll switch off their power supply for ten minutes, that oughta quieten 'em down for a while." Dave's mind drifted back to the ball game. Bill was feeling nervous and dawdled a while, glancing back at the monitors to satisfy himself that everything on level 14 really was OK. He moved over alongside his colleague

"I'll tell them we've had a small alarm, but nothing to worry about. That should keep us in the clear and convince them that we're on the ball."

Dave looked directly at him, putting his fingers to his lips. "OK, OK, but shush, Kosko's coming in to bat."

Bill moved away from the screen so as not to give their secret away. Picking up the microphone he turned his back to his colleague, signalling to his colleague to turn down the volume, in the hope that the radio commentary would not be heard, and pressed the send button.

"This is security unit14 here, security unit 14 here. We've just had a small blip on the audible alarm control. Nothing to note on CCTV, presume it's the usual power systems kicking in. Everything is A OK - I repeat everything seems A OK."

Putting down the microphone he returned to his colleague's side.

"You're still one down. Want to up that bet to twenty dollars?"

Below them on level 14 an unknown alliance had formed.

Several of the 'greys' believed that they had been mistreated and ignored and wished to return to their home planets. These requests had been blocked with promises of a later deal. They were well and truly pissed off. Tesman realised that this was a breeding ground for allies to his cause and had promised to help them escape if they helped him with his task.

The power unit for the phaser system had been secretly dismantled and then re-assembled with the Greys dark corridors, the perfect hiding place in full view of their 'hosts'. As word spread of a possible escape many more 'guests' vowed to help. They combined as one unit to break into the main power cables which supplied each separate area with heat, light and life support systems.

Tesman had calculated that, by taking a small amount of energy from several different areas, the combined power would fuel his phase machine without creating the one large power surge which would certainly be noticed. Bit by bit small, un-noticeable, amounts of power were fed into the phaser power unit.

He was right.

In the darkness his phaser began to build up power; enough power to help him phase and teleport to retrieve the ultimate weapon from his jailers.

If he could take it from the president that would surely send a message to his new allies; he will have a ready formed army of followers all keen on retribution.

If Bill had looked for longer and more intently into the CCTV monitor he would have seen Mr. Tesman, dressed all in black, staring back and smiling at him. His eyes reverting back to their natural state, those of a pure born Pleiadian.

Eyes as black and as smooth as haematite.

Chapter 54

As the president moved towards his lectern, acknowledging the applause rained on him by his staff, Johnno noticed two of the security guards put their fingers to their ears, obviously receiving some kind of message. They looked at each other and gently nodded, acknowledging whatever message had been received. They both surreptitiously checked their handguns inside their jackets, just as if reassuring themselves that they would be instantly available if needed.

Glancing sideways he noticed other guards making the same gesture.

He glanced at Rick, gently gesturing towards the guards and their subtle movements.

Rick frowned slightly, unsure as to why his friend seemed concerned.

Johnno felt slightly alarmed. Slowly, almost casually, he retrieved the cigar box from the table top, placing it securely in his lap. Turning to face his president he opened the lid for several seconds, seemingly checking that all was where it should be before closing it again.

The president spoke.

"Today, gentlemen, in this time of world-wide chaos and mistrust we need to be reminded occasionally just how great the United States of America really is, and today is one of those days. Ever since JFK made his rousing and prophetic speech in May 1961, and the desire to complete project Lunex, we have strived to make these two dreams a reality, and we are on the cusp of success. However, when things conspire against us and threaten to kill those dreams we become in need of an old fashioned hero to help us out. Today we are in the presence of not just one hero who came to our rescue, but two. I speak, of course, of the two heroes sat here in our presence. Gentlemen I give you Flight Lieutenants John O'Ryan and Richard Abrahams."

The President gestured towards Johnno and Rick and led the round of applause and table thumping which came from all those present, none louder and more demonstrative than Commander Pazzaro in support of his two team members.

Rick and Johnno both looked suitably proud and yet embarrassed at the same time.

As the applause began to die away eyes turned back towards the president for the continuation of his speech. Everyone was stunned when they noticed a strange anomaly by his right shoulder. It was as if the area around the president had transformed into a huge TV screen, with the image fluctuating much like ripples on a pond.

Within seconds a dark image appeared, transforming itself from a haphazard array of dark dots into the unmistakable shape of a man. As the image finally became fully formed there stood Tesman, at the president's side, with a weapon aimed at his head.

Instinctively one of the president's security entourage drew his weapon from his shoulder holster, his much favoured 1911 automatic, and lifted it to aim at the interloper.

Tesman was quicker. He directed his own weapon towards the guard, a fine red beam of light emanating from his weapon appeared on the wall just below the guard's outstretched arm. He then opened fire, the red light began to burn a hole in the wall, accompanied by a high pitched whine. Raising the weapon at speed the red spot tracked up the wall, leaving a fine line of damage cut into the wall. As it reached the agent's outstretched arm it continued upwards, cutting his weapon in half, removing his forefinger in the process. There was a thud as the severed weapon hit the ground along with the accompanying trigger finger. The agent recoiled in agony but no blood was to be seen, the stump on his hand having been cauterised by the intense heat.

It was over in the blink of an eye, Tesman quickly placing his weapon back against the president's head. Tesman smiled and began to shake his head, much like a parent berating his young son or daughter. He looked directly at the guard, who was clutching his hand in agony, having placed a clean handkerchief from his jacket pocket.

"Tut-Tut. That was a silly move young man; that was a VERY silly move."

Turning to face his audience he continued. "Please do not try any pointless gestures like that again or your president will die," pressing his weapon into the president's neck to make his point. "Imagine what this weapon could do, separating your president's head from his shoulders." He paused for effect. "Still, you wouldn't have to listen to any more boring and repetitive speeches, would you?" Reaching into his pocket he took out what appeared to be a piece of plastic tubing in the shape of a circle. He placed it over his captive's head, squeezed it gently and it immediately appeared to contract around his neck. The president lifted his head, as if to relieve any pressure he felt, but it was pointless.

As it just began to create painful pressure on the president's neck it stopped.

"You know what this is, don't you lieutenant Abrahams?"

Rick nodded slightly, his face trying to mask what horrors could befall if it were activated.

"Our neighbours on Auriga developed this as a weapon of torture. It can literally remove the head from your head of government, slowly, but ever so surely."

"Go ahead and kill me Tesman," the president had had enough, "as soon as you do my men will cut you down where you stand." His security men stood to attention as if to reinforce his words.

"Not before I aim my weapon at that box," he gestured towards Johnno, "it **is** in the box, isn't it?" Johnno's grip tightened almost imperceptibly, but it was enough.

"I thought so. One shot at that box would set off a chain reaction and, before you know it, we shall all be gone, as will your precious Groom Lake Complex, your secret area 51, and everyone else within a 50 mile radius. Is that what you really want?"

The president struggled as he spoke "If that's what it takes, you bastard."

"And what would you tell your adoring public when they discover evidence showing the secrets WAY below ground in Area 51. Why, there may even be some survivors who decide to live above ground for a change. That WOULD cause problems with your government, and your standing in the world, wouldn't it?"

Everyone around the table was looking for an opportunity to do something, anything, that would save their president, but they were helpless. They kept looking towards their colleagues for inspiration, as did the guards, but the situation seemed hopeless.

"All I want is what is in that box. Then I'll leave you all in peace. That's not a lot to ask, is it?"

"Mr President, we need to accede to his demands, the risks otherwise are too great." Johnno decided to be the mediator. "If he gets the package I'm sure we can track him and prevent its use." His voice was full of confidence. "We've taken it back once and we can do it again."

Rick kept his composure, fully aware that once the weapon was in Tesman's hands they had no way to track its movements. What the hell was Johnno thinking?

"At last, a sensible statement." Tesman directed his smile towards Johnno and the box. "Now, pass it over please, and no sudden moves."

Johnno opened the box and reached inside.

"NO!". Tesman shouted, obviously fearing that Johnno might be able to use the weapon inside. He levelled his own weapon towards Johnno, who looked down, a red dot appeared menacingly in the middle of his chest.

"NO - Leave it inside the box."

Johnno took his hand out of the box, closed the lid and got to his feet.

"Now bring it here, slowly, and no tricks. No-one wants a headless president, do they?"

Johnno slowly moved towards Tesman, the box in his outstretched arms.

"I don't have any tricks. I just want to save my president."

"Very touching, you may even get a medal for this, who knows." Pushing his weapon against the president's temple for effect. "You WILL give him a medal, won't you, Mr President?"

"I'd like to give you something, you alien bastard."

The tension in the room was electric. Each individual wanting to save their president whilst knowing that one wrong move could spell the end for all of them. Tesman's threat was uppermost in their mind. The only sound was the occasional painful moaning of the injured guard, now being tended to by a colleague.

Keeping his own weapon in his left hand aimed at the president he reached out and took the box from Johnno, clutching it to his chest. His faced beamed with a smile of intense satisfaction and smugness, he had won! Single handedly he had defeated the United States of America, and who knows which nation would be the next to succumb, once his new weapon was in action. He took one step back from his stance by the president. He moved his left hand down towards his belt and pressed at the buckle.

"Thank you for your help gentlemen. I am sure that we shall meet again in the near future, and I warn you, I may not be so benevolent next time."

Ripples seemed to appear around him again as he spoke. Then his image seemed to fade in layers, much like those on a TV screen as it was switched off.

Then he was gone.

Rick jumped to his feet and raced over towards the president. "Don't move, sir, we need to remove this band before it's activated." Frantically searching for the activation button he moved around the president fingers feeling feverishly for the tell-tale button. As he pulled gently on the band it suddenly came away in his hand and fell to the floor. The president felt his throat, just making sure that there was no blood, and no damage done. His security men rushed to his side.

Rick was puzzled. An Aurigan neck band did not just fall off. On close inspection he noticed that it was clear plastic tubing with a fine coiled spring inside, a coiled spring which had given the tubing the appearance of a deadly weapon.

"It's a fake. This is no Aurigan neck band. The bastard played a trick on us."

Johnno took the band from him and inspected it.

"So he did. Clever, very clever"

Rick was stunned.

Their enemy now had the package and had escaped, why did he seem so calm? Any moment now there could be an almighty battle, why was Johnno was smiling?

Errol Gilmore addressed his colleagues. "We need to find out where that alien bastard has gone and take him out." There was a general murmur indicating agreement.

Johnno smiled. "He just played a trick on us sir; If he loves playing tricks on people he'll just love this one."

Gilmore now looked amazed. "What the f ......?"

His sentence was cut short as the ground below them began to shake, followed by a dull rumble, much like thunder in the distance. Fine sprites of dust appeared from gaps in the ceiling tiles and the lights flickered on and off. Everyone seemed unsteady on their feet, putting their arms out for balance as the ground trembled. The air was filled with the smell of ozone.

"It's an earthquake." Gilmore sounded alarmed.

Then all was calm. The floor stopped shaking, the dull rumble was gone, the fine dust had settled in small piles on the table, but had ceased to fall. It had passed

Johnno turned to Gilmore and smiled.

"Actually, sir, it's probably called a space quake."

Chapter 55

Down below, in the security office the two guards had been listening intently to their radio, following the Dodgers v Braves game. There was a twenty dollar bill riding on the result. Just as the Dodgers scored their second home run in the 8th innings the crowd erupted, as did Dave as he saw twenty dollars coming towards him. He jumped up from the radio and danced a little jig around the room.

At that moment there was an explosion deep below them on level 14.

The room began to shake violently, the radio sliding off the table and smashing on the floor. The VCR's on the shelves threatened to fall off, as did the monitors fastened on the wall above them. Alarms began to sound from all sides of the office. Dave rushed over to inspect the CCTV screens to see exactly what had happened. Many of the screens were just showing static, obviously now defunct due to damage or electrical failure. Two monitors seemed full of static but, on closer inspection, were registering the dust and debris thrown up by an explosion.

Bill was now panicking.

"Play it back, play it back. Check the tapes, let's see what the hell just happened."

Dave performed a fast rewind on several tapes, eventually locating one which showed a bright flash by a power station, followed by a visible streak of light shooting across the screen. An explosion followed and the screen went blank.

They stared at each other in disbelief.

"I think we need to report this. They may not know upstairs."

"Yeah, but let's ditch the radio first, no sense asking for trouble."

Dave hid the radio inside a locked desk drawer as Bill contacted the security team in the conference centre. "This is security unit 14 here; security unit 14 here. Level 14 seems to have been badly damaged by a huge explosion. I think one of the power transformers has blown."

Chapter 56

The security team each pressed their fingers to their earpieces, listening intently. They looked towards each other desperately looking for confirmation that they had all received the same message.

'Bud', who appeared to be the team leader, spoke. "Sirs, we've just had a report from security unit 14. It seems that level 14 has been damaged by a power unit overload."

Johnno smiled. "Oh no Bud, it's much more than that."

Everyone was bemused. They had just witnessed their president being taken hostage, and survived an attack of some kind, and this young lieutenant seemed nonplussed by it all.

Tom Gerarty spoke up. "Can you tell us anything that would help explain what just happened, son? … and why you seem so cocky?"

"Yes, but first of all can I suggest that everyone takes a seat, especially you Mr President." The president acknowledged the gesture and concern shown, taking his seat at the head of the table.

"Please be seated gentlemen, and let Mr O'Ryan explain why we shouldn't be worried. And get some medical help down here for my injured guard." Everyone ambled back to their seats, puzzled by Johnno's apparently casual behaviour, wanting to know what they could do next. All eyes were on him.

"First of all I need to apologise to my friend Rick here. I wanted to keep a souvenir of my exploits and so I kept one of his weapons, a neuroliser, for myself." Adding "I was never going to use it, just keep it safe in a drawer at home , and maybe show it to my kids one day when I finally settle down and have a family." He turned to face his friend "Sorry Rick."

Rick was still puzzled, but smiled in acceptance of the apology.

"And , Mr President, to put your mind at rest, I need to give you this."

Unbuttoning the top of his uniform he reached inside the jacket and pulled out the 'package', the weapon that Tesman believed he had secured. He passed it to the President. "Be careful Mr President, I think the safety catch is on, but I can't be sure."

Everyone was stunned, amazed, and relieved to say the least. Rick shook his head in disbelief, Pazzaro beamed with pride. The president leaned over and took the package, unable to hide his sheer joy at this unexpected turn of events.

"Johnno, I think I should call you Johnno, I cannot express my gratitude and that of my colleagues and the millions of US citizens who are indebted to you. You are an amazing young man. Now tell us how you pulled of your amazing trick, we were all taken in as well as that bastard." His face suddenly froze, concern etched across it, as he then glanced at the lectern. "Can he come back? He can't get back, can he?"

"No Mr President, he certainly cannot come back."

His shoulders dropped in relief. "Come on Johnno, tell us more."

As he prepared to tell his story he glanced around the table. Everyone was hanging on his every word. Placing his arms on the table, to help steady his shaking hands, he began.

"When I heard from Commander Pazzaro that Tesman had been discovered checking through plans, especially the dining room, I felt a pang of suspicion, it's similar to the twists and turns we had with Maia. I felt he may be trying to misdirect us. I mean why attack your target in a room full of people where someone may just be lucky in taking you out? In our lessons on battle strategy at 'boot camp' we were taught that the best way to kill a movement was to take away it's leader. If you can do that in full view of his followers you strike even more fear into them."

The president turned to Errol Gilmore "Take the head from the snake!." Gilmore nodded.

"I strongly believed that Tesman would probably strike here. The head of the snake, sorry Mr President, is present alongside his ranking followers," Johnno looked around the table, "sorry gents." He was met with a bank of smiling faces. "So, when we reached our room to shower and change I replaced the package weapon with my souvenir. I'd carried the package within my shirt for so long that it became second nature."

Dr. Payne coughed and cleared his throat. "But how could you be so sure?"

Almost apologetically Johnno replied. "I wasn't sure, but my Aunt Freya always advised me to follow my gut instinct."

Rick leaned forward and placed his arm on Johnno's shoulder "So that's why you fly by the seat of your pants." Johnno tilted his head and smiled nervously.

"When I saw your security team touch their earpieces and then check their weapons I knew something was possibly amiss. I pulled the box back onto my lap and started the first sequence for the explosive self-destruction of my secret neuroliser. If I had been wrong it would have been easy to cancel the action and no-one would be any the wiser." He could feel his throat drying up as he battled his nerves to continue his story. He reached over the table and poured some water from the obligatory jug into a glass and took a sip, and then a deep breath. There was a knock on the door. Several medical attendants entered, apologising for the intrusion. The president was keen to get attention for his personal guard.

"Get him to your hospital as quickly as you can. I'll call and see you later Jeff." The injured guard acknowledged the gesture, thanking the president as he was led out of the room. As the door closed Johnno continued.

"When he appeared I was, just the same as everyone here, fearful for Mr President's life. When he fired his weapon at just one guard I was baffled. If he was trying to scare our government and build on our fears he could so easily have taken us all out and just collected the package. It's possible that no-one would have been aware of our fate for hours. I believe that his weapon would no longer fire, or needed time to recharge, and he was doing his best to trick us."

"Well reasoned lieutenant, but what finally convinced you to take the final action and prime your weapon?" Vasey was intrigued.

Looking pensive Johnno replied. "I noticed that Tesman did not stray from Mr President's side, even after placing that ...... that….. "

"Aurigan neck band," Rick helped out

"Yes that neck band. If it was so deadly he would have had the confidence to walk over to me and just take the box from me, secure in the belief that no-one would stop him. I believe he stayed at the president's side for security. He was sure no-one would take a shot at him for fear of missing him and killing their president."

The president relaxed back into his chair, placing his hand to his chin and smiling broadly. "You son of a gun! Just when did you finally arm the weapon? How were you so sure he wouldn't check the contents before he went?" leaning forward again and placing his arms on the table, "and how were you so sure that it wouldn't explode right here and now?"

Turning to face his friend he replied "Well sir, Rick had given me full and explicit instructions on how to set the self-destruct mechanism on a neuroliser, you know, just in case."

Rick smiled and thought "You're making this up buddy, but it does sound right and makes me look even better."

He continued " ... and he told me never to use it unless in a dire emergency. I believe this was a dire emergency. I had already completed my calculations and gone over them again and again in my head until I was sure I was right. I knew that we had sixty seconds from activation.

It would take Tesman thirty seconds or so to phase and teleport back to his power source. If he took the package and disappeared within, say ten to fifteen seconds, and then he wouldn't have enough time to return here. If it was successful then the charge would destroy him and his power source whether he was back at base or trying to escape by teleporting. I armed the neuroliser when I pretended to remove the weapon. I knew he would be afraid of me removing it in case I used it against him. I closed the lid when he ordered me to, clicking the lever on the lid to stop it opening by accident. When we felt the earthquake, sorry the space quake I knew we had won. He tried to win by subterfuge and trickery. I believe that our subterfuge and trickery was even better."

He relaxed back into his seat. His nervous smile hiding the pride he felt inside. He had completed his mission and saved the life of the president of the USA.

After several seconds of silence the room erupted with applause, everyone keen to get round to him and shake his hand and slap him on the back. He stood nervously accepting the plaudits as everything in the room became somewhat of a blur. As his body kept reacting to the slaps and handshakes, in his mind's eye he could see his beloved Freya alongside his parents, faces full of pride, smiling down on him. Eventually the president got to his feet and took his place back at the lectern gesturing with his arms for everyone to sit down.

"Take your seats gentlemen, I have a speech to complete." He collected the sheaf of papers which had fallen to the floor and began to re-arrange them as his chiefs of staff took their seats once more. The mood in the room was now buoyant, jovial even, the usual air of 'business as usual' had been replaced by a bonhomie and feeling of optimism. Ties were re-straightened and jackets buttoned up to give an air of formality.

Even the security team seemed to visibly relax, their calm business like demeanour giving way to broad smiles. One of them was then seen to place his hand to his ear as he received an incoming message.

"A message for Flight Lieutenant Abrahams sir. Your team members from Orion are all safe and sound and ..." there was a slight delay, "they can confirm that Mr. Tesman and several of his allies have literally disappeared sir. They will be in contact later this evening."

The room erupted with cheers again, the president leading the way. It was more like the Dodgers v Braves game than a formal presidential staff meeting. Once the ritual slapping of hands on the table ceased the president waved his arms again, looking to restart where he had left off. He stood there; in his right hand was his formal speech, papers in disarray covered in shoe prints and dust. He took a long look at them before throwing them up in the air, leaves separating and fluttering down onto the desk and floor. He placed both hands on the lectern and smiled.

"I don't need these, do I? When I started my speech earlier today I mentioned dreams and heroes. Well today I have met two such heroes and our dreams are becoming reality. When this package is returned as promised, having been recovered as promised, then our dreams of space exploration become just a little more real, a little more solid. With Project Lunex about to start and our alliance with our friends here from Orion," he gestured towards Rick, "then not only is the world our oyster, but so is the Universe. Our past has been secured thanks to our two heroes present, and now our new and exciting future begins today." He stood as upright as he could, placing his right arm across his heart. "God bless America."

The atmosphere in the room was electric. Each member of his team stood and solemnly placed their right hand on their hearts and bowed their heads. If ever there was a short speech which could raise their spirits then this was that speech. The president continued as his team sat down once more.

"We shall reconvene this meeting in eleven days at the White House. July 20th will be a special day for us all, indeed for all of the world, and I wish to share it with all of you assembled here." He looked over to Johnno, Rick and Pazzaro. "I shall be most honoured if you will be my guests on the day. Without your input I doubt if the planned events for that day would ever have occurred. Oh, and by the way Johnno, you can leave your Blackbird at home; we will provide your transport." A gentle laugh erupted from several of the guests.

Johnno looked slightly sheepish, but was bursting with pride. Commander Pazzaro rose to his feet and stood to attention.

"On behalf of myself and my two lieutenants with pride I humbly accept your invitation."

"Thank you Joe. Please remember to bring your lovely wife along too. What's her name again?"

Pazzaro smiled, knowing just how excited she would be, an invitation from the president himself.

"It's Linda, Mr President"

"I dare say Linda will need a new dress for the occasion Joe," added the president, winking.

He passed the cigar box to Richard Elms. "Keep an eye on it Richard, as head of CIA please remember history is literally in your hands."

"Yes sir Mr President."

"And now gentlemen we can finally change for dinner, I could do with a stiff drink. Let's reconvene in one hour."

Everyone around the table slowly rose to their feet, making small talk with each other as they made for the door. The president left first, flanked at front and rear by his security details. As he passed one of his security staff he paused and spoke quietly.

"Mike, ring and find out how Jeff is doing. I'll go and see him later."

"Yes sir Mr President."

Johnno lingered in his chair, savouring this special occasion and it's heady atmosphere. Eventually he got to his feet and turned to face Rick. They looked at each other, each finding it hard to accept what had happened in the last half hour. They clasped each other's' hands, and then went into a man hug

"It's been one hell of a day buddy. I can't believe how calm you were when you saw off that bastard Tesman."

"Calm? Calm did you say? I was shaking like a leaf inside. What if I'd been wrong and killed our president? … and his staff … and us too? I've never felt so stressed."

"Call that stress?" Pazzaro joined in the conversation. "I have to go with my wife and buy a new dress for next week."

He winked and winced as if in pain.

"Is this the right colour? Is it too long? Is it too fussy? Does my backside look too big?"

He shook his head, eyes closed as if in prayer.

"Gentlemen, now THAT's stress."

Chapter 57

The next day the two pilots were summoned by Richard Elms, chief of the CIA, for a full debrief of their mission. John Vasey, head of the armed forces, was with him. As they entered his office Johnno was surprised to see his cigar box on the desk in front of him, assuming that the president would have it locked away in a deep secure facility somewhere.

"Is that the actual package sir?"

"Yes it is Johnno, and please call me Richard. Mr President has asked me to fully debrief you on your very successful mission and to see where this wonderful weapon fits in and actually works. Please take a seat. There are drinks on the table should you need them. This is to be an informal session, let's not stand on ceremony."

Rick was concerned. "I believed that the deal was to return the weapon, using human input in the form of our friend here," Rick gestured towards his friend, "and to do that a s a p."

"Don't worry Lieutenant Abrahams; it's here just for demonstration purposes only."

"And to motivate us as well," added Vasey, rather nervously.

"Please take notes Miss Heaton." Elms looked towards his stenographer for confirmation that everything was being noted and recorded. He glanced back towards his guests. "For the record gentlemen, it will all be kept hush-hush and marked for the president's eyes only." He opened the cigar box and handed the weapon to Johnno. "Can you confirm that this is the weapon you managed to rescue on your mission?"

Taking the weapon in both hands Johnno examined it closely, turning it around to view everything fully. He passed it over to Rick, who did likewise. Rick nodded. "That is the weapon we rescued, and please be careful with it as it is powered by small nuclear power cells. Small, but extremely powerful," passing it back to Johnno, who placed it back securely within the box. Elms looked towards Vasey, exchanging smiles and raising their eyebrows in an air of success and satisfaction.

"Now tell us everything lieutenants, please do not leave anything out, not even the smallest detail. We're keen to know how a small force of five outwitted the German army, and then the alien enemy as well."

Although wary of their intentions Johnno began to recount his story, with Rick adding the occasional snippet of information which Johnno overlooked. They occasionally paused to allow Miss Heaton to keep up with their tale, as well as confirming with each other certain aspects of their story.

When Rick mentioned the rockphaser weapon Vasey's eyes lit up as he leaned forward on his seat.

"And where is this weapon now?"

Still wary of their intentions Rick looked towards his buddy.

"Transported back to Orion for safety."

Johnno cottoned on immediately.

"Alien technology, and all that, sirs."

Realising that it was safely stored by a time portal in Poland didn't seem to be a sensible answer. Rick made a mental note to have it removed.

Vasey relaxed back into his seat. "Pity."

Both Johnno and Rick were careful to mention that any technology used by themselves was now destroyed, culminating in the last neuroliser being used to destroy Tesman and his teleportation device. Vasey showed a great deal of interest when the 'watchers' were mentioned.

"They can film the enemy, but can they fire a weapon of any sort? only in self-defence, of course."

Again Rick was wary of providing full details.

"They are powered by small engines which suck in the surrounding air, ignite it and then force it out of small jets. The four jets allow for movement in any direction and can be programmed to follow a heat source or set to infra-red for night time. But we do not use them as weapons, they are far too small, and do not remain airborne for long."

Vasey's eyes narrowed as if deep in thought. "Pity, I could see those as a potentially useful tool," before adding, "for search and rescue, ideal in situations where our soldiers may be missing and in need of being rescued." His reasoning sounded slightly hollow. "Tell me again, how do your neurolisers work?"

Rick sounded vague. "I can tell you what they do, and how they are powered, but as for HOW they work I haven't a clue I'm afraid. All the internal technical stuff is beyond me. They have been developed by scientists back on Mintaka, scientists who guard their secrets closely."

"Nice one buddy," Johnno thought, "this is no normal de-brief."

After thirty minutes or so the de-briefing came to a halt.

Elms stood up and moved around his desk towards his guests. He proffered an outstretched hand "Thank you for your valuable time Lieutenants, and for your amazing story. The whole of America owes you a debt of gratitude. Unfortunately only a select few will know of your actual exploits." After he had shaken hands with both Johnno and Rick, Vasey rose from his seat to their sides and shook their hands as well. "Thank you gentlemen for everything you have done, helping keep America safe and a land of the free. Oh, by the way, the president has granted you ten days R and R. Enjoy it to the full."

Acknowledging their thanks Johnno and Rick formally saluted and then left the room.

As the door closed behind them Elms looked towards Vasey and grinned. "Delete and destroy everything on file Mary, this meeting never happened."

"Yes Mr Elms, this meeting never happened."

Elms and Vasey watched as Miss Heaton left the room.

"What do you think John? Is any of this within our reach?" Vasey was deep in thought.

"The neurolisers would be an excellent hand weapon, but it's just the stuff of sci-fi movies, the same as the rockphaser. We could never manufacture those, even in our black ops units."

"What about those watchers?"

"The same again I'm afraid. They would need to be propeller driven to be of any use here as we don't have any of their jet engines. They would be too noisy and difficult to control. I could never see them being practical."

"Not even if they were capable of carrying weapons?"

"Sorry, it's a 'no' yet again. I mean, could you possibly see us flying an unmanned aircraft towards the enemy. How could we see where we were going? And it would need one hell of a lead on the remote control to guide it."

A thoughtful grin flashed across his face "Just think of the droning noise it would make, how the hell would it be able to creep up on our enemy? No, I have a better idea; let's feed these details to Tom. He can pass them on to his skunk works and give them something to do"

Elms grinned broadly. "And he would owe us a favour too. Good thinking John."

Elms reached forward and pulled the cigar box towards him, opening it as he did so.

Reaching into his jacket pocket he took out a pack of cigarettes, proffering one to Vasey.

He lit his own and took in a deep lungful, blowing the smoke to one side. "Now we have this little baby, for a week or so anyways, we have tangible proof of space weapons. We can pass it on to our research unit, but for fuck's sake don't let the president know."

"What about Giller and Ratchford?"

"Oh no, not those two. With a bit of luck blue book will be closed this year and we can continue in area 51 with impunity."

Vasey rose from his seat, took one last draw on his cigarette, stubbing it out in a large glass ashtray on the table. "I'll leave it in your hands then Richard. Good luck." He turned to leave. "See you at the White House for cocktails. Good luck with your retro engineering your package."

Elms nodded. "Make mine a Jack Daniels on the rocks."

As Vasey closed the door Elms leaned forward, taking a long hard look at the weapon. "It was a bitch of a job retrieving you. Let's hope you can give up your secrets."

Closing the lid he leaned back and opened the top drawer of the desk. Reaching inside he lifted out a small tape recorder, placing it on the desk in front of him. "My evidence. Just in case John, just in case." He switched it off, replaced the lid and carefully placed it in a large brief case at his feet, followed by the cigar box. He picked up the telephone receiver on the desk and dialled.

The receiver clicked, a quiet voice replied "Yes?".

"I'm bringing the package over now. Remember you have seven days maximum, make sure you are successful. Failure is not an option. And DO NOT damage it in any way. Understood? And, for God's sake, do not fire it accidentally."

The receiver was replaced in its cradle. He stood and smoothed the creases on his jacket and closed the brief case spinning the dials to set the combination lock.

"Today's been a good day Richard my boy, a very good day indeed."

Chapter 58

"Did you sleep well, any more nightmares ?"

"Like a log buddy, like a log. No more bad dreams for me."

It was a gloriously sunny day as Rick and Johnno sat in the diner enjoying a long, luxurious breakfast of steak and eggs, pancakes with maple syrup and an endless supply of coffee. It was the iconic American diner, red vinyl topped bar stools with Formica covered tables and counter top. The homely smell of coffee mixed with griddled bacon was a heady mix, one that Johnno had all but forgotten. In the background the juke box was playing their newest record, aptly named 'space oddity' by David Bowie. Sandra, their waitress, came by the table and topped up their coffee with clockwork regularity, eventually persuading her 'boys' to have blueberry pie to finish.

"Well buddy, we've lazed around for five days, drunk beers, let old shovel transport us here and there, and generally chilled, what shall we do for the next five?"

Rick smiled and sensed the time may be right for more revelations.

"Fancy a little sightseeing? I mean REAL sightseeing."

"Sounds good to me buddy, where do we start?"

"I fancy Sedona, where you and your beloved Aunt Freya lived."

Johnno's eyes lit up and seemed to drift away in the distance. He could visualise the serenity of the desert, the inky blackness of the nights, and the security it gave him in a strange country. "Count me in," Johnno was excited at the prospect, "will Freya be there to meet us?"

"Sorry buddy, she's still with the Federation ironing out the wrinkles from our adventures. They're still a little concerned at the demise of Maia and Tesman, but I'm sure she'll come through for us."

Johnno was fired up. "Do we have a map on 'shovel'?"

"No need buddy, I've done it before. We can take the '93' down through Vegas and then onto the '40' towards Flagstaff and down to Sedona." Johnno began to get up out of his seat.

"Whoa there buddy, what about my blueberry pie?"

Johnno grinned and sat back down. Sandra reappeared with two of the largest pieces of pie you could imagine. With it came a jug of pouring cream and two dishes complete with vanilla and chocolate ice cream.

"I can tell you're in one of our services boys, and I'd like to feed you up as a thank-you for keeping us safe here back home. I know you can't say anything and that you've probably been to secret places far, far away," a knowing wink followed, "but God bless you both." She walked back toward the counter, preparing to serve a new customer. "Good day sir, what can I get you on this fine day?"

Johnno took a large scoop of ice cream and placed it beside his pie. Looking up towards Rick, who already had a melting mouthful of pie in his mouth, Johnno grinned.

"If only she knew buddy the full story, if only she knew."

The ride down to Sedona was uneventful. They passed through Las Vegas, marvelling at the city in the desert, but resisted the temptation to stay and gamble. Johnno did insist on having his photograph taken in Williams, next to the iconic route 66 sign, the Rolling Stones version being his favourite. Rick was more laid back and preferred Nat King Cole's velvet voice. They reached Sedona as the evening sun was setting, Johnno directing his friend towards Red Rock Crossing to view it at its best. The red stone rock pillars seemed to reach up and grab a piece of the sky. The birds were imparting their evening chorus as they prepared to roost and sleep in the abundance of trees nearby. The creek was giving out a gentle murmur as it passed through on its long path towards the ocean. As the sun went down the rocks took on a vivid fiery red glow, the shadows slowly overtaking the 'flames' as night intruded on them.

"This is what we saved buddy, this is what a free world is all about."

Johnno sounded almost poetic. "I'm with you my friend, I'm with you. Aunt Freya would regularly bring me here just to sit and relax, soak up the beauty of the dark skies with their pin pricks of light giving me a hint about the marvel of the universe. Hot chocolate with toasted marshmallows .. I can taste them now. Occasionally we'd travel to airport mesa and camp there, it was so magical." In the low light of dusk Johnno failed to recognise his friend's 'knowing' smile.

As the night began to encroach on their peaceful idyll they took one last look and set off to find Freya's house before darkness overtook them. Rick pulled up on the drive and switched off his engine, silence surrounded them like a blanket. There were no lights showing to Johnno's dismay, he had hoped that his beloved aunt had returned to greet them. As they entered the cabin and turned on the lights his face was greeted by a scene forever etched in his memory.

Native American rugs hung on the wall. A bronze cowboy and horse sculpture was still on the dresser. As a child he would picture himself riding the range and rescuing a damsel in distress. Over the fireplace was a Winchester rifle, one that Freya would never allow him to get down, he had to make do with a Daisy BB gun when he took pot shots at the empty tin cans in his back yard. It even smelled like home.

"Let's hit the sack and start our adventures in the morning." Rick made his way to the guest room, leaving Johnno wondering how he knew where it was.

Rick saw the look on his friend's face and smiled. "I've been here before. It will all become clear in the morning. Sweet dreams." Closing the door behind him he left Johnno alone with his memories. Moving towards his old room he stopped to touch the bronze figure. "Hi Roy, how are you and Trigger doing?"

His room was just the same as he left it. Posters on the wall showing the latest jet fighters; model kits of World War 2 aeroplanes, the Spitfire was his favourite, at its side was a P.51; a large poster showing the stars in their constellations. An old pair of motorcycle goggles, donated by a kindly neighbour. He would wear these when he 'flew' on top secret missions as a young boy. By the windows was his telescope, a prized gift from his Aunt when he showed an interest in the stars and the universe. Evidence of its use showed on its body, as did the wear 'suffered' by his constantly taking outside to get a better view of stars and planets he'd read about. He sat on his bed, still made up and looking exceptionally tidy. Kicking off his boots he swung his legs up, lying with one arm under his head "It will all become clear in the morning. I wonder what that's about?"

His eyes could no longer stay open. It had been a long day.

He drifted into a contented sleep.

Finally his nightmares were a thing of the past – literally.

Chapter 59

The smell of freshly brewed coffee was too much to resist, dragging Johnno from a deep sleep back into the reality of life. Sitting up he wondered where the slightly acidic smell was coming from. Sniffing around he realised it was him. "Phew, I need a shower and a change of clothing. I don't suppose ..." he walked over to his wardrobe and found his clothes all neatly in place, washed, pressed and ironed. "Trust Freya, she's a mind reader."

He passed through the lounge area on his way to the bathroom and shower. Rick was busy in the kitchen.

"I'll be ten minutes tops."

"Better had be buddy, the pancakes are stacked and the bacon is about to go on. Eggs over easy to follow."

Showered and changed Johnno felt ready to meet the world. As they ate breakfast the conversation drifted to their de-briefing and how Rick had managed to hold back so much, and keep a straight face.

"What they don't know cannot hurt them. And we're still heroes!"

Johnno washed and stacked the dishes, just as he had done so many times for his Aunt. She had a thing about responsibility and doing chores.

Rick was standing by the fireplace as Johnno came in and sat down in his favourite chair, draped in a Native American 'throw over'. He caressed the well-worn wooden arms and all seemed right with the world.

"Where are we going today, Monument Valley?"

Rick smiled. "No, I thought somewhere further. Mexico perhaps, then maybe onto Northern Arizona, or Montana, perhaps even Peru."

"Stop taking the piss, where are you REALLY taking me."

"On a voyage of discovery my friend. You've earned it."

Rick turned to face the chimney breast. "Ever wondered why Freya never let you touch this old Winchester?"

"I was too young I suppose" He grinned. "She was probably afraid I'd shoot myself in the foot."

Rick reached up pulling back on the rifle's hammer whilst pulling down on its barrel. There came a sound of scraping, accompanied by a hissing sound that Johnno had heard before. The wall to the right of the stone chimney breast was clad in layers of pine trunks, apparently sliced in half to leave the bark in situ as a feature. It began to move gently backwards, apparently detaching itself from the adjoining wall and chimney breast. After it had regressed back inwards by around two feet or so it began to slide left, behind the chimney breast, revealing a dark open void.

"I've seen this kind of thing before. Are we …?" His sentence was cut short.

"Come on, it's time that you knew more about our part in Earth's history."

Rick moved into the dark void, with Johnno close on his heels. As they entered the wall slid back behind them, and locked itself back in place, ensuring their secret was still secure. An ambient light appeared around them, lighting the room in an eerie blue glow. It was enough to see by, but not enough to dazzle and hurt their eyes.

"Remember this?" Rick was pointing to a dull glass like screen on the wall.

Johnno peered closely as his eyes became accustomed to the light. Recognition arrived along with a smile on his face. "It's the route map for you portals, isn't it? How long has this been here?"

"The portal itself? Thousands of years. This control is relatively new; the original property was built around sixty years ago and we added these new controls when Freya bought the property. Do you ever remember hearing noises in the night?"

"Freya told me they were the happy spirits of the Honanki reaching their happy hunting grounds." He paused. "So … how did you get in here without me noticing?"

"We came from a direction that you never knew buddy." Rick turned away and activated the screen by locating his key in the touch keypad where it 'sank' activating the control panel. As the keys appeared he touched a combination of six numbers with amazing speed, he'd obviously done this before. Immediately a myriad of lines appeared, crisscrossing many times, but all leading to a central point, Federation central of Orion. This map seemed to be more elaborate than the one in the forest hut, the lines creating a 3D effect as each line took on a different hue. Using his hands on the actual screen with a mixture of sliding and pulling the lines became fewer as he zoned in on his target, portal links on planet Earth. Johnno was impressed by the speed of his friend's actions, peering over his shoulder to see if he could recognise any locations.

"Is it faulty? I can see several locations in the oceans."

Rick was still fine tuning his map, and answered without looking around. "No faults there buddy. We have several locations under the seas where our craft can submerge and not be seen. Water pressure is very similar to the vacuum of space so locating there is no problem, no problem at all." As the screen finished its acrobatic motions Rick moved to one side allowing his friend to take a closer look.

"I can see points in the oceans by San Francisco, that looks like Santa Catalina and ..." he moved over towards New England "Shag Harbour?" He continued downwards towards South America "Where's that? It's inland but appears to be underwater."

"That is Lake Titicaca, one of our earliest portals in the Americas."

"I've never been to South America, is there much there?"

"It all depends on what you want to see , or what you need."

Rick moved back over to the screen, looking closely for his first destination. "We need a couple of points to visit so I'll start .... Here." As he touched the screen his first location turned green. "And finally, there." Each press caused the location to change colour, first green red and finally blue as pathways emerged and highlighted the route between them.

While Johnno was trying to make out where Rick had chosen for them to visit Rick moved back over to the control keypad. He pressed a combination of keys and the destination paths began to flash.

"Nearly there. Can you do me a favour and collect those two belts on the side wall please?"

Johnno peered but could see nothing. "Over here?" he walked towards the wall. Two unseen panels swung open to show two matt black belts suspended as if in mid-air.

"Whoa, this is magic stuff, this alien technology."

"I don't think so, try magnetism."

Feeling rather sheepish Johnno collected both belts and took them over as instructed. Rick took one, instructing Johnno to wear the other one.

"These are dynamically linked to each other, programmed with our destinations. Where you go, I go and vice versa. It just ensures that we travel together safely through the portals and beyond. A major upgrade on our cabin in the woods. "

As Johnno put the belt around his waist, it moved around and closed itself, reducing its size to a perfect fit.

"Come on buddy, time for lesson one." He moved to the second screen to the right of the room, the portal itself. As Johnno stood alongside his friend the screen in front of them seemed to bounce in and out as if it were made of a transparent rubber. Eventually the appearance of bouncing subsided and the screen was still.

"Go ahead. Touch it." Rick encouraged his friend in his first step into the unknown.

Johnno gave an embarrassed look, he was still quite wary of what was about to happen.

"Go on, it won't bite"

Thoughts flooded in as he decided what to do. "I've travelled back in time, fought off the German army, beaten aliens and I'm afraid of this gloop." He eventually leaned forward and tentatively touched the screen. Ripples emanated from his fingers as if he had dipped it into a pool. As he pulled his fingers back the screen seemed to be as if made of jelly, stretching back with him until it finally snapped away causing yet more ripples to appear. He felt slightly embarrassed at his initial reluctance, but soon repeated the action amazed at the vertical wall of liquid.

"See, that wasn't too bad, was it?"

Johnno's sheepish grin said it all.

"Now follow me." Rick stepped into the screen, the 'gloop' enveloping his body as he did so before disappearing.

Johnno tentatively stepped forward. "Here goes nothing." He disappeared into the void. He felt as if he were travelling in slow motion, with each step seemingly taking seconds to complete, following as close behind Rick as he could. He tried to speak, but could only hear distorted sounds, the kind you hear when coming around after anaesthetic, or waking with a mild hangover.

Within seconds they had reached their destination.

Johnno looked around; he was obviously in some form of cave. The air was thick and humid and smelled of damp vegetation and waste. As he adjusted his eyes he could see a shaft of light in front of him, reminding him of the images he'd seen as a child of heaven's light illuminating the infant Jesus. And it was hot; the damp heat that seeps into your bones and causes sweat to trickle down your back.

"Mind your step; we have a small walk over this mossy ground. Be careful of the uneven steps and … here we are."

Johnno was more concerned about hidden creatures lurking in the dark, but eventually joined his partner directly under the amazing shaft of sunlight.

"OK, where is here exactly?"

"Just one more step and then we ....."

Johnno felt his feet leave the floor as he slowly rose into the air. It was as if the sunlight was being used as an elevator. He looked around, feeling slightly unsteady, watching as the darkness of the cave gave way to the vivid greens of tropical vegetation. He glanced down to see the dark floor slowly receding into the distance "Is this safe? I mean, how the hell are we levitating?"

"Not levitating buddy, just good old anti-gravity again. And, before you get too concerned, you're linked to me, and I *have* done this before."

Soon they were bathed in daylight at ground level. Rick guided them over to a gap in the trees, where they gently touched down on solid ground.

"That was unreal, it must be at least a hundred feet to the bottom."

"At least buddy, if not a little more."

As he looked around Johnno realised he was in a jungle setting. The sun was shining directly overhead, its shafts of light breaking through the canopy here and there highlighting the green carpet of tropical plants. The smell was less damp, more of a sweet heady smell of ripening fruits. A strange bellowing noise suddenly began to surround them, coming from all directions at once. Rick noticed his friend's look of concern as he began to follow the narrow path ahead of him.

"That's just howler monkeys. We're in their domain now. Keep up , not far to go now."

Johnno obediently followed. "Snakes? Are there any snakes?"

"Probably, but they're more afraid of us than we are of them."

"That does NOT reassure me one bit."

"Here we are, what do you think of that?"

They entered a clearing and there, in front of them, almost growing out of the undergrowth, was a ruined building. "Jeez, what's that?" Johnno was stunned.

"That, my friend, is all that remains of Yaxchilan, a city in the jungle created by the Maya people over 1,000 years ago. Let's take a walk and I'll fill you in with the details."

As they walked around the ruins Rick pointed out the structure, almost pyramidical in shape, and several stories high. There were elaborate carvings strewn around; some within the building and many lying as if cast aside on the jungle floor. Johnno couldn't resist feeling the stonework, running his fingers along the elaborately carved faces of inhabitants long since gone.

"This is just stunning; there must have been hundreds of people here to build this."

"Tens of thousands actually and they lived here as well." Rick took a seat on a low wall and began to elaborate.

"Many years ago we had an alliance with the inhabitants of the Pleiades system and agreed to a system of non-interference with any cultures and civilisations we visited. When we discovered the Maya, and their innate ability to learn, we took them under our wing you might say. We taught them about such things as agriculture, building, medicines ... but they were amazingly adept at astronomy and mathematics. They even adopted our system time in katuns, baktuns and so on, even counting in a base of twenty." Noticing his friend's bemused expression Rick added. "We count our toes as well as our fingers."

Johnno looked down towards his feet, back up to his friend, and smiled "Makes sense."

Rick continued.

"As they prospered and built many more cities such as Chichen Itza, Palenque and Uxmal, we took our leave and just maintained a watching brief. While they built cities we quietly installed our portal, deep down in the cave where we felt it was safe from prying eyes."

"And that's where we arrived?"

"Yes. We first arrived by what you would call a spaceship, first arriving when your planet Venus was bright in the sky. The Mayans believed that's where we came from. We believed this was an ideal cover story, especially if we had to return quickly for any reason. For years they prospered and we felt we had helped a civilisation prosper purely by providing knowledge – the first decree of the Federation."

Johnno looked around at the ruins, and the encroaching jungle. "Something obviously went wrong."

"The climate changed due to natural occurrences on Earth and the crops began to fail. Many thousands of lives were in danger. The Federation sent a contingent of so called diplomats to offer assistance. They were less than cautious and were seen exiting the cave system. Unknown to us they were led by Snneldaay, a local commander not known for his, shall I say, diplomacy. When he realised he could offer no assistance he decided the civilisation needed culling, only the pure to survive and thrive. Remind you of anyone?"

"All dictators and autocrats are the same, whatever the planet, whatever the millennia."

"And so he advised them that human sacrifice was the answer. Start with child bearing women; add children, plus any prisoners. He even advised them that removing the hearts would please them, the Gods, and all would be well."

Rick looked deep in thought as he shook his head. "And so it continued until another envoy from Orion visited and saw the carnage. This amazing, civilisation, which had so much to offer, was sliding into a hell of its own making. The populous blindly followed, hoping for safety and salvation."

Johnno looked pensive, and smiled "A little like Germany and the third Reich."

"As well as ritual sacrifice they had even begun throwing people down into any cave system they could find in the belief the Gods would notice more quickly. We had to act and help them."

"I thought the Federation was dedicated to help through knowledge alone, with no direct interference."

Rick's eyes closed as he recalled the actions taken, gently nodding his head. After several seconds he turned to face his friend, eyes wide open and a broad grin on his face. "Politics buddy, we used politics to save them."

"OK, enlighten me further."

"We gave them more, relevant, knowledge; we advised them that the stars were affecting the Earth's climate and sacrifice was useless. We showed them, mathematically, how their race would die out if they continued to live there. We then gave them the knowledge about other planets out there in the wide universe which would benefit from civilisations such as theirs; where life was good, the crops grew every year, and there were new stars to learn about."

"What did they think of this knowledge?"

"They wanted to live. We wanted them to live. So we arranged an exodus, very much like your biblical version, and took them to a new promised land. I am not allowed to tell you where, only that they now prosper and thrive."

"Did they all go?"

"No. Some of the older ones wished to stay and live where they had been born. These were often supported by their children, who could now eke out a living as the demands for food were not nearly so high. Many travelled out of their cities to thrive elsewhere. Locally, tribes such as the Lacandon still survive, but essentially the Mayan civilisation ended on Earth hundreds of years ago." Johnno stood and looked around, the howler monkeys still acting as the backdrop.

"Hence the ruins."

"Yep, hence these ruins and many more besides I presume." Johnno stood in stunned silence. "Needless deaths for a needless cause.". Hitler was repeating the Mayans' actions and would, hopefully, fail just as the Mayans did hundreds of years ago. He took a deep breath. "Thanks for the history lesson. History repeats itself and all that."

"Where are we going to next? Could it be somewhere a little less damp? I'm sweating buckets here, and I'm sure I can hear snakes," nervously scanning the ground around them as they spoke

"One more trip, and then home for our presidential appointment."

Rick stood up, dusted the dust off his trousers, and headed back to the portal deep within the cave. As they approached the cave entrance Johnno suddenly remembered the shaft opening and the 100 feet drop to the floor.

"Have faith buddy, and follow me." Rick stepped out over the vertical shaft and began to slowly descend. Johnno followed nervously, now that he was fully aware of the depth of this shaft, but was amazed at his slow and safe steady descent. As they neared the bottom darkness began to envelop them once more as the daylight began to recede until, eventually, solid ground was beneath their feet once more. Johnno peered into the darkness of the cavern before them.

"This ain't gonna be easy, I can't see a thing."

Just then the floor below them lit up creating a pathway towards the darkness which lay before them like a door. The soft blue lighting was weaving a path before them, highlighting the contours of the cave floor as well as providing direction for their exit. As they neared the end of the illuminated pathway Johnno saw the vertical 'water wall' appear before them, emanating from the floor upwards.

"Are you ready for our next destination buddy?"

"Hell yes. I could get used to this. Even better than our Blackbird."

Rick disappeared into the ripples of the portal, Johnno confidently following close behind. As they passed through their 'gloop' the doorway behind them 'sank' into the ground and the illuminated pathway disappeared.

It was merely a deep, inaccessible, cave once more.

As Johnno exited the portal for the second time he recognised he was in a room in some form of a simple building structure. Glancing behind him he realised that he had just left a solid stone rock face. He watched as the portal door disappeared, something he could not see in the dark cave.

Walking forward towards daylight Johnno recognised the basic outline of a stone built building, attached somehow to the natural overhang of a butte. As they exited the room they were confronted by a series of buildings all linked together, with ladders in place allowing movement between them.

"This way, buddy. It looks a damn site more impressive over here and looking back."

Rick climbed down a series of ladders, crossing floor ways which seemed to form the roofs of the structure below them. Despite the intense heat and location the area around the building was quite fertile with trees and grasses being quite abundant. Rick settled below one of the trees in the shade, gesturing for his friend to join him. From his jacket pocket he took two pouches, passing one over. Johnno looked baffled.

"Just tear off the top, put it to your mouth and squeeze. You'll feel all the better for it."

Johnno did as he was told and, though the pouch had a slightly metallic taste, he was pleasantly surprised as he swallowed the contents. He felt immediately refreshed as the liquid first quenched his thirst and then seemed to satisfy the gentle pangs of hunger.

"What is this stuff? You should market and sell it."

"It's a food and drink substitute, which also helps with the effects of portal travel, although it can give you a blinding headache."

"What's in it, it's quite addictive actually."

Rick smiled and tilted his head.

Johnno understood. "I know, alien technology and all that."

Rick looked back at the structures in front of them. "Impressive, isn't it? Where our Hopi brothers lived."

"It sure is impressive. I've seen photographs in the National Geographic but I don't know a thing about them." Rick picked up a handful of soil, letting it slip through his fingers as he spoke.

"We thought we had learned our lesson with the treacherous Pleidians and when we heard that Snneldaay had been visiting thc plains of your early America we despatched our own contingent of advisers once more. Due to our ability to traverse time we were fully aware of what was to happen to this continent and felt duty bound to offer knowledge to the indigenous peoples who lived here. Our first landings were on your West coast and, as we move eastwards we met the Hopi peoples and so began our quest to enrich their lives. As you can see we taught them how to build structures like this, and pueblos houses, in order that they may live in groups and not isolation, in peace and not in friction. They welcomed us and called us Kachinas, after our expedition leader Ka-cheena. They were suffering a drought so, this time, we helped by seeding the clouds and bringing rain. No more thoughts of bloody sacrifice."

"What of Snneldaay, did you stop him?"

"He managed to convince the Sioux tribe of his desire to help them. However when he began to defile their land with deep excavations, and taking a liking to killing the buffalo for sport as well as food, the Sioux nation rose against him."

"Defile their land? How?"

"He was searching for gold. Although we do not value gold as much as everyone else on earth, it is a valuable resource for manufacturing alien technology, circuit boards, electronics and the like."

"What happened to him and his alien army?"

"We believe that there was a surprise attack as they worked within one of their mine shafts. The story is they began firing arrows into the entrance and rolling in flaming tumbleweed bushes. Streaks of 'lightning' were seem coming out of the entrance ... probably from weapons ... then the shaft collapsed as a ball of flame shot out from the entrance. This was then filled with the soil and rubble left outside and the Sioux went back to revering the earth and it's bounty."

"Forgotten?"

"More or less. Many of Snneldaay's workers were what are now termed as 'Greys'. Their images can be found in many Native American etchings. We even believe some lived here before the Hopi, probably a downed craft. They spoke to us of 'Ant People' who lived underground ... probably searching for a portal back home."

"What about your Hopi guidance?"

"Sorry, I drifted a little there. As I said before we were fully aware of what would befall the native Americans in their future and tried to prepare them with knowledge and information- you know, forewarned is forearmed and all that."

"Did it? Work I mean?"

"Well when the Spanish conquistadors arrived they set their leader, Pedro De Tovar, a series of quests which we had suggested."

"What happened then?"

Rick's face broke into a wide grin.

"He failed and was seen as a failure by his men. They got back on their horses and promptly left."

"Can they still survive?"

"Their elders noted our warnings and, with our help, set out nine prophecies. They have been passed down from father to son, generation to generation, to this very day."

"How many of these prophecies have passed to date?"

"Eight, and the ninth could be the final one. We are doing all we can to prevent it becoming reality and very soon everyone on earth will have their part to play. You have a beautiful blue oasis in the middle of the cold, starry desert of space. Let's hope that your leaders and its inhabitants realise how valuable and rare ALL life is."

"We've done a small part by denying Hitler his fourth Reich, haven't we?"

Rick placed his hand on Johnno's shoulder with a reassuring squeeze. "We have my friend, yes we have..." pausing, he looked towards the skies adding, "but there's a damn sight more to do if we are to prevent the Hopi ninth sign from becoming reality."

They both relaxed against the base of the tree and took in their amazing surroundings. Nearby a cactus wren was busy singing in the hope of finding his mate. The sun was shining gloriously in a clear blue sky tempting lizards to dart out of their hiding places to bask in the heat, powering their fine frames with solar power. The wind rustled gently through the Palo Verde trees causing the sunlight to create abstract shadows on the dusty floor.

"It really is a beautiful world, isn't it?"

"It sure is buddy. However your history lesson is now over. Let's make tracks back home, we have a president to meet."

"Will we be in time?"

"We're due in Washington DC and the Mr President is expecting us at 1800 hours on the dot."

"1800 hours ... on the dot...Are we using Alien technology and all that?"

"Not this time. The commander has pulled in a few favours with his friend the governor and managed to borrow his Lear jet for the day. Apparently it was his wife's idea."

"Ah hah - female technology and all that."

They climbed back up into the pueblo buildings, Johnno still marvelling at their construction. Carefully checking to see that no-one was in their vicinity Rick activated the portal and they quickly passed through. They spent the next day firstly in Sedona, visiting Johnno's favourite place for contemplation, the Chapel of the Holy Cross. Rick was impressed as it seemed to mirror the Hopi traditions of being rooted in the surrounding mountain.

The afternoon was spent in Monument Valley where Johnno's main wish was to visit John Ford's point. He was an avid John Wayne fan and spent his time pointing out the locations where he had starred in his favourite movie, the Searchers. As the sun set Johnno insisted in viewing the 'Mittens', watching the shadows move across their faces in a magical dance. They finally climbed back onto shovel ready for the journey back to Freya's home and a good night's sleep before returning to base and then on to their meeting with the president.

"I'm nervous about this meeting, are you?"

"Why should we be, we've met him before, and I think he liked us." Johnno sounded upbeat.

Rick looked deadly serious "No, not meeting the president, it's the commander's wife I'm worried about," then his broad grin gave him away.

"Whatever you do don't mention the dress!"

Chapter 60

Johnno and Rick presented themselves, as directed, to Commander Pazzaro's office at 0900 hours on Wednesday 16th July.

Pausing outside his office door they checked out the creases in the trousers of their dress uniforms, taking the opportunity to polish their shoes one last time on the back of their trousers. Ties checked too, they knocked on the door. "Come in gentlemen." The commander waved them in as he listened intently to a radio in the corner of his office. "We're busy catching up with the latest news of our boys in Apollo 11 approaching the moon, they're almost there boys, they're almost there." Johnno and Rick looked at each other rather sheepishly; they had forgotten about the planned lunar landing.

"It's not my fault," Rick did his best to whisper from the side of his mouth, "perhaps if it had been a full moon I'd have remembered."

Pazzaro turned to face his men. "You're both looking very smart gentlemen; you are both shining examples of air force efficiency and style."

At Pazzaro's side a lady stepped forward and gently coughed.

He turned his head in her direction. "Are you alright dear? – it's the dust you know." She gave him a withering look, followed by a nod of her head towards Johnno and Rick, and then smiled graciously. Pazzaro cottoned on.

"Let me introduce my lovely wife Linda."

Pazzaro's wife was an elegant lady, perhaps slightly younger than her husband. She has quite a petite build, around 5ft 4ins tall, with mousey blonde hair which had obviously just been trimmed and styled for this important occasion. She was obviously proud of her husband's achievements as an air force wife and she oozed confidence as she stood by his side.

"Good morning ma'am, it's a pleasure to meet you," was spoken in unison.

Stepping forward in front of her husband she moved elegantly to meet the guests.

"And it's an honour to meet two brave men who serve alongside my husband," offering a gloved hand for them both to shake. "I don't know the full details of your recent mission, only that it was VERY successful and my Joey, sorry, Commander Pazzaro is very proud of you both."

Pazzaro looked slightly embarrassed as his pet name was revealed.

"What do you think of my wife's dress?" trying to move on the conversation.

As they looked towards their commander to reply he looked back at them nodding his head slightly as his eyes opened wide in the hope of a positive response. They turned and made a grand gesture of looking the dress, and its wearer, up and down. It was an elaborate evening style dress, in vivid colours, which had obviously cost their commander a great deal of money. Rick spoke first.

"It's beautiful ma'am, it really is."

"I bet my husband ordered you to say that," She turned to look at him. Pazzaro flashed a nervous smile and shrugged his shoulders.

Rick continued. "No ma'am, it really is beautiful. It's an Oscar de la Renta, isn't it?"

Mrs Pazzaro looked really flattered. Pazzaro was amazed.

Johnno was stunned. "How the hell does he know that?" flashed through his mind.

"Yes it is lieutenant, and may I congratulate you on your knowledge of fashion."

The sound of coughing resonated again, this time from Pazzaro. "It's time to go. The jet is fuelled and ready and Dave is waiting to fly us personally."

"Dave? Who is Dave sir, we don't recognise that name. Is he in our squadron?"

Linda leaned forward and whispered, as loudly as she could.

"He's the governor, a friend of ours. He insisted on loaning us his plane." She put her right hand to her mouth as if to muffle the conversation. "SO much better than a bench seat on a dirty cargo plane, the ones we're normally shipped about in, don't you think?"

Rick turned on the charm again ."I fully agree, we can't have your beautiful dress creased before you meet the president, can we?"

Johnno turned and opened the door, standing back to allow Mrs Pazzaro to leave feeling quite regal and happy with life.

The commander passed through the door. As he did so he paused, smiled and winked at both of his men.

"Well done boys, you truly deserve a medal. Meeting the president will be a piece of cake after this."

Chapter 61

'Dave' flew his guests into Hyde airport, Pazzaro having been given presidential permission to do so. As the Learjet finally pulled to a halt the sound of seat belts un-clicking was partnered with Johnno's comment. "Boy, I could sure get used to this."

Dave came through from the pilot's cabin, dressed immaculately in a crisp white shirt and dark slacks, sporting a broad grin on his face. "I just had to come and meet you boys. You must have done something really special to warrant a presidential invite. Shoot, even I can't get one of those."

Rick was the first to shake his outstretched hand. "It has been an honour to have you fly us sir." Johnno proffered his as well. "A true honour sir, thank you."

As they descended the plane's steps Dave was heard to say "I LOVE your dress Linda. You must come by one evening to one of our cocktail parties."

"Thank you Dave," came the blushing reply.

Pazzaro smiles as Dave winked at him. "Was I sincere enough?" he whispered.

"You can never be too sincere in politics Dave. Thank you again."

As the party finished exiting the plane Rick turned to see where the terminal was located. "Don't look over there lieutenant … look over there." Pazzaro gestured towards a large helicopter.

"Shit ... sorry Sir, sorry Mrs Pazzaro ... it's got the presidential shield on the side."

"That shows you just how much importance the president has attached to your mission gentlemen. Let's hope the others complete their task just as successfully."

Johnno looked quizzically to Rick. "Others?"

"The final piece of the jigsaw buddy, the final piece."

Minutes later they landed on the White House lawns and were met by a ceremonial guard consisting of US marines, again in full dress uniform. The sergeant at arms approached them and smartly saluted. "This way lady and gentlemen, you guest suites are ready for you." They were then escorted across the lawns and over towards the White House.

Johnno marvelled at its size. "It doesn't look this big on TV, it's huge."

The marine sergeant spoke without breaking stride. "In the White House sir we have one hundred and thirty two rooms and thirty five bathrooms located over six levels." As he spoke they reached the doorway leading them in. Two marines had been placed at arms to welcome them , opening the doors as they approached. The sergeant continued. "We are bound for the President's personal guest suites, you certainly must be VIP's for such an honour, sir, and it is my pleasure to take you there."

"We're just a couple of air force pilots and their commanding officer, an ex-air force pilot, son." Pazzaro spoke humbly, before adding "And, of course, my beautiful wife in an elegant dress," moving to one side, "after you dear." A broad smile adorned Mrs Pazzaro's face as she elegantly entered the building. The sergeant, obviously a man of the world, remarked as she passed. "You look lovely ma'am, perfectly adorned to meet a president"

As Pazzaro passed the sergeant he mouthed a silent 'thank you."

Smiling he took the lead again "Please follow me."

After passing through a myriad of corridors, and using an elevator to move up a couple of floors, he abruptly stopped.

"Your guest suites await." The Pazzaros were directed to the 'New England suite'. Linda Pazzaro beamed with delight as she entered. "I always wanted to go to New England."

Johnno and Rick were taken just further along the corridor to the 'Montana' suite.

"Please enjoy your suites, food and beverage are available, and you'll find your luggage has already been delivered. I shall collect you at 16.00 hours for your personal tour of our wonderful facility. The president is expecting you for an informal meal in his private dining room at 20.00 hours. Please relax; Oh, and can I suggest that you turn on your TV, something amazing is happening that I feel will be of interest to you. Indeed, I am off to my quarters to witness this historical moment myself."

Stepping back he stood to attention, then smartly saluted and left.

Johnno noticed cases placed outside further guest rooms just along the corridor from theirs. "I wonder who our other VIP guests are?"

Rick looked and shrugged his shoulders. "Fancy cases, but they look as if they've travelled somewhat."

All four guests entered their rooms and made their way to the TV sets as recommended. After a brief warm up time they were rewarded with hazy black and white images which were difficult to discern at first. Then a moving landscape came into view.

"Apollo 11 is approaching touchdown buddy, let's pray they can land safely."

In the next guest room Mrs Pazzaro wasn't quite as interested as her husband. "Darling, you should see the soaps and lotions in this bathroom, they are to die for."

"Yes dear." Pazzaro's eyes were glued to the screen.

The four guests watched in awe as Apollo made a successful landing, small puffs of dust rising as its legs made contact on the moon.

"Engine arm is off Houston. Tranquillity base here. The eagle has landed"

Both Johnno and Rick punched the air in triumph, and then shook each other's hand.

"Roger, Tranquillity. We copy you on the ground. You got a bunch of guys about to turn blue. We're breathing again. Thanks a lot."

"And two more here in the Montana suite." Rick slumped onto the bed.

Johnno made his way over to the drinks cabinet and tentatively opened the door. "Should we?"

"Too damn right buddy, any Jack Daniels in there?"

Johnno reached in and took out a bottle of their favourite tipple. "Oh yes, " reaching inside, "we have a full ice bucket too."

Commander Pazzaro also found the Jack Daniels in his cabinet but reluctantly made do with a strong black coffee as recommended by Mrs Pazzaro.

"We can't have you drunk in front of the president."

"No dear."

The marine sergeant returned as promised at 16.00 hours, his face beaming.

"Did you see it on your TV? We're on the moon this very minute. What a day for the United States, what a day." Regaining his composure he asked his guests to please follow him as he escorted them on their VIP tour. Johnno noticed the cases had gone from the corridor.

"Do we need to collect our fellow guests for the tour?"

"No sir, this is to be your own personal tour, just the four VIP's I see in front of me sir. Please step this way and feel free to ask any questions at any time."

Mrs Pazzaro looked concerned.

"Are we viewing EVERY room sergeant? I'd hate to be late for the president."

"Don't worry ma'am, we'll be back in plenty of time for your important appointment."

"Can we go in the Oval office? I have my instamatic camera and I'd love a photograph to hang on the Commander's wall."

"Out of bounds I'm afraid ma'am; perhaps Mr President will show you his office this evening."

Mrs Pazzaro beamed with delight. "One can hope, sergeant, one can hope." Commander Pazzaro raised his eyes to heaven, smiled and ushered his wife ahead to follow the sergeant.

The VIP party made their way along the designated VIP tour route, ably led and kept fully informed by the sergeant. Mrs Pazzaro managed to visit three 'powder rooms' , checking on the colour schemes used as a guide for her quarters back at Groom Lake. As they strolled along the corridor towards their guest suites the Commander thanked the sergeant for his patience and, glancing towards his wife, and his professionalism.

"It's a day we shall all remember sergeant. The important events happening in space, and our own special day on Earth."

"It has been my pleasure and a privilege to show you around our beautiful edifice sirs, and madam. It will also be my honour to collect you at 1945 hours and escort you to the president's personal dining room."

He saluted smartly and left them in the corridor.

Rick and Johnno were keen to return and watch events unfolding on TV.

On entering their suite Mrs Pazzaro was keener to check out the furnishings. "How do you feel about powder blue sheets edged in pink Joey?"

The Commander sighed and followed his wife into the room. "Whatever you wish, dear."

The Commander was an obvious advocate of 'happy wife, happy life'.

Chapter 62

At 1945 hours precisely the Sergeant at Arms collected his guests and escorted them to the president's private dining room. The room was large enough to comfortably contain all of the guests, yet small enough to be informal.

In the centre was a large dining table topped with a highly polished walnut veneer. It could easily accommodate all the guests present with ample room to spare. In the centre was a range of small floral settings, impressive in appearance yet small enough to allow all guests to see each other quite easily. Ashtrays were set out which would presumably allow any of the gentlemen to enjoy a cigar with an after dinner brandy .There were two doors at the far end, mirroring those at the end where the guests entered. Behind the president one led to the corridors which eventually reached the oval office, whilst opposite was the second door, which led towards the kitchen and preparation areas where the banquet was to be prepared. The walls were adorned with an array of pictures, each one chosen as an addition by the incumbent president. Landscapes and modern art seemed to incongruously blend with each other in a display of wildly varying tastes.

Around one side sat the now familiar faces with their respective wives, each one obviously taking the opportunity to purchase a new dress for the special occasion. The president sat at the head of the table, his wife facing him at the other end. To his right was the vice president, with his wife sat alongside.

The seated guests all rose to their feet and applauded as the final guests arrived.

"So pleased to meet you at last," the president's wife sounded sincere, "my husband has told me something of your bravery and the resounding success of your mission," adding in a loud whisper, "of course he won't share the full details but this IS the first private function arranged for serving members of our wonderful armed forces."

"Thank you ma'am, we're both deeply honoured to be here." Rick was on top form, Johnno surmising that he'd been honoured before in this fashion. As he glanced along the side of the immaculately laid out dining table he noticed that there were seven vacant seats, and not just four as he would assume.

"This way please gentlemen" the sergeant led the way placing Rick by the fourth seat from the head of the table, a noticeable gap between himself and the Second Lady. She smiled as he sat down.

Rick reached over and kissed he hand. "So pleased to meet you ma'am."

Johnno was then directed to his seat, leaving a gap between himself and Rick. He could only smile and nod towards the vice president and his wife as he sat down.

Finally one more seat was left vacant before seating the Commander and his wife, whose face lit up when she realised she was sat next to the president's wife.

She was immediately put at her ease when the first lady complimented on her choice of dress for the occasion. "Oh, this old thing, I've had it for ages." The commander's eyes rose towards heaven … again.

"And Linda, I hope you don't mind if I call you Linda, we girls can all go for a good gossip when the boys do their official stuff later," she said, gesturing towards a door in the bottom corner, "it's my girly hideaway."

Seizing her opportunity Linda replied. "Oh, I'd love that, Patricia – you don't mind if I call you Patricia do you?" squirming with delight at chatting with the first lady.

"I'd rather you call me Pat."

"So be it … Pat."

The commander did his best to ignore the girls' small talk but was impressed by the way that the First Lady had set his wife so much at ease. He also realised that it could well cost him more new dresses when they returned home where she organised weekly cocktail evenings for the officer's wives. She would have enough material for at least a dozen evenings by the time this evening was through. Though he looked a little nonplussed on the outside, deep inside he was proud of the way she was handling this special day.

The sergeant at arms smartly marched towards the door where he had entered, performed an about-face, stood rigidly to attention, saluted smartly and announced.

"All guests officially seated Mr. President. I shall take my leave of you and collect our final party." At the head of the table the president rose to his feet and tapped gently on the side of his wine glass. The acoustics in the room were admirable as the slightest 'chink' brought about immediate silence.

"Thank you sergeant, please go about your duties."

As the door gently closed all eyes moved back towards the president, who rose to deliver his prepared speech.

"Today is a special day in the history of our great American homeland and I have invited you all here, as my special guests, in appreciation of all of your hard work and dedication leading up to this moment. For the first time in our history we have managed to send three brave astronauts out of Earth's natural domain, across many thousands of miles, to land on our nearest neighbour, the Moon. I have the pleasure to inform you," he dipped his head slightly, allowing him sight of his guests over the rim of his reading glasses ,"though I suspect you all know already, that at 3.17 this afternoon we landed our craft safely on the surface of the moon. Not only has the eagle landed safely, but it has roared our intentions to the rest of the world."

The room burst into spontaneous applause, accompanied by the customary slapping of hands on the table.

The president raised his hands in acknowledgement. After several seconds he slowly lowered them, prompting his guests to fall silent once more. "I must thank everyone here, but a special mention must go to Tom here and his predecessor John Webb, for admirably leading their teams at NASA, and ensuring that the promises made by a great man in 1961 have been honoured."

More applause, and shouts of "here, here," accompanied by table slapping met with an embarrassed look from Dr. Payne, although the plaudits were gratefully received.

"Our Air Force certainly supplied pilots with the 'right stuff' throughout our space programmes from Mercury, through Gemini and onto Apollo whilst John and Richard ensured our country had the security needed to complete those monumental tasks," he paused, and looked towards his Joint Chief of staff, "admirably organised and led, of course."

The president moved his attention to his right, smiling benignly at his mildly embarrassed guests. "And now we must all pay thanks to our esteemed guests sat to my right, whose actions will directly affect the safety and security of our beloved borders, and way beyond, not just for today but for generations to come." The commander shuffled in his seat slightly, as a mixture of pride and embarrassment set in.

"First of all today our thanks must go to Commander Pazzaro, who organised and controlled this operation with total efficiency, allowing us the luxury of one of his amazing aircraft to help successfully right a potential wrong." His voice rose in volume, his voice adopting a serious tone. "A potential wrong which would have had dire consequences not only for our beloved nation, but for the entire world."

The table resounded with hand slaps; so much so that the vibrations caused ripples in the glasses of wine which were laid out for the first course.

"Thank you Mr President," Pazzaro was glancing towards his lieutenants, "but I think we all know where the praise for the success in this undertaking must go."

"Well said Joe, well said my friend." The president turned his attention to Johnno and Rick. "Two intrepid explorers who successfully completed a mission so daring and so dangerous -yet they never wavered from their duty. We cannot yet reveal the intricacies of this mission, but I can reveal that we are in the presence of two genuine

American heroes. I ask you to raise your glasses for Flight Lieutenants John O'Ryan and Richard Abrahams."

Around the table everyone rose and collected the wine glasses laid out in front of them, raising them high in the air. "Lieutenants O'Ryan and Abrahams." The loud chorus of approval filled the air.

Rick and Johnno accepted the plaudits, smiled and gently nodded in acknowledgement.

Rick's thoughts turned to his many trips around the Universe, realising that they all began with his ancestors short journeys to nearby moons and neighbouring planets.

Johnno's thoughts were linked to the president's speech. If only he'd known about him being totally unaware of his mission, and the real heroes were Rick and his companions. Manni and Astrild had kept him alive. His dear Aunt Freya had given him the ability to survive and complete this mission. His mind wandered briefly. "I wonder what she would say if she could only see me now. My little spaceman sat at the president's table, being feted and dined as a hero." Then his mind drifted towards the slaves he had seen in the mine and his attempts to free as many as possible. "They are the real heroes, unsung and unloved by a brutal regime, but never forgotten."

Slowly the sounds of the room drifted back into his mind, the sound of applause and table slapping slowly gaining volume until his thought were back at the president's table.

"And finally, ladies and gentlemen," the president appealed for calm, the noise began to subside, "And finally, ladies and gentlemen, I realise that while we are all keen to eat and not let our superb meal spoil, you may have noticed that we have three empty places around our table." There was a murmur of agreement as everyone wondered why they were there, but had not had the courage to ask why.

"I have the pleasure of inviting in our three final guests. Although they are not US citizens their courage and bravery on behalf of our nation has been exemplary." He signalled to his marine sergeant, who had entered the room quietly, un-noticed by the guests.

"Please show in our esteemed guests."

The sergeant opened the door, moving aside to allow the president's final guests to enter. The corridor behind them was in darkness, making it difficult to recognise anyone until they were finally in the room.

Johnno and Rick leaned back in their chairs, wondering just who was about to enter.

"Probably an admiral, we're only missing the navy," Johnno murmured sarcastically.

As they finally entered the room both Johnno and Rick's eyes widened as they grinned from ear to ear. It was Freya, Manni and Astrild, all looking slightly perplexed as they entered a room full of strangers. Johnno tried to get to his feet, stumbling with his chair, before he remembered where he was and sat down again. Freya smiled as she recognised him and waved a gentle wave in his direction.

"Go and give your aunt a hug Johnno, then we can all sit down to eat."

Johnno turned towards the voice and saw the president smiling at him

"Go on son, she deserves it."

He didn't need telling twice and made his way down the room, where he grabbed her in a bear hug. Eventually he loosened his grip to look his aunt in the face. She reached up and cupped his face in her hands lovingly. There were tears in both their eyes; she kissed his forehead gently.

"I thought I'd lost you. I thought you'd returned to Alnilam. I thought I might never see you again."

"I'll tell you everything later. I think the president wants to eat, shall we take our seats?"

Meanwhile Rick had made his way to Manni and Astrild, warmly greeting them both.

"Is everything OK with the Federation?"

"It took a while and a LOT of diplomacy from Freya but yes, everything is now sorted."

Rick guided them to their seats at the table. As Johnno passed them with his beloved aunt he leaned down to gently hug them both. He felt as if his life was complete again.

Pulling the chair out for his aunt to sit down he glanced at the president, standing at the head of the table, smiling as he were Kris Kringle delivering Johnno's best ever present.

Johnno smiled back and mouthed the words "Thank you sir."

"You're most welcome Lieutenant, most welcome."

Everyone now seated, the president tapped on his wine glass again.

"That sounds kind of empty; I think I need a top up."

The assembled gathering laughed gently.

"And now we shall sit and enjoy this marvellous meal, the night's excitement has only just begun." He turned to his maitre'd. "We are ready Francois, please serve the first course."

Whilst the meal and the service provided went like clockwork, with courses arriving simultaneously for all the guests, to Johnno it was all just a blur. In between mouthfuls of food and a very enjoyable selection of wines he was keen to quiz his dear Aunt on her adventures since he left her so long ago and so far away.

"I was worried that I may not see you again, you know, in case the Federation had somehow banned us from meeting again after we failed to follow their directive when we first dealt with Maia and then with Tesman. Once we had acquainted them fully with all of the details the Federation was more concerned with the treachery shown by these two so called allies, contravening the spirit and ideals of Orion's treaty with the Pleiades." Freya looked pensive for a moment. " It is very much like your 'cold war' and the uneasy alliance with the USSR, each waiting for the other to blink first."

"So, everything is OK for you then? You're not in trouble?"

"Far from it. We have been commended for our discreet and decisive actions taken which prevented a paradox which could have changed earth's history in preventing the development of the Bell machines. We have also been lauded by saving the president's life and destroying the phase shift. Either one of these could have moved history along different paths with potentially disastrous consequences."

Johnno smiled. "Manni and Astrild, were they commended too?"

"Yes, and both have been promoted. You did well Min Lille Romfarer. Everyone alive on Earth today owes you a great debt. The only problem is that they don't know it, and probably never will."

"I can live with that," came the pragmatic reply.

The meal came to a close and coffees were served.

Cigars were lit, filling the air with an aroma of banned Cuban smoke. A very nice cognac was offered. Johnno refused, Rick accepted. Turning to face his friend he raised his glass and smiled. "A toast to you buddy, the best damn partner anyone could wish for." Johnno nodded and collected his wine glass, still half full of the red wine from the main course. Glancing towards each of his three colleagues in turn he raised his glass and quietly spoke.

"To the best team I could ever wish to work with, three friends strong and true"

The room was drawn back into silence once more by the clinking of the president's glass.

"Ladies and gentlemen we must thank Francois and his team for a wonderful meal." The room filled with the sound of applause and a gentle tapping on the table. Francois looked suitably embarrassed, and bowed gently in appreciation.

"Now Patricia, could you please take the ladies away for further coffee and chocolates whilst we visit my Oval office to deal with business," glancing around the table he smiled, adding, "and please leave some of the chocolates for me." Freya and Astrild rose to join the ladies who were preparing to enter the lounge at the rear of the room.

"Excuse me, Freya and Astrild, could you please join us in my office. I'm sure the girls will save you some coffee for later."

Pleasantly surprised at the invitation they turned around and followed the men as they left the dining room for the Oval office, the president leading the way.

Chapter 63

The party made their way along the plush carpets and veloured corridor walls towards the Oval office. More faces of past presidents watched their progress along this well-trodden route. The president let himself in, manoeuvring past the temporary furniture laid out inside.

"We may be a bit cramped in here Errol, but I'm sure no-one will mind for once."

The president stood in front of his desk, with Errol Gilmore to one side and Tom Gerarty to the other. In front of them were two rows of high back chairs. Freya, Vasey, Elms and Payne sat in the rear row leaving Johnno and his three colleagues to sit in the front .

The president noticed the look of mild panic on Johnno's face.

"Relax, lieutenant, it's just tradition."

He leaned back against his desk. "Before we move on to the exciting activities planned for this evening some quarter of a million miles away, I have a pleasant task to perform. We have before us four genuine heroes. Whilst only two of them serve in our armed forces, the actions of two foreign, and I use the word wisely, agents," a gentle murmur of muted laughter followed, " they have also acted very much in the interest of this great United States of America. As a token of my gratitude, and that of countless millions around the world, I should like to present them personally with the Presidential Medal of Freedom."

Gilmore passed over two ornate boxes, from which he took out the medals.

Manni and Astrild felt rooted to the spot and, almost reluctantly, rose to their feet and approached the president. He pinned the medals to their chest, Manni allowing Astrild to go first.

"God bless you both, and thank you for your courage."

Everyone began to applaud, no-one more so than Johnno. He and Rick rose to their feet in unison and applauded as though their lives depended on it. To the rear Freya was beaming with delight, proud of her team's achievement. (She had reluctantly refused such a medal, wanting her team to be recognised. She believed being fooled by Maia made her ineligible, her team being the real heroes.) After accepting the accolades they both sat down, holding their medals in disbelief at the honour bestowed upon them. Johnno and Rick were still applauding long after they had regained their seats, eventually the room became silent once more.

"And now we must also reward our serving heroes, Lieutenants John O'Ryan and Richard Abrahams. The mission you undertook was perilous, with many unknown dangers laid out before you. In spite of those unknown dangers, and the threat of interference from foreign agencies intent on the failure of your mission and ultimately your demise, you carried out your brave actions with total success. We owe you both a debt of gratitude that can never be repaid and, sadly, cannot ever be fully recorded."

Gerarty passed over the two boxes he had been holding.

"To you I have the pleasure of awarding the Medal of Honour. Please step forward gentlemen."

Johnno stood, looking quite awkward, gesturing for Rick to go first. Rick took a small step backwards, and shook his head.

"You first, my friend, you deserve this far more than I do."

Johnno stepped forward hesitantly, stood to attention and smartly saluted. The medal was pinned to his chest. He stepped back and remained to attention. The process was repeated with Rick. Who also stepped back smartly, remaining smartly at attention.

The pride that both men felt ensured their backs remained ramrod straight.

"At ease lieutenants, now turn and face your audience." As they did so there was a spontaneous round of applause from everyone present.

Freya was having trouble focusing on her heroes; the tears in her eyes had begun to flow freely. Elms leaned over and offered his handkerchief, it was gratefully accepted. As the office was relatively small the applause seemed even louder as it resonated from the walls. Even the bust of Winston Churchill seemed to smile and approve of what had happened as it gently vibrated on its plinth with the echoes of appreciation.

As they prepared to regain their seats the president spoke again.

"Not so fast gentlemen. Please about face again."

As they turned to face the president they moved back to attention, wondering what was happening next. The president raised his arm towards the rear of the room, summoning forward Tom Payne, the head of NASA. "If you please Tom."

Payne made his way to the front, standing alongside the president in the place vacated by Errol Gilmore, who had stepped to one side. "Thank you Mr President"

He turned to face Johnno and Rick, who were still bemused by what had already taken place and were wondering just what came next.

"Having taken into account your recent mission, and taking into account the unusual craft that you have encountered demonstrating that you do indeed possess the right stuff, I would like to enrol you onto our current Apollo programme, with a planned flight to the moon in Apollo 18, currently planned for launch in the Summer of 1973." Cheers filled the room.

Johnno and Rick beamed with delight and just stared at each other. Johnno glanced back at Freya, who was holding her face with both hands in disbelief. The president leaned forward, placing the back of his hand to the side of his face.

"I think you'd better say yes boys, it's a golden opportunity."

Rick was the first to step forward and grab Gilmore's hand in a strong and hearty handshake.

"I ... I mean we ... we would both be honoured to join your esteemed Apollo programme sir, highly honoured."

Johnno followed, in a daze, accepting Gilmore's proffered handshake. "We will NOT let you down sir, I promise."

"I know. I've had a word with Commander Pazzaro, who is understandably devastated at losing two of his best pilots, but he joins me in wishing you well on your training. Please report to Cape Kennedy on August 1st to begin training."

Johnno was now on cloud nine. He had dreamed of travelling into space since he was a child and now all of his dreams were about to come true. He wondered if Freya's nickname of 'my little spaceman' was prophetic, or did she know something? After all, she was used to time travel. Perhaps she saw him actually launch on one of her travels in the future. But why was she smiling, and crying? He was brought back to reality as Rick threw his arms around him, slapping his gently on the back.

"We made it buddy, we made it. We're going to the moon. Can you believe it?"

"Not really ... but we've got four years to get used to the idea."

"Gentlemen, gentlemen," the president raised his voice slightly "now that the niceties are over we have a chance to witness history being made and to see the culmination of our mission, please take a seat, relax and enjoy."

Scattered around the room was a selection of leather arm chairs, all luxurious and deeply buttoned as you'd expect in such a high office. One by one they were taken by the guests, each apparently having a favourite that they had used before. Johnno and Rick waited until everyone was seated before they took their own place, still feeling rather embarrassed at being in such auspicious surroundings, yet still elated at the honour just bestowed upon them.

"Is everyone comfortable? Anyone need a drink? No? OK, bring her in for the late show."

From one side of the room an aide pushed in a large TV set on a trolley, placing it to the wall on the right hand side. He plugged it in, ensuring all the communication leads were safely in place, and switched it on. Slowly a grainy picture appeared on the screen, difficult to make out at first, it soon became recognisable as the 'Eagle' – Apollo 11's craft on the moon.

"Someone dim the lights, untold history is about to happen, and we're about to witness it live."

Chapter 64

"That's one small step for man, one giant leap for mankind"

"They've done it, by God they've done it." The president was ecstatic. The room broke out in a deafening wall of cheering and whooping. Cries of "Yes" emanated from around the room. Tom Payne jumped to his feet and punched the air. "Mission accomplished, one hundred per cent."

The president turned to face his guests. "If only the world knew just how giant that leap really was. Now play the medical tapes Tom, let's hear what was said during our 'convenient' radio silence."

"Wilco Mr President."

Johnno and Rick looked at each other with a look of curious amazement.

"Our convenient silence?" Johnno mouthed the words.

The President saw the puzzled looks on his guest's faces. "We have a secret radio channel which transmits only between astronauts and their ground crew. It's not broadcast to the public in case there's a medical emergency," winking slowly he followed with, "or something else of real importance."

He signalled to the aide who had brought in the TV. Tom Payne smiled at him.

"You heard Mr President, replay the medical transmission tapes."

The aide opened the front of the TV stand where a large video cassette recorder was housed.

"Gentlemen, we shall now hopefully hear the news about our reclaimed package finally being safely delivered."

The transmission started;

"What's there? Mission Control calling Apollo 11."

"These babies are huge, sir … enormous….Oh, God, you wouldn't believe it! I'm telling you there are other space craft out there… lined up on the far side of the crater edge… they're on the moon watching us."

"Do you have the package ready for delivery?"

"Yes sir. The hatch is open, I'm lifting the package outside and … it is making its own way across towards the crater as if by magic. It must be something magnetic or some kind of retrieval beam.

They, they have it now and … they appear to be moving back out of sight into the crater.

Package delivered successfully Houston.

Now we have another mission to complete."

"Roger that. Now go and complete your experiments on the lunar surface. Congratulations commander, you guys have done a wonderful job, now enjoy the rest of your trip."

The transmission ended.

Johnno looked around to a sea of smiling faces. Rick leaned over and grabbed his knee. "Well done buddy, well fucking done."

The president rose to his feet, moving around his desk to face his guests. "Today has been a momentous day in the history of not only the USA but also the world. We have helped secure our future by the actions you have just witnessed, and the universe now beckons us."

Turning to face Johnno and Rick he added "Thanks to you two brave patriots we can all sleep soundly in our beds tonight. And speaking of beds, your Aunt and her two colleagues are making their way downstairs to the rear lawn and wish you to join them. We have my personal guest suites reserved for you all for this evening and tomorrow my personal helicopter will take you to wherever you wish to go. Enjoy the rest of your evening."

As he moved forward Johnno and Rick realised that it was their cue to leave. They stood up to attention and saluted.

"No need for that, boys," the president offered a parting handshake, "no need for that at all. I am deeply in **your** debt, as is everyone else here. God bless you both. God bless your colleagues. And God bless America."

He smiled at Pazzaro. "Commander, Joe, your wife awaits, still resplendent in her new dress." The commander smiled, and moved forward to shake the president's hand.

"It's been an honour Mr President, one that neither my lovely wife of myself will ever forget." Standing to attention he saluted, performed a smart 'about face' and moved towards the rear of the room. As they turned to leave they noticed that the marine sergeant had returned , almost anonymously, and beckoned for them to follow him.

The door to the Oval office gently clicked shut behind them.

"This way please gentlemen, we need to go down one level to the lawn area. Your colleagues are waiting there for you."

Back in the Oval office the president had resumed his seat behind his highly polished desk.

"Are you ready for the next steps Richard?"

"We believe we are Mr President. Our new friends have already done us a favour with Luna 15. Confirmed destroyed as it began its descent. Our secret alliance is still safe."

"Can it be done? Do we have the technology to engineer one of these weapons yet?"

"Not just yet Mr President but, given the 'facilities' and craft we have in Area 51, I believe we shall have a working prototype completed in a couple of years."

"What about Denver? Is the planned construction on time?"

"Yes Mr President – the new airport will be a joy to us all and a safe area to store our products. Areas 51 and 52 are becoming too well known."

"Are you sure they won't notice that we've 'looked' at it, the weapon I mean?" John Vasey added a note of concern.

"No way, we treated it like the Madonna's child. They'll never know."

"Are members of Majestic 12 aware of this latest mission and its outcome?"

"They are fully aware Mr President. It has top security clearance. No one outside of this room will ever know."

The president relaxed back into his chair, reaching for his box of Cuban cigars in his top left hand drawer. As he placed them onto his desk he pulled out a bottle of Jack Daniels, closely followed by an array of shot glasses. "Gentlemen, please join me in celebration. One mission accomplished successfully, the cold war is about to get hot. Tomorrow is the dawn of a new era for our great country. God Bless America"

"God bless America" came a chorus of replies.

Chapter 65

As they re-entered the dining room the commander's wife was waiting with a beaming smile on her face. "You'll never guess what we've been chattering about."

"No dear, but I'm sure that I soon will."

"An aide will take you to your guest suite commander, whenever you are ready."

"Now would be a good time sergeant, before my wife plans a new kitchen as well."

Johnno and Rick slowly made their way towards their rendezvous on the rear lawn.

Moving downstairs towards the rear of the building they passed several security men, hands crossed in front of them, each touching their ear piece as the party passed them.

"There you are gentlemen," the marine sergeant opened the door which led onto the White House lawn, "and may I say it's been an honour to meet you both. I shall be waiting inside when ready to show you to your guest suites." He stood smartly to attention, saluted and re-entered the building.

Although it was late evening it was still quite warm. The smell of fresh cut grass was a reassuring gift to their senses, bringing back memories of forest walks and star gazing adventures for Johnno. Around the building was a series of lights, mostly positioned towards the magnificent white edifice, a symbol of law, order and purity for all those who came to gaze upon it.

"It's been one hell of a day buddy."

"It sure has. And we're going to the moon."

Johnno was ecstatic. Rick seemed unimpressed and just grinned. "You've been before, haven't you?"

Rick smiled a 'knowing' smile. "Possibly. But never with you."

Their conversation was cut short as Freya approached from behind putting her arms around both of them. "Come, let's sit and talk awhile on this beautiful evening."

As they turned to walk away Manni and Astrild appeared, just visible in the reflected light, sitting and relaxing on the lawn. Soon they were all sat down on a green velvet carpet, gazing up at the sky in wonderment.

"Pity it's not a full moon." Johnno sounded disappointed. Freya smiled and held his hand.

"Maybe not, but just think for the first time in your history someone from Earth is looking back down at you."

"And they have you to thank for that buddy."

"Nah, not just me, it's all of us. We're like the three musketeers 'All for one and one for all'."

"But there are five of us."

"OK – the five musketeers."

After a brief pause Astrild spoke. "What's a musketeer?"

Manni smiled. "I'll tell you later."

"OK Aunt Freya, apart from it being a beautiful evening, and the end of a perfect day, why are we sat in near darkness on the White House lawn approaching midnight?"

Freya looked towards her colleagues and smiled. Each one smiled and nodded in return.

"Go on, tell him the good news."

"As you know we had to report back to the Federation with full details of the mission, including the demise of Maia and Tesman."

Johnno frowned and looked concerned. "But we had no other way of succeeding."

"I know that, we all know that; and finally the Federation accepted our version of events. In fact they were so impressed with your actions and integrity that," she paused, "that, they want you to join our team as a permanent member and complete more missions on their behalf."

Johnno's emotions did a somersault as he was surprised, impressed and flattered all at once by the invitation.

"Can I think it over? Why me? I'm not from Orion... What can I offer?" He paused for several seconds, his eyes losing focus as his thoughts took over. "And what about our plans for Apollo 18?"

"Your mother was from Orion. Think how proud she would be. And yes, Apollo 18 is still yours for the taking."

"You said more missions? I thought this was a one-off."

"I'm afraid not Min Lille Romfarer. As technology begins to speed up on Earth we have many problems to solve, much like the Bell which was left in error millennia ago."

"Such as?"

Rick joined in the conversation. "There is the map room in Egypt – a map of the inhabited planets and their resources. Then there are the discs of accumulated knowledge hidden in Ecuador when one of our earliest scouting craft got into difficulties; plus a crashed craft at the bottom of Lake Titicaca. The hidden operations base in the Antarctic – remember Byrd's expedition just after World War 2?"

Manni leaned forward "And now that you are travelling to your outer planets we need to recover items from Mars, especially in the area you call Cydonia. Not to mention what will be discovered if the Moon is fully investigated for artefacts, or for its true composition."

"It all sounds tempting, where can I find the time to do all these things and still qualify as an astronaut? It's impossible."

"Not when you can travel in time buddy. We can complete our new missions and still be back in time for tea. What do you say buddy? The five musketeers, the dream team."

"I'm still not sure. This operation was supposed to be a one-off."

"If you still need motivation," Freya's voice took on a note of urgency, "we believe that Tesman may still be alive, trapped somewhere in an alternative dimension. The blast may have propelled him into his phase shift where he is currently imprisoned. He does have many followers, especially greys and renegade Pleidians. We have heard they are searching for him now as we speak. If he somehow returns he will be out for vengeance, and you are now his number one enemy. We may even have to enter into his dimension to neutralise his threat."

"I've dealt with him once, I'm sure that I could do it again, couldn't I?"

"Not if he time travels back," Rick paused and looked towards Freya for approval, " not if he time travels back and kills your parents before you were born. Then everything changes, and we're back to dealing with the Bell and the third Reich ... all without you."

Johnno's face took on a look of desperation. His eyes closed as his imagination took over.

His heart began to race until he could feel it beating so hard he felt his shirt begin to gently move in unison. The balmy evening air now caused him to sweat profusely. Had all his work been in vain? He couldn't let that happen. "OK, I'm in. What's next?"

A sea of smiling faces surrounded him.

"You ask what's next Min Lille Romfarer .What's next is that we go back and rescue your mother and father and get them to safety before Tesman finds them. If you recall they 'disappeared' as they entered the complex. Perhaps **we** can help them to disappear somewhere safe where Tesman cannot find them"

Johnno was ecstatic. He punched the air as elation replaced his despair.

"We can do that?" he asked.

Freya smiled and nodded.

"I think for the sake of security both on Earth and throughout the galaxy it would be a prudent thing to do."

"YES-YES-YES count me in"

Finally he could save his parents.

Finally he could hold his mother again, just as close as he'd held his dear Aunt Freya.

Finally he could hug his father again.

Finally he could become part of a whole family once more.

He had a new future to look forward to; and, of course, his parents would be so proud when he flew with Apollo 18.Then reality dawned. His smile disappeared. Desperation began to creep in. His elation was gone. He 'came back to earth'.

"Whoa, what about the Federation? They would not allow it, you told me already."

"I think I speak for all of us."

Freya glanced towards her three colleagues. They smiled as they spoke in unison.

"To Hell with the Federation!"

Meanwhile, in another dimension, somewhere in the space between space, a badly injured figure with a disfigured face was peering out of the darkness, willing his followers to find him and bring him home.

A home where he could plan how to take his revenge on the upstart earthling who had sentenced him to a living hell.

A disfigured face with eyes peering into nothingness,
desperately pleading for help …

Eyes as black and as smooth as haematite …

Appendix

(Facts that may have influenced my story telling
which may also be of interest to you)

Area 51 is well known as the top secret section found in Groom Lake, Nevada. It is renowned for its links to the UFO phenomenon, with wreckage from the (denied) UFO crash at Roswell 1947 being transported there.

As well as wreckage from the craft it is believed by many ufologists that alien entities are being kept there, safe from prying eyes beneath ground in a myriad of levels and tunnels. It is also reported that many of these 'guests' are not happy with their lot.

https://www.gaia.com/article/is-there-proof-of-aliens-inhabiting-the-dulce-secret-air-force-base

https://www.express.co.uk/news/weird/1062753/Aliens-greys-UFO-Dulce-battle-Roswell-New-Mexico-alien-news

.. or just Google 'Bob Lazar'.

Although 'top secret' the USSR would send over high altitude spy planes photographing the base, usually at night. Initially the ground crew would put all its aircraft into hangers each night believing that would keep their activities secret. 'Leaked' inside information informed them that the aircraft would leave a 'shadow' on the ground, caused by the high intensity of the sun causing a real shadow in the daytime. This loss of heat could be photographed by the spy planes and information gleaned about the development of US aircraft. Staff at the airbase then began to paint fantastic aircraft shapes on the runway with a matt black paint to fool their Russian adversaries.

Speaking of fooling adversaries; when 'Oxcart' was being developed to replace the U2 spy plane it became obvious that the aircraft needed to be manufactured from titanium. Flying high in the atmosphere it would be subject to temperatures of 550 degrees Fahrenheit, and no ordinary metal could withstand the pressures that would place it under. At that time titanium was in short supply in the US and difficult to find. The answer? The CIA set up a dummy business company and bought it from the USSR! In 1962 it took off on its first test flight…

An airbase at Malmstrom had noticed intense UFO activity around its perimeter, and then by the site's main gate, on March 16, 1967. There was some concern raised as there were nuclear missiles located on the site.

Almost immediately all missiles on 'Alert' switched themselves to 'No Go'. No reason for such a shutdown was ever found, nor could it be repeated. The 'best guess' was that a 10 volt pulse was directed onto a data line. This could only be done from outside the shielded system by an electromagnetic pulse. Full details at: https://www.ufocasebook.com/1967malmstrom.html

It is well documented that Adolf Hitler and his acolytes were deeply interested in the occult, and had sent many expeditions to find 'lost' artefacts which they believed would help to support their cause. Heinrich Himmler was a particular devotee who re-modelled Wewelsburg castle to function as his SS centre of excellence *("Germanic pre- and early history, folklore studies, etc. as an equipment for ideological-political training")*

As well as turrets and castle battlements he designed a 'round table', along the lines of King Arthur, a place for his 'knights' to sit. He named one of the study rooms as 'grail', another as 'King Arthur' and so on. More details can be found on the website *https://www.thevintagenews.com/2017/12/11/wewelsburg-himmler-occult-rituals/*

According to the Bhavagad-Gita and Mahabharata , epic tales of battles on the Indian sub-continent, battles raged using weapons of amazing power, latterly compared to nuclear war. As these records date from the 2nd century BCE it seems incredible that such weapons could have been used then. One such weapon was called 'brahmastra', created by the god Brahma, which produced something today we would recognise as an IBM. The weapon produced "*an incandescent column of smoke and flame as bright as 10,000 suns that rose in all its splendour. After, corpses were so burned as to be unrecognizable. Their hair and nails fell out; pottery broke without any apparent cause, and the birds turned white… After a few hours, all foodstuffs were infected.*" "*Any target hit by the brahmastra would be utterly destroyed; land would become barren and lifeless, rainfall would cease, and infertility in humans and animals would follow for aeons of time.*" Does this sound like the aftermath at Hiroshima and Nagasaki?

There are still several highly radioactive sights in this subcontinent such as Harappa and Mohenjo-Dara where ruins, dated back to 2500BC, include vitrified glass(a by-product of nuclear explosions) and a skeleton with 50 times the level of radiation it should have.When Robert Oppenheimer, who masterminded the 'Trinity' project that produced the nuclear bombs used in 1945, was asked if this was the first ever detonation of a nuclear device. His reply? "Yes, in modern times". More details available at; *https://www.gaia.com/article/evidence-nuclear-war-ancient-times*

Die Glöcke (the Bell) was a weapon (some say supposedly) being developed by the Germans in World War 2. It was purported to be a device used to allow time travel. Developed at the Wenceslaus mine, near Ludwidsdorf in Lower Silesia (now Ludwikowice in Poland) all that remained at the end of the war was the remains of a metal device and a henge, which Hitler presumably thought would provide supernatural support when it was 'launched'.

Experimental work was also done on UFO development, mostly following Germany's 'Roswell' incident in Freiburg, 1936.

https://www.thinkaboutitdocs.com/1936-black-forest-germany-ufo-crash/

On December 9th 1965 a large fireball was seen over Kecksburg Pennsylvania. The unusual thing about this fireball was its flight path, seemingly not 'natural', making deliberate turns. When it landed the area was totally sealed off to the residents and general public. Although the official report states that 'nothing was found' an army lorry was seen to leave the area with a 'Bell shaped object' partly covered by a tarpaulin on the back. As the craft appeared on the horizon two brothers, Robb and Ray Landy witnessed its approach. and witnessed what happened immediately after the UFO crashed. See what they have to say at .. https://unsolved.com/gallery/kecksburg-ufo/

On June 30th 1908 there was large explosion near the Tunguska river in Yeniseysk, Russia. The explosion over the sparsely populated area flattened 2,000 square kilometres of forest. It was as if a nuclear explosion of 10-15 megatons had occurred above ground, very much like modern nuclear weapons. The 'official' story blames an air burst from a comet entering the atmosphere, but no crater has ever been found and many ufologists believe this to be a cover up.

We know what really happened, don't we?

Did the Nazi regime really try to access alien technology? You may ask why they sent an expedition to the South Pole in the 1930's, setting up a base there after reports of alien activity and bases being located there. Were they successful? Consider …

https://history.howstuffworks.com/history-vs-myth/was-hitler-building-advanced-ufos-in-antarctica.htm

https://mysteriousuniverse.org/2022/07/A-UFO-Battle-at-a-Secret-Nazi-Antarctica-Base/

https://www.ufoinsight.com/conspiracy/government/base-211-nazi-antarctic-mission

If this was merely a 'pipe dream' why did the USA mount Operation High Jump in 1946? A very expensive 'research' project?

https://coolinterestingstuff.com/operation-highjump-declassified-pictures-ufo-evidence

https://www.ancient-code.com/the-nazi-antarctic-fortress-base-211-and-operation-highjump/

https://www.express.co.uk/news/weird/748249/John-Kerry-Antarctica-secret-Nazi-UFO-base

Why the Pleiades?

https://www.gaia.com/article/who-are-the-pleiadians

https://www.annunaki.org/pleiadians-nordic-aliens/

https://cayelincastell.com/the-pleiades/

https://thehiddenrecords.com/tikal.php

https://keysofenoch.org/the-pleiades/

https://www.earthgoddessrising.com/who-are-the-pleadians-and-was-lemuria-in-hawaii

And Orion, how does it relate to early civilisations?

https://www.ancient-code.com/the-origin-of-our-civilization-the-constellation-of-orion/

https://osr.org/blog/astronomy/pyramids-of-giza-and-orions-belt/

https://in5d.com/the-connection-between-the-pyramids-and-orions-belt/

https://thehiddenrecords.com/angkor.php

Shag harbour, (perhaps where Tesman 1st arrived before re-locating to Manset, Maine) Lake Titicaca, Malibu? Underground UFO and alien bases, portals ..

https://exemplore.com/ufos-aliens/Unidentified-Submerged-Object-the-Underwater-UFO-at-Shag-Harbor

https://www.coasttocoastam.com/article/video-transmedium-ufo-photographed-submerged-in-lake-titicaca/

https://stillnessinthestorm.com/2020/02/10-alleged-underwater-alien-ufo-bases/

https://duckduckgo.com/?t=ffab&q=manset+maine+map&atb=v273-1&iax=images&ia=images&iai=http%3A%2F%2Fwww.thedirectory.org%2Fcities%2Fmaps%2FME%2Fmanset.gif
https://files.abovetopsecret.com/images/member/ab2b77fa1f63.gif
https://history101.com/gate-of-the-gods-hayu-marca-peru/

Jacob Sporrensberg was an SS-*Gruppenführer und Generalleutnant der Polizei* in Minsk, Belarus and Lublin, Poland. After the war, Sporrensberg stood trial in Poland and was convicted in 1950 of war crimes and sentenced to death. He was executed in December 1952.

Sporrensberg has since been linked to the alleged German secret project *Die Glöcke* (The Bell) by Polish writer Igor Witkowski, who claimed to have discovered the existence of *Die Glöcke* from transcripts of an interrogation by Polish authorities of Sporrensberg. Witkowski claims to have gained access to read the transcripts through an unnamed contact in the Polish intelligence service.

Erich Muhsfeldt was an SS NCO who served in two extermination camps during World War II in occupied Poland: Auschwitz and Majdanek. He was arrested and charged by the Allies originally in 1946, then transferred to Poland where the full extent of his war crimes was revealed thanks to new evidence. He was retried by the Supreme National Tribunal at the Auschwitz Trial in Kraków, and found guilty of crimes against humanity. Muhsfeldt was sentenced to death by hanging in December 1947, and executed on 24 January 1948.

Hans Kammler was a German civil engineer and SS commander during the Nazi era. He oversaw many SS construction projects, including concentration camps, gas chambers and crematoria. His willingness to use arbitrary execution and brutality gained him eventual promotion to Oberführer (Brigadier General). Towards the end of the Second World War he was put in charge of the V2 rocket and missile programmes, codenamed project Riese, building underground facilities in Lower Silesia (Poland).

He 'disappeared' in 1945, his whereabouts or fate have never become known.

Werner Von Braun was the recognised architect of German rocket science. Initially a base was developed at Peenemunde on the Northern peninsula of the Baltic island of Usedom.

It was here that rockets were designed, manufactured and tested, the most famous of which being the V2 'Wunderwaffe', the Miracle Weapon. Two Polish janitors of Peenemünde's Camp Trassenheide in early 1943 provided maps, sketches and reports to Polish Home Army Intelligence, and in June 1943 British intelligence had received two such reports which identified the "rocket assembly hall", "experimental pit", and "launching tower". As the opening attack of the British Operation Crossbow, the Operation *Hydra* air-raid attacked the HVP's "Sleeping & Living Quarters" (to specifically target scientists), then the "Factory Workshops", and finally the "Experimental Station on the night of August 17/18, 1943. The Polish janitors were given advance warning of the attack, but their co- workers could not leave due to SS security and the facility had no air raid shelters for the prisoners. As a direct result of that raid production of V2 rockets was moved to several underground sites, the main site being in Austria. Another reaction to the aerial bombing was the creation of a back-up research test range near Blizna, in south eastern Poland. Carefully camouflaged, this secret facility was built by 2000 prisoners from the Pustkow concentration camp.

Von Braun, and many of his fellow scientists, were all spirited out of Germany at the end of the war under 'operation paperclip'. Many were granted US citizenship and were instrumental in the success of America's race into space,(hence Johnno's concern that Von Braun was not to be targeted) beginning with the Mercury projects in the 1950's, developing into the Gemini programme , Saturn and , finally, the Apollo moon missions. As Germany developed the V2 rocket they were also engaged in developing UFO's (Flying saucers) for which plans have been found, but no actual craft. American pilots reported 'Foo fighters' shadowing them on their high altitude bombing missions. They initially believed them to be a new secret German weapon. However these were seen by German pilots who believed them to be American secret weapons! To date no real explanation for their appearance has been given. Without Von Braun, and Operation Paperclip the Apollo landings may never have taken place, hence the need to keep him safe in the raid on Peenemunde.

https://www.theguardian.com/commentisfree/2022/may/14/wernher-von-braun-former-ss-officer-nazi-us-space-programme-nasa-apollo

https://www.sciencemuseum.org.uk/objects-and-stories/technology-it-took-get-moon

https://eu.usatoday.com/story/news/factcheck/2020/09/16/fact-check-nazi-scientists-brought-u-s-operation-paperclip/5690870002/

Many civilisations have their heritage based on visits by 'star people' originating from the Pleiades cluster, and/or the Orion star system. Native American Indians talk of visits from these 'star people' who guided them in agriculture and so on, similar to tales told by the Mayans, Aztecs and so on, even prehistoric man saw something.

Not convinced? Consider …

https://www.gaia.com/article/ufos-ancient-art

https://www.express.co.uk/news/weird/952299/ancient-alien-proof-Earth-UFO-cave-drawings or even ..

https://www.express.co.uk/news/weird/939342/Ancient-aliens-ETS-UFOs-native-American-rock-art

The Hopi prophecy mentioned by Rick?

https://en.wikipedia.org/wiki/Blue_Star_Kachina

Many cultures around the globe tell a similar story of civilisation being almost destroyed by a colossal flood. Many cultures around the globe have developed the art of building pyramids, though their cultures (we are told) never met. Many cultures developed the skills to build huge stone structures and monoliths in places such as Stonehenge, Carnac, Baalbek, Dolmens, and Ggantija and so on, which litter the globe. Look at the Yonaguni Monument found in Japan.

Perfectly 'carved' and fitted stones in places such as Puma Punku in Bolivia – and Saqsaywaman in Peru, all weighing many tons and all completed and laid perfectly using rudimentary tools?

When we are told about 'star people' who come from the skies they are usually categorised as;

Nordic Aliens - *Humanoids with stereotypical "Nordic features" (tall, blond hair, blue eyes) and have featured in several cases of contact. It is said they are from Ancient Earth but presented themselves as ET's in the past, they moved from living on the surface to live underground around the Himalayas area after a natural event.*

The 'Greys' - *Grey-skinned humanoids, usually 3–4 feet tall, bald, with black almond-shaped eyes, nostrils without a nose, slits for mouths, no ears and 3-4 fingers including thumb. They have been the centre of quite a few cases of alleged alien contact over the years. Due to their large heads (which would trouble any birth canal) and lack of visible genitalia some Ufologists believe they may be a form of autonomous android.*

https://www.express.co.uk/news/weird/1062753/Aliens-greys-UFO-Dulce-battle-Roswell-New-Mexico-alien-news

https://www.soulask.com/alien-species-advanced-humans-greys-and-reptilians
/

Little Green Men – *a by-product of 1950's sci-fi films, but never actually seen, except at the movies.*

Replicants – *beings who can transform themselves into other living creatures, usually managed by touch, but possible by sight alone. Perhaps Adolf Hitler himself was 'replicated' in order to kill off ideals of a 4th Reich. As his body burned the two replicants made their escape in order to 'lead' their followers to oblivion. They both flew out of Berlin as the allied net closed in on them. One travelled via Hohenlychen to Rjukan in the North of Norway, where he boarded U-Boat 3253 bound for Misiones in Argentina and onto Paraguay, where he was then supported by Juan Peron. The second replicant flew out of Berlin and travelled overland via Austria with papal support (and a large amount of cash). It is not sure whether this replicant then moved onto Chile and stayed there, or moved via U Boat to a base in the Antarctic. The US mounted an expedition there in 1946, Operation High Jump, led by Rear Admiral Bird in order to establish a 'research base'. 'Task Force 68', its official title, included 4,700 men, 13 ships, and 33 aircraft ... and returned in 1947! Doesn't that strike you as a lot of men and equipment just for research?*
Perhaps the real reason may never be known, or may even lead to another book!

Shape shifters , and skin walkers – *have the ability to transform themselves into a variety of entities at will. Embedded in native American folklore, and still affecting us today.*
https://science.howstuffworks.com/science-vs-myth/strange-creatures/skinwalker.htm
https://nativeamericanloveforever.com/navajo-skinwalkers-and-shapeshifters/
Finally if the above hasn't convinced you that we haven't had visitors from other planets just consider the following…
Our first aeroplane flew on December 17th 1903, managing to cover the width of a Jumbo jet! Today, just 120 years later we have visited the moon; sent Landers to Mars where they constantly sent back information in preparation for future visits; we have a permanently manned space station orbiting the Earth every 90 minutes or so; we have sent missions to Neptune and beyond into deep space beyond our solar system, photographing and making new discoveries as they go.
Imagine where we will be in just 1,000 years!
Imagine then what a civilisation just 1,000 years older than us could be capable of achieving!
The Universe is around 13.8 billion years old. The Solar system is 4.6 billion years old.

Imagine another system that developed 1 billion years before ours, or even 'just' 100 million years! Or even just 10,000 years …

What would they be capable of doing now?

How would their capabilities and advancements compare to ours on Earth?

How would we appear to them?

Would our development of nuclear weapons be of concern to them?

If so, would they need to keep an eye on us?

Just how did we progress so rapidly in just over 100 years?

I suggest you Google Philip Corso, Lieutenant Colonel (retired) – that's a start.

The President latterly mentioned the 'Majestic 12'.

You can make up your own mind by visiting the following ..

https://www.gaia.com/article/new-documents-add-to-the-majestic-12-conspiracy?utm_source=google+paid&utm_medium=cpc&utm_term=&utm_campaign=1-UK-DYNAMIC-SEARCH&utm_content=UFOs+&+Aliens&ch=DimensionNotFound&gclid=EAIaIQobChMIkMCZoaeL5gIVBrDtCh2guwgqEAAYAiAAEgJR0fD_BwE

Denver Airport mentioned by the President? Take a look at;

https://www.mentalfloss.com/article/61740/5-weird-conspiracy-theories-surrounding-denver-international-airport

or..

https://www.independent.co.uk/travel/the-darkest-conspiracy-theories-about-denvers-bizarre-airport-a7808376.html

Could there possibly be any form of 'alien' settlement on the Moon already keeping an eye on us as benevolent 'minders'?

Remember what Neil Armstrong has been reported as saying on his 'medical' channel.

"These babies are huge, sir … enormous….Oh, God, you wouldn't believe it! I'm telling you there are other space craft out there… lined up on the far side of the crater edge… they're on the moon watching us.

https://www.ibtimes.com/nasa-moon-photo-captures-alleged-200-meter-alien-base-expert-says-3024313

https://news-intel.com/china-captures-a-massive-alien-outpost-on-the-moon/

When Apollo 13 flew on its 'failed' mission to the moon in April 1970 the astronauts still had to fly around the back side of the moon to gain the 'slingshot' needed to get home. Mission control added an extra experiment and directed the crew to jettison the S-IVB upper stage and allow it to crash onto the moon's surface. The resultant impact surprised everyone. The moon began to 'ring like a Bell', the reverberations lasting for an hour. It was as though the moon was actually hollow. The same effect has been witnessed again in similar explosive experiments.

Scientists have since discussed that if the moon had been created by an impact on Earth all those years ago then its composition, mass and density should be the same – it is not. Others have proposed a theory that the moon itself is an artificial satellite 'placed' where it is. It is just large enough to block out the sun in an eclipse – how 'lucky' is that? If interested one such book is "Who Built the Moon" – Authors Christopher Knight and Alan Butler – get it on Kindle.

Web reference? Try

https://hackernoon.com/our-funny-artificial-moon-576c5c6d9930

Neil Armstrong, credited with being the first man to step onto the moon, undertook an expedition to Cueva De Los Tayos, Ecuador, in 1976 in search of artificial tunnels, lost gold, strange sculptures, and a "metallic library," supposedly left by a lost civilization aided by extra -terrestrials. Nothing was discovered unfortunately but why would such a down to earth scientist, astronaut and all American hero undertake such an unusual task?

Perhaps he saw something on the Moon!

Did he know something that we didn't?

Consider these ...

https://www.youtube.com/watch?v=mppf7AdlV10

https://www.express.co.uk/news/weird/1096115/Nasa-moon-landing-apollo-11-lost-two-minutes-ancient-aliens-ufo

In 1994 Neil Armstrong delivered a speech
in the White House where he said ...
"To those who can remove one of truth's protective layers
there are places to go beyond belief."
I wonder what he meant?

About the Author

Mike Brameld completed an apprenticeship as a precision engineer. In his 30's he ran a training centre in a large blue-chip company, as well as teaching engineering at a local FE College. He retrained as a high school teacher in his 40's , before retiring in 2013, having achieved the role of Assistant Head Teacher, where he taught Design Technology as his specialist subject.

Mike has always written poetry as a hobby, as well as the occasional short story, seeing these two pastimes as a way to help keep his mind busy and active during his retirement.

As an avid reader of science fact as well as science fiction, along with his interest in Ufology and conspiracy theories, he eventually decided that was where his first full length novel should be directed.

One of his first short stories inspired him to develop these themes, incorporating them into one tale. The Führer's Time Machine is the result.

Mike's other hobbies include photography, painting & sketching and enjoying walks and holidays with his wife, enjoying each day to the full.

Mike donates a percentage of all royalties to charity

Printed in Great Britain
by Amazon

23672762R10209